CATCHING STARS

LAURA RUDACILLE

Wild Hair Wednesday Press
Red Lion, PA

ISBN: 978-1-7373446-0-5 (print)
ISBN: 978-1-7373446-1-2 (ebook)

Printed in the United States of America

For Tina

(my real-life Nina)

Nods & Waves

The support for *Catching Stars* spans years. I'm eternally grateful to my family—Mom, Carol, and Keith who've patiently championed me through the finial tedious revisions.

Thank you to my content and clarity readers Gene, Julie, Kim, and Kristen. Your insight breathed layers of life into my characters and storyline.

To my proofreader and revision partner Amy, thank you for beginning your assessment notes with a "Ten things I loved about your book" list and for championing the best for and from me.

Demi Stevens, editor/publisher, Year of the Book Press. Thank you for insisting I return to my craft and for your persistent pursuit of excellence in this ever-changing industry.

Thank you to the creative professionals who contributed their time and talent to this project:

Teague Rudacille, graphic design—Thank you for the beautiful cover. You captured the vision and heart of *Catching Stars* brilliantly. GraceBoundDes77 on Redbubble.com

Jamie Greenwood, ceramic artist, Turtle Hollow Pottery—Thank you for giving me a glimpse into your imaginative genius and for answering my countless questions. Thanks also for encouraging me to get my hands dirty behind the wheel. www.turtlehollowpottery.com

Georgene Novak, jewelry designer, Georgene Novak Designs— Thank you for bringing my *Catching Stars* pendants to life. Dreams are for everyone... catch yours at www.georgenenovak.com

Finally, my husband Adam who loves to steal away and savor time where natural beauty inspires full-hearted dreaming. Thank you most of all for honoring the time I dedicate to crafting stories.

Beginnings...

humbled, challenged, scarred or blessed,
set the stage for what you aspire to become.

For any woman finding her feet
and standing shoulder to shoulder
with friends to begin again.

Chapter 1

"Put your safety gear on."

"But Mom." Lindy plopped on the floor and started to put on her knee and elbow pads. "Isn't a helmet enough?"

"No, it's not." Susie smiled at her precocious eight-year-old. "Especially since you've decided it's more fun to ride without using your hands."

"It *is* more fun." Lindy tied a second knot in her sneaker laces. "I'm getting really good. Well better," she amended before her mother could remind her of the spectacular wipeout she'd suffered three days earlier.

"Be grateful they make things to protect you." Susie dumped a box of noodles into salted boiling water. "At my age, there's no such thing as a soft landing." She set a digital timer.

Lindy did as she was told and rushed outside.

Susie carried her watering can to the front porch to soak her thirsty flowers. It was the simplest way to keep a covert eye on Lindy while she rode the loop from driveway to street and back again.

Summer was ending on the Eastern Shore. Shorter days and cooler rays meant the flood of beach-loving vacationers would begin to recede, returning tranquility to the small island of Chincoteague, Virginia.

Susie pinched expired blooms from her flourishing planter and wondered where time had gone. In two weeks, school bells would ring and Lindy would return to the classroom.

Over her shoulder, the kitchen timer dinged. "One more lap, Lindy," Susie called, "then come inside for dinner."

Susie turned off the burner and dumped the pasta into the colander.

Lindy dropped her helmet and pads in a heap by the door. "Can I help?" She kicked her sneakers into the corner.

"You may. Go wash your hands." Susie added margarine and milk to the strained noodles.

Lindy was back in a flash. She pulled a chair beside the stove, climbed on, and circled the wooden spoon. Carefully, she sprinkled the packet of flavored powder into the pot. Like magic, a vibrant burst of color drenched the pale pieces of starch, making her mouth water. "That looks really yummy."

"It certainly does." Susie smiled. "Grab us two bowls and…" The rumbling sound from a rust-eaten muffler carried through the window.

"Is Daddy home?" Lindy hopped to the floor.

"Sounds like it." Susie tucked the chair under the table.

"I can't wait to show him my no-hands trick." Lindy eagerly bounced on her toes.

"I'm sure he'll love it." Susie worked to keep her voice light. She wasn't expecting Lindy's father for another week.

A union welder, Frank traveled most of the year. His early arrival meant one of two things. The crew had finished ahead of schedule and earned a cash bonus, or he had been kicked off the job, again.

Tires squealed. The truck angled onto the property and skidded to a stop straddling grass and pavement.

The playful energy of the afternoon vanished.

"Mommy?"

Susie hugged Lindy's shoulders and pulled her away from the door. "Go to your bedroom, sweetie."

"Come with me." Lindy clung to her mother's hand. "Come with me to my secret spot."

"You go." Susie kissed the top of her daughter's head. "Everything will be okay. Hurry now."

Lindy scurried from the room.

Susie pressed her hands to her churning belly, then worked quickly to tidy the kitchen.

Frank cursed and kicked Lindy's bicycle out of his way. "My money, sittin' out for anybody to run over." Steel-toed boots stomped up the splintered porch steps. The head of an unsuspecting purple petunia snapped and took flight over the railing. He jerked the screen door open.

The temperature of the house plummeted.

"Spoiled kid left her bike in the damn street."

"I'll g-go—" Susie set the can of unopened peaches aside. "I'll move it, right now."

Frank slammed his cooler on the counter. "What you'll do, right now," he tossed his dirty work shirt at her feet, "is fix my dinner."

Lindy trembled in the pitch-black closet. Words hurled like an avalanche of rock on the opposite side of the door. Topics switched and made little sense. Dinner was cold or the meat was dry. The house was dirty or the tea was weak.

"Don't worry, he'll leave," Lindy whispered to her stuffed lion. "He always leaves." She jolted as something shattered. Fragments of splintered glass tinkled over the tile floor.

The shouting stopped. A door slammed and an eerie hush replaced the echoing cruelty.

Lindy patted her lion's soft head and tucked her beside the bag her father used for baseball league. "I need to check on Mom." She scooted forward and pushed the door open an inch. Her shoulder bumped a wooden handle jutting awkwardly from the bag's open zipper.

Petite fingers closed around the grip. Lindy shuffled over threadbare carpet dragging the bat behind her like a child's blanket. She tiptoed around broken dishware and kneeled on sticky, macaroni-soiled tile beside her mom.

Frank was on the porch.

Through the porous mesh, Lindy watched the molten tip of his cigarette burn brightly as he pulled air through the filter.

Frank drained the last droplets of beer into his mouth. He hurled the bottle like a shortstop making a double play toward a metal trashcan.

Glass exploded against the side of the house sending razor-sharp debris over the grass and driveway.

He laughed and staggered into the kitchen. His mirthless chuckle crawled over Lindy's skin like maggots. The refrigerator opened, casting a splash of muted light across the small room.

Lindy got to her feet and tried to raise the heavy bat.

"Well, look who thinks she's something special." Frank twisted the cap off the long-necked bottle. "You're not." His eyes drifted to the wooden baseball bat in her hands. "Feeling brave, little mouse? You're not." He sneered. "You're not special or brave. You're nothing."

The following morning Lindy sat down to breakfast with Daddy. Different from Frank, Daddy laughed and played. He spoke with kindness and gentle affection.

For Lindy the unbalanced influence felt like no-hands riding minus the thrill. She cautiously scrutinized every interaction like a section of crumbling roadway, knowing the smallest pebble could initiate a turbulent wobble, loss of control, or a painful crash.

As Lindy got older, her world widened and naivety fell away.

She heard the whispers around town and knew her family was a topic of discussion at more than a few dinner tables. Lindy tolerated the pitying looks and snickers on the playground and simply kept to herself.

Self-isolation proved to be an effective strategy until fourth grade when a spunky girl moved to the island. Her name was Nina. She had a freckled nose, dimpled cheeks and blonde braided pigtails which dangled to her waist and ended with perfect, pink polka-dotted bows.

"You're Lindy, right?" Nina slid on the stool and unwrapped her peanut butter sandwich.

"Yep." Lindy bit a hunk out of her apple.

"Thought so." Nina laid the triangle of bread on top of a napkin printed with smiley faces. "Want half? I have chips too."

Lindy stared blankly at the food.

"What's the matter?" Nina's head tipped to the side. "You allergic?"

"No."

"Then eat. I'm going to be your best friend."

Lindy rode home delighted by the prospect of having a best friend. She lifted her hands from the bars and wiggled her fingers in the spring sunshine.

Cutting through the alley, Lindy glided through the final turn and spotted her father's truck in the driveway.

Frank had been working in Florida for several months. His homecoming, like a cloud overhead, would either bring soothing shade or a torrent of...

A fierce bellow cut through the afternoon.

Joy shriveled like a worm on hot pavement.

Frank had never aimed anything but words in her direction. Mostly because as a child, her mom had been sure Lindy was tucked safely away.

Lindy hopped off her bike and shrugged her heavy backpack from her shoulders. "I'm not a child anymore." She'd been studying self-defense clips on YouTube for months, waiting for the day when she'd stand shoulder to shoulder with her mom and face the dragon. "Today's your unlucky day, Frank."

A violent crash interrupted Lindy's confident march across the patchy grass. She took a deep breath, jumped to the porch, and opened the door.

Her mother was on her knees against the stove. Her arms were wrapped around her head, bracing for the next fist or boot.

Frank tossed a casual look over his shoulder. "The Princess has returned to the castle."

"Lindy, honey." Susie staggered to her feet. "I lost track of time. Please go to your room and start your homework."

"No." Lindy stepped into the madness. "Get out, Frank." She had stopped calling him Dad years ago.

Hate fired his eyes. "You'll mind how you speak to me."

"Why?" Lindy taunted him with a brazen smirk. "Get in your truck and drive forever."

"I'll teach you to mouth off." Frank clenched his fist and stepped toward Lindy.

Fearing for her daughter, Susie lunged for Frank's leg.

He kicked Susie hard, propelling her into the refrigerator.

"Mom!" Lindy rushed forward.

Frank spun and slammed his elbow into Lindy's temple.

Lindy's vision swam in layers of pain. A wave of nausea washed over her and the world fell into darkness.

Frank knew he had gone too far. While Lindy lay dazed and Susie bleeding, he packed his duffle and fled.

Lindy watched her mom prepare breakfast. Bruises bloomed on her face and arms. The makeup she'd applied to conceal the damage only amplified the brokenness.

Frank didn't come home, but that wasn't unusual after a big fight. When days added together and became weeks, Lindy, who understood more than she should, hoped he'd never return. Each night she snuggled beneath the covers and made wishes, little and large, on the stars winking against the night sky.

Summer passed in a humid haze and a new school year began. Lindy transitioned to sixth grade and moved to the high school. Her hope for a clean slate and fresh start quickly faded as gossip and town-talk took the desk beside her.

Holiday decorations went up and as the frigid months of winter swept over the island, it became clear Frank had abandoned them.

Determined to keep food on the table and a roof overhead, Susie added extra hours at the café and took a second job at the hotel in housekeeping.

Despite her effort, the bank sent a certified letter. The date for foreclosure was marked in bold print across the top. Lindy and Susie had one week until they'd have to select their cardboard box and choose a street to squat upon.

That was the day Kate Cocheran showed up for dinner. Kate owned the Bayside Inn. She'd been friends with Lindy's mom forever.

Lindy opened the screened door and stepped aside. Kate entered the small kitchen with a folder under her arm and a warm pie in her hands.

"Lindy girl, take this pie and bring me a plate of whatever smells so delicious." Kate pulled out the chair reserved for Frank and sat with an irreverent plop. "Susie, I'm here to beg a favor." She patted the binder. "I'll warn you, it's a doozie, hence the pie." She winked at Lindy. "Figured I might need to sweeten you up."

Lindy hurried to the stove, filled a plate, and brought it to Kate. She grabbed a clean glass, lifted the pitcher, and poured some tea.

"You're such a darling." Kate raised the cup and drank deep. "Ahh, your mom makes the best tea."

After dinner, Lindy dallied on her way to the tub. She listened closely through the crack in the door as a wish-laden star streaked across the sky and landed in the kitchen.

Kate asked her mom to quit the maid service at the hotel and run a bed and breakfast on Main Street. The property included a two-bedroom manager's residence and a large fenced yard.

Lindy fell asleep to the sounds of weeping, but for the first time in her life, she heard relief and hope in her mother's falling tears.

Chapter 2

Lindy lived in the big house on Main Street for three years and in that time her mom transformed. Susie completed a beginner computer session at the Community Center then enrolled in an online business course. As her skill set expanded, so did her confidence.

Kate sang praises about the B&B and its proficient proprietor to anyone who'd listen. The noise reached a journalist intrigued by the herd of wild ponies living on the barrier island. She booked a room so she could experience the island hospitality firsthand. Following her stay she asked for permission to photograph the rooms and interview the manager. The article graced the cover of *Coastal Living* magazine and included a stunning picture of Susie watering the lush window boxes accenting the deep café styled front porch and patio.

Lindy and her best friend Nina sat at the wrought iron table with yogurt parfaits and tall glasses of chocolate milk between them. They were doing a sleepover to celebrate Lindy's upcoming sixteenth birthday. Her mom told the girls to pick any bedroom and she'd treat them like paying guests.

"Miss Susie," Nina scooped up a berry and a bit of granola, "your flowers always look really pretty. My mom is so jealous of the zinnias and vinca."

Susie blushed. "I've told her many times my secret is watering twice a day, first thing in the morning and again at sunset."

"And she says it can't be as simple as that or hers wouldn't look like stems and sticks knocking at death's door."

Lindy began to gather the dirty bowls and cups.

"No, you don't," Susie said quickly. "Guests don't tidy." She lifted the dishes to her tray. "You girls headed to the beach?"

"Yes, all day if that's okay."

"Of course, just mind the traffic on your ride to and from, and take your phone so I know you've made it safely."

Nina spread the blanket across the hot sand. "I think you should do a boy-girl birthday party. You could do a cookout after the final night of the carnival."

"Maybe." Lindy joined Nina and draped her Van Halen towel over her legs. The beach was beginning to fill with families.

"Tucker's growing up well." Nina nudged Lindy. "Look at those muscles. Ooh," she giggled. "You should invite Tucker. He's into you and he is H O T."

Lindy didn't need Nina to point out Tucker Brandt. She'd watched him pilot his surfboard for the past two summers. She appreciated the way he moved across the sand and the water.

"Oh Lindy, he's coming this way." Nina flipped her hair over her shoulder and angled her curvy body across the blanket. "Hey Tucker," she called. "Planning on catching some waves?"

"Sure am." Tucker smiled fully at Lindy. "Hi, Lindy."

"Hi," she answered softly. "Looks like a great day for it."

"Do you surf?"

"No, I've never tried."

"Want to?"

"Dude," the other boys hollered from the water. "Ditch the chicks."

Tucker kept his back to the ocean. "Swim out if you change your mind. I'll give you a lesson."

The girls swallowed their giggles as Tucker jogged toward the waves. Nina flopped to her back. "Oh, he could give me a lesson. I repeat yummy, yum, yum."

Lindy snickered.

"You don't think so? He's totally into you."

Lindy shrugged and brushed the sand off her knee. "You saw him first."

"It's not like cute shoes, Lindy. Plus it kinda helps if the boy likes you back."

Lindy noticed Kate walking toward them.

"Hello, girls." Kate opened her beach chair and sat beside them. "Pretty day to catch some rays."

"Sure is," Nina said, "but we were watching the boys."

"Certainly a nice side benefit," Kate chuckled. "Lindy honey," her voice grew serious, "your father is in town."

Lindy's eyes filled with heated tears. "How dare he come back here?"

"It will be okay, sweetie. Your mom has prepared for this day and she won't be alone, I promise you. She just wanted me to let you know she's meeting Frank for lunch. We're going to stay here together until she calls. Then I'll drive us all back to my house for a nice dinner."

Lindy knew Kate meant well, but unless you lived the horror, you could never understand. "I'm going for a swim." She pushed to her feet and ran toward the water.

Nina's lower lip quivered. She crawled across the blanket and laid her head in Kate's lap. "Should I go with her?"

Kate stroked her hand over Nina's hair. "Let's give her a few minutes."

Lindy swam out beyond the break to a familiar silhouette straddling a surfboard.

"Lookie here," Tucker brightened, "I found myself a mermaid. You change your mind about the lesson? The waves are flattening, but we could give it a try."

"Just needed a swim." Lindy grabbed the end of his board. "You mind if I hang on a few minutes?"

"Not at all, but why not climb on? There's a pod of dolphins moving through. You can see them better if you're out of the water."

"Okay." She kicked hard and hoisted her body to the long board. "I'll probably tip us over."

"No worries if you do, we're already wet," Tucker laughed. "Spin around and look toward the horizon."

Lindy folded her legs under her. Tucker balanced them as the board drifted farther out. A few moments later the pod breached the surface.

The group moseyed along unconcerned with the bobbing humans a few yards away.

A paddleboarder invaded their comfort zone and the family divided.

"Why'd he need to do that?" Lindy clucked her tongue.

Tucker snickered, "Everyone wants a close encounter."

"Spoiled it for the rest of…"

"Shh…" Tucker lifted his heels to the surfboard. His legs framed Lindy's. "You're about to have a close encounter of your very own."

Lindy held perfectly still. The water stirred and a small dolphin exhaled. Her heart pounded as another larger mammal broke the surface. "Amazing."

Tucker allowed the water to carry them along the shoreline. The pod regrouped and disappeared into the depths. "That was pretty great." He lowered his legs.

"You joking? On a scale of zero to great that was off the chart." Lindy's delight was as bright as the sun.

"Finally," he said. "I've been waiting to see you smile."

"I smile all the time."

"Sure, but that one was just for me."

Lindy flushed. "I thought I was going to pass out. Did you see the little ones? I'll take that as my birthday present and be one hundred percent content."

"It's your birthday?"

"Next week." Lindy turned so her feet hung over the side and tried to hold on to the beauty of the moment. Despite her effort, the weight of her father being on the island was brewing like a summer storm. "I should go back in."

"Hang tight, we're out a little farther than you may realize." Tucker maneuvered the board easily, and in a few minutes, they waded from the surf. He unzipped his wet suit. "You want to grab a sandwich or something?"

Lindy wasn't allowed to ride with boys but today she didn't care much for rules. She could see Kate down the beach, deep in conversation with another woman. If she was going to make a break this was her shot. "Sounds great. I'll meet you at your Jeep."

Nina, caught between envy and concern, sputtered in protest. "Lindy, you need to stay here. Kate said…"

Lindy toweled off and pulled on shorts. "Go for a swim, Nina." She gave her a tight hug. "Tucker will bring me right back."

Tucker hopped in the driver's seat. "Where to?"

Lindy knew her mother's face-down-Frank plan to the letter. "The deli on Deep Channel Drive."

Tucker pulled into the deli. "Wow, they're swamped. Want to go to the BBQ on Main instead?"

"Nope." Lindy was already climbing out. "This place is serving the only thing I'm hungry for."

Tucker hurried after her and pulled the door open. "You must be starving."

"You have no idea." Lindy surveyed the room and zeroed in on her target. "You may want to hang back."

Tucker followed her gaze and saw the source of Lindy's temper. He reached for her elbow and eased her to a halt. "He's not worth it, Lindy."

"You're right, but she is."

Susie's skin was pale against the bright-colored sundress. She held her hands together in a position of prayer on top of a stack of papers separating her from Frank.

"I just need a moment, Tucker, and then I think you're right. BBQ will hit the spot."

Conversations in the small room silenced as Lindy cut a path through the busy tables like a rescue swimmer navigating rough seas.

"Hey, Frank." She snagged a vacant chair and aligned with her mom. "I'd hoped you were dead."

Susie placed a palm on her daughter's arm. "I expected you to stay at the beach."

"And miss this? Not a chance."

The vein along Frank's temple pulsed and his fingers clenched, whitening his knuckles. "The brat grew up."

"That happens when months add up to years, you idiot." Lindy's head tipped to the side. "Funny, I remember you being much bigger."

"Still a disrespectful little cuss."

There it is, she thought, the muscle had always been in his mouth. "So, tell me, Frank," Lindy lingered over a bored sigh. "You finally run out of road? What are you doing on the island?"

"I live here."

His barbed tone pricked her confidence. Knowing Frank would delight in the slightest flash of fear, Lindy met his steely scowl with one of her own then lifted her mother's cup and sipped. "Nothing for you here, Frank." She glanced at the clipped stack of divorce papers. "No profit in hanging around. I'll be going to college in a few years. You want to foot the bill for that?" She tapped the documents. "Better to sign on the dotted line and cut your losses. Don't, and I'll come after you for half or more, seeing as you never paid a red cent toward my upbringing."

"Ungrateful twit," he seethed. "I gave you life."

"Yeah, thanks for that." Lindy crowded close. "Crawl back in whatever heap of metal you're driving, Frank, and go."

Tucker moved tight behind Lindy and rested his hand on her shoulder.

Susie covered the shock of the strapping young man allied with her daughter. "Hello, Tucker." She forced the corners of her mouth into a slight smile. "It's nice to see you. Lindy, I have a few things to discuss with your father. Tucker, would you mind seeing Lindy home?"

"Sure, Miss Susie. We were going to get a bite to eat first if that's okay with you."

"That's fine." Susie nodded to Lindy. "Go with Tucker now. I'll call you in a little bit."

Tucker and Lindy drove to the BBQ. They ordered three to-go boxes then returned to the beach.

They crossed the sand to where Nina was frantically pacing. "I was so worried. Are you alright? You left your cell phone in your backpack."

"I'm good." Lindy had lost her appetite. "Nina, could you text your mom and tell her we're staying on the beach until dark?" She turned to Tucker. "Thanks for the ride and," she lifted her hands and let them fall, "I'm sorry."

Tucker watched Lindy walk to the water's edge. He passed the bag of food to Nina. "Try to get her to eat something, and when you talk to your mom tell her, tell her I'm staying with you guys until Lindy's ready to go home. If she's okay with it, I'm happy to load your bikes in the Jeep and drive you both."

"Okay." Nina wrung her hands. "Was it awful?"

"Yes, but she handled him," and Tucker had never seen anything quite like it.

Chapter 3

A week had passed since the scene at the deli with Frank.

Lindy studied Tucker as he looked over the water. As if he sensed her gaze he turned and locked eyes with her. Lindy didn't look away and instead allowed her lips to turn upwards and gave him a second just-for-him smile.

Tucker's face brightened and he jogged toward her.

"Want to take a walk?" she asked.

"Heck yes." He offered his hand and pulled Lindy to her feet.

They strolled away from the crowd to the north beach where only a few sunbathers remained savoring the end of the day. Tucker didn't press her on the details of the confrontation with her father. Instead, he asked her about movies, books and music.

"Are you doing anything special to celebrate your birthday?"

"Nothing exciting." The summer wind tossed and tangled her hair. Lindy gathered the strands in nimble fingers and made short work of securing the mass in an intricate braid. "Nina and I are going to the carnival tonight."

"Cool, I'll be there." Tucker bent down and picked up a shell and skipped it across the surf. "If you could go anywhere for your birthday where would you go?"

"New York City." Lindy lowered to the sand.

In the distance, a crew of kiteboarders harnessed the powerful current of air and surged across the ocean's surface. "That's what I want, the freedom to go fast and tackle any adventure. To fly at warp speed without thought or worry about what's lurking below or hiding behind the next wave."

"Is that the appeal of the city?"

"Part of it, I guess." She traced circles in the loose granules. "I have no idea what I want to be professionally, but I do know I want to be free to travel. Los Angeles, Atlanta, New York, and anywhere else I'm drawn whenever the mood strikes. I won't be chained to a single location or be stuck in a life dictated by another person, that's for sure."

Tucker sat down beside her. "I think I'd die without the salty breeze and pounding surf."

Lindy laughed for the first time all afternoon. "A bit dramatic, don't you think?"

"Maybe," he chuckled.

"You're going away for college, right? I mean, I heard you got accepted."

"Keeping tabs on me?"

Her blush gave her away. "Small island news circuit, Tucker. Everyone knows everything about everyone."

"True." He scooped up a handful of sand and let it funnel through his fingers. "I'm going to the University of Delaware. Lucky break to play football a little longer and get my education at the same time. I'd always thought I'd pick up my degree online or go to a small community college." He shrugged. "The sea is in my veins. I can't imagine living anywhere else."

Lindy sat quietly as the kiteboarders, mere specks in the distance, faded from sight. She didn't understand how anyone could feel that way when they hadn't been anyplace different. "You leave soon?"

"Another month." Tucker studied Lindy's profile. "Plenty of time to squeeze some quality out of this summer."

"Make a wish." Nina held up a lighted cupcake.

"A one-way ticket off this island."

"Oh, come on. Wish for something happy." Nina's head tipped to the side. "Like a pony, a house on the water, or an official date with Tucker."

Lindy rolled her eyes and extinguished the flame.

"Wonderful, now let's go to the carnival and flirt with the vacationing boys."

Tucker was running the Ferris wheel. "Hey Lindy, it's time for my break. Want to take a ride with me? Tickets are free to workers."

"Of course she wants to ride." Nina guided Lindy forward. "It's her birthday. Hi, Mike." She fluttered her lashes at Tucker's friend. "Are you going to take over the controls?"

Mike blushed. "Want to watch?"

Lindy and Tucker took the next available seat. The car rocked as the wheel stopped and started until all passengers had been refreshed. Fully loaded, the speed increased making Lindy's belly light.

"Are you having a nice birthday?"

"I am." The revolutions slowed and paused. Lindy and Tucker were teetering on the very top. They had a clear view looking over the bay.

"Happy birthday, Lindy." Tucker leaned in and gave her a swift kiss on the cheek.

Lindy's heart raced. He held her hand on the second circle, keeping their hands low so no one could see.

"You want to play some games or listen to the band?" Tucker asked as their ride came to an end.

"My mom is picking me up soon."

"Want to call her? I'd be happy to drive you and Nina home."

"I pushed the limits riding with you the other day, Tucker." Lindy shrugged. "I'm not allowed to date 'til I'm sixteen."

"Which you are now, right?" Tucker smiled. "Call your mom, Lindy."

Chapter 4

Lindy hopped out of Tucker's Jeep and ran up the steps to the B&B's private residence. She pulled open the door and stopped short. Frank may have been absent for more than four years but she recognized his work.

Her mom was sweeping broken glass into the dustpan. "You enjoy the rest of your birthday?"

"That cowardly bastard."

"Now, Lindy," Susie winced as she straightened. "I did..."

"Nothing to deserve his fist." Lindy crossed to her mother, took the broom and finished gathering the shards.

Susie reached for her daughter's arm. "I'm sorry."

"Nothing to be..." The porch planks creaked. Lindy angled the broom across her body and charged the door.

"Hey." Tucker stepped back and held up his hands. "You forgot your backpack."

Lindy released a weary breath. "Sorry." Her anger shifted to shame. "Come in."

Tucker entered the room and placed her bag on the floor. "Is everything..." His voice trailed off as Lindy's mother turned. Her lip was split and an angry welt pulsed like an unhatched egg beneath her eye.

Lindy leaned the broom against the wall and moved to the kitchen counter. She gathered an ice pack from the freezer and a bottle of aspirin from the cabinet. She poured a glass of cold water from the pitcher in the refrigerator, snagged the tea towel from the drawer, and walked to her mother.

Tucker had heard the stories of what had gone on within the walls of the Colton house but had never seen the results of domestic violence firsthand. "What can I do?" he asked quietly.

"You could hunt that prick of a man down and dump him in the back bay. He'll be at the bar blowing off the rest of his rage with a bottle of Jack, or in the event he's feeling particularly proud of himself, he'll be carousing like a frat boy playing pool or darts and looking for an easy lay."

"Lindy," her mom's voice trembled.

"What?" Lindy snapped, then knelt beside her and offered the pain reliever. "Frank doesn't get to burst in here and undo all you've worked to build."

Susie whimpered when the cold water contacted her lip.

Lindy waited for her mom to swallow the tablets, then carried the glass to the sink and looked out the window. She faced Tucker and saw the helplessness she felt reflecting in his eyes. "You should go home." She lifted a heavy shoulder. "Crappy way to end our day, but…"

"Lindy, I can stay and…"

"No, thanks but no." She crossed the span and ushered him to the porch. "I need to deal with this and then I'm going to bed."

Lindy straightened the house, settled her mother between the covers, and closed the bedroom door. She went to the closet and pushed the clothing aside. Her fingers wrapped around the grip of her softball bat. The weight felt solid and good.

She stood on the porch and looked at the beautiful star-dappled sky. Since childhood, Lindy had given her dreams to the twinkling orbs. Tonight was the first time she wished for resolution at any cost.

Clash or align? Lindy wondered as she stepped inside and locked the door. Either way, she was prepared to finish it.

Lindy turned off the kitchen light and pulled a chair away from the table. She sat in darkness with the wooden bat across her lap, hoping her father would be misguided enough to try to call this house his home.

It was nearing two in the morning when she heard the rumble of his truck. She rooted to the seat, not in fear, but defiance, and waited for his boots to pound the wooden steps.

Frank tugged on the locked screen door and snickered, "Dumb woman thinks that will keep me out?" His hand punched through the mesh.

Lindy moved to the center of the room. "A little breaking and entering to end your evening, Frank?"

His eyes trailed over the young woman in front of him. "Little mouse thinks she's brave."

"I'm not a kid anymore." Lindy tapped the bat against her palm and noticed Frank's brief flicker of apprehension. "Last chance. Get out of this house and leave us alone forever." Her fingers flexed and adjusted for a secure hold as she readied to defend her home.

"I'll go where I want, when I want." A feral sound erupted as he charged toward her.

Heart and fury banded together, adding power to the blow. A horrid crack of bone meshed with Frank's wail, producing the sweetest symphony she'd ever heard. Lindy lifted her foot to his midsection and thrust hard. He flew backward through the door and sprawled across the porch cradling his broken arm.

"You stupid twit," Frank spit out the words as he tried to regain his feet. "You're nothing."

"So you've always told me." Unaware of the sirens racing to her aid, Lindy pushed the tip of the bat into the center of Frank's chest. "Got any new lyrics? This song is tired and overplayed."

Police cars angled across the yard. Frank screamed for medical attention and demanded Lindy be arrested for assault.

Strong fingers covered Lindy's and the weapon slid from her grip. Her vision filled with faces, familiar and not, as arms banded around her waist and pulled her into the safety of the house.

The investigation was tedious, but in the end revealed the truth. Protection orders were issued and Frank's plan backfired. He was found guilty of trespassing and received a harsh penalty for domestic violence.

In an act of goodwill, Frank signed the divorce papers. Susie and Lindy were finally free.

The court encouraged twelve months of interactive counseling. Lindy embraced the avenue to healing and spent the next year immersed in art therapy. The sessions exposed her to varied mediums, and her passion for creative works flourished. She was introduced to a pottery wheel and her love for ceramic arts was born.

The months passed in a flash, and the time came for Lindy to leave the program. The instructor encouraged Lindy to continue learning. She prepared a folder listing websites that sold used equipment, and a directory of studios and colleges on the east coast that offered workshops.

Lindy sat in the car and paged through the information. A flyer for a summer session at the Academy for the Arts in New York City slipped to the floor. She retrieved the paper and read the description. The three-month immersion program was led by renowned artists from all over the world. Students would study firing techniques and the properties of glazing. They would take field trips to forage shallow streams for natural clay and tour prominent museums. The session would conclude with exhibitions in three major cities.

"If only I believed in fairy tales." Lindy sighed and drove to Kate's for a simple picnic to celebrate her seventeenth birthday.

Susie carried the lighted cake to the deck and placed it in front of Lindy. The candles fluttered in the breeze. "Make your wish, honey."

Lindy closed her eyes and blew, extinguishing the flames.

Nina cheered as the smoke swirled and lifted. "Are you ready for your presents?"

"I don't need gifts." Lindy watched the group begin to exit the deck.

"Would have saved me a lot of work if she'd mentioned that sooner," Kate's husband Rudy muttered.

"Hush now." Kate playfully bumped him with her shoulder. "Lindy girl, we couldn't be more proud of you."

Susie held out her hand and wiggled her fingers. "You coming?"

Clearly confused, Lindy took her mom's hand and followed them across the yard. She obeyed their request to close her eyes as they led her toward Kate and Rudy's garage. The door rattled as it opened and she was directed to take a few steps forward.

"Happiest birthday," her mom whispered. "You can look now."

Lindy's eyes fluttered open and the sight before her filled her heart. Work tables, drying racks, a variety of sculpting tools, a metal scale, square and round wheel-bats for throwing, and her very own potter's wheel. She wandered among the equipment and discovered a container of raw clay, an assortment of basic glazes, and a rapid-fire kiln.

She was utterly speechless. Lindy lowered to a piano stool positioned behind the wheel and looked at the faces of the people who had worked in secret to outfit the perfect studio. The people who loved her, understood her, and only wanted the best for her.

"Thank you."

Chapter 5

Creating became as vital as breath, and although she made more mistakes than finished work, Lindy found nothing held her interest like a rapidly rotating wheel loaded with malleable clay.

The hammock inside the studio had become Nina's favorite place to dream out loud. The ropes ached as the fabric swayed and Lindy offered the occasional "Umm" "yeah" or "uh-huh" to keep the conversation going.

"Mike's the one," Nina gushed. "He's my after-ever."

Lindy laughed at her friend's term for blissful happiness.

Recently Nina determined she was too wise to believe in cartoon-inspired tales of lasting affection. She wanted larger than life, can't hold it in your heart, devoted love, that expanded beyond forever.

"How on earth can Mike be *the one* when you've barely met anyone?"

"We've been together a whole year, and we want the same things. You and Tucker have been together a whole year too."

"Tucker and I have been talking and texting regularly for a year," Lindy corrected.

"Come on, Lindy. He's the one. You love each other."

"Sure, I love him. He's my friend." Lindy flipped the power to her wheel on and pressed the pedal. "Love," she muttered under her breath, "isn't always enough."

Lindy didn't buy tickets to Fantasy Land. She'd witnessed the struggles of love, and the hollow shell fear and belittlement produced.

"Love can look very different after a few years." Lindy reduced the speed and held a tool against the base of the wet clay to sharpen the edge. "Not all after-evers are happy, some end in bruises and brokenness."

"Oh, Lindy."

"My point is Tucker and I have lives to live. We both know it's important to find our own path. Besides, who knows what will happen in five or ten years?"

"I know." Nina sat up and draped her legs over the side of the fabric. "I do," she insisted. "We'll have a double wedding then Mike and I will buy the house down the street from the B&B." She popped up and twirled. "We'll get pregnant the same month, and go into labor on the same day. I'll have a boy, Eric, and you a girl," she pressed her finger to her lips. "Sophie?"

Lindy wrinkled her nose. "I'd prefer Charlie."

"Perfect," Nina clapped. "A sweet baby girl named Charlie. We'll raise our kids here on the island and stay 'til we're withered and gray."

"You're crazy." Lindy glanced at the fading Academy for the Arts flyer she'd pinned to the corkboard a year ago. "I'm sorry to say, my dream looks a little different."

"Well, Mike and I will give you an example of after-ever that will change your mind." Nina grinned. "I have to run. I'm helping your mom set up for tomorrow's bridal shower." She plopped a kiss on Lindy's head. "Couldn't love you more."

"Me too, bye." Lindy inserted her earbuds and selected her favorite classic rock playlist. Bret Michaels and "Every Rose Has Its Thorn" filled her ears as she carried her finished piece to the damp box. Humming, she cut another section of clay, placed it on the scale to check the weight, then the intricate dance began again.

What will you become? Lindy pondered as the clay responded to the movement of her fingers. She dipped a sponge into the jar of muddy water, adjusted the angle of her body, and reached inside the cone. The form grew taller and bowed outward like a belly growing with promise.

A figure shifted on the edge of her vision. Lindy squealed and the clay collapsed. "Tucker." She turned off her music and pressed her hands to her stomach. "You startled me."

Regret washed over his features. "I'm so sorry."

"No worries, happens more often than you'd think." She powered off the wheel and the awkward rotation stopped. "When I'm in it I'm oblivious to what's going on around me." She dragged a length of wire beneath the base of the ruined clay and pressed the separated mass between her hands.

"It was a really cool shape."

"And it will be again." Lindy tossed the hunk into a bucket. "It's one of the things I love most about clay. There will always be another day. I thought you were working."

"I made arrangements. Thought I'd try to talk you into taking a break. Maybe grab a pizza and steal a few hours at the cove. We could go for a swim then grab an ice cream on the way back. Figured you might want to practice playing hooky for your senior year."

"All of that sounds really great, but I can't leave right now. I'm waiting for the kiln to finish."

"How long will that take?"

Lindy glanced at the clock. "Three more hours."

"Okay."

Lindy watched as Tucker wandered along the shelves where dozens of pieces were in the process of drying.

"Green-ware?" he asked.

Lindy nodded. "Yup, and that's…"

"Bisque-ware, I remember." Tucker cradled a bowl in his hands. "Fired in the kiln once and waiting for you to dip or brush on the color."

Lindy smiled, pleased he remembered.

"You are really getting the hang of it."

She blushed. "I've begun to experiment with glazes." Lindy washed her hands then grabbed a towel. "Wanna see?"

"Yeah."

"This particular glaze is fired using the Raku method." She pointed to a grouping of finished mugs and bowls. "I like the way the color transforms in the heat. These are…"

Tucker had no idea what she was talking about. Firing techniques, zinc oxide, and kiln temperature settings, the subjects rebounded in his brain, but he didn't care. It was obvious Lindy was completely and passionately endeared to her art. "Your last year sitting in school is going to be very painful."

"Actually, I switched to online classes so I can work in the studio more." Lindy grabbed her water bottle.

"Really?"

"Senior year is more about celebrating the last this or that. I'm more interested in what's next." She tapped the flyer on the bulletin board. "I'm planning to apply for an art program in New York City."

"Wow, why didn't you tell me?"

"Because most people think my dreams are odd enough as it is," she shrugged. "Applicants must be twenty years old and I'm virtually a beginner."

"You can learn a lot in two years."

"That's the plan." Lindy smiled at him. "The submission packet requires current physical work and a portfolio of professional photos. In addition, I'll have to render colored pencil mock-ups of prospective designs." Saying it out loud made her knees knock. "It's crazy to even think about it, but it's all I can think about."

Tucker laughed. "You can do it. My friend Zak is a brilliant photographer. If you want to connect or consult with him just let me know."

"When I'm ready, that would be great." She checked the dials on the kiln. "Want to try to throw a few?"

"Sure."

Lindy weighed a hunk of clay then took him to the canvas-wrapped table to pound out the air pockets.

"Great way to work out frustration."

"It certainly is." Lindy adjusted the piano stool to accommodate Tucker's height then placed a dry circular bat on the wheel head. She dropped an apron over his head and smiled. "Step one, have a seat. Step two, slam your clay in the center of the disk."

Tucker was a wonderful student. He patiently listened and applied her instructions.

"This is not as easy as you make it look."

"I bet your summer surfing and paddleboard students say the same thing."

He chuckled. "Every day."

"But you encourage them and they try again, right?" Lindy handed him another portion of prepared clay.

"They do." Tucker hunched over the wheel and braced his elbows as Lindy had shown him. He added pressure and willed the mass to stop wobbling and find center. The clay slipped through his fingers, narrowed, and grew taller. He inserted his thumb and the divot became a hole. The revolving wheel and noise from the machine began to cast its spell.

Lindy saw the moment Tucker was lost in the process. His hands stopped fighting and accepted the adapting shape. The clay responded to the pressure and widened. A few moments later, a bowl emerged.

"I think I may have done it." Tucker released the pedal and straightened. "Kind of."

"You absolutely did. Great job."

"Now what?"

She checked the gauges monitoring the kiln and turned off the power. "We clean up and grab that pizza."

Chapter 6

The Jeep bumped over sandy ruts in the narrow lane on the north end of the island. They passed Ole Man McCoy's house and continued until the headlights skimmed the tattered plywood and pylons of a poor man's boat launch. Tucker killed the engine and for a moment allowed the beams to shine across the bay.

The cove was Lindy's favorite place on the island. She hopped out and put the pizza box on the hood then moved to the tall grass marking the border between wet and dry. The view begged for wishes and stirred the endless string of "what if's" slumbering inside her.

Lindy tipped her head back and scanned the twilight sky for the first sign of stars. She stretched her arms high and wiggled her fingers. "I just want to touch one and hold it in my hands."

Tucker reached behind the seat and lifted the gift he'd brought then joined her by the water. "I might be able to help you with that." He passed her a bundle wrapped with a t-shirt and twine.

Lindy's brow furrowed. "What's this?" She smiled as she made out the Aerosmith *Dream On* logo. "Great group."

"Great song." Tucker shifted his weight. "This is your favorite place to dream, right?"

"It is." Her belly fluttered. She leaned against the bumper and pulled the ends of the string. The t-shirt opened and revealed a small wooden box with three carved stars on top and a tiny silver clasp on the front.

Tucker held out his hand. In his palm were two tiny keys on a length of silver chain.

With a soft click, the lock gave way and the lid opened. Inside Lindy found a pen and dozens of stars cut from pastel paper.

"I thought maybe this could be a place to hold your dreams until you catch them." As he said it out loud the idea felt corny and weird.

Lindy lowered the top and traced each etched star with her finger. "You made this?"

Tucker jammed his hands deep into his pockets and nodded.

"It's amazing," Lindy rested the box carefully on the bumper then wrapped her arms around Tucker's waist. She pressed her cheek against his chest and his arms encircled her body. If she were the kind of girl who believed in the fanciful, she'd wish for this, but she wasn't.

Lindy patted Tucker's back. "You know I'll probably lose the keys."

Tucker's laugh rumbled against her cheek. "I made duplicates."

"You know me so well, Tucker Brandt." Lindy stepped away and climbed on the hood. "Let's eat." She opened the pizza box.

Tucker snagged their drinks from the cab and joined her. He leaned against the windshield as he enjoyed a second slice. "Tell me how you heard about the New York program."

"My art therapist." Lindy sipped her soda. "Who would have guessed clocking Frank with a Louisville Slugger would turn out to be a good thing? That doesn't mean I have to send him a thank-you note, right?"

"Certainly not, but it's nice such a beautiful gift is coming from the bad."

"True. I've had the flyer tacked to my corkboard for a year and it'll still be twenty-four long months until I can do anything about it. Even then, I'll just meet the minimum age requirement and will still be a novice by the academy's measure. Most of the applicants will have formal training and completed college degrees."

"Expensive pieces of paper," he said absently. "You're committed and you have the time."

"I still can't believe mom went for the virtual schooling. I expected to have a harder time convincing her but it turned out she was already researching it."

"Moms tend to always be several steps ahead."

"Weird, right?" She rattled the ice in the bottom of her cup. "Anyway, it's scary to hope and terrifying to not."

"I get it, no safe zone or guarantee, just balancing the parts that matter."

"This matters." Lindy slid off the hood, inserted the key and removed a light blue star. She scribbled her dream across the paper and pressed her lips against the ink. "I have two years to improve my skills." She closed the lid and locked the chest. "Worst case scenario, I'll get a professional review of my work, and if by some miracle I get in..."

Tucker gestured to the sky. "You'll have touched your first star."

Chapter 7

The time passed in a blur of wet clay on a rapidly spinning wheel. Lindy produced signature styled mugs for the B&B and sold a few pieces in a downtown gift shop. In between, she waitressed part-time for Kate at the Bayside Inn.

Nina earned an associate degree in event planning and was working side by side with Susie to host small events at the B&B. The pair had grand plans to expand the offerings to include intimate weddings.

Nina and Mike would be the first couple to test the venue. Their ceremony was a week away. The two had been entangled since high school. Mike was as smitten as Nina. He'd recently finished his HVAC certification and was planning to open his own business.

"Can you believe it's really happening?" Nina stood on the pedestal for her final fitting. "I'm getting my after-ever."

"You certainly are." Lindy smiled. "You've always known exactly what you wanted."

"I have," Nina beamed. "Is your first step to after-ever ready to be postmarked?"

"Nearly." Lindy had worked for weeks to finalize her portfolio. In addition to producing three pieces representing her skill level and style, she hired Tucker's friend, Zak, to do the photography.

Zak was imaginative and meticulous. He'd stayed at the B&B for a week and worked with Lindy as a dedicated partner. They'd spent hours together on the beach maximizing the hues of sunrise and sunset. They incorporated the textures of beach grass and sand. Zak set up his equipment in the small bedroom and experimented with dimensional lighting and fabric drapes. The result had exceeded anything Lindy could've imagined.

Lindy helped Nina out of her dress. "I'm heading to the studio when we're finished to meet Zak and check everything for the hundredth time." She laughed. "He wants to be certain I've protected the images in a manner he feels acceptable. He also wants to kiss the boxes, and me of course, for luck."

"Zak's a shameless flirt." Nina pursed her lips. "How is it he can look like a bohemian roughneck, behave like a Neanderthal, and still be appealing?"

"I'm sure he would say it's a gift," Lindy snickered. "In light of all his flaws, Zak is as invested as I am. Anyway," she wrung her hands nervously, "in a few hours I'll seal the boxes, and first thing tomorrow morning, they'll be out of my hands and on the way to New York City."

"I'm coming with you tomorrow." Nina tugged her jeans over her hips and her sweater over her head.

"You don't have time for a trip to the post office."

"Nonsense, we're standing together, like always. No argument." Nina narrowed her eyes. "I will always stand with you."

Lindy found Zak stretched out and fast asleep in the hammock beside the garage. His ripped flannel shirt was buttoned crooked and his frayed cargo pants showed more skin than they covered.

"I hope you weren't waiting too long."

"Just long enough to catch a few winks. I need to be refreshed for the nuptials."

"I'd think a man like you would run away from weddings like your skivvies were in flames."

"Not looking to wear the penguin suit myself," he clambered to his feet, "but I'm always happy to entertain an enthusiastic bridesmaid."

"Only one?" Lindy's brow arched. She opened the door and walked inside the studio. "I think you'll be..." The words dried on her tongue. "What have you done?"

"A little forcible entry," Zak leaned against the door frame, "with a skosh of property damage."

Lindy wandered to the long wall absorbing a collection of seven matted and framed photographs taken during their portfolio session on the beach. "I was an intense and overbearing stage mom, wasn't I? Positioning my pottery, checking the light and directing each grain of sand." She laughed. "How you must have wanted me out of your way."

"Quite the opposite, sugar."

"Oh Zak…"

The next candid series showcased Lindy spinning across the sandy dune. Wild spirals of blonde-streaked hair were frozen in flight like rays of sunshine. The three-panel sequence ended with her laughing into the camera lens with her arms thrust victoriously to the sky.

"I wanted you to have something to look at while you waited for your acceptance letter from the academy."

"They're beautiful." Lindy trailed her fingers over the custom framework. "I love… love…" she shuddered, then buried her face in her hands and wept.

"Well hell, this isn't the reaction I was hoping for." Zak crossed the room. "Easy." He gathered her close. "Take it easy, sugar."

Lindy wrapped her arms around him. "I'll never be able to repay you."

Zak scooped Lindy clean off the floor and hugged her tight. "I'd be happy to suggest a few enjoyable ways we could settle your account. But," Zak set Lindy down and dropped a kiss on the top of her head. "You, gorgeous, are out of my league."

"Tease." Lindy playfully swatted his chest. "Seriously, you've given me a real shot, and I'm grateful."

"Your talent is giving you the shot," Tucker said from the doorway.

Lindy jolted. "And the surprises keep coming." She eased from Zak's embrace and wiped her face. "Nina and Mike's wedding is certainly bringing the men to town."

"Well, this man has a hot date." Zak walked toward Tucker and extended his hand.

Tucker gripped Zak's hand firmly and pulled him close. "A date?"

"A hot slippery and sudsy hour with the barber. I need to freshen up if I want to hook a bridesmaid." He winked at Lindy then added, "Or two." Zak patted Tucker's shoulder and lowered his voice. "And clearly this maid of honor is spoken for. I'll see you both later."

"I thought you said you wanted to check my packing?" Lindy asked.

"Cloak and dagger, baby." Zak winked. "Cloak and dagger."

Lindy stared at Tucker. She hadn't seen him since he'd landed a coveted internship in Virginia. The last few months, between his work and her drive to complete the submission, their conversations had become sporadic.

"I owe you pretty big too." Lindy pointed to the framed photos. "Zak was the perfect recommendation for cataloging my portfolio."

"I can see that." Tucker moved to her side and studied the collage.

Lindy was suddenly nervous. Tucker hadn't seen any of her recent work.

"Clearly, Zak's as gifted with his camera as he is with women."

"Truth," Lindy laughed and busied herself with the bubble wrap. "So tell me something, Tucker Brandt. What have you learned on the mainland aside from the fact you can survive away from the sea?"

"Yes, you were right. I was able to exist off the island, but I'm ready to come home. I'll be bringing my degree and my experience back for good in the spring." He lowered on the stool beside her wheel. "I'm developing a plan to expand the summer water sports business to include a brick-and-mortar store."

"Wow."

"It won't happen quickly, but I'm clear on what I want in my future." His gaze locked with hers. "I'm all about catching those stars."

"Yeah…" Lindy's mind tangled with soft, sweet memories. She swallowed the lump in her throat. "As you can see, I'm still stretching." She gestured to the boxes on the table. "Your timing is perfect. I'm shipping everything to New York tomorrow." She released an uneasy breath. "I'll be a wreck 'til January."

"I knew October was the target date but I was afraid to hope." Tucker laughed at her surprised expression. "I wanted to see your portfolio in person." He walked to the table. "May I?"

Lindy nodded. She watched Tucker cradle the vase gently and angle it beneath the light.

"This finish looks alive." He returned her piece in the nest of protective packing and focused his attention on the bowl. "You were so irritated that you weren't old enough to apply."

"Time has taken care of that detail." Lindy smiled. "I'm all grown up now."

Tucker faced her. "You certainly are."

The world tilted slightly, taking Lindy along for the ride.

"Wanna go grab some pizza?"

"Huh?" She blinked like an owl.

"I'm hungry." Tucker jammed his hands in his front pockets. "You still like meat lovers?"

"Pizza sounds good." Lindy busied herself with the postal box. "If we follow it up with some ice cream."

"Deal."

The next morning Lindy and Nina stood in line at FedEx to get her portfolio and entry pieces on the way to New York City for review.

"So exciting," Nina grinned.

Lindy swallowed the butterflies trying to escape her belly and passed the clerk her submission package as if it were gold. They waited while the parcel was weighed, labeled, and placed in the appropriate bin for transport.

Lindy tucked the receipt and tracking information in her tote then lifted her shoulders and tried for a relieved smile. "Nothing to do now but wait."

"I wouldn't say nothing." Nina linked her arm through Lindy's. "Your best friend's getting hitched in a matter of days."

"True, thank you for the well-planned distraction."

"Speaking of distractions, Mike said Tucker should be home today. Are you anxious to see him?"

"I've seen Tucker."

"What?"

"He dropped by the garage while I was packing up my submission. We went for pizza and ice cream."

"Interesting."

"It was, actually."

"Tell me everything."

Chapter 8

To the delight of the wedding guests, Mike dipped Nina and sealed the deal with a kiss. Lindy caught the bouquet, and shed a few tears, then stood on the porch and waved as the newlyweds drove off to enjoy their honeymoon.

Lindy worked in the studio every chance she could and allowed the hum of the space heater and spinning wheel to distract her from counting the days until January.

Fat flakes of snow fell as Lindy wound buffalo plaid ribbons around the porch pillars and dangled garland from the railings. She filled the window boxes with fresh greens, holly and twinkle lights. The storm persisted until a thin blanket of snow covered the island.

In a finger snap, New Year's Eve arrived. Lindy huddled with Nina and Mike as the traditional sparkling Pony Island Horseshoe dropped, marking the end of another year. Well wishes circulated throughout the crowd, and a moment later the newlyweds were wrapped in a private bubble of celebration.

Lindy shrank away from the festivity. She pulled her hat low and allowed the icy wind to propel her down Main Street.

Heavy footsteps sounded behind her.

"I hope you aren't going to make me chase you all the way home." Tucker laughed and fell in step beside her. "It's freezing."

"It's winter. Where's your Jeep?"

"Zak met someone earlier tonight so..."

"Say no more."

The B&B was in full party mode when they arrived. "I see the Hummers still know how to celebrate."

"They certainly do." Lindy smiled. The clan from Pennsylvania had visited Chincoteague every summer since the '60s. Generations of island love had yielded a hearty family tree. Six years ago the Hummers began renting the entire house from Christmas to the New Year. "Want to join them? They traditionally wind down the evening with karaoke and Twister."

"I'll pass." Tucker kicked his toe against the step. "Want to sit on the swing for a few minutes?"

"Not really." Lindy shrugged. "I was thinking about driving over to the cove. You up for it?"

Lindy drove through town and turned on the narrow sandy strip which led to the water. She parked but left the engine on to keep the heater running. "There's a blanket in the trunk if you want to grab it."

They stepped from the car and were met by the quick, crisp breeze off the bay.

"Wind carries the luck to shore," Tucker said as he opened the hatch.

"I could use some luck." Lindy unzipped her fleece and invited the wind to baptize her.

Tucker hurried to her side. "You'll freeze."

"Just trying to catch a little New Year's good fortune."

"You know there's a better, not to mention warmer, tradition for ringing in the New Year."

"Har har." Lindy fastened her jacket.

"I'm not kidding. You have a big year ahead of you."

"I'm not in the program yet, Tucker."

"Precisely my point." He draped the blanket over her shoulders. "I'd hate to see you miss an opportunity to align the fates in your favor. What's a little New Year kiss going to hurt?"

She shook her head. "I won't risk our friendship."

"I think we can handle one friendly kiss." The wind kicked up as Tucker turned her toward him.

Lindy clutched the blanket tightly to her chest as a tangible barrier, then closed her eyes in an attempt to maintain a speck of emotional distance.

"Happy New Year." Tucker brushed his lips lightly over hers. "See," he whispered, "nothing to it."

Lindy was more aware of Tucker than she'd ever been. She pressed her lips together and tried to hold the sensation a moment longer. Aiming for casual, she lifted her gaze, but when her eyes found his, the punch of power threatened to topple her.

There was nothing friendly about the next kiss. The blanket fell to the sand and they grappled to get closer. Tucker fought for reason but Lindy arrived first.

She shoved against his chest to gain separation. "Whoa."

"Indeed." Tucker stepped away, seeking to bathe in the chilly air. "And definitely not friendly." He scrubbed his hand over his face and looked toward the dappled sky. Focusing on a single star, he said, "I love you, Lindy."

She gathered the blanket and stood beside him. "I know." She rested her head against his shoulder. "I love you, too."

His arm circled her waist. "But..." Tucker picked up her unspoken clarification. "I have college to finish and you're only beginning."

As Tucker squeezed her tightly to his side, Lindy thought some stars would have to wait.

Two weeks later, Lindy pulled the mail from the box and the return address for the academy in New York City leapt out at her. She walked carefully up the steps knowing this was a moment she wanted to remember in microscopic detail. She opened the front door and laid the pile on the desk.

Heart thundering with hope and fear, Lindy pressed the envelope to her chest. "Mom?" The first tear slid down her cheek. "Can you come here a minute?"

She heard her mother scrambling to join her in the foyer. "Okay, okay." Susie pressed her hand against Lindy's damp cheek. "I know, honey." She took a deep breath. "Here we go."

Sweaty fingers fumbled as Lindy zipped her thumb under the flap and withdrew the packet of papers. The single word blurred as her mother's delight erupted... *Accepted.*

Chapter 9

The three-month academy began June first and ran straight through to the end of August.

The intensive schedule left little downtime. Students began each day in theory and lectures, afternoons in experience, and their evenings in workshop. Lindy established Sunday night check-in calls with her mom and texted Nina and Tucker whenever she could. She sent videos when they did cool things like combing streams and creek beds for natural clay.

Lindy was the youngest enrolled by far but age seemed of little consequence. Her workshop partner and newest bestie was a seventy-year-old man from Arizona. Cal was a retired Navy cook who discovered his passion for stoneware on a trip to Europe.

"I fell in love with jugs," Cal said. "Any shape, any size, I just love 'em."

The group snickered.

"I'm not sure why everyone giggles so much when I say that," Cal confided in Lindy later.

"You do know 'jugs' is another word for breasts, right?"

"Well, gravy biscuits," Cal blushed. "That explains a great deal." For the rest of the session, he'd sent them both into hysterics, occasionally muttering, "Any size, any shape."

At the close of the summer session, the academy presented the students' works through a series of exhibits in Baltimore, Washington D.C., and New York City. The events were designed to expose the budding artists to all manners of the social elite and create an opportunity to make a big splash into a supportive art-collecting community.

Lindy prepared two pieces, a hand-built basket and a wheel-thrown vase. Striking in size and color, the line of the vase was complemented by a woven leather sash accented with intricately carved beads.

"You have to come. It's only a three-hour drive," Lindy said during her routine Sunday call. "It's like my coming out party. The display will be open for seven whole days in Baltimore's Inner Harbor. There's a banquet on the final night, kinda fancy, but I get six tickets."

"Sounds very exciting."

"Please say you'll come."

Susie came for the entire week. She and Lindy shared a room overlooking the harbor. They ate good food, listened to live music, and toured the National Aquarium. On the last night, they entered the banquet center. The student art was positioned at the front of the room, backlit with subtle hues to enhance each design.

"Your work is simply beautiful." Susie's voice wavered with pride.

"No weeping, Mom." Lindy gripped her hand. "I'm trying to be a professional."

Etiquette went out the window as Lindy spotted Nina, Mike, Kate and Rudy. She squealed and ran to her friends.

"What about me?"

Lindy released Nina as the timbered voice washed over her. She turned and tried to focus through ruined mascara.

"Surprise," Tucker said quietly and wrapped her in a warm hug.

Cal and his wife joined their group and together they enjoyed every moment of the incredible evening. The academy presentation included remarks from each instructor and images from the student sessions and field trips. One picture captured Lindy and Cal sitting in a dry creek bed combing the rocks for natural clay fragments.

"I didn't know that was a thing," Nina mumbled.

"Not a practical, modern-day thing but yes, for centuries, people have harvested raw clay to make what they've needed."

"Fascinating."

"Lindy would have sat alongside me all day," Cal commented. "Not just 'cause she loved it, but because she knew I couldn't get up."

The next snapshots showed Lindy and Cal lost in laughter as they attempted to hoist one another off the loose pebble and silt.

"We were a troublesome pairing." Cal winked at Lindy.

The balmy breeze surrounded the group on their stroll back to the hotel. Mike and Tucker followed the brick walkway to study the historic warship docked in the harbor. The night exceeded Lindy's wildest imagination and her heart was full. "I can't thank you enough for coming."

"We wouldn't have missed it, Lindy girl," Kate said.

"So," Rudy asked, "your next stop is Washington, D.C.?"

"Yes, we leave first thing in the morning."

"Then you kids better squeeze the minutes out of this moon. We old folks will head back to the rooms and into the air conditioning."

Live music from the bars and restaurants drifted above the chatter of the late-night crowds. Nina threaded her arm through Lindy's. "Hard to believe summer's over already."

"Harder to imagine you've been married a year."

"Just about," Nina laughed. "Best eleven months of my life. After-ever is really something you should put on your to-do list."

"Forever the romantic."

"I'm not the only one." Nina angled her head toward Tucker. "How 'bout we give you a little room? Mike, my love, let's wander toward the aquarium and finish the evening properly."

"You mean, find a place to make out?" Mike grinned at Nina. "I'm down for that."

"Crazy kids," Tucker chuckled as they dashed off. "Here's your ship, Lindy. The USS Constellation, built in 1854 according to the sign."

"Built to wage war," she smiled. "Is that how you think of me?"

"As a fighter? For sure, but I was thinking the name suited you. You're beginning to catch your stars."

"Well, one anyway." She glanced to the sky. "I still can hardly believe I got into the program, and now I'm facing the other side. Why do the things we love fly past at warp speed?"

Tucker reached into his pocket and pulled out a small satin pouch. "I have something for you."

Lindy watched as Tucker unsnapped the fabric and dangled a delicate silver chain from his fingertips. A star-shaped pendant floated freely and two tiny diamond chips sparkled in the moonlight.

She lifted her hair, and just for a moment, the world did slow down.

"Whenever the moment is moving too fast you can touch this and remember tonight." Tucker fastened the clasp then brushed a kiss over her cheek. He took her hand and smiled when her fingers linked with his.

Lindy hugged everyone one final time, then climbed on the student van and was on her way to Washington, D.C.

The itinerary included private tours designed to fuel their inspiration. Lindy was enthralled by the National Museum of the American Indian. The building itself was a work of art and appeared as if the structure had been chiseled from a mountain of compressed earth, sand and stone. Inside, countless rooms were filled with cases of stoneware.

Lindy tried to grasp the magnitude of beauty and rich history as she strolled among the naturally cured wide-bottom pots and vases, accented organic with color. She longed for each piece to share its secrets of origin and tell the tale of the artist whose hands had birthed it.

That evening when the students arrived at the convention center their teacher pulled them aside to make an announcement. "We've just been informed that one artist's work will be selected and featured during the Art Academy Presentation Series final exhibit, our crown jewel event, in New York City."

The murmur of excitement passed among the students.

"The artist selected will receive a six-month extension for studio use at the academy and a complimentary apartment in the building. In addition," she continued, "the honoree will be interviewed and their piece photographed for an article in *Clay Times* magazine."

Lindy nearly choked on her cheesecake when her name was announced. She had won a home and a studio. Most importantly, her work would be featured in a major publication and seen by a national audience.

Holy catching stars with both hands.

Chapter 10

Lindy sat in the hotel's elaborate bathroom and reapplied her lipstick for the millionth time. She was not accustomed to painting herself up and being the center of attention.

Her vase was front-page news. She'd scoured resale shops for an appropriate gown. Even at second-hand rates, the ensemble put a hefty dent in her dwindling checking account.

She gave up trying to work the clasp on her necklace and placed an emergency video call home. "Mom, I'm so nervous."

"You're going to be just fine."

Nina shouted greetings from the background.

"I can't get my hair right and my hands are shaking so badly I can't fasten my choker."

"Stop stalling and show us the dress." Nina squeezed into the frame.

"You've seen it already."

"Not on your body," Nina giggled. "Prop the phone so we can see you better."

Lindy positioned the camera. "Ready or not." She stepped into view.

"Wow, Lindy, just wow," Nina gushed. "You look like magic."

"Oh…" her mother sighed then sniffed.

"Mom, are you crying?"

"No." Susie blew her nose.

Nina handed Susie a tissue. "Pull yourself together." She laughed as she lifted the phone. Her face filled the screen. "You look sooooooo beautiful, forget the necklace. We're thrilled for you. Call us tomorrow and tell us everything."

The door opened and an exotic woman entered adorned in confidence from head to designer dressed toe. Her bold black hair angled in an arrow-straight line from nape to jaw and was punctuated by brilliant blue bangs.

She moved to the vanity, tossed her clutch on the counter, and straightened her pencil skirt. She caught Lindy's eye in the mirror and smiled. "That's a great dress."

"Yours too." Lindy forced her lips into a smile. "I love your shoes."

"Weakness." Her eyes twinkled. "Hope my arches hold out until I meet the featured artist. She's the next big name."

Lindy swallowed. "She is?"

"And barely twenty, can't even sip the champagne they'll be toasting her with. Have you seen her piece?"

Lindy nodded dully and sank to the settee.

"It's magnificent and makes my shoes look like rubber dime store flip-flops." She ran her fingers over her sleek cobalt fringe. "I'd kill to be able to do what she does but," she wiggled perfectly manicured fingers, "I'm all thumbs. Publicity is my thing."

"Are you good at it?"

"Very good." She noticed the hairclip lying in Lindy's lap. "Making a last-minute style change?"

"I took it out." Lindy fumbled the jeweled comb. "Shouldn't have, and now I can't get it right."

"May I?"

Lindy blinked. "Sure."

Deft fingers tousled and weaved the strands of her wild hair. In an instant, a section was secured, leaving wispy curls falling naturally at her temple and cheek.

"Not sure about the all-thumbs comment, thank you."

"Anytime." She winked and tucked her clutch under her arm. "We girls have to stick together. Clock's ticking on my toes. I better get out there and find my girl."

The door swept closed leaving her words *"the next big name"* to play again and again in Lindy's mind. The echo was swift and gnawed like a dog on rawhide... *You're nothing*.

"Not tonight, Frank." Lindy pushed her father's favorite barb aside. "Tonight, I'm somebody."

The evening, sponsored by the Hayward Livingston Foundation, was steeped in sophisticated style and grace. Elegant gowns, layered jewelry, tailored tuxedos and polished shoes. The air smelled of lavender and roses, and the food was infinite and luscious.

Twinkling white lights reflected in tall champagne flutes and mirrored ceilings, reminding Lindy of fireflies against an August sky.

Hayward Livingston asked her to dance. He placed a strong hand on the small of Lindy's back and together they glided as if floating on air. "You're extremely talented, Belinda."

Lindy opened her mouth to correct him.

His charming laugh washed over her cheek. "I'm calling you Belinda because it suits you and your ability. Lindy Colton is a girl who longs to be seen, whereas *Belinda Cole* has aspirations beyond a simple headline. Belinda Cole is a woman whose ambition will propel her reach to farther than she's ever imagined. Belinda Cole is world-renowned."

Lindy's gaze lifted to his and she fell into the vision he cast. "Belinda Cole," she whispered.

"Yes." His smile bloomed. When the music ended Hayward ushered her from the dance floor. "It was an honor to meet you, Belinda." He pulled a business card and pen from his lapel pocket and scrolled quickly across the back. "Pass this on to your representative." He neatly tucked the card into her palm. "I'd like to discuss a commission for the Livingston Foundation's Starving Artist Gala in December." He lifted her hand and feathered a kiss across her knuckles. "Until next time."

Lindy watched Hayward fade into the crowd then stared dully at the card. On the back in clean strokes of bold ink, he'd written Belinda Cole.

Lindy scanned the room for the woman she'd met earlier. She spotted her standing beside the display highlighting Lindy's vase. Admiration painted her features as vibrantly as the blue streak accenting her hair.

"You weren't blowing smoke." Lindy stood at her side. "You really are a fan of her work."

"Oh, I'm more than a fan." She pivoted on her high-rise heels and smiled knowingly. "I hear you know Lindy Colton pretty well." She offered her hand. "Celeste Wilde, promotion. Want to help me convince her to give me a shot at representing her?"

When Lindy's hand closed over Celeste's an anchoring calm passed between them. "I never thought I'd need an agent." Lindy released a long breath. "It's been a dazzling few weeks."

"My primary focus would be to allow you to enjoy the dazzle while I handle the day-to-day, whatever that may bring."

"Ever hear of the Starving Artist Fundraiser?" Lindy passed the card Hayward had given her.

"I certainly have." Clearly impressed, Celeste turned the card over. "Belinda Cole?"

"That's what he called me." Lindy shrugged then lifted two flutes of champagne from a passing tray and offered one to Celeste. "I turned twenty-one in July."

Celeste raised the glass in cheers. "We're going to have so much fun."

Chapter 11

The next morning Lindy arrived at the academy's student studio early. She walked through the quiet workspace and tried to process the whirlwind which had unfolded over the last few hours.

Celeste Wilde was meeting her for lunch to talk about the particulars of doing business together. A quick internet search had revealed Celeste was more than an exquisite package of trendsetting style. She had started her company at twenty-five and in three short years had complied a client list that rivaled her exclusive taste in shoes.

Lindy settled at the wheel to warm up by throwing a few small pieces. Hands moved and water dripped, and within minutes she was lost.

In Celeste's opinion, new partnerships were best forged with food. She walked into the deli near the address Lindy had given her and scanned the menu. Until she learned Lindy's preferences, she decided to cover all bases. She ordered two large salads with salmon, cut fruit, cold beverages and a bar of dark chocolate.

Celeste entered the Academy for the Arts building and hopped the elevator to the sixth floor. She'd left messages to confirm their meet-up but Lindy hadn't responded. Although she hadn't pegged Lindy for the brush-off type, artists were an interesting blend of DNA.

The doors opened to a wide hallway ripe with shape and color. Photography, paintings, tapestry, and more were combined in a riotous mosaic of creative energy. Celeste took her time absorbing the power of a monochromatic portrait, then shifted her attention to a woven textile panel. At the end of the mini-exhibit, she discovered the space designated for the dirty work.

Lindy was in the corner postured over a rapidly rotating wheel. Hands, arms, shoulders contorted with flowing movement as she manipulated the clay.

Celeste set the deli bag on the counter and settled in to watch the show. Several artists came and went, completing one project or finishing another, but Lindy, engrossed in the creative process, continued to work through lunch.

Lindy released the pedal. The revolving disc slowed and eventually stopped. She straightened her spine, pressed her hands into her low back, and groaned.

"I should say so," Celeste laughed richly. "I'm adding weekly massages to your schedule."

"Holy cow." Lindy startled and in a flash remembered their meeting. "I'm so sorry. I completely lost track of time."

Celeste unfolded her legs and stood. "May I?" She moved closer. "I've never seen anything so intense and concentrated." She shook her head. "You are amazing."

"Today was a good day." Lindy dipped her head toward the rack.

"You made all of those today?"

She nodded and pushed to her feet. "I'll pay for it, I assure you."

"As I said, massages on the regular." Celeste grabbed the bag from the deli. "You hungry?"

"Now look who's amazing."

They chatted about simple things as they ate. The natural kinship Lindy felt the evening before expanded.

Celeste passed her a hunk of chocolate. "Now for the business of doing business."

She lifted a file from her bag and laid the drafted letter of intent to partner with the Livingston Foundation in December. "Please read this over in the next twenty-four hours. I'll adjust any language or details to your liking and send it on to the executive board." She rattled the keys of her laptop and cued a spreadsheet mapping her plan for branding and marketing for the first half of the year. "This is tentative, pending a few questions and answers from you."

"About what?"

"Specifically, what is your ultimate vision for your career? Where do you want to work? Is travel important? Do you want to study from any ceramic art masters? Personal time, exercise routine, trips to the spa, sporting events," she gestured to the baseball bat propped against the work table. "Are there hard and fast holidays or blackout dates around special events or family traditions? What do you do for yourself to maintain sanity?" When Lindy paled, Celeste laughed. "I'm not expecting answers on the spot."

"That's a relief." Lindy released a shaky breath.

"Your dream." Celeste reached out and cradled Lindy's hands in hers. "What do you see when you close your eyes? I want to give you a foundation to build on. The structure can and will change as you've barely begun. My business is to put the steps in place so you have room to nurture the gift inside you and see what this world has to offer."

"Okay," Lindy relaxed. "Overall, I'd say I'm pretty uncomplicated. I was twelve when I saw a bowl in a gift shop and something inside fired to life. At sixteen I did a stint in therapy and got my hands in clay. I was lucky to have a pod of people around me who made it possible to dive deeper into the craft. I don't look too far ahead. Even now," Lindy shrugged absently, "this studio and the apartment are secure for six months. I won't think about the next move until a week before." She gestured broadly. "Everything is a gift. I learned early on gifts slip through fingers and shatter all the time."

"Hmm, very true," Celeste said thoughtfully then waited for Lindy to continue.

"I can work anywhere with the right equipment and I want to learn from everyone. My mom is my everything. She, well we, survived domestic brutality the hard way." Lindy pointed to the baseball bat. "She lives in Virginia and I video call her every Sunday night. We celebrate No Reservation November the first two weeks of the month. I guess that would qualify as a blackout."

"I've never heard of it."

"That's probably because my mom invented it," Lindy laughed. "When you run a bed and breakfast you have to carve out a vacation

51

somewhere. Each year she blocks the reservations, and we spend fourteen days stripping the B&B of summer décor and shifting the canvas in preparation for the holiday season."

"Smart." Celeste scribbled a reminder to protect the Sunday night calls with Lindy's mom.

"It's been our tradition since I was fourteen. What else?" Lindy sipped her water considering. "Travel, yes. Big cities but also I'd like to visit the national parks and go to a state in the Midwest and dig up a triceratops. What I'm attempting to say is, my dreams are disconnected and unfocused. I was given an opportunity to stretch, a chance to try and, I think, more than anything, I'd like to inspire others to try. It's bigger than just me, you know?"

"Triceratops big." Celeste laughed.

"Exactly," Lindy grinned. "It's imperative I make my own way. I need to focus and establish a creative routine. I don't want to be bound to one location or become reliant on generosity or charity to keep my head above water."

Celeste jotted furiously, capturing the no-compromise factors in Lindy's vision.

"Speaking of dollars and cents," Lindy released a worried breath. "I don't know what you charge but I'm pretty sure I can't afford you."

"When you do well, I do well." Celeste set her pen down and reached for Lindy's hand. "It's my job to make sure you do well."

"Me time," she sighed. "I practice yoga to stay flexible but if I'm to maintain social skills in any capacity, I need to attend a class once a week in a studio. Most of all, Celeste, it's important you understand today wasn't a fluke. I lose time, forget appointments, rarely turn on my phone or remember to charge the battery. I cut my own hair, prefer t-shirts to fancy duds, and the gown you saw last night is the only one I own."

Celeste noted alternate methods for seamless communication and Lindy's aversion to shopping. A courier entered the room carrying roses in more colors than Lindy knew existed.

"Belinda Cole?"

Lindy cradled the crystal vase.

"Somebody made an impression last night." Celeste plucked the card from the perfect blooms and turned it so Lindy could read the signature.

Hayward.

Chapter 12

Lindy carried her coffee to the elevator and descended three floors. She followed the windowed hall to the student studio enjoying the occasional fat snowflake swirling hundreds of feet above the city streets.

She certainly couldn't fuss about the commute or the view.

The prize of additional time at the academy was a gift Lindy refused to squander. She spent the next two months attending countless advanced workshops and lectures and every free moment perfecting the nuances of her art.

Celeste established an easy routine. Throughout the week they exchanged information via email and text and met in person once a month.

The nonintrusive setup allowed Lindy to create without pressure or stress. The result of Lindy's dedication greeted her as the studio lights blinked to life. "Good morning, children," she said as she passed twin shelving units filled with completed and in-the-process projects.

The only decision Lindy had been faced with that made her slightly uncomfortable was whether or not to follow Hayward Livingston's suggestion of marketing under a unique name. Celeste was coming today to help select the pieces she'd offer at the Starving Artist Holiday Ball the first weekend of December.

Lindy fastened the "do not disturb" sign on the door, put on her headphones, and opened the tub of clay. She worked for a few hours and finally eased back, studied the form on the slowing wheel, and said, "I like it."

"You should."

Lindy jolted and nearly fell from her stool.

"Careful," Celeste laughed. "I've never met anyone who can tune out the world the way you do."

"Am I late for our meeting?" Lindy flushed.

"No, I came early because of the storm. I thought better to get stuck with you than to not be able to get here later."

"Stuck? What are you talking about? The snow was so pretty this morning."

"Flurries are beautiful, even a few inches, but I'm not a fan of trying to navigate through feet of slop and slush."

Lindy hurried to the window and her heart sank. "I had no idea they were calling for this." She reached for her satchel and rummaged for her phone. "Mom is going to be so disappointed."

"I assumed you rescheduled."

"No." Lindy powered on the device. "It would help if I watched the forecast." Her phone began to chirp and vibrate. "Or turned on my phone." She scrolled through a dozen missed calls and text messages.

"Call your mom." Celeste rested her hand on Lindy's shoulder. "I'll go grab us a bite from the cafeteria. Be back in a minute."

Lindy washed and dried her hands then waited for the video call to connect.

"Happy No Reservation November," her mom's face filled the screen.

"Happy No Reservation November," Lindy responded with less enthusiasm. "I can't believe this."

"Classic nor'easter according to the weather channel." Susie walked to the foyer and opened the front door. "Look at this." She turned the phone so Lindy could see the covered front walk. "The seagulls are very unhappy."

"I can relate."

"Hi, Nina." Susie stepped aside and Lindy's best childhood friend hurried inside. "Perfect timing, Lindy's on the phone. Get out of your coat and I'll hand her to you."

"What's she doing there already?"

"Nina stayed here all last week to help bring the things down from the attic."

Lindy frowned.

"Don't be upset, honey. Since you only had the weekend I wanted to get a head start so we could maximize your visit." She lowered her voice. "Nina misses you and I think being here helps. Plus she's whipping things into shape. We have a new computer with a touchscreen and have added social media marketing to the business plan."

"Awesome." Lindy fought a swell of jealousy.

"It truly is." The oven timer chimed. Susie slid her hands into hot mitts and lifted a perfectly crusted quiche to the cooling rack.

"Mom," Lindy whined even as her mouth watered. "You are not making this any less painful. That looks amazing."

"Want me to send you some Fed Ex?"

"Yes."

The phone jostled. Lindy heard Nina and her mom laughing and a second later Nina's face filled the screen.

"Hi, hi, hi." She walked to the front room. "I miss you so much."

"Me too." Lindy's eyes filled.

"Tell me all about everything, especially the Holiday Ball," Nina gushed.

"The Starving Artist Ball is the first weekend in December. The event raises funds for community art programs throughout the city. A few of my pieces will be auctioned to help the cause."

"You say that like it's nothing." Nina flopped on the couch and positioned the phone so Lindy could see the snow drifting over the bay. "A year ago we were fretting over you getting into the summer session, and now the highest rung of society somebodies will be bidding on your art."

"I guess."

"And the man connected with it all, Hayward Liv-ing-ston," Nina dragged out the syllables. "Even his name sounds regal. Is he as yummy in person as he is online? I confess, I Googled him, very upper crust. Did you know he owns a vineyard in Napa Valley?"

"No, I didn't," Lindy laughed fully. "I only met him once at the final student exhibit."

"The night that changed your life," Nina said dramatically.

"The evening certainly shoved doors open for me."

"Did you know celebrities will be at the Ball? I'm talking real live movie stars," Nina swooned. "Did you know they start the bidding at two thousand dollars? What are you going to wear?"

Lindy's stomach lurched. "What am I going to wear?" Her head was swimming. She hoped Celeste had her wardrobe covered.

"I'm sorry, I'll be quiet. I'm just excited for you."

"I probably should get my hair cut by a real professional." She slid from the windowsill to the chair.

"Might be a good idea," Nina snickered. "Oh, hold me up to the window. Look at that view. Susie," she shouted over her shoulder. "Come look at Lindy's city. It looks just like a snow globe."

Celeste found Lindy with her head between her knees. "Everything okay in here?"

"I need to get a haircut and a fancy dress."

"Right now?"

"For the Holiday Ball."

Celeste set the tray of lunch items on the table. "I made a salon appointment in two weeks—color, cut, and wax—and I put a few dresses on hold for you."

"You did?"

"Yes." Celeste pulled a chair beside Lindy. "Your choices are chicken noodle or Italian wedding soup, turkey sandwich or ham-and-cheese croissant."

Lindy took a deep breath and released it slowly. "Thank you, Celeste, for everything."

"Don't mention it."

Chapter 13

The Livingston Foundation's Starving Artist Holiday Ball was the cherry on the top of the multilayered sugary goodness. Social elite and gallery owners from across the nation would be in attendance.

Celeste sipped hot coconut tea as she finalized press packets for the public launch of Belinda Cole. "You've done the hard work. Tonight you'll enjoy, mingle and meet the people. I'll be next to your display all night handling interest and making connections for your tour."

"You won't mingle with me?" Lindy pouted. "You're the only person I'll know."

"You'll be fine. Rumor has it Bradley Cooper may be there."

"Holy cow, I'll certainly make a fool of myself if I run into him."

Celeste laughed. "Don't know a woman who wouldn't."

"I'm still having trouble believing any of this is happening. I don't believe in fairytales."

"Well, whether you like it or not," Celeste glanced at the time, "your fairytale is beginning right now."

"What have you done?"

"Not me," Celeste laughed at Lindy's panic. "The Livingston Foundation is sending a car. You are being treated to a spa day at the exclusive Madame T beauty salon, and dinner prior to the opening."

"I can't possibly."

"You can and you will. I messengered your outfit to the salon yesterday." Celeste laughed and grabbed Lindy's hands. "I'll meet you in the ladies' room promptly at seven forty-five. We'll tweak anything you don't like and walk out together."

"Then what?"

"Then, you'll enjoy the Ball."

The salon technician showed Lindy to the changing room. She stripped, stowed her personal items in the locker, and pulled on the luxurious client robe. Each shift of the silky fabric amplified her nakedness.

Lindy nibbled on her thumbnail and studied her reflection. She released the elastic securing her hair. Haphazard layers, streaked naturally by coastal living, fell in waves over her shoulders. The chunk of bangs she typically sheared in annoyance, had grown long enough to tuck behind her ear.

Knuckles rapped lightly against the door. "All set, Ms. Cole?"

"As set as I get." Lindy tightened the sash at her waist and followed the technician down the hall.

The experts at Madame T's worked their magic. Four hours later Belinda emerged and the girl from the island had been erased. Lindy gaped at the woman reflecting back at her. A brunette bombshell with coifed razor-textured edges that stopped just shy of her collarbone. Angled bangs framed sculpted brows and tinted lashes. Her skin was radiant and hydrated, her nails shaped and polished.

Beside the locker holding her belongings was a large box with a huge pink ribbon. The note taped to the top read, "I'd be honored if you'd wear this tonight, Hayward."

The sleek crimson silk hugged the length of her body and ended at her ankles. The scalloped hem flirted over shoes which appeared carved from glacial ice.

Hayward Livingston picked her up in a limousine and whisked her to a rooftop restaurant he'd reserved just for them. A harpist sat in the corner by a large fountain.

He handed Lindy a glass of champagne. "We're marking a significant moment. The first of many, I hope."

Wishing to slow time, Lindy's fingers drifted to the star pendant at her throat. She tapped her glass to Hayward's and the crystal chime rang into the night. The liquid bathed her tongue and the bubbles tasted like gold.

Celeste's heels rattled against the marble-tiled floor as her call to Lindy went to voicemail for the millionth time.

The hotel's massive doors would open any second. The lobby would fill to capacity with people dressed head to toe in holiday glitz and glamor. An assembly of Tony award-winning vocalists was scheduled to perform a mini medley after dinner, followed by a showcase by the Radio City Rockettes.

"And the artist is a no-show." Celeste braced her hands on the porcelain sink. How would she explain her client's absence? "Pull yourself together." She straightened and ran a hand over her platinum bob tipped for the occasion in holiday plum. "You're a professional." She adjusted her necklace and took a long settling breath. "Do your job."

A representative from the Livingston Foundation welcomed guests and hors d'oeuvres began to circulate. For the next half hour, Celeste handed out informational flyers and collected business cards. The buzz was positive, and the crowd was eager to set eyes on the artist herself.

"So am I," she murmured.

Just as her worry was beginning to get the better of her, Celeste saw Hayward crossing the lobby with a living work of art attached to his arm. The object d'art was Lindy.

Her hair, now dark brown, had been ribboned with subtle strands of caramel and rich cherry. Her makeup accented every feature yet remained natural. The gown, not what Celeste had selected, embraced each attribute in festive red from shoulder to floor and ended on heels of glass.

All eyes tracked the couple as they moved to the raised platform in the center room. The lights softened, and a spotlight framed Lindy and her intricate vase. Hayward stepped to the microphone. "Good evening, ladies and gentlemen. It's my honor to present the Holiday Ball's featured artist, Belinda Cole."

The modern-day fairytale unfolded as Hayward guided Belinda Cole through the room and introduced her to an endless sea of people.

Celeste's brain was working overtime. Seeking a moment to regroup, she tucked herself into the corner, thumbed through the mass of business cards, and began to sort the genuine interest from the unlikely leads.

She opened her phone and dictated a quick list of people she needed to reach out to in the morning. Then in a manner of effective organization, she noted the "do not call" list.

"A 'do not call' list," Hayward remarked. "One would certainly say that's a unique method of managing Belinda's budding career."

"Efficient actually." Celeste refused to be flustered. Hayward hadn't hidden his opinion that a larger agency would provide a higher level of exposure and in turn an increased market value.

"Belinda will learn what is best for her." Hayward raised a hand acknowledging someone across the room. "Excuse me."

The sun was about to take its turn over the city as the driver pulled to the curb.

"A moment of privacy please, Baxter," Hayward said and the driver stepped from the car. "Thank you for allowing me the honor of presenting you tonight, Belinda."

Lindy laughed nervously. "I still want to look over my shoulder when I hear that name."

"With proper direction, you'll grow into it." He angled his body toward her. "I'd like to be the one to guide you. I'm well connected and will gladly provide introductions as well as assist you in navigating the subtle nuances and formal etiquette expected in my world."

"I would be very grateful."

"I'm sure." He held her gaze for a few lingering seconds then leaned back. "I'll have my assistant email your representative tomorrow with a few options to get us started."

Exhausted in the most delicious way, Lindy fell into bed and dreamed of Hayward. He escorted her up a polished marble staircase to massive glass doors lettered in gold, *Belinda Cole Gallery*. The capacity audience turned and applauded as she stepped into the spacious room.

The reverie twisted and the door that slapped at her back was the one from her childhood. Her beautiful pottery was sitting on a rickety kitchen table, and her father stood beside it tapping a wooden baseball bat against his palm.

Frank's face contorted with loathing as he lifted a glazed and fired bowl and tossed it into the air. The weapon circled and impacted the fragile vessel. The shattered fragments pierced her skin and littered the tiles at her feet.

"Small town nothing brat from the beach, eager for a slice of fame. Why would any man pave your way to success? You better be just as eager to lie on your back with your feet in the air. That's the only way you'll get anywhere. You're nothing."

Lindy woke trembling and covered in sweat.

Chapter 14

With the support of the Livingston Foundation behind her, Belinda Cole exploded onto the art scene.

Celeste managed the firestorm brilliantly. Capitalizing on the surge, she booked Belinda on a one-month spring tour to the western part of the country… a hopscotch circuit with stops planned in Colorado, New Mexico and Arizona. In addition to displaying her work, the adventure would include visits to Native American reservations, hiking, sightseeing, and opportunities for Belinda to offer demonstrations and speak to aspiring artists in classrooms and community centers.

"What kind of clothing should I be packing?" Belinda pushed hangers aside in her closet. "Please don't say fancy."

"No sequins or heels required for the next four weeks, I assure you." Celeste selected a pair of lightweight cotton pants and a carefree tunic. "I'd think you should pack what you're most comfortable in plus a few casual dinner outfits. March weather can be unpredictable. You may encounter many climates, so layers will work best."

"Can I take this?" Belinda cradled a rag sweater her mom and Kate had worked in tag-team to create for her. "I know it's not a name-brand designer, but it is so cozy."

"I love that sweater," Celeste smiled. "The colors are gorgeous and clearly whoever made it knows and adores you."

"They do." Belinda hugged the garment close. "It would work well for layering, right?"

"Perfectly."

Belinda tossed the sweater on the pile. "When are you joining me? I know I'm being needy but are you sure you can't come the whole time?"

"I'd love to run away, trust me."

"But," Hayward stepped into the room startling both women, "as your representative, Celeste understands advantageous association is not a tool employed by individuals practicing ethical management. In other words, Belinda darling, traveling with you would be self-serving and unprofessional."

Belinda hopped off the bed. "I didn't hear you come in."

"The door was unsecured." He crossed the room and placed his lips against hers. "I knocked and sent you a text message before I entered."

Hayward had shown a keen interest in Belinda since the Holiday Ball. He'd taken her to Café Carlyle on the Upper East Side to ring in the New Year. He continued to fill her weekends with Broadway openings, sporting events, and gallery unveilings. On Valentine's Day, they'd dined at an exclusive restaurant in Tribeca and ended the evening with a sunset helicopter ride.

"Celeste and I were getting started on packing for the trip."

He pinched the sleeve of the handmade sweater and frowned. "We can certainly do better than this." Hayward lifted a gift bag in manicured fingers and held it out to her.

"You shouldn't have." Belinda removed the colored tissue and revealed an exquisite cashmere sweater with an angled hem. "You've done too much already."

"I enjoy doing nice things for talented, beautiful women. I hope you'll wear it tonight." He smiled at her puzzled look. "Also in the message you've not read." He angled his body to exclude Celeste from their conversation. "You will be away for quite a while. Take the sweater with you on your tour and think of me." His fingertips trailed over her arms. "I'd like to be the last person to share time with you. I was thinking a late dinner and lingering dessert."

She shivered. "I need to finish packing."

He glanced toward her closet. "Perhaps if I lend a hand."

In record time Hayward nipped six hangers from the rod and draped the articles across the bed. Next, he selected an array of complementing tops and lifted four pairs of dress shoes from the floor.

"Add the studio clothes you prefer but keep in mind you'll be photographed by strangers. Those pictures will land on social media and be tagged with your name. Even your working clothes should say Belinda Cole. You're branding yourself on this trip, not vacationing. Understand?"

She nodded.

"Toss in your intimates and bathroom essentials and you're ready to travel." Hayward dropped a kiss to the top of her head. "I'll pick you up for dinner at eight. The charcoal Ponte pants and suede mid-calf boots should complement your new sweater nicely." He brushed past Celeste as if she were a lamp on a side table.

Celeste waited for the door to close behind him. "The man is…"

"I know," Belinda said breathlessly, "confident and generous." She held up the sweater. "This is so gorgeous and soft. He has tremendous style and look." She gestured to the stack of clothing. "All I need to do is add socks and undies and put it in the bag." She grinned. "He shaved off an hour of my procrastination and indecision."

"Yes, he was very helpful." Celeste looked at the clothing and heels Hayward had chosen. "Why don't I do the packing while you shower for your dinner date? When you're finished we'll finalize the itinerary and then you'll be ready to go."

"Sounds great." Belinda moved to the bathroom. "And Celeste, for the record, I disagree with Hayward. I think it would be in the best interest for all things Belinda Cole if you're with me for as much of the tour as possible." Her eyes pleaded. "Tell me you'll think about it, okay?"

"Okay."

As promised, the tour had been a perfect marriage of business and pleasure. Belinda sent postcards to her mom from every location and phoned home every Sunday. Her individual and collaborative presentations sparked interest in potential workshops and established valuable contacts for the future.

The final week began in Phoenix. Celeste and Belinda toured Botanical Gardens and enjoyed a hike outside the city. They mar equally over the towering saguaro cacti and the phenomenon of Celeste wearing hiking boots rather than heels.

The historic stretch of Route 66 to Flagstaff delivered spectacular sights and a rowdy night at the Museum Club. A local man at the downtown coffee house recommended an offbeat pathway to reach the south rim of the Grand Canyon. The winding trip had added the Cameron Trading Post and a walking path marked by fossilized dinosaur tracks to their adventure.

It wasn't a triceratops, Belinda thought as she returned to the car, but it was still really cool.

The region was ripe with inspiration and visual contrasts. They wrapped up the month immersed in the beauty and power of the Red Rocks of Sedona.

Celeste hooked her sunglasses over her knee and opened her canteen. She leaned on a ledge to absorb the natural sandstone creation, Cathedral Rock. "Thank you for not making me hike this one." She took a long drink of water.

"Next time," Belinda chuckled when Celeste groaned. "I only have a few weeks left on my complimentary use of the studio and apartment at the academy. I need to lock down working space and housing."

"I have a number of leads on available residences as well as artist co-ops." Celeste slid her sunglasses back in place. "When we get back I'll schedule walk-throughs on the ones you feel have the most potential and we'll weigh your options."

"You're always one step ahead, aren't you?"

"I try to be," Celeste smiled. "Now that you've experienced another aspect of travel and sharing your passion face to face, what has made an impression?"

"I think for once I have a loaded answer to your simple question." Belinda rubbed her hands together. "I liked teaching and leading discussions more than I'd expected. I guess I shouldn't be surprised—art therapy was a huge avenue of healing for me."

"Would you be interested in pursuing classes or earning a degree?"

"Social work or psychology would require six years of education even online. Hayward says I should be careful not to confuse obstacles with opportunity."

"He's not wrong but there are many ways to give back and tutor without being a counselor or licensed therapist. You could align with an established program or organization that already has something in place. You could design a workshop or flexible component which could be added to an existing presentation. Mini segments would be, in my opinion, an ideal way to beta test a few layouts before diving into the deep end."

"Then I could modify or bolster the offering to best suit individual groups." Belinda nodded her head. "That's a really good idea."

"Ready to head back?"

"Never." She reached her hands toward the sky, inviting the vitality of the expanse to infuse her entire being. "It does make it easier to leave knowing I'll be coming back." She sighed. "I guess it's time to return to the real world."

Celeste followed Belinda's lead and stretched her arms wide. "Speaking of returning, I wasn't able to switch my flight, so I'll be an hour behind you on our trip home. I'll arrange transportation for you from the airport to your apartment."

"Actually, Hayward sent an email this morning." Belinda started along the descending trail. "He's picking me up at the terminal. He said he has a big surprise for me."

Belinda was speechless.

Hayward had secured a trendy loft apartment just outside Manhattan. The spacious upscale unit boasted mammoth windows and exposed brick through the main level and the second-floor layout was well suited for her pottery studio.

"I've spoken with the property manager regarding approval for kiln installation with proper venting." Hayward walked into the kitchen and opened his briefcase. "I've also received an estimate from an electrician and structural contractor for the minor renovations I expect you'll need."

Belinda's head was spinning.

"I've taken the liberty of reserving the equipment you prefer. You will need to look over and approve the invoice. I think Celeste can manage the timely coordination and move." Hayward turned and faced her. "And finally, I've contracted and paid in advance for personal services including weekly cleaning, food delivery and laundry service."

Belinda's mouth opened but she failed to produce a sensible response.

"I assure you, hiring someone to pick up after you is a reasonable extravagance. You do not have time to waste at the market selecting fruits and vegetables." Hayward paused. "The top priority is for you to remain focused and produce quality works of art."

Dumbfounded, she watched Hayward lay clipped stacks of papers across the marble counter.

"Talk it over with Celeste. Any question either of you may have," he tapped the documents, "is answered here." Hayward snapped the leather briefcase closed and walked to the door.

Belinda texted Celeste the address and sat in the middle of the floor until she arrived.

"The studio will flood with natural light in the morning, and wait until you see the balcony," Belinda chattered with excitement about features and square footage as she led Celeste through the second-floor galley kitchen. "I can just imagine sitting under the stars at night with a glass of wine. There's even room for a twin bed where I can sleep if I pull an all-nighter. In my first studio, I had a hammock. Did I ever tell you that?"

"No, you didn't."

Belinda laughed at the memory. "Anyway, I mentioned getting one to Hayward and he said I'm no longer a penniless hippie so I should have a real bed." They returned to the lower level. "Hayward said timing is everything and this is my opportunity to sustain my creative output and claim a seat at the global table."

Celeste bristled. She may have missed the pitch but she was up to speed. Hayward was so slick and polished. He moved effortlessly, so masterfully it nearly masked his bid to control.

"Can you believe it, Celeste? Me, in a private residence with a personal studio in the most esteemed city in the country?"

"I can, yes, but as Hayward said, timing is everything." Celeste shrugged out of her suit coat and spread it out on the wide-planked floor. She snatched the neatly stacked papers from the counter. "Let's take a breath and look at the fine print. The last thing I want is for you to make any decisions without absolute clarity."

"You do know real talk is a lot less fun." Belinda sighed and then settled on the floor beside Celeste to pour over the details.

Chapter 15

Belinda dipped the vase in a bucket of glaze and turned the piece to allow gravity to shift the liquid.

"I've forwarded the Sedona workshop proposal to your email." Celeste's voice floated from the computer. "Look it over when you get a moment and we'll discuss it in detail next week. You're all set for tomorrow. The presentation will include three other former art academy students. They are expecting you at nine and you should wrap up by eleven-thirty. I'll be joining you onsite for the Jubilee at the Hotel Marquis. We will tweak any dates or events to your specification then. Sound good... Belinda?"

"Yes, I'm here, sorry. I'm trying to finish up and I'm running out of minutes. Hayward has returned from his trip and I'm to meet him at his apartment in an hour." She placed the vase on the rack and leaned toward the camera. "I'm jumping in the shower now. I promise I'll read the email tomorrow and look forward to seeing you at the event."

Belinda hurried across town and let herself into Hayward's high-rise Manhattan residence with ten minutes to spare. He had supported her like no other and she never wanted him to think she was unappreciative. She was standing along the wall of glass overlooking Central Park when he entered.

Hayward rested his hands on her shoulders. "I missed you."

"Me too." She leaned into his embrace.

"Come with me. I have something to show you." Hayward led her to the second bedroom and opened the doors to the walk-in closet.

Belinda gaped at the array of gowns, tops, slacks and skirts. She was stunned by the meticulous organization of even the basic denim and everyday clothes. Necklaces and earrings were paired with handbags and shoes. "This is," she didn't have the words, "way too much."

Hayward simply smiled. "You're welcome." He opened the armoire and revealed intimates and shapewear. "You have an important role to play and in my arena, you need a wardrobe to support the task. I've decided it's time for you to travel with me and meet new people. New alliances are the key, and the next-level connections I have in mind will elevate not obligate you. Will you allow me to cherish you?"

"Cherish," Belinda shuddered, "is not a word I have much experience with."

"I feel there are many things you should become accustomed to." He lifted her hand and brushed his lips across her knuckles. "A fashionable wardrobe is the least of them."

"Thank you." Belinda lifted a silk camisole from the drawer.

"One of my favorites." His gaze heated. "Try it on." He watched as she shed her shirt and slipped the fabric over her head. He crooked his finger inviting her closer.

Belinda stepped toward him and he turned her to face the full-length mirror.

"How beautiful you are."

She flushed.

"Nearly perfect." He tapped his phone. "This is Hayward Livingston. I spoke with Madame T this morning and reserved a block of... yes... Belinda Cole, that's correct. She'll need the works... yes, everything... I agree. If we could only convince her to prioritize personal appearance... A classic facial with lymphatic massage and a vitamin C mask would be magnificent..." Hayward lifted Belinda's hand and examined her nails. "Definitely add extensions, even though she'll fuss and ruin the full set in a day... You couldn't be more right on all accounts... Excellent." He disconnected the call.

Belinda walked to the closet, selected a black and white slip dress, and held it in front of her.

"Madame T is expecting you tomorrow morning at ten." Hayward jotted the appointment on a notepad. "You'll take," he reached past her, "this dress and," he selected shoes, a purse, and jewelry, "these accessories to the salon. I'll join you in the lobby following my afternoon meetings."

71

"I'm committed at the elementary school until eleven-thirty." Belinda tried not to squirm under the weight of his stare. "You remember the collaborative assembly I've been organizing to promote art and creative expression? The children will be so upset if we were to cancel."

"Disenchantment is a difficult lesson." Hayward continued to hold her gaze. "Have Celeste rearrange your day."

Fresh from the salon, Belinda met Hayward in the lobby. "Exquisite." He pressed his lips to her temple. "Your presence alone will up the ante this evening."

"They're courting you, Hayward. Why would I be of any curiosity to anyone?"

"Because you'll have arrived with me," he laughed. "What sells a story is the image presented. What sparks and amplifies the interest is the mystery. What sustains and captivates is scandal or envy. We, darling, are the perfect combination of all three." He placed her arm over his. "Tonight I'd like you to pay attention to the volley of conversation. First word and last word in an exchange shows who is leading and who is chasing the pack."

"Okay." She was doing her best not to gawk at the lavishness of the private club, not to mention the attire and jewelry displayed by the people in attendance.

The room was filled with an ocean of heavy hitters. The social swirl reeked of wealth, influence and clout. Belinda was out of her depth and alone would have sunk to the bottom.

"Don't shrink, darling," Hayward whispered and gathered her close. "Your place is on my arm." He lowered his lips to her ear and murmured, "And in my bed." Her quick catch of breath fueled his ego.

An older man approached them. "Evening, Livingston." He ogled Belinda as he jiggled the ice in his empty whiskey glass. "This is the shiny new plaything I've been hearing about."

"She's my secret weapon," Hayward joked.

He licked his lips. "A weapon with benefits, I imagine."

"Filthy man." Hayward patted his shoulder. "One of the reasons I like you so much."

Belinda was acutely aware of the eyes on her as Hayward took her hand and moved to the center of the ballroom.

"Let them look." He took her waist and whispered, "Image, mystery, envy." Belinda followed his lead as if they'd been dancing together for decades. "Let them gossip and speculate. The attention is good for both of us."

Chapter 16

A portion of Belinda's collection was featured in the Hotel Marquis's elaborate atrium. The strategic positioning maximized exposure and would be captured again and again by the media swarm documenting the Jubilee.

Additional auction items were on display throughout the ballroom. Skillful service staff weaved through the throng of bodies balancing trays burdened with cocktails and tidbits.

"Who can eat at these things?" Celeste whispered.

"I know." Belinda brushed her hand over the open midsection of her gown. "I'm too concerned with standing up straight and remembering who's who."

"Yours is the name folks are going to remember." Celeste adjusted Belinda's double-tier necklace as she angled her head toward the group of people gathered around her stoneware. "You just keep smiling and let me worry about who's who."

"Darling," Hayward's voice lifted above the conversations. Photographers jostled to get a better angle and captured the kiss he pressed to Belinda's cheek. "You look lovely."

The man certainly knew how to maximize an entrance, Celeste thought. "Good evening, Hayward."

"Celeste," he said briskly without shifting his focus from Belinda. His brow lowered as he studied her necklace. "This is…" Hayward turned the charm dangling from the end of a crude, chunky chain, "not what we'd selected."

"I found it at a flea market in Sedona."

"Choosing a yard sale accessory to compliment haute couture is an interesting option."

"I couldn't agree more, Hayward." Celeste passed Belinda her vintage beaded purse. "A bold and unique choice."

"Yet you claim your specialty is promotion." Hayward turned his back on Celeste and offered Belinda his arm. "Keep your shoulders back, darling," he said as he glided toward the elevator, "or the dress will wear you."

The next hour passed in a blur of names and handshakes dripping with influence and power. Hayward was a master at this particular dance. He led with compliments then sprinkled subtle hints regarding his willingness to support certain individuals in their quest to pursue political office.

"There he is." Hayward ushered Belinda toward yet another distinguished-looking man. "Darling, I'd like you to meet Congressman Keyport and his wife Kimberly."

"It's so nice to…" Belinda's phone rang, interrupting the introduction. "Excuse me, I'm so sorry." She fumbled with the clasp on her clutch.

"Who could possibly need to reach you?" Hayward bit down his annoyance as the couple moved on. "Everyone of importance is in this room." He took her bag, opened the snap and silenced the phone.

Kimberly Keyport noticed the exchange and gently squeezed her husband's arm. "Sweetheart, Belinda is one of the artists featured this evening. The vase you admired in the vestibule is her work."

"Exquisite." Congressman Keyport's expression brightened. "Don't tell my wife," he leaned close to feign secrecy, "I plan on placing the winning bid and surprising her on Christmas morning." He laughed richly. "Now Hayward, what did you want to discuss with me?"

Kimberly rested her unpolished fingers on Belinda's arm. "Why don't we slip off and powder our noses? These men want to talk business, and frankly, I don't want to listen."

In a room of starch and polish, Belinda found Kimberly's unassuming nature refreshing. "Sounds perfect, Mrs. Keyport."

"Please, call me Kimberly." She hooked her arm through Belinda's. "Your pottery is captivating. Do I call it pottery? I don't want to embarrass myself."

"Captivating works for me," Belinda laughed.

Inside the bathroom suite Kimberly settled on the chaise. "If they expect a woman to be speedy then why put such comfortable furniture in the restroom?" She patted the seat next to her. "Sit a minute and check your messages, dear."

Belinda opened her purse and retrieved her phone. "I apologize for forgetting to turn the ringer off."

"Nonsense, you're building a career, aren't you?"

"I am," Belinda smiled. She had seven missed calls. Worry bubbled as she accessed her voicemail.

"Lindy honey," Kate's voice cracked with emotion, "it's your mom." The rest of the message was a blur. Belinda's heart sank along with her body into the settee.

Kimberly's arm came around her. "Breathe... breathe... that's it, easy now."

"I'm sorry... I need to... I should... I don't know..."

"Take a moment and return the call." Kimberly rose and moved to the door. "I'll make sure you're not disturbed."

Her hand trembled as the call connected.

"Lindy girl," Kate's voice was heavy with sorrow. "I don't know much other than your mom collapsed, was taken by ambulance and went directly into surgery. We're waiting to hear from the doctor. You're needed at home right away."

"I'm at an event." Lindy pushed to her feet and began to pace. "And I have commitments tomorrow..."

"Some things can wait, others cannot," Kate said firmly. "Do not make me drive up to that concrete island and fetch you. You get yourself home now."

Kate had never spoken anything but the truth her entire life. That fact more than the harsh command had Lindy's insides melting like ice cream in the sun.

"I'll be on my way within the hour."

Belinda gathered the hem of her dress in one hand and her shoes in the other. She raced down three flights of stairs, burst into the lobby and hurried to Celeste. In a sputter of syllables and broken breath, she said, "My mother... emergency... I... leaving immediately."

"Should I get Hayward for you?"

Scenting a hot story, members of the media aimed their cameras in her direction. Belinda fixed her smile as shutters snapped in rapid staccato. "No." She leaned closer to Celeste and lowered her voice. "It's an important night for him." She continued to move toward the exit. "I don't want him inconvenienced. I'll touch base with him later."

"You're very upset." Celeste touched her arm. "Do you want me to come with you or do anything to help you get on the way more quickly?"

"I'll be okay, I just need to grab a few things from the loft and get on the road. A car..." Belinda's face fell. "Where can I rent a car at this hour?"

"You'll take mine. The spare key is hanging on the pegboard in the studio." Celeste walked Belinda toward the door. "No argument. That's part of our deal. I handle the details." She opened Belinda's clutch and tucked a clip of cash inside. "I'll text you the garage address and key code for access. There are a few snacks and bottled water in the trunk and the gas tank is full." Celeste opened the taxi's rear door and relayed the address for Belinda's apartment.

Tears threatened to spill. Belinda gripped Celeste's hand. "I can't remember anything you just told me."

"Take a deep breath." Celeste squeezed her hand. "As soon as you pull away I'll text all the information to you. Okay?"

"Okay." Belinda released a quivering breath. "Thank you, Celeste, thank you so much."

Chapter 17

Belinda rested her head against the seat and closed her eyes. The driver navigated the bustling streets. Her cell alert chimed. Celeste's text came through complete with a do-not-forget-to-pack list.

Eternally grateful, Belinda gathered the items and tossed everything into her canvas tote. She carefully wrapped a few finished pieces from the studio, engaged the security and returned to the waiting cab.

On the ride to the garage, Belinda dictated a personal statement to the Livingston Foundation expressing sincere regret for her abrupt and unavoidable departure from the event. She sent the announcement to Celeste and in a gesture of transparency granted permission for the release to be read prior to the auction.

Next, she texted Hayward to clarify her reasons for exiting discreetly and apologized for any disruption she may have caused for the remainder of his evening.

They'd only been seeing each other regularly for a few months. He'd never asked about the details of her childhood and she had never offered.

Traffic in Lower Manhattan was uncharacteristically light as Belinda descended into the Holland Tunnel. One and a half miles later, it was Lindy who came up for air. She navigated to the interstate, eased the car onto I-95, followed the ramp toward New Jersey, and then on to Delaware.

Kate called again as Lindy crossed the state line and relayed the address to the medical facility. The update on her mother was grave. The news stripped away her dream life and dumped her into the callous reality.

"How can this be happening?" Lindy shouted into the void. She exceeded the speed limit the rest of the way. A few hours later, she raced across the parking lot and entered Atlantic General.

The surgeon's explanation made little sense. An ulcer as a result of chronic gastric erosion had hemorrhaged. A complication according to reported cases which affects one in one hundred thousand patients and Susie just happened to be the unlucky one.

Lindy's eyes filled and spilled over as she moved into the stagnant room. Kate was in the corner knitting. She had a mask over her face to protect her dear friend from outside germs. "Here's your girl, Susie."

Susie's breathing was labored. "So... proud of you."

Kate stood, lifted a paper gown and mask off the table, and offered them to Lindy. "She's groggy from the fever. They're giving her morphine to keep her comfortable. Hurry and wash your hands and then cover up."

Lindy did as directed then sat beside the bed for the next five days and watched her mother's life slowly drift out of reach.

"Lindy?"

"I'm here, Mom."

"So glad... fearless dreamer... you always dreamed life-sized... bold... so strong and talented... I wish I'd been..." Susie attempted to lift her hand and winced in pain.

"You were everything, Mom. Everything I could've ever asked for."

"Are you happy?"

"Yes."

"Your Hayward is kind... respectful? I'm sure... you'd never settle for less." Her body shuddered.

"Try to rest." Lindy adjusted the oxygen.

"Kate?"

"I'm here, Susie..." Kate moved to the side of the bed. "We're both here."

"Take... care... of my..."

"I will." Kate leaned over and kissed Susie's forehead. "I promise I will, always."

"Lindy… you are," her words rode on a wisp of breath, "stronger than you know… I love you…"

Lindy folded and buried her face in her mother's abdomen and wept.

Oppressive humidity greeted Lindy's shocked system like a lost friend and carried her across the parking lot. She leaned heavily against the hot car and sent a brief text to Celeste and Hayward, to let them know she'd be staying a few extra days to settle her mother's affairs.

Lindy navigated the summer traffic and parked on the street in front of the B&B.

Nina was sweeping the porch. She heard the car, set the broom aside, and hurried down the steps.

The girls met on the sidewalk and for a fleeting moment the comfort of reuniting overshadowed the heaviness in their hearts.

"Lindy." Nina's voice was weary with mourning. "I still can't believe it."

They moved as one unit into the air-conditioned house. The instant the door closed at her back Lindy fell captive to the rush of memories.

The desk was the same, the rug different, the same mirror, a new lamp. Odd, Lindy thought, how everything seemed smaller, like a dollhouse. She trailed her fingers over the banister and wondered if she had the energy for the climb.

"I relocated the reservations for the next two weeks," Nina said. "I figured you'd want the house to yourself, and wasn't sure how long you were staying."

"Three days."

Nina gasped, "Only three?"

"Four, tops." Lindy touched the flowers in a glass vase at the foot of the steps, a simple arrangement of bright blossoms with a single pink rose standing a few inches above the blooms. "What room am I staying in?"

"Well, yours of course. I was about to move my things."

"That's silly. I'm a guest, and guests stay upstairs."

"Lindy…"

"I've been sleeping in a chair and am wearing the same clothes I had on when I left New York however many days ago." Lindy's shoulders drooped. "I realize there are many things to be dealt with but, right at this moment, I'm not fit for human company. I need an hour to regroup."

"Take all the time you need." Nina watched Lindy tackle the stairs like a hiker on the brutal stretch to the summit, then ducked into the kitchen.

Lindy's legs threatened rebellion as she arrived on the second floor. She followed the cheerful, lemon-painted hallway to the front of the house and chose the master suite with an indulgent private bath and king-sized bed. Her bag hit the floor and she continued to the large-paned glass window which offered an unobstructed view of the bay.

She turned away, sank to the bed, and allowed the mattress to support the weight of her grief. She traced the seam, running down the center of the feminine eyelet coverlet, where two twin bedspreads had been sewn together to achieve the size needed to drape the massive bed. Even as her heart split wider, Lindy didn't resist the memory of her mother's laughter as she wrestled the fabric into the sewing machine and then gave up and finished the stitching by hand.

The colossal claw foot tub beckoned. Lindy stripped as she walked into the bathroom. She selected a cucumber melon bath-bomb, tossed it into the porcelain-lined cask, then spun the knobs to a degree under scalding. With every barrier shed, she stepped in and sank to her chin.

An hour later, Lindy followed her nose to the kitchen and found Nina busy at the stove. "Smells good in here."

"Fresh bread and soup. Grief food," she shrugged. "Predictable, I know." Nina leaned against the counter. "Feeling better?"

"Than what?"

"Sheesh, Lindy," Nina laughed. "What they say about the gruff nature of New Yorkers is true."

Lindy shook her head. "I'm a miserable person."

"Give yourself a break. You were busy with your work and then got upended with this," Nina gestured broadly, "horribleness."

Lindy studied Nina's face and saw for the first time the layers of sadness fresh makeup couldn't hide. She laid her hand on Nina's arm. "I'm sorry for your loss too."

Lindy's eyes filled. "I swear to you, I worked side by side with Susie nearly every day for the last year and hadn't a clue she wasn't feeling well." Nina dabbed at her eyes. "I don't know how she fooled us."

"Mom was a master at hiding pain." Lindy grabbed Nina's hand and squeezed. "Thank you for being here and loving me even when I'm being a brat."

Nina's eyes spilled over again. "I'll be empty sooner or later right?"

"I doubt it." Lindy's wet laughter bubbled. "Before we eat a bowl of your delicious sorrow soup, would you want to walk to the water with me?"

Nina turned the burner down. "I would like that very much."

Looking over the water was a ritual her mom had begun when she and Lindy moved to the house on Main Street. At the time they'd been in survival mode, enduring and healing. In the morning, she'd carry her tea across the street and greet the day. In the evening, she'd say farewell as the sun dipped from sight.

The girls linked arms and crossed the street.

"Why do you think Susie did this each day?" Nina asked. "I always wanted to ask but it seemed like sacred time."

"I think for her it was." Lindy stepped to the edge. "A quiet reflective moment before her day got crazy or a gratitude practice when the day was over. A simple reminder to celebrate life while she was living it."

The sun was fading slowly just like her mother had hours before. Lindy and Nina watched the bay swallow the bright orb, casting hues of pink across the sky.

Chapter 18

Lindy woke early. Her footsteps echoed in the hollow house. She found a smiley face resting on a basket of fresh-baked mini muffins and a note taped to the coffee maker that said "push me."

The rich aroma roused her senses and challenged her grief. Lindy decided choices lacked inclusivity, so she wrapped one of each flavor in a napkin and carried her breakfast to the front porch.

Vibrant life met her on the other side of the door. Early morning cyclists, walkers and runners passed the house. Some smiled or lifted a hand, others were lost in the process of traversing from here to there.

Lindy nibbled and sipped. Her mom's flower boxes were thriving with rich color. The fragrance permeated her gloom and partnered with a gentle memory of her sixteenth birthday.

"Miss Susie, your flowers always look really pretty," Nina said.

"My secret is watering twice a day, first thing in the morning and again at sunset." Susie's laughter carried lightly on the breeze...

A hummingbird whizzed past, breaking Lindy's mind mosey. He zipped from bloom to bloom, gathering moisture and sustenance, then hovered directly in front of her.

"Good morning," Lindy smiled. "Want some breakfast?" He disappeared in a flash over the banister. "More for me."

She contemplated a quick yoga flow to release the tension in her back and legs then spotted the watering wand. "Morning and evening," Lindy mumbled. "I hear you, Mom." She finished her coffee, turned on the hose, and began to soak the soil.

"Lindy Colton." A woman bustled up the front walk, arms loaded with foil-wrapped pans. "We're all in shock. Susie was such a good woman and you, well she couldn't have been more proud of all you're doing."

"Thank you." Lindy pulled the hose out of the way.

"I'm Hazel from the YWCA." She mounted the porch. "Where shall I put these? Casserole, gingerbread, and such." She stepped to the door and managed the knob. "The kitchen would be the best place, right?"

"Um, sure." Lindy started to follow Hazel inside when a delivery van pulled to the curb. A man hopped out and slid the side door open. He lifted an enormous bouquet and hurried up the sidewalk.

"One of five." He offered a gentle smile. "I'm sorry for your loss. Where would you like me to put them? How about the dining room? Then you can move them wherever you feel is best."

Lindy watched him disappear into the house. *What the heck was happening?*

The news of her mother's death spread across the island. Food and flowers poured in like beach lovers during peak season. Thankfully, Nina arrived and took over.

"They just keep coming." Nina carried another arrangement into the kitchen. "I've spread them all over the house, which is a shame as nobody will see them. I have a list of people who would like you to call, but that can wait of course."

"Did Mom have a will?"

"The safe in the office would be my guess. I have the combination but didn't feel comfortable going into it without you."

Lindy groaned when the chimes sounded again and the front door opened and closed. "This is insane."

"Good heavens, you're overrun," Kate's voice rumbled from the foyer. "Nina dear, stop whatever you're doing and call Mrs. Chapel and tell her to shut it down." She bumped the swinging door with her hip and entered the small kitchen. "Ask her to encourage people to make donations in Susie's memory to the charity of their choosing."

"Right away." Nina relieved Kate of a basket of fresh fruit and a pumpkin pie.

"I brought healthy and not, so pick your poison. Where's my girl of the city?"

"Right behind you." Lindy took the hand Kate extended.

Lindy would always remember when Kate arrived at her childhood home days before the bank was set to foreclose. Much like today, she'd opened the door, arms filled with pie. *"Susie," she'd said. "I'm here to beg a favor."* Then she'd plopped down in the chair reserved for Lindy's father and presented the opportunity that changed their lives forever.

"Did you girls get any rest?"

"A bit," Lindy said.

"To be expected." Kate cupped her cheek. "Let's heat the kettle for tea and have some pie."

"Pie fixes everything?" Lindy asked as a tear trickled slowly over her cheek.

"Too tall an order for one pie." Kate brushed the droplet away with her thumb. "Which is why I brought two."

For the next several hours the trio busied themselves with the business of death.

"The reception could be here," Nina said. "That would give us an opportunity to make use of the flowers and food. However, parking would be a problem."

"Plenty of off-street parking at the Inn," Kate suggested. "You're welcome to use the hospitality room, Lindy. We can keep the food simple and handle a large crowd."

The discussion was adding to Lindy's heartache. "This all seems a little excessive, not to mention a lot of work." She pushed from the table and moved to the back door. The butterfly garden she planted for Mother's Day when she was fourteen was pushing buds. "Grief is private and personal, or it should be. Why do I need to receive people?"

"Memorial services provide moments of comfort for those of us who continue on. But I understand why for you it feels intrusive."

"Because," Lindy huffed, "it *is* intrusive." The front door chime sounded again and an instant later the phone rang. She tossed her hands in the air. "This place is like Grand Central Station. Why can't people wait for the services to pay respects? I need some peace."

Kate signaled Nina with a curt nod.

"I'll take care of it." Nina hurried into the office.

Kate gathered her notes and collected her basket. "You need a bit of downtime." She tipped her head to the side. "An evening out will do you good. Come by the house tonight around six."

"Okay," Lindy relented. "I'm sorry for earlier."

"Nothing to be sorry for." Kate kissed Lindy's cheek.

Like a wrench to a drippy faucet, the flow of visitors and calls stopped. Nina and Lindy climbed the narrow steps to the attic.

"Susie had been on a mission the past few months to get everything incredibly organized." Nina pulled the chain, and the light bulbs illuminated tidy rows of totes neatly labeled with contents. "I realize this is not a task for today but I thought you should see for yourself so you can get an idea of what's here."

"I don't want any of it. I'll make arrangements to have an auctioneer pick up everything."

"That's the grief talking." Nina lifted a large container marked "Lindy" and set it on the floor. "I'm going to go downstairs and sort through some of the food. Good Lord knows we aren't eating anything Hazel made. The woman's heart might be in the right place, but she's never mastered the art of edible cooking."

"You can leave whenever you're ready, Nina. I'm sure you need a break, and Mike would love to have his wife at home. Besides, I've been ordered to report to Kate's tonight."

"If you're sure." Nina moved to the steps. "Be careful coming down."

"I will, and please tell Mike thanks." Lindy popped the lid on a tote and lifted a book of poems her mom had given her.

"See," Nina smiled, "not all trash. I'll touch base tomorrow morning."

"Sounds good." Lindy packed a few items from the attic, a snow globe Nina had given her, and a few candid pictures. She reached inside the next container and pulled a lanyard with two tiny keys from the nest of paper. Her heart bumped as she rushed to push the packing out of the way and looked down at the chest Tucker had made for her.

She laid the precious gift in her lap as the memory of the night he'd given it to her flooded her heart. They'd picked up a pizza and driven to the dead-end circle after he'd waited hours for her kiln to finish cycling.

She traced each etched star with her finger. "You knew me so well, Tucker Brandt." Lindy smiled. The little chest was filled with a wide range of unsophisticated and outlandish dreams. The lock had guarded them from the world and now many were coming true. Afraid to let the magic out of the box she set it aside unopened, turned off the light, and returned to the first floor.

The idea of being in the rooms her mother would no longer occupy loomed. "Baby steps," Lindy muttered. In the hallway connecting the kitchen to the residential quarters, she discovered a mural of sorts, marking every achievement of her past year. Candid photos from the academy summer session and her tour were printed on various sized canvases.

The corner curio cabinet in the small sitting room displayed several of Lindy's earliest creations. Unpracticed hand-built forms, trinket dishes, and chunky jars, rustic pieces she'd made in her garage studio as she mastered the wheel. The evolution of diligent practice was evident.

On the center shelf, all by itself, was the vase from the student exhibit in Baltimore. Lindy opened the glass door and with a trembling hand lifted the delicate piece from her debut. Beneath it, an envelope held the tickets to the banquet. On the back, Mom's handwriting noted "Lindy's coming out party." She listed who had been there and a few highlights from the week they'd spent together.

"Oh, Mom." Lindy sank to the floor and wept.

Chapter 19

Lindy pedaled her bike into Kate's driveway at five-thirty. Kate's husband Rudy was standing beside a car with the hood propped open.

"Hey, Lindy girl." He smiled and wiped his hands on a rag. "Come here, you."

She walked into his sheltered embrace. Rudy didn't offer canned sentiment or fluffy words. He simply held her.

"Know anything about carburetors?"

"Nope."

"Me neither." He released her and returned to studying the car engine.

"I told him he'll only make things worse," Kate called from the doorway. "Dinner will be ready in thirty minutes."

"I don't have time for…"

"Don't be prickly. I know you have no plans to stay forever but that doesn't mean you can't take a moment to have a family meal. Besides, I'm making your favorite."

Lindy walked to the deck. "Can I help?"

"I don't know," Kate grinned. "Can you fix a carburetor?"

Lindy laughed. "No."

"Then you can chop the carrots for the salad." Kate moved into the cozy kitchen and handed the peeler and cutting board to Lindy.

Dinner was the distraction she'd needed. Rudy wanted to hear about everything she'd been doing in "the city that never sleeps."

Lindy talked, chewed, and swallowed until her belly was painfully full. She had immediate regret when she realized somewhere a pie was lurking.

"I'm doing the dishes." Lindy gathered the plates. "So don't get *prickly*."

Kate snorted as Lindy used her favorite phrase against her.

Rudy excused himself to tinker with the car.

"Troublesome man," Kate smiled as she opened the back door. "Excuse me a minute, sweetie. I need to see how far south Rudy's amateur fiddling has gone."

Lindy looked out the window toward the garage, and her heart squeezed. She recalled the night she'd come to Kate's for a simple picnic to celebrate her seventeenth birthday. She remembered the cake but not her wish. She could smell the smoke from the extinguished candles and hear the door rattling as it opened.

Little did she know how the perfect pottery studio would change her life.

Lindy brushed a tear from her cheek as Kate returned to the house. She was on the phone with the island mechanic, making arrangements for the car to be collected at his earliest convenience.

"Well, that takes care of that." Kate picked up the tea towel and dried the dishes as Lindy filled the strainer. "It's nice to have you in my kitchen, Lindy girl. Feels like old times."

"Yes, it does. I was just remembering the night you guys surprised me with the studio. I can tidy the garage before I leave. I'm sure Rudy would appreciate having the space."

"You'll not touch a thing out there this trip. You have plenty to handle, and your pottery-making things are in no one's way." They finished the task at hand and moved to the deck.

Lindy settled on the cushioned rocking chair. The wind moved through the trees, and for a few moments, the world was at peace. "I think Mom would have preferred the reception to be held at the B&B. Nina would also probably like to handle the fussy details herself—plates, napkins and food. I think we could probably use the church lot for parking and folks can walk to the house."

"That sounds lovely."

The tow truck arrived and backed into the driveway. Rudy fisted his hands on his hips and shook his head.

"Just thinking of you, my love," Kate called to him, "and saving you any further frustration."

"Saving our marriage is more to the point."

"Well yes, there is that."

Lindy smiled at the pair. They made relationships look easy but she knew good days and bad days were part of the deal. Rudy blew Kate and Lindy a kiss, then climbed in the truck to supervise the repair.

"I know your burden is beyond measure, Lindy girl, but there are some things I must discuss with you. Nothing needs to be decided today but if you wouldn't mind, I'd like to lay out the details. You'll save me from making a trip to the towering concrete city you adore."

"Okay." Lindy turned toward Kate.

"The B&B has reservations through the next year. I'll work with Nina to continue managing the business until you decide how to proceed."

"Whatever you think is best, Kate. I'll make arrangements to get everything personal out."

"Did I say anything about you moving out?"

"No, but..."

"Shall we start again?" Kate took Lindy's hand in hers. "The decisions regarding the business are yours."

"Huh?"

"The B&B belongs to you." Kate allowed the words to settle. "Your mother never took a salary for working. We argued about it 'til I was blue, but Susie felt she owed me." Sadness threatened to spill over. "I provided a way through. That's all. She did the work." Kate cleared her throat. "So while Susie thought she was being clever, only drawing money for groceries and the few extras you needed, I invested the salary I would have paid anyone who did the job. A few years ago I transferred the property, furnishings, and the business to her." Kate handed the folder to Lindy. "As her sole heir, the business is now yours."

"Oh, Kate." Lindy opened the folder and stared at the deed and formal documents. "I don't... I couldn't possibly."

"This is not a trap or trick to get you to stop pursuing what you're meant to do. It is simply the truth. You have an asset that functions and earns."

"How in the world will I manage a business from New York?"

"I think the question you mean to ask is who. Who would be thrilled to manage a successful business on your behalf?" Kate pushed against the planks and her chair began to rock back and forth. "Who do you trust implicitly and even holds a degree in hospitality?" Kate patted Lindy's knee as the bulb fired. "There you are."

They sat in silence as the last part of the day slipped away. "Would you mind if I stayed a bit longer and worked in the studio? I think it would do me good to turn my mind off for a few hours."

"One condition." Kate squeezed her thigh. "You let me drive you home or you stay through until morning. I don't need to add worry to my plate if you decide to ride your bicycle home in the dark."

"Deal."

"I'll put some blankets and pillows on the couch for you."

Lindy wasn't dressed for it but she didn't care. Having her fingers immersed in slippery clay was the therapy she desperately needed. At some point, she tested the threads of the dusty hammock and surrendered to fatigue.

Chapter 20

Lindy rode through the park and past the marina. Morning boat crews were scurrying to prep for a day at sea while the captains stood back and sipped coffee. She followed the streets home and eased into the driveway.

The chains of the porch swing rattled. Lindy flinched and pressed a hand to her pounding heart, then released her strangled breath as Tucker's large body unfolded from the seat.

"I didn't see you sitting there."

Time hadn't lessened his effect on her. Lindy had worked to shore up her defenses before crossing the bay but still found herself focusing intently to put one foot in front of the other as she climbed up the steps.

Tucker held a bouquet of fresh flowers tied with a cloth ribbon. "I'm sorry about your Mom. It stinks."

A torrent of emotion rose from deep within her and when his arms came around her, she didn't have the strength to suppress them.

Tucker lifted Lindy off her feet and carried her to the swing. He settled into an easy rhythm, rubbing soothing circles over her back. Eventually, she fell silent and he knew by her breathing she slept.

Lindy came awake as the day broke fully. She opened her hand across Tucker's chest and allowed the steady beat of his heart to link and anchor with hers.

"I didn't think to look for you in the garage," Tucker said quietly. "I guess I should have."

"An impromptu art therapy session."

"Did it help?"

"As much as anything could, I guess." Lindy released a steadying sigh. "So tell me, Tucker Brandt, where are you in the process of executing your perfect island business plan?"

"I'm getting ready to investigate properties."

"That's exciting."

"It is. Zak moved down for the summer. I think he'll be an island resident by August. He's been helping me with the water sports and we've added video to our packages."

"Wow."

"You should come take a ride before you head back to the hustle. Do you good to get some wind in your hair." Tucker brushed her bangs to the side. "Looks nice, by the way. Your haircut."

"Not at the moment." She blushed and raked a hand through the tangled strands. "But thanks."

"Enough about me. You, Lindy Colton, are the one on the fast track. Or should I call you by your fancy professional name?"

She swatted his belly playfully. "Goes with the hairstyle."

"You've caught a few stars and accomplished a great deal in the last few months."

"Lucky break."

"Talent recognized, I'd say." Tucker watched a town car pull to the curb. "Are you taking reservations or do we have ourselves a lost mainlander?"

Lindy sat up and gawked as Hayward emerged from the vehicle. She wiped her face and hurried down the steps.

"Belinda, I've been so worried. Your phone is going straight to voicemail and there's been no response on the business line."

Tucker watched from the porch as the well-dressed stranger enveloped Lindy in a protective embrace.

"I'm covered in clay."

"When aren't you?" he chuckled. "Clothing can be cleaned. I'm sure there is a reputable dry cleaner somewhere in the county." He eased back and framed her face. "I brought you appropriate funeral attire and a few essentials I noticed you'd forgotten to pack. If you'd only answer your phone from time to time you wouldn't be surprised by generosity and affection." He lowered his lips to hers.

Tucker turned away from the display and gathered his stainless steel coffee mug.

Hayward's driver opened the trunk, set two bags on the sidewalk, and retrieved a garment bag from the rear seat.

"One moment, darling." He released her to converse briefly with the man. "I'm all set. Show me to our room."

"You're staying?"

"Only for the night. I'm catching a flight to Atlanta tomorrow." Hayward shifted his gaze toward the house. "A guest, Belinda?"

"What? No." She folded the clothing bag over her arm. "That's my friend Tucker." She grabbed his hand. "Come on, let me introduce you."

"And here I was concerned you were going through this horrible ordeal alone." Hayward extended his hand. "Pleasure to meet you, Mister..."

"Brandt." Their palms fused. "Tucker Brandt."

"Tucker just stopped by to pay his respects."

Hayward's brow lifted. "Interesting hour to come calling."

"Actually Lindy and I have a long history of sharing sunrises." Tucker was pleased when a muscle twitched along Mr. Sophisticated's perfect jawline. "I'll see you tomorrow at the service." He gathered Lindy close again. "Let me know if there's anything else I can do for you."

Chapter 21

Susie had been well-liked and respected in the community. Lindy stood in front of the chapel as mourners offered sympathy and words of comfort. She politely refused dinner invitations, assuring everyone she needed to return to the city.

Tucker stood in the condolence line. His starched white shirt screamed against his seafarer's skin. The tails hung loose over his tight-in-all-the-right-places best dress cargo shorts.

What an awful daughter I am, Lindy scolded herself and wiped her brow, *using libido as a distraction for bereavement.*

The minister delivered a message of hope and promise. Lindy listened as people relayed personal stories and shared pieces of her mother she'd never get an opportunity to know.

Lindy moved through the day on automatic pilot. She maintained her poise until the last person filed out of the B&B. The deadbolt turned with a hearty click. She kicked her heels into the corner by the base of the stairs then joined Kate and Nina in the kitchen. "Everyone is finally gone."

"You sure? Did you check under the table?" Kate laughed. "I got the impression old man Knapper was planning to stay until he'd eaten enough to carry him through to winter."

"I fixed him a plate to go," Nina confessed.

"I'd like to finish the rest of the cleanup if you don't mind." Lindy pulled her mom's apron from the peg and slipped it over her head. "You both have done so much and I can't begin to thank you. This I can and want to do." Lindy smiled. "Please."

"If you're sure." Kate set the tea towel aside and gathered her purse. "Rudy is asleep on the back porch. Will I see you before you head back to the city?"

"You will."

Kate nodded. "Get yourself a piece of pie." She brushed Lindy's hair away from her eyes. "Then go upstairs and crawl into bed."

Lindy smiled. "Pie fixes everything."

Kate kissed her cheek. "You're a good girl."

Nina made one more pass through the first floor looking for random dishes then settled at the table. "I won't help if you insist, but I'm not ready to go home just yet."

"Okay." Lindy dipped her hands into the soapy water. They shared the silence and held space for each other the way they had countless times. Nina's friendship was one of a few constants she'd ever known.

Kate was right. Nina was the perfect person to handle the bed and breakfast in her absence.

Lindy dried the final platter and removed her apron. The weight of the day arrived as the fabric fastened to the hook. "Is this really happening?"

Nina was out of the chair in a flash. "It's unimaginable. I keep expecting to see her in the garden or hear her laughter carrying from the front room."

"She's really gone." Lindy grabbed Nina's hand. "I don't know how to ask more of you, but I need a favor."

"Anything, Lindy. You know that. I'll do anything, just ask."

Nina's eyes widened with shock and fresh emotion. She listened as Lindy laid out the concept of her running the B&B.

"You and Mike can move out of the small apartment and live here." Lindy paused and took in Nina's baffled expression. "Or not... whatever works best. You don't have to commit to forever but just until I can settle into the changes and figure out how to manage things. There are reservations through the next year and there's a salary and other details. I'll let Kate explain." Lindy sat across from her dearest friend and took her hands. "I know you've always had the perfect after-ever plan and this was certainly not part of it, but would you consider it?"

Nina was speechless. "I don't know if I want to bawl or throw up."

"Is there a third option?"

"Under the circumstances, I'm appalled to say I'd love to, but Lindy, I would love to. One hundred million percent. I'd be honored to run your business for as long as you need me to."

"Let's take a bottle of wine across the street and tell Mom the news."

Nina stood with Lindy on the shore as the sun raced to meet the horizon. They raised their glasses to her mother's life and legacy, to Nina's new position, and Lindy's pursuit of her passion. Then together they tipped the bottle and poured a bit of wine on the sand.

Arm in arm the girls crossed the street, stood on the walk, and looked up at the building. "Mom's okay," Lindy said. "That may sound crazy but I think she's okay."

Nina squeezed Lindy's arm. "And we'll be okay too."

They climbed the steps. "I'm going to take Kate's advice and grab a piece of pie and go to bed. I'll be pushing hard to get out of here tomorrow."

"I don't want to think about saying goodbye," Nina sighed. "You sure it has to be tomorrow?"

"There's a function I promised to attend, and yes, they'd certainly understand under the circumstances if I'd cancel." Lindy turned off the lights as they wandered through the house. "If you could spare the afternoon, I'd appreciate your support," the words caught in her throat, "as I pack up mom's room. I'm not sure I can face her personal things by myself."

"Of course. I'll help you, however I can."

Unable to sleep, Lindy climbed the steps to the attic. Her hands sorted through fragments from her childhood and other inconsequential things that had accumulated and gotten stored for another time. She loaded a single tote and moved it to the foyer.

Memories swirled as she walked into the small bedroom and ran her hands over the painted mirrored dresser, a four-dollar flea market treasure her mom decided just needed a fresh coat of paint.

The cavernous ache deepened. Oh, the mess they had made sanding, scraping and repainting. "We called it our perfectly hideous masterpiece. Do you remember, Mom?" Lindy's heart yearned for a reply.

She sighed as she wrapped the mirror in a blanket for safe transport then carried the sections downstairs to the front room.

"I apologize in advance for invading your privacy," Lindy said as she lined up the empty drawers on her mother's bed, "but this is the option you've left me with."

Delaying the inevitable, she went to the kitchen to make a pot of coffee.

She worked slowly, beginning with her mother's pottery collection and the pictures she'd recently hung. Next, she folded sweaters that still carried her mother's scent and cried her way through the vintage holiday pin collection.

Lindy moved to the bathroom hoping the act of discarding half-used shampoo would be easier. It wasn't. The medicine cabinet exposed the elephant her mother had masked so effectively. Prescriptions for pain and inflammation as well as countless over-the-counter treatments for upset stomach and indigestion.

The moan that passed Lindy's lips was unnatural and fraught with misery. Her knees buckled and she collapsed to the floor.

Nina let herself in the back door and hung her coat on the rack in the mudroom. The washing machine and dryer were churning, and the house smelled of coffee and bleach. The kitchen table was lined with sorted clothing and the floor with containers of shoes. She followed the noise overhead and found Lindy on the second-floor elbow deep in the linen closet. "Wow, you've been busy."

"The project took on a life of its own. I'm leaving all the linens for you to decide what's what." Lindy closed the door and jogged to the first floor. "Mom's closet is cleared and the bathroom is empty, scoured, and sanitized. I set aside a couple of sweaters I remembered you giving her, and I chose a few tchotchke pins I thought you may want to keep. What else?" She ran her hands through her hair. "Oh yes, the comforter is in the wash and the curtains are in the dryer."

"Did you sleep at all?"

Lindy stepped over a trash bag. "Most of her clothes and shoes are bagged or boxed and are in the foyer. I called Community Aid to have them collected so you just need to put them out front tomorrow afternoon, or we can do it now. I just figured you'd prefer not cluttering the porch." She tipped her thermal cup and was surprised to discover it empty. "You want coffee?"

"Lindy, sit for a minute," Nina spoke gently. "You're shaking. Let me get you some water or food. You have to be exhausted."

"You got that right," Lindy snapped. "But I'm not nearly as worn out as I am furious." She scooped up the trash bag at her feet and shook it. "Forty-seven bottles of belly fixes. Some of them dating back to before we even moved into this house. Forty-seven, can you believe that?" She paced in frantic strides to the kitchen. "What kind of daughter is so immersed in her own life she doesn't know her mother's indigestion is killing her?"

"Lindy…" Nina trailed behind her.

"I don't want to hear the post-operative infection was rare and things happen. If she'd prioritized herself sooner, I could've had years with her. Years, Nina. Not to mention she could've had an opportunity to find happiness. She settled again and again so I could do what I wanted." Lindy tossed the trash bag into the hallway. "Forty-seven bottles… it's just incredibly ridiculous."

Nina eased on the corner of the bed and sank into the weight and misery of grief. She lifted the cable knit cardigan she'd given Susie from the pile Lindy had mentioned. The perfume was slight but it was there. She hugged the soft fabric to her chest and waited for the storm to pass.

"The bulk of the attic will have to wait until my next visit. The only piece of furniture I'm taking is the painted dresser with the mirror. We can shift something else into the room to replace it. After you and Mike decide on the living arrangements, you can use your discretion on selling or donating the other stuff. Honestly, I just can't tackle anymore right now."

"Okay."

"I need to get on the road if I want to make it back to the city in time for the banquet. I'll be damned if I miss a single event or opportunity. My mother killed herself so I could chase after what I wanted."

In less than an hour, the car was loaded. Lindy hugged Nina for the hundredth time. "I'll be in touch in a few days. I'm sorry about the explosion."

"We're good, Lindy. Everything will be okay."

"I'm stopping at Kate and Rudy's to grab a few things before I hit the road."

"Promise me you'll pull off and get a hotel if you're too tired."

"I promise. Good luck with your adventure."

"You too."

Lindy drove to Kate and Rudy's. She wrapped and packed the mini gallery wall and secured the studio.

"Slip this behind the seat." Kate handed Lindy a bag. "A few slices of pie individually vacuum sealed and ready for your freezer. Just a bite or two to remind you of home from time to time."

Lindy wrapped her arms tight and held on. "If I don't leave now, I won't go."

"You will go and you'll do big, beautiful things." Kate placed her hand on Lindy's cheek. "We'll watch from here and be bursting with pride."

Anxious to disconnect from the island and release the anchor of her emotional history, Lindy climbed behind the wheel. Distance was what she needed. She'd swallow strong coffee and drive all night if she had to… or so she thought.

There was one loose string that needed to be tied up tight or deliciously unraveled before she could cross the bridge to the mainland.

Tucker Brandt.

Lindy pushed the profound heartache of losing her mother aside as she pulled into the marina. Her heart thundered in her chest when she spotted him framed against the late afternoon sky. She knew the choice she was making was selfish and bordered on cruel, but somewhere deep inside she reconciled the potential fallout and climbed from the car.

Brimming with unfriendly intentions, Lindy crossed the lot. The sensation of longing swelled as Tucker's gaze lifted and locked with hers. She unfastened the nylon stern-line, wound the length in tidy loops and stepped from dock to deck.

Tucker moved behind the console and fired the engine. He guided the vessel through the water and arrived at their secluded cove.

He knew the moment was as much a beginning as an end. On the other side of night, he'd face the harsh reality of Lindy's absence all over again, but as the soft rays of twilight streamed through the cabin highlighting her features, he decided the pain would be worth it.

Hours later Tucker held Lindy's hand as she returned to dry land. The radiant moon captured their single silhouette as they came together for one final embrace.

Then, the shadow widened, split in two, and she was gone.

Chapter 22

Celeste ran her hand over the painted dresser and listened as Belinda told her the tale of its creation. "Such a beautiful story."

"I should probably have it refinished, but I just can't."

"No, you can't." Celeste knuckled a tear away and joined Belinda by the studio's large window. "Is there anything I can do to help you with the estate details?"

"Hayward recommended an attorney to sort the assets, though there aren't many. I own a bed and breakfast, which I find hilarious. My friend Nina will run it for now. I brought a few things back with me, pictures and knick-knacks." Belinda gestured to the stack leaning against the wall. "No idea where I'll put them. There's still room in my storage closet, I guess. Why I keep adding things to the room is beyond me."

"Someday you'll have a home that suits them."

"Maybe," Belinda sighed and walked to the galley kitchen. "Anyway, Hayward says death is merely a speed bump for the living, and the best way to process my grief will be to stay focused on maintaining my momentum."

Celeste snorted. "That's not very compassionate."

"Perhaps not, but the impromptu trip to Napa he planned is. The change of scenery may be just the emotional palate cleanse I need to put my grief," *and my misguided jaunt with Tucker,* "in perspective. Are you all set for your all-inclusive resort vacation with Mr. Perfect?"

"You better believe it." Celeste had been dating an international art dealer for six months. The trip would be their first real test of compatibility. "The bikini I got is nothing but scraps and strings. He may require frequent mouth to mouth resuscitation," she winked. "No worries, I'm certified."

"Lucky for him."

"How about you? All packed for your getaway?"

"Of course she is." Hayward strode into the studio. "Time to finish up, Belinda. We're leaving early."

"But I'm not..."

"Celeste," Hayward rolled on, "you will verify that Belinda's email auto-response it set for Do Not Disturb. That goes for you as well. Anything you suppose emergent, handle on your own." Hayward walked to Belinda. "We will be uninterrupted for two whole weeks."

"I could really use another hour to..."

Hayward angled his head. "Everything will be waiting for you when we return." He dropped a kiss on the top of her head. "Get showered and meet me on the lower level."

"On that note, I'm off. Give me a hug." Celeste wrapped her arms around Belinda and squeezed. "Enjoy Napa. Eat tons of good food, drink too much wine, and soak up those California UV rays. Most of all, relax."

Belinda worked quickly to tidy her studio, showered in record time and tossed on comfy clothes. She grabbed her socks and sneakers and hurried down the stairs.

Hayward was opening and closing every cupboard in the kitchen. "Where did you put the heavy goblets I prefer?"

"They're on the second shelf, next to..." Belinda set her shoes on top of her luggage. "No, wait. Here let me..."

She stepped forward and in a swift simultaneous motion his elbow drew down and caught her hard on the cheek. The tumbler dropped to the granite. The detonation punctuated her grunt and sent shattered glass across the tile floor.

"What the—" Hayward scooped her off her feet. "Careful, you'll get cut." He placed her softly on the island. "I had no idea you were behind me." He opened the freezer and began to rummage. "An ice pack or vegetables?"

"Freezepop?"

Hayward grabbed a sheet of rainbow kids pops and wrapped them in a clean dishtowel. He held the makeshift compress to her cheek and kissed her forehead when she winced. "Shhh," he soothed. "Grab hold of me." He lifted her into his arms and carried her to the lush sofa.

"I'm fine, Hayward."

He released a shaky breath. "Let me see." Marks were already announcing themselves. The impact had narrowly missed her eye. "Not as bad as it could have been."

Hayward cradled her in his lap and rocked back and forth until the icy treat softened to liquid, then he nestled her into the cushions and went to the kitchen to swap the melted for firm. He returned with a second frozen cluster and handed her an opened sleeve of blue raspberry.

Belinda sucked on the popsicle and watched as Hayward straightened the mess. He gathered, swept and discarded the broken glass, then moved the remaining three goblets in the set to the first shelf.

An hour later she boarded the Foundation's private jet and headed to Hayward's family property in fertile Napa Valley countryside. They spent two weeks strolling through precise rows of groomed grapes and sampling gourmet food from the region. Hayward treated her like a treasure and promised next time they'd tour other wineries and visit the nearby hot springs.

On their final morning, Belinda sat on the stone wall and watched the fog crawl through the gorge. The dense mist toiled then began a lazy climb, rising to greet a hot air balloon gliding through the clear blue sky.

"Everything is so beautiful here," she said as Hayward joined her.

"As are you, darling." Hayward lifted her chin toward the light. The bruising had faded considerably. He feathered a kiss over her unpainted lips. "I know this has been a difficult time for you."

"I'm feeling better, stronger, over the hump."

"I received an email from the attorney and have set an appointment for you to review your inherited assets when we return. You'll sign and move forward."

"Oh." The thought rattled her.

"No, you don't." Hayward kissed the tip of her nose. "Being stronger often means releasing what we've outgrown, and you, Belinda Cole, were made for more."

Chapter 23

With Celeste's expert guidance, rigorous routines were established over the next two years, and all things Belinda Cole flourished. Time was managed with incredible efficiency, striking a balance between studio production, community outreach, and personal time.

The creative workshop series had taken on a life of its own. Following a beta test, it was determined that adding prerecorded and virtual components would allow Belinda to reach specific groups and provide them with flexible viewing options.

"Your summer session buddy's flight arrived on time." Celeste briefed Belinda while the clay turned beneath her hands. "Cal and his lovely wife Jane will check in to the hotel and join you for an early dinner downtown—the Grill, at five o'clock."

"Good..." she dipped her sponge in the container of water and squeezed out the excess.

"Tomorrow morning, the video team will arrive at the Academy's Student Studio at six-thirty. They'll begin recording the first segment promptly at seven-fifteen. The director's plan is to shoot all four segments."

"Hmm, yes, that's good," Belinda mumbled, as she guided the clay.

"Cal agrees everyone should be buck naked for artistic effect."

"Uh-huh... right." Belinda leaned back and blinked. "He what?"

"I knew you'd stopped listening," Celeste laughed. "All written down in here." She tapped the binder. "You need to be dressed and hailing a cab by four-thirty. I set your alarm."

"Perfect." Belinda returned her focus to the form at her fingertips.

"The veterans' workshop is set for the last week of the month," Celeste continued. "Would you like me to begin the promotion or would you prefer I wait until the course editing has been completed?"

"I say green light on the promotion. We've worked with this team before and I'm sure Cal will knock his portion out of the park." Belinda used the trim tool to sharpen the base edge.

"Bringing Cal on board was a stroke of genius."

"I agree." Belinda turned off the unit's power and grinned. "A hundred bucks says he works the jugs story into his presentation."

Celeste snickered and jotted a few notes. "Last question. Thinking ahead to your in-person commitments, would you like to partner with Cal a few times a year on the east coast or only when the workshop locations make sense with your current calendar?"

"The schedule is getting chaotic, isn't it?" Belinda detached the bat from the wheel head and carried it to the drying rack.

"Hectic but doable."

"Okay, let's say three purposeful partnerships with Cal. One should be during the upcoming two weeks in Sedona. Could you look into veteran organizations in and around Phoenix?"

"Certainly." Celeste made a final notation while she moved to the table used for packing finished work. "May I continue wrapping the gift for your friend Nina?"

"Please." Belinda washed and dried her hands. Nina had transitioned to running the B&B and balancing her life brilliantly. She and Mike were expecting their first child in December. "I still can't believe my best friend is having a baby."

Belinda could picture the young family tucked inside the B&B, just like Nina had always envisioned.

"Winter will be a cozy time to settle in with a newborn." Celeste wound bubble wrap around a lid of the canister set Belinda had created for the nursery and placed it into a nest of brown paper. "I'm so happy you decided to deliver your gift personally." She walked to the closet.

"Me too," Belinda grinned. Kate and Nina had coordinated a surprise attack by video call and worn her down. "Hayward has arranged a car. I'm heading out as soon as we wrap up the shoot tomorrow."

"I picked up a few additional items last week." Celeste lifted a small bag from the closet. A wide-eyed plush giraffe peeked over the top. "I couldn't resist, and you'd mentioned Nina's fondness for these long-necked fellows." She laid an assortment of colored tissue, curly bows, and pastel paper across the table. "I can handle the fussy part for you if you'd like."

Belinda cuddled the toy and shook her head. "When do you find the time to shop for this kind of stuff?"

"We all have our strengths."

"As if cruising for stuffed toys and ribbon can be considered a strength," Hayward remarked from the doorway, walked to Belinda, and kissed her fully. "I've conferred with the pilot. You'll fly directly to the Hamptons for the Fall Festival. I'll pack your things for Boston. There's no need for you to cart extra luggage south." He dropped a kiss to her head. "Be sure your phone remains charged in case anything changes with the travel arrangements. I'll see you in a few days."

He was out of the room as abruptly as he'd arrived. "He's always five steps ahead." Belinda stood in amazement.

"Uh-huh." Celeste bit back the rest of her sentiment as she attached the final bow. "Enjoy your time. And Belinda? The file you may want to take with you is in the top drawer of your work table."

"File?"

"Top drawer," Celeste winked and moved to the door. "Safe trip. Call me if you need anything."

Cheerfulness flickered to life as Lindy glanced through the documents her attorney had prepared. Hayward wasn't pleased with her decision to gift the property and ownership of the B&B to Nina. He felt strongly the asset held great value and should be sold. In the end, he was happy Belinda was severing her final tangible tie to the island.

Chapter 24

October was a sleepy time along the eastern shore. The harvested farmlands were bare and the soil was preparing to restore. The fresh market stands were bursting with pumpkins, gourds and fall decor.

The driver passed through Girdle Tree and Stockton, then made the turn toward the sea. Countless rows of satellites at NASA's Wallops Island Flight Facility pointed to the sky seeking to give or gain insight from worlds beyond. The car accessed the causeway and crossed the stretch of water separating Chincoteague from the rest of the world.

She harbored no nostalgic pangs for strolling down memory lane, revisiting old hurts or rewinding the years. She was Belinda Cole—a successful artist, admired woman, and envied companion to one of the most powerful men in New York City.

It was like stepping back in time, Belinda decided, as she looked at the house that had been her home for the last part of her childhood.

A red Radio-Flyer wagon overflowed with orange and white pumpkins and nubby gourds. Swags of grapevine garland woven with silver ribbon draped the windowsills and porch railings. The enchantment was amplified by miniature white lights flickering like forgotten summer fireflies within the blooming golden and burgundy mums.

The only thing missing was her mother, balancing on the ladder, fussing over the seasonal wreath on the front door. Lindy's heart skipped as the wooden door opened and for an instant, she saw her mom crossing the threshold.

"Lindy!" Nina squealed and gathered her sweater around her burdening belly. "I'm so glad you came." She hurried down the steps and swallowed Lindy in a hug that smelled like warm cookies.

"Look at you," Lindy said with wonder.

"I know," Nina beamed with joy and turned in a full circle. "Can you believe it? I haven't seen my toes for weeks."

"And it's all you ever wanted." Lindy gathered her dearest friend close again.

"Everything I wanted and more."

The aroma inside the house had Lindy's mouth watering. She followed Nina to the kitchen and whimpered at the sight of dozens of cookies and muffins, a variety of scones, and even a frosted cake.

"I went overboard." Nina bit her lip.

"You think?" Lindy slid her coat off and over the back of the chair. Suddenly famished, she picked up a chocolate chip scone and bit it in half. "Yummy," she mumbled and sprayed crumbs across the table.

"Want milk?" Nina reached for a glass. "I bought ice cream too," she grinned, "and pickles." She pressed her hands on her lower back. "There are a few pieces of fruit and the makings for salad in the refrigerator somewhere, in the event you want a little bit of nutritional balancing."

"I'll help myself later." Lindy took in the sight of her radiant friend. "Sit down and put your feet up."

Nina snatched a pillow from a basket by the pantry. "I require bolsters to do just about anything these days." She lowered into the chair. "Now, tell me everything."

The girls picked up like friends who'd lost no time.

"I read about the programs in Sedona." Nina's hand rubbed her belly. "I'm so proud of you. We all are." The tears were fast. "Hormones." Nina waved her hand. "Ignore me as I leak." She snagged a tissue and dabbed and wiped. "You are so incredibly busy. I'm sure it's a lot to balance."

"It is and I appreciate your understanding." Lindy smiled. "I've been straddling the water for too long. In order for me to really focus, I need to release some baggage. On that note I have something for you." She pulled the file from her tote and slid the papers across the table.

Nina scanned the documents. "Lindy, no…" Waterworks came full force, and not a tissue manufactured would be up to the challenge. "I couldn't possibly… Does Kate know?"

"She does."

"But your things."

"None of it's mine, not really. It was Kate's, then Mom's, and now yours." Lindy grabbed the box of tissues and placed them in front of her. "It's always been yours, Nina. A piece of your after-ever. If I'm ever going to find mine I need to move forward. There's too much history on this island."

"Not all of your past was terrible."

"No, certainly not, but that fact doesn't change the truth." Lindy rubbed her hands over her face. "You're the love of my life and that won't change if your name is on the deed to this property. Mom would have been pleased for both of us. She knew I needed to go and somehow I think she hoped you'd succeed her here."

Nina's hands trembled as she held the papers. "After-ever," she said quietly. "Is Hayward part of your after-ever?"

"He certainly checks many of the boxes."

"Boxes?"

"He's secure financially, driven to achieve, supportive of my work, and of course incredibly handsome."

"Drive and achievement can make for a lonely life," Nina said in a low voice.

"Hayward and I share an ideal no-strings entanglement," Lindy defended. "He's taught me a great deal about navigating business and advocating for myself in intimidating rooms. He believes in me and has built my confidence. He's a tremendous companion."

"With benefits I hope," Nina wiggled her brows. "The man is yummy."

"He most certainly is," Lindy laughed.

"What about love?"

"You know how I feel about love." Lindy shifted in her chair. "Hayward and I enjoy each other. I have no delusions about the time he spends with me. Hayward doesn't want or expect more and I'm not capable of anything else." She shrugged. "He says he wants to cherish me. I'm still wrapping my head around that."

"That's lovely." Nina's eyes filled again. "I want you to be so happy."

"I think for me, safety and security will always come before contentment."

"Contentment isn't..." Nina instantly waved her hands signaling for a truce. "My point is you deserve to be surrounded by people who love you, who really, really, love you."

"Isn't that why I keep you around?" Lindy laughed and pointed to Nina's expanding belly. "To produce humans who'll be raised to love their Aunt Lindy whether they want to or not."

"Aunt Lindy," Nina inhaled sharply. "Someone likes the sound of that."

"What's happening? Are you hatching?"

Nina giggled. "No, I'm not hatching." She took Lindy's hand and pressed it firmly against the life growing within her.

"What the heck?" Lindy marveled at the gentle bumping against her fingers. "I think he wants out."

"He?"

"Yep, my money is on a boy and if I remember correctly you'll name him Eric."

Nina's face glistened with tears. "Thanks for being my best everything."

"You didn't give me a choice." Lindy leaned in and wrapped Nina in a tight hug. "Thank you for being my best everything too."

"Now, help me out of this chair." Nina gripped Lindy's hands for leverage and groaned as she attained vertical. "Mike and I have baby class tonight. Your dinner is make-your-own salad, more pastry, and a side of pickles."

"Sounds amazing." Lindy looked out the window. "I'm going to do these dishes, then walk across the street and talk to Mom."

Chapter 25

The gear and accessories required to birth and rear an infant were as endless as they were baffling. Lindy watched as wrapping and tissue paper flew through the air in chunks and wads. Another tiny human outfit was revealed and was met with a boisterous chorus of Oooos and Ahhhhs.

"Clearly I'm missing a gene," Lindy muttered to Kate and carried a stack of dirty plates to the kitchen.

"You hiding out?" Rudy sneaked in the back door.

"Not exactly." Lindy leaned in for his kiss.

"Any cake left?"

"Plenty," she chuckled as she rinsed and loaded the dishwasher. "Would you like coffee, milk or whiskey to chase it down?"

"Yes." Rudy grinned and grazed the counter, sampling leftover tidbits and treats. "Get your hands out of the sink and sit with me for a few minutes. It's been a long time... bring me up to speed."

Minutes later Kate pushed through the swinging door.

"Hi, my love." Rudy's cake-loaded fork froze midair. He smiled broadly at his wife. "I've found the sweetest of sweets."

"Well, I can't say I'm surprised. You've always had a knack for it." Kate refreshed her coffee and settled at the table beside Rudy. "Before I forget to pass on the message, Tucker texted and his meeting ran later than expected so he'll catch up with you tomorrow."

"Excellent," Rudy grinned. "Now we can enjoy our girl without watching the clock. Rewind, Lindy girl. Kate will want to hear everything you told me firsthand."

"Tucker's not home?" Lindy asked.

"He's around. I'm sure you'll make time to see him before you go." Kate rested her hand over Lindy's. "Tell me about your studio. I read an article on the line."

"On the line?" Lindy chuckled.

"Don't poke fun. I'm on the web, toes in, as much of it escapes my brain, but I can surf and twit."

"I think you mean tweet," Rudy offered helpfully. "Like birds singing."

"Either way, the pictures looked lovely. Fancy digs to make your lovely pottery." Kate added a teaspoon of sugar. "Drives the price sky-high, so we who've known you since the very beginning can only dream of collecting a piece or two."

"Hold that thought." Lindy retrieved her tote from the pantry. "I was going to mail this for the holidays but hand delivery is much better." She passed a bundle of paper to Kate.

The protective sheets fell away and revealed a stout bowl etched with fall leaves accented with a red glaze that had become one of Lindy's signature finishes.

"Oh…" Kate cradled the bowl like a precious child. "Lucky, lucky me."

Time was evaporating. Lindy had just enough for one final farewell before catching her flight to the Hamptons. She wanted complete closure with her former life before departing, and that included facing Tucker.

She borrowed Nina's car and drove to Tucker's apartment and boat slip only to find them both vacant. "I guess life has moved on for more than just me." Lindy decided to do the next best thing and traveled to the north end of the island.

The bumpy lane jarred her spine and her memory. She parked where the sand ended and water began and looked across the cove toward the mainland. As a child she'd felt the expanse had mystical powers. She'd offered her dreams to the waters beyond the bank and had seen many of those wishes come true.

To another it may have seemed foolish to feel gratitude to a location but for Lindy, the freedom to dream had given her hope and that hope had given her a life.

She climbed from the car and wandered toward the dock hidden in the tall grass. The coastal storms had weakened the structure, so Lindy decided her plan to walk to the end wasn't worth the risk of a late-season plunge into the bay.

The weathered planks and view of the cove beyond triggered a rush of unexpected emotion. The surge of sentiment fell in fat droplets soaking her shirt. No longer concerned about rushing, she sat and offered her heart to the cove as she'd done dozens of times before.

Tucker lifted his ten-week-old puppy, Boop, from the front seat and set her on the compressed sand. The brisk wind lifted her ears and threatened to carry her away. As he hoisted the zipper on his fleece, his grandfather's words flooded his mind. *"Winds crossing the water to carry good luck to shore."*

"I'm wide open for luck." Tucker had gambled everything when he decided to launch his business in October, but he had a plan. Step one, wear Boop out. Step two, return to the store and initiate a tactical marketing blitz to capitalize on the holiday shopping season.

Laughter joined the breeze. Tucker rushed to where Boop was molesting a woman sitting in the marsh grass. "I'm so sorry, ma'am."

"Ma'am? What am I, forty?"

"Lindy?" Tucker thought he was dreaming. She looked different and it was clear she'd been crying. "Is everything okay?"

"Everything is..." She giggled as the puppy bathed her face. "...fine. I was just saying goodbye to the cove. Lots of memories here."

"Some of my best."

"She yours?"

"Yes." He reached down and pulled the puppy back. "Boop, this is Lindy. Lindy, this is Boop."

"As in Betty?" She laughed richly and climbed to her feet as Boop bounded into the cold water.

Tucker jammed his hands in his pockets. "You've had a busy few years, knocked some of the cities off your list. Sedona is somewhere I hope to go someday."

"You know they don't have ocean, right?"

"Yeah," he chuckled. "Figured I'd rough it. What's returned you to this stretch of sand?"

"I was in town for Nina's baby shower. I'm catching a flight to the Hamptons in..." Lindy checked her phone. "...less than an hour."

"Busy." He kept his attention on Boop. "We've missed your personal updates, especially Nina."

"Nina understands that I need to stay focused, Tucker." Lindy crossed her arms over her chest.

"Since when is friendship a distraction? Being determined is one thing, cutting us out is another."

Lindy's eyes filled. "That's not fair, Tucker."

"You're damn right it isn't." The words came out more harshly than he intended.

"Do you want me to be something I'm not?"

"Never." Tucker's voice softened and he framed her face. "I just wanted to be included or at least invited to watch you soar." He pressed his lips to her forehead to stop the words he longed to say.

Lindy's resistance softened. Her arms found their way around his waist and she clung to his warmth and gentleness. They stood much as they had countless times before looking over the cove.

Tucker gathered the wet and sandy puppy and they walked across the crushed shell lot. "I'd like to show you something. It will only take a few minutes," he added quickly as he placed Boop into the Jeep. "Will you follow me?"

She checked the time. "I only have twenty minutes."

Lindy pulled into the newly built retail strip and parked in the area designated for a business called Sea Surge. The grand opening banner was stretched between the brick pillars and the signage byline read Surf -Skim-Paddle-Plunge. She climbed from her car. "Oh my gracious, Tucker. You did it!"

"Beach gear, surf, skim and paddleboards." He moved past her and unlocked the door. "Only open weekends now, but in season we'll offer lessons and rentals plus apparel and sunglasses." Tucker held the door and watched her wander through the store.

He wanted her to be proud of him, or at least a little impressed. Just as she had when she was younger, Lindy revealed nothing. She was a master at holding her feelings in check. When she finally faced him the smile lit her eyes.

"Your store is amazing, Tucker." She turned in a slow circle with her arms outstretched. "Really, really amazing. Congratulations."

"Sure you can't delay your departure? My apartment is upstairs."

Her phone alert sounded. "I'm sorry, Tucker. I have to go." She turned again and soaked in the sight of his accomplishment. "I'm so proud of you."

As the jet launched into the air, Lindy decided the quick trip to Chincoteague had been an incredible success. Nina had received everything she needed to welcome the baby, the property transfer would be finalized as soon as the lawyers double-checked the fine print, and she had faced Tucker without incident.

On the final evening of their East Hampton trip, Hayward took Belinda to the exclusive Maidstone Club. Over dinner, he spoke in terms of their future. The importance of Belinda playing the role of leading lady opposite him, the leading man. Then in the flickering candlelight, he handed her a small box and asked her to be his partner in life.

Belinda's mind flooded with a single thought as the dazzling sparkle of rock slid over her knuckle and rested against her hand... Tucker.

Nina squealed and bobbled the phone.

Mike ran from the bedroom half asleep. "Is it the baby?"

"No, sorry honey. Go back to bed." She scanned the trending headline a second time: *Hayward Livingston Bachelor No More.*

Hayward Livingston popped the question to his long-time
companion sculptor Belinda Cole. Publicity reps for both
Livingston and Cole hinted at a quick spring wedding, raising
speculation of a possible pregnancy.

Nina clicked the video link capturing Lindy as she unfolded from
the stretch limousine bathed in a fluttering flash of the paparazzi.

"Things certainly do move fast on the Mainland." Nina released a
baffled breath and texted her bestie offering congratulations and
requesting a FaceTime ASAP for all the details.

"His partner in life?" Nina wrinkled her nose.

"Don't dissect the language, please. I thought you'd be happy for
me."

"Of course I'm happy, Lindy. This is exciting news. Show me the
rock again."

Lindy leaned close to the camera and lifted the chain around her
neck. "Looks better on my finger of course, but I'm working today so
this is the best option."

"And you're okay with not setting a date?"

"Dates are for weddings not partnerships," Lindy sighed. "Let's
change the subject. How are you feeling? Any twinges?"

Nina rubbed her hand in circles over her belly. "Nothing yet." She
laughed. "Can't wait to meet him, or her. When do you think you'll be
able to squeak in a visit? I know your schedule is really kicking into
overload."

"It is, but I'll figure something out. First babies often arrive late,
right? I'm headed to Sedona for two weeks and it's possible the session
will be extended. Back to New York for the Starving Artist Holiday Ball
the first week of December, then we're going to Italy for Christmas and
Napa for Valentine's Day."

"Wow," Nina said. "We'll be here whenever you can come."

On the fifteenth of December Nina sent a horrifying video capturing
the moment baby Eric roared into the world. Thankfully countless less

frightening pictures followed and Aunt Lindy was delighted beyond words.

Chapter 26

Belinda Cole, in association with the Livingston Foundation, continued to garnish focus from influential powerhouses nationwide. Prestige was wielded like a wand of magic. Every move, like an elaborate game of chess, was designed to lead to the next.

The pictures on the studio calendar had changed in a flutter of days spent. Belinda opened the bottom drawer of her small painted dresser and lifted an artificial wreath to her lap. The red ribbon wrapping the faux pine glittered with her mom's vintage holiday pin collection.

She anchored the decoration to the center of her mirror alongside pictures of Nina's rapidly growing son. Eric's first birthday was around the corner. Belinda grabbed a pen and scribbled a quick reminder to ship the gift she'd purchased on her last trip to Arizona.

The demands of her schedule put a strain on her free time. Regular check-ins with Nina drifted to random emails and social media exchanges. Hayward didn't approve of the ties to her past and reminded her often, *"You discard things you've outgrown."*

Celeste arrived and began to deliver her weekly report over the noise of the spinning wheel. She studied the clay taking shape at Belinda's fingertips. Barely birthed, she could already see the genius.

Belinda released the pressure on the pedal and the turning ceased. She stood, stretched her back and washed her hands in the utility sink.

Beneath the baggy clothes Belinda preferred, Celeste could see she'd lost weight. "When was the last time you ate something that actually grew from the ground?"

Belinda shrugged. "I've got so many concepts in my head right now. I want to get them out of me."

"But you need to sleep and eat too." Celeste dug in her tote and pulled out a bag of almonds. "Eat these, and then for the love of all things holy, take a shower."

Belinda grinned. "What's that?"

Celeste laughed. "We need to discuss the dates for the next tour and frame in the spring workshop series in Sedona. Also, we need a final decision on which pieces are being photographed for this year's Holiday Ball. The board of directors approved the meal—Peruvian."

Belinda walked to the table to retrieve her water bottle. "Couldn't they, just once, host a barbeque? Everything is always so fussy. The food, although delicious, is often exotic, impossible to pronounce, and way too pretty to eat. Give me a sloppy roll of pulled pork or a stack of brisket... maybe I am hungry." She tore open the almonds and tossed a few in her mouth. "Hmm, yes, hungry. Thank you."

"You bet." Celeste jerked her thumb toward the adjoining room. "Shower."

"Can we multitask?" Belinda stripped her clay-streaked sweatshirt over her head as she strode to the bathroom. "Grab the iPad off the desk so we can make sure I'm not double-booking over Hayward's events."

"Certainly." Navigating Belinda's career around Hayward's agenda was becoming an issue. Celeste balanced on the counter and rattled off Belinda's commitments as the steam swirled.

Belinda felt dizzy. She leaned forward to steady herself then turned off the water. "Celeste, can you hand me my robe?" She eased the curtain back and wrapped the plush material around her body. She tried for a smile as she lowered herself to the edge of the tub.

"You have to take a break."

"Impossible. Hayward says focusing on my work is the only way to remain relevant and recognizable."

Celeste was growing increasingly concerned that the best interests of Belinda's health and welfare might be getting lost in a string of sentences beginning with "Hayward says."

"I think you should leave your career track to me."

"Belinda?" Hayward called from the studio.

Celeste hopped from the counter. "We're in here."

120

"Conducting business in the bathroom?" Hayward scowled. "Extraordinarily unprofessional."

As usual, Hayward did little to hide his dislike for Belinda's chosen agent. He'd been working to undermine her at every turn.

"Celeste and I were just going over my schedule."

"I find it a little late to review the agenda as your salon appointment was an hour ago."

"Oh!" Belinda gasped. "The fancy dinner."

"Yes, darling." Annoyance rebounded off the tile. "The fancy dinner." His gaze finally landed on Belinda. "Are you ill?" His tone bode heavy with exasperation rather than concern.

"No, I think the water was too hot and I'd skipped lunch."

"Ridiculous." Hayward shoved past Celeste. "Crafting should never override taking care of your basic health." He lifted Belinda into his arms. "The salon is sending a styling team here. Hopefully they're worth the money I'm paying. They only have an hour to pull off a miracle and make you presentable." His eyes narrowed on Celeste. "I'm hiring a chef. Meals will be prepared each and every day. You will be certain to clear space in her calendar and make sure she eats them."

"I can do that."

"I'm not too confident as you clearly forgot to add today's salon appointment and this evening's dinner." Hayward carried Belinda from the room. "Your competency continues to be a concern."

Celeste freshened her lipstick as his rant continued. Hayward's digs at her proficiency would need to seek a softer target. She would continue to look out for Belinda on all fronts. Especially where Hayward Livingston was concerned.

"Tonight we will be in the company of powerful, connected individuals. This is a vital networking opportunity. Remember, timing is everything." Hayward adjusted his tie. "You'll be certain to treat everyone as if they are the most important person in the room. Stick to the topics we've discussed and if you aren't sure of a proper response, don't speak. A random comment can sink a ship in harbor." Hayward turned to scrutinize her dress and jewelry. "You've forgotten your ring, darling, and the other shoes will add more height and allow the fabric to float freely."

Belinda made the adjustments and slid the ring over her knuckle.

Hayward lifted her hand to his lips. "One final reminder. Keep your remarks brief regarding our personal life. No one needs insight beyond what they see with their own eyes."

Conversation swirled as Hayward guided Belinda through the room. Belinda's growing reputation as a compassionate voice in communities nationwide had begun to spark interest.

"We are so impressed with your dedicated philanthropy, Ms. Cole. Tell us about the workshops you're putting together. I heard veterans and young children are your focus."

"Yes, for now." Belinda beamed at Hayward, pleased she was contributing positively to the energy of the event. "We will be launching additional programs to specific groups in the next two years. I want everyone to know how art can change lives and inspire healing."

Hayward was tolerant of the attention Belinda was receiving. He smiled with polite indifference then guided the discussion to a topic which benefitted his objectives for the evening. Eventually he grew tired of the patient pretense and excused himself to refresh his beverage.

"She's lovely, Livingston." Congressman Larell did nothing to mask the desire in his gaze as he focused on Belinda. "Not to mention young. It's so nice to enjoy them while they are pliable and eager."

"Certainly raises the appeal." Hayward glanced across the room as a swarm of people gathered around Belinda. "I better go and bail out my fiancée."

"She appears to be holding her own." Larell tossed back his drink. "There's a real future for you in politics, should you ever throw your hat in the ring officially. Not to mention with her at your side you'd win constituents in any arena you decide to enter."

"But why would I want to play by the rules when I can make them up as I go along?"

"Regardless," the stodgy congressman chuckled, "you're very smart to align with a bleeding heart."

"Yes." Hayward's smile was rigid. "I am clever."

Chapter 27

The arrival of spring pushed bulbs from the earth and living color erupted throughout the courtyards in the city. Annual blooms added fragrance to the oppressive heat of July, August and September. In an instant crisp winds and cooler temperatures replaced summer's humidity.

Colored leaves danced across the walkway as Belinda strolled through Central Park. The chill and barren branches matched the solitude perpetuated by her daily routine.

The last six months she'd spent more time at what Hayward deemed "important social engagements" than in her studio. They attended Tony award-winning musicals, opening nights on Broadway and the Met, and now he wanted her to travel to California for a red carpet movie premier.

The continued interruptions and added pressure felt like a weighted blanket, but rather than inducing comfort, the demand to execute at the highest standard was creating immense anxiety.

"Be flexible, Belinda. This studio is available to you twenty-four hours a day. Haven't you always said you can work anytime?"

"Yes, but I…"

"You will finish the pot when we return from California." Hayward snatched her sweatshirt off the chair. "How hard is it to hang up your clothes?" He rammed the fabric over the peg by the door and turned back to her. "It's a quick trip. Surely you can spare four days and then find a moment later to work in the mud."

Belinda watched Hayward frown as he stalked the racks of her most recent work.

"May as well offer some mass-produced knick-knack from China," he quipped cruelly. "Perhaps you're losing your touch. You realize it isn't too late for the Foundation to select another artist's work."

Belinda flinched as the piercing pain of his remarks landed.

"Forget the premier. I'll fly to California and attend the red carpet alone. In fact, since undoubtedly you're having difficulty harnessing your skill, I'll stretch my stay to a week. That will give you the uninterrupted time you obviously need to produce quality results." Hayward turned abruptly and left.

Belinda locked herself in the studio determined to make something Hayward would be proud of. She forced the clay to shift and swell, only to watch the shape collapse over and over again.

Everything she had produced was flat and insignificant.

Celeste entered the room with Belinda's lunch. "I asked the chef to make your favorite—fresh spring rolls and sliced melon."

"What am I going to do?" Her voice shook with anguish as she dragged the wire beneath the ruined form. "Hayward said I haven't created anything worthy of national attention."

"What does he know?" Celeste set the meal on the table. "Come on, wash your hands and eat something." She gathered the discarded protein supplement wrappers. "You have more than a dozen finished beautiful pieces."

"But Hayward wants something different, something unique, something..."

"Good thing I'm in charge of showcasing your talent." Celeste walked along the racks of completed work and lifted the nesting bowl set Belinda had made following her last trip to Sedona. She carried the trio to the packing station and set them out.

The smallest was glazed in a soft blue with a single line etched in the side. The color on the medium-sized bowl shifted from light to navy and the linework was interwoven and slightly more intricate. Finally the largest boasted a depth of color which transitioned navy to midnight blue. The accented scrollwork was sweeping and complex. Celeste wiped each with a soft microfiber cloth then began to wrap them in protective paper.

"But those are…"

"Striking." Celeste held Belinda's gaze, making sure her words landed. "My job is to highlight your astonishing gift, and yours, in this moment, is to chew and swallow." She angled her head toward the plate and smiled as Belinda complied and tossed a wedge of melon into her mouth.

"The focus for the event is children growing through art. What better way to depict growing up than a grouping that gets bigger, more colorful and multifaceted?"

Belinda sighed. "I guess you know what's best."

"I absolutely do." Celeste moved to the corkboard and unpinned an invitation shaped like the Incredible Hulk. "Speaking of little ones growing up too quickly, any chance you've decided to attend Eric's super-hero party? I'm sure he'd love to see his Aunt Lindy in the flesh."

Little Eric was turning two and she had yet to meet him in person. "I can't travel right now. Hayward says I need to protect my time. Besides, Eric would be traumatized if he saw my entire body. He's only ever seen my face on a four-inch screen."

"I'm going to start a deep hot bath for you and then let myself out. You are going to finish every bite on your plate, then strip, soak and sleep for at least eight hours. Got it?"

Belinda plucked Nina's picture from the mirror. How she missed her best friend. She should call her right now, but what would she say? *"Sorry I've been so self-centered and never met your child. Sorry I can't seem to rally enough energy to leave the studio, eat or bathe."*

She felt the tears rise. What a dud aunt she was turning out to be.

Chapter 28

Belinda dreamed of the ocean. She could feel the swell lift her body and cradle her weightlessly in a sustained salty float. Nina's rich laughter swirled with the mist as she chased Eric across the sand. They dashed into the surf, jumped the waves and called out for her to join them.

Sometime around three, Belinda slipped from bed and tiptoed into the studio. She a fed a mass of clay through the roller then transferred the evenly compressed slab to the work table. Her hands pinched and pushed and a portrayal of moving water took shape.

Lost in the creativity she worked for hours. When her body finally gave in, she slid from her stool and curled up where she landed.

Hayward let himself into the loft and shouted her name. Music drifted from the upstairs studio. Annoyance simmered as he climbed the steps. He was dressed for dinner and entering the workshop meant risking his suit.

He found her sound asleep on the floor, hands and forearms caked in mud. "Ridiculous." Hayward grabbed a clean rag from the table and shook her shoulder. "Wake up. How long have you been in here?"

Belinda blinked the sleep from her eyes. The sun was soft around the shades. "I don't know. What time is it?"

Hayward huffed, "Nearly seven."

"I couldn't sleep so I worked a bit before breakfast."

"Don't be coy. Breakfast was hours ago." He gripped her arm and lifted her roughly to her feet. "We're due at the supplicant social in an hour."

"What?" She hurried past him and dried clay marked his suit.

"Damn it." He brushed the dust. "Be careful."

"I'm sorry," she said as she stripped in a flurry. "I'll be ready in fifteen minutes."

Belinda showered quickly and dressed. She stood in front of the mirror for one final check. The skirt hugged her hips and ended well above her knees. The sleeveless blouse was the style Hayward preferred for public dinner engagements.

"What is…" She leaned closer and studied the marks circling her bicep, puzzled over how a bruise could form with so little pressure. "Well, I guess it's official. I'm a fair-skinned city girl."

Swiftly she exchanged the garment for a long-sleeved tunic with an open back, then scooped up a pair of narrow heels which would torture her toes and make the skirt appear even shorter.

Hayward's eyes heated as Belinda descended the stairs. He consumed her figure as she balanced against the couch to put on her shoes. He swirled his finger in the air and stepped behind her as she began to turn. His hands settled on her hips then he teased the exposed skin from the base of her spine to her neck. Hayward dropped a kiss behind her ear and whispered, "Perhaps we could be a little late."

"I had so much fun tonight." Belinda slid into the back seat and removed her shoes. "For once I barely noticed how badly my feet were hurting."

"That's charming, darling."

"Everyone was so complimentary about the press coverage I received for the workshops. First word and last word, just like you've taught me, but this time I was leading and it was exhilarating. Regi was so kind and not at all what I expected. He said he may have a connection for me at Apple TV. Can you imagine? I can't wait to tell Celeste."

"Regi?" Hayward's tone was aloof and mocking.

"Are you upset with me?"

"Reginald," Hayward crowded so close his nose brushed hers, "is a Kennedy. You are familiar with the family. They're practically political royalty."

"No, I didn't realize." His breath smelled of liquor.

"Of course you didn't." He clasped her jaw tightly in his hand. "You were too busy throwing yourself at him while the entire room watched. Too busy making a fool of me. Who do you think you are?"

His eyes were dark and unrecognizable. Belinda laid her hand on his wrist. "Hayward, you're hurting me."

He released her face and sat back against the seat. "Reginald Kennedy is active in global endeavors. There were several people in attendance whose primary goal was to have his ear for sixty seconds." Hayward cursed and clasped her thigh as the driver pulled aggressively into traffic. "You monopolized the evening regaling him with pottery throwing how-to's."

Belinda threaded her fingers through his to lighten the pressure. "He seemed genuinely interested."

"As if he was even listening." Hayward petted her flesh as if to erase the discomfort. "He was merely being polite. In the future I expect you to recognize the difference and be prepared to hold intelligent tête-à-tête or remain silent."

The remaining miles passed in hurtful silence. The car pulled to the curb. Hayward reached across and shoved the door open. "I have no time to escort you in." He relayed the address for a popular nightclub to the driver as the door closed between them.

Belinda stood on the street dismissed. Loneliness threatened to swallow her whole. She unlocked the loft, dropped her purse on the floor then kicked her shoes into the corner. The echoing thuds amplified her dejection.

She climbed the stairs to the studio. In the center of the room on the raised worktable sat her dream-inspired piece encased in plastic. Belinda shed her jewelry, set it aside then gently removed the sheeting exposing her work-in-progress.

She closed her eyes and imagined the ocean breeze lifting her hair and bending the beach grass. She pictured the movement of water and sound of crashing waves. Engrossed in her vision she selected a small carving knife and began to etch minuscule details in the pliable clay.

The memory of Nina's laughter flooded her mind and filled her heart. *"Get in here,"* her best friend called and gestured for Belinda to join her in the water. Joy swelled like a cresting wave then peacefully raced across the shoreline.

Hours later Belinda stripped and showered. She gathered her wet hair into a messy knot, pulled a silk nightgown over her head and fell into a deep and restful sleep.

She dreamt of a glaze that shifted with unpredictability. The vibrant image roused her to wake. She switched on the bedside lamp then grabbed watercolor pencils and a tablet from the nightstand. Lying on her belly she worked to fill the sheet with shades of sky and sea, of sun and sand. The blended tints conveyed peace and contentment and felt a little bit like home.

Belinda strolled into the studio and opened the bottom drawer of her painted dresser. She rummaged through the stash of t-shirts she kept hidden and lifted the one Nina had sent for her birthday last year. She snipped the tags and pulled it over her head. The oversized cotton hung well past her waist and ended mid-thigh. Framed in the wavy glass mirror Belinda saw a hint of the girl she'd been once upon a time. "Hi, stranger," she said and moved to the narrow galley kitchen to fix some tea.

The cleaning staff arrived early and placed the morning paper on the counter. Belinda sipped her tea and snagged a bowl of berries and yogurt from the refrigerator. She added granola and honey, tucked the paper under her arm and returned to the café table in the studio.

Natural light streamed through the large windows highlighting her impromptu swatch board. Happiness and gratitude filled her as she sipped, swallowed and scanned the news.

The spoon froze midair. The grainy image in the upper corner of page six had captured Hayward as he exited a trendy bar with a NYC socialite wrapped around him.

Belinda's cheerful mood evaporated.

Hayward's playboy antics were just another on a growing list of things Belinda had been expected to tolerate.

At what point would the cumulative cost of a life with Hayward Livingston be too high?

Belinda looked at her beautiful workspace and thought about the closet filled with expensive garments he'd provided. Once upon a time a tiny garage on a small island had been enough. Once upon a time she had no idea what designer clothes were.

She abandoned her breakfast and walked to the bathroom. Perhaps Celeste was right. A few days out of the studio, a change of scenery, would be good for her, and may provide the breath of perspective she desperately needed.

Cal and his wife, Jane, had said she was welcome anytime… Did they mean it?

Belinda picked up her phone. "Good morning, Celeste. I'm taking your advice and skipping town for a few days. I don't even know where I'm going. Out of the city, I know that much."

"Where isn't important. How can I help?"

Belinda relaxed. Celeste wouldn't ask questions, she would simply support. "I loaded the kiln. I know you're familiar with operating the unit but I laid the instruction booklet on the counter just in case. You'll need to stay here while it's cooking, I hope I'm not asking too much. Feel free to move in until I get back and do what you do."

"A mini vacation for me too. Sounds perfect."

"There's a list of supplies to order including a few new ingredients for a glaze I'd like to play with." Belinda tossed clothes into a bag as she spoke. "What else? I don't know. I can't think."

"Good, no thinking is exactly what you need. I've got you covered."

"Thanks Celeste, I'll check in when I get settled somewhere."

Chapter 29

Cal picked Belinda up at the Flagstaff airport. She looked like a battle tested warrior after the six-hour flight. He loaded her luggage and watched her surrender to sleep on the ride to his home.

Jane greeted them in the carport holding a wiggling ball of white fluff with a polka dot bow perched on top of her head. "Welcome, this is Lady Bug." She passed the dog to Belinda. "Apologies in advance, she will need to sniff and kiss you to death."

"I don't mind a bit." Belinda cradled the dog. "I like your bow. Thank you for letting me invade with virtually no notice."

"Family is always welcome, dear." Jane guided her to the living room.

Determined to rally, Belinda accepted a cup of coffee and settled on the couch with Lady Bug curled close to her side. Moments later, her head bobbled.

Cal lifted the untouched mug from her fingers and passed it to Jane. He studied the shadows of sadness showing through even as Belinda slept. "Something else going on here," he said quietly and covered her with a blanket.

"I'm glad she called and felt she could come." Jane rubbed Cal's shoulder. "We'll give her the space she needs and let her tell us when she's ready."

Belinda stirred and curled into the fuzzy warmth beside her. A steady beating heart kept rhythm as a chest filled and emptied beneath her cheek.

She jolted and shoved upright. Her eyes were glazed and wild as she took in her surroundings. "Foolish of me, foolish." Belinda scrambled from the couch. "I'll be ready in five minutes. We won't be

132

late." Still half asleep, her frenzied panic built. "We won't miss anything, I promise. Wait, what day is... I mean time... what time is it?"

"Day is right," Cal spoke softly. He pushed from the recliner and opened the back door for Lady Bug. "You zonked out big time and slept clean through."

"My phone, where's my phone?" Belinda hurried to the dining room. "I need my phone." Anxiety squeezing her lungs, she raced to the couch and scooped up her shoes. "I have responsibilities. I need to..."

"Wake up, Belinda." Cal approached her with care. He placed his hands on her shoulders and squeezed. "Come around now." Then sharply he added, "Wake up."

Belinda blinked once, then twice, and disorientation dissolved to embarrassment. She sank into the cushions and buried her face in her hands. "I left the city to relax."

Cal kneeled in front of her and smiled. "Then how 'bout you try and relax?"

<hr />

"Belinda," Hayward shouted as he stalked through the apartment's lower level. "I've been attempting to reach you for hours and don't appreciate having to..." Soft music drifted down from the second level. "Ludicrous." His irritation rose as he climbed the stairs. "If you'd answer your phone or respond to my..." He pulled up short at the sight of Celeste sitting by the window sipping coffee.

"Good morning, Hayward."

"Afternoon is more accurate."

"Huh," Celeste glanced at the clock. "I guess it is."

"I've been attempting to reach Belinda." Hayward lifted Celeste's coat from the chair and hung it on the hook by the door. "I assumed I'd find her working since she's made nothing decent lately."

"She's not here."

"Clearly," he snapped. "The Holiday Ball is less than four weeks away."

"As her professional representative, I'm very well aware of her next contracted obligation." Celeste sipped her coffee. "Belinda Cole's piece has been selected, photographed and is in transit. The media criterion has been satisfied as per our agreement with the Livingston Foundation. All i's dotted, Hayward. All t's taken care of."

He took a deliberate breath to calm his brewing fury. "Do you know where Belinda is or when she plans to return?"

Celeste turned to the next page in her book. "I do not."

Hayward studied Celeste's bare feet and fuzzy robe. "You appear to be very much at home."

"I am, thank you. The Jacuzzi tub was a special treat and the bed was quite comfortable."

"You're staying here?" he squeaked. "In the apartment I provide?"

"Last account reconciliation, I noticed Belinda's rental checks were still being deposited."

"The Livingston Foundation secured this studio and..."

"Apples and potatoes," Celeste clipped his tirade. "Simply a matter of efficiency and juggling." She spun the newspaper and tapped the image of him exiting the club with the scantily clad socialite. "You, of all people, understand juggling."

Heat crawled along his starched collar. "I'll not debate with you." Hayward waved a dismissing hand. "Once again your lack of professionalism and integrity astounds me. After Belinda and I marry, your services, whatever they may be, will no longer be suitable."

"Well until then," Celeste carried her mug to the kitchen nook, "I'd like you to leave Belinda's apartment. I'm waiting for the kiln to complete the cycle and cool. The next item on my to-do list is to strip naked and sit on every piece of furniture."

Hayward's face contorted with disgust. He grabbed his briefcase and exited the loft.

Chapter 30

"I'm delighted you're enjoying the pie," Jane grinned as Belinda helped herself to a second slice. "With your slim figure I doubted you indulged in treats."

"I was taught that pie fixes everything." The phone rang. Belinda's hand jerked, sending coffee over the rim of her mug. "I'm so sorry." She mopped up the spill with her napkin.

"No worries." Jane passed her an extra cloth. "Cal spills things all the time."

"True enough." Cal grabbed the carafe to pour her a refill.

Belinda flinched when the sound pierced the room again.

"Before I answer," he returned to the table and stood by her chair, "tell me how badly you want to avoid that man of yours."

Her head fell.

"I think we'll let the machine get it," Jane said and lifted her cup. "Then we're going to turn the ringer off altogether so we can finish our dessert. Sound good?"

"Sounds perfect." Belinda smiled. "Thank you both again for—" Her email notification sounded.

"Gracious, the man's persistent." Jane sipped her tea.

"I should return his call. Excuse me a moment." Belinda stepped into the living room. "Hello, Hayward... Yes... I'm visiting Cal and... a few days... No." She softened her knees and lowered into the wing chair.

Cal and Jane stood beside her like bookends of support.

"...Yes... No... of course not." The one-sided conversation continued. "I was... I didn't appreciate... Yes... later tonight." The base of her skull was pounding. "Yes... before eight... I'm certain. Goodbye."

Belinda powered off her phone and dropped it into her lap.

Jane signaled her husband and Cal rested his hand over Belinda's. "How 'bout you give me that and we take a drive?"

Two hours later Belinda was standing in the shadow of the Desert View Watchtower on the south rim of the Grand Canyon. The picturesque immensity stole her breath and her equilibrium.

"Never gets old," Cal said with awe as he gazed over the Colorado River.

"I don't know where to focus. I can't believe I left my phone behind."

"Did that on purpose," Cal chuckled. "Too many things filtered these days behind a screen or lens. Minimizes the power and the effect." He turned her attention to the seventy-foot Puebloan styled tower perched on the lip of the chasm. "Look at the structure Mary Jane Colter envisioned and brought to life in 1932."

Belinda shielded her eyes and took in the purposeful, precise imperfections Mary Colter had insisted on to allow the stone tower to unobtrusively blend into the surrounding canyon walls. "I read a little about her when Celeste and I passed through on my first trip. She certainly was enchanted with the region and the culture."

"A female architect working in a male dominated world." Cal blew out a breath. "Woman had to have moxie in spades to accomplish what she did."

"Moxie to be sure, but I'm thinking balls. Big, brass balls."

"All sizes and shapes," Cal chuckled. "Go on, wander inside and take your time. The panoramic view is to be savored. I'll be right here whenever you're finished." He lowered to a large rock. "Never gets old," he whispered again.

Belinda did linger and welcomed the unhurried pace. She marveled over the colors Hopi artists used to paint murals on the ceilings and curved walls, then sat in the Eagle's nest and allowed her sight to be transported through the telescope lens to the terrain below.

She rejoined Cal on the ledge. "Beyond words."

"Yup." He offered Belinda a canteen. "Feeling a bit better?"

"I am." She took a long drink of cool water.

"It's humbling to think of the obstacles the tribes of the canyon faced making a life in this environment, and in comparison what modern culture deems difficult." Cal laughed. "What simple things we allow to overwhelm us."

"Very true, but when you're in it…" she trailed off.

"All about perspective." He draped his arm over her shoulder. "So what do you say… wanna sit on the edge of the world, lean on a solid shoulder and give me a crack at offering some unsolicited advice?"

The opportunity to talk openly was a gift Belinda hadn't thought to register for. She shared with Cal the story of her childhood and the urgency she'd felt to escape the narrow picture youth had painted. She spoke of her hopeful quest to learn and become someone else and how the comfort and care Celeste and Hayward had offered felt safe. Ultimately, she laid out the personal heart-shift growth had required and the weight cumulative compromise had brought with it.

Cal soaked up the innocence of Belinda's designed boundaries and the unsettled result she was facing now.

Hearing her own voice while she sat on the canyon rim looking into the fathom depth shook her. "Okay, I'm ready. Give me your wisdom."

"For starters I'd like to see you be gentle with yourself." He bumped his body against hers. "Growing pains are part of the process and releasing is necessary. Not all the plummets you're facing are as threatening as the drop appears. Even here," he gestured to the canyon, "there are trails, some prepared and some uncharted. If you want to get to that river, you have to take a step."

They sat quietly as the day drew to a close. Belinda thought about the many sunsets she'd witnessed in twenty-four years. Maybe it was the canyon, maybe it was Cal… regardless, the stirring in her was new and for the first time in a long time she felt hopeful for the promise of dawn.

Chapter 31

Belinda allowed Cal and Jane to spoil and coddle her for the first few days. Then she heartily pitched in, taking Lady Bug for daily walks and prepping meals with Jane.

One evening she accompanied Cal to the community center for his veteran's artistic discovery session. Belinda was grateful to observe the effect of her workshop on real people. Reading the reports was nothing compared to seeing and hearing it firsthand.

"What an amazing night." Belinda held the door for Cal. "I'm so glad I came."

"You needed to see the impact you're having." Cal loaded the crate of supplies into the car. "When you have more years under your belt, the nonsense falls away and what matters becomes the light you bask in." He closed the trunk. "Life isn't about chasing and pursuing next and more. Life, the fullness of life, is being in the moment." He opened the driver's door. "You, your programs, your compassionate heart are spilling over and making an incredible impact."

Belinda looked at the star-filled Arizona sky. Wonder poured into the sad, lonely and barren places deep inside her. "Cal," she said as she climbed in. "Do you think Jane would mind if I stayed for Thanksgiving?"

For the next two weeks Belinda observed Jane and Cal. She studied their interactions and listened to their banter and discussion over subjects in the news. She thought of Nina and Mike, how they'd grown up together, and were expanding their family while working full-time. She considered Kate and Rudy's devotion to one another, how they'd decided to fearlessly embrace love much later in life.

Lindy examined her personal thoughts on relationships following the example she'd seen as a child. She scrutinized the conclusions she'd drawn and barriers she'd put in place to maintain safety and control over her heart.

Belinda worked side by side with Cal and Jane to prepare and serve the holiday feast. They were joined by some of the new friends they'd made since relocating.

"What a wonderful day," Belinda said as she dried the final dish and placed it into the cupboard. "I'd love to stay forever, but the real world won't allow it."

Jane took the cloth and draped it over the oven handle. "You'll come again soon."

"I'd really like that."

Cal walked into the room. "You've finished cleaning up already?"

"You were napping, dear." Jane playfully snapped the towel at his belly. "Belinda was just promising to visit again soon."

Cal pulled her close and dropped a kiss on the top of her head. "You better."

"I need to gather my things. Are you sure you don't mind driving me to the airport?"

"Mind?" Cal smiled. "I'd be insulted if you didn't let me."

Belinda dashed into the Flagstaff coffee shop to grab a pound of coffee to thank Celeste for covering her extended time away. On impulse, she added a few extra souvenirs and hurried back to the car.

"Looks like more than coffee," Cal laughed as Belinda tried to stuff the items into her carry-on.

"A whim." She held up the lime green graphic t-shirt. "I've never seen Celeste wear anything as simple as a cotton v-neck."

"Corruption by comfort, I like it." Cal merged into the lane for departures and found a space to unload. "It was so nice to have your body in my home and not just your face on a screen." He rested a warm hand on her cheek. "Meeting you was a lightning bolt for my life. When I applied for the summer session I never expected to get in, let alone find my soul child. That's what you are to me, Belinda—family. I may not be able to dial up a canyon view but the shoulder is always available."

"I appreciate every—" Her phone chirped. "It's Hayward. I should answer. Hello."

"Belinda, finally," he huffed. "If you aren't boarded and in the air within the hour, you'll never arrive on time. Do I need to approve a jet to cart you back?"

"I'm outside the terminal right now. The flight will have me be back in plenty of time. I'm going directly to the salon, and Celeste will deliver whatever clothing you've selected. I'll join you onsite. Is that acceptable?"

"It's adequate," he said curtly. "Do not dally, Belinda. The Starving Artist Holiday Ball is an important night of exposure for both of us."

The call disconnected. "You mean you," she mumbled. "Reality has returned."

"Is he violent?"

"Cruelty has many faces."

Cal watched a single tear slip down her cheek. "Then you'll leave."

"It's not that simple."

"Doing may be difficult." Cal gathered her close. "But like the path to the river, you must decide to take the first step."

Chapter 32

The strength and confidence Belinda discovered during her visit with Cal and Jane wavered then fell as the mandatory season of cheer descended. Belinda turned on holiday music in the loft to boost her mood and climbed the steps to the studio.

She fixed a pot of tea and sat at her mirrored dresser. Her heart ached as she tugged a snapshot of her island family free and laid it in her lap. The picture had been taken at the student debut in Baltimore. Her mom, Tucker, Nina and Mike, Kate and Rudy… she grabbed her cell and dialed Kate, then just as quickly disconnected the call and turned off her phone.

What would she say? Belinda released a weary breath. She returned the photograph to the mirror.

Celeste hustled into the studio, stripped her coat and tossed it over the chair. "The first snow makes the Christmas decorations extra pretty, don't you think?"

"I do." Belinda shoved her personal pity party aside. "The tea's hot if you'd like some."

"I would." Celeste added honey and cream and joined Belinda by the window. "The Inner City Arts Club was thrilled to be chosen as your highlighted organization for the Hearts United Celebration in March. The Livingston Foundation has requested we repeat the bidder dance again since the revenue generated last year was immense."

Belinda looked at Celeste and her sadness returned. The Hearts United Celebration would be the final event Celeste would handle as the agent of Belinda Cole.

Hayward had finally acted on his disdain for Celeste. Insisting competent management was not friendship. Celeste would fulfill the remainder of her contracted obligations and then under a cloak of efficiency would be phased out and replaced by a management team selected by the Livingston Foundation.

The holidays were lost in a pile of ribbon, tissue and tape. December gave way to January, then February and moved forward to March.

Belinda moved among the starched shirts and overstuffed wallets assembled for the Hearts United Celebration. She was dressed in a vibrant, flowing, floral dress slit to her hip. Rubies and diamonds, on loan from Harry Winston, adorned her wrist, neck and ears. The ensemble was just one of the many elaborate outfits required for the occasion and for the woman gracing the arm of Hayward Livingston.

For two hours Belinda ignored her aching arches and exchanged pleasantries. She smiled as expected and did her best to ignore the shutters clicking in rapid succession as the media captured every moment.

"Don't falter," Hayward whispered sharply and pressed his hand against her spine.

Belinda straightened her shoulders. "I need to use the ladies' room."

"Soon," Hayward commented absently and turned to the next connected face. "Good to see you, Michael."

"Livingston," he clasped his hand to Hayward's. "I appreciated the tip on the equity account."

"Don't mention it," Hayward winked. "Tonight is about the children and my lovely fiancée's work to better their little lives."

Russo, Belinda remembered. Michael Russo—a man with very deep pockets and ties to Texas oil. He had a reputation for shady business, swift marriage and speedy divorce. The current Mrs. Russo, twenty-five years his junior, was chomping on gum while she held fast to her slippery husband's arm.

"Angelique." Hayward took her hand and raised it to his lips. "More beautiful every time we meet." The woman's eyes sparkled, rivaling the sequins accentuating her cleavage.

Michael's focus zeroed in on Belinda. "May I offer the same compliment to you, Belinda?" He leaned in and hugged her. "You look delicious." His palm dipped low on her back as he held her a moment beyond cordial.

Belinda angled her body away. "Excuse me, Mr. Russo, I need to visit the ladies' room."

"I'll come along." Angelique cracked her gum. "Always important to refresh." She winked at Hayward and trailed her finger over his arm.

In the restroom Angelique primped and fluffed her over-lightened Texas tresses. "We're so lucky to be attached to such powerful men. I'd do anything to ensure Michael's success."

"Anything?" Belinda asked.

"Well yeah, wouldn't you?"

Belinda quickly shifted gears. "Of course, I'm just a bit tired tonight."

"Well, find your second wind, girlfriend." Angelique cupped and lifted her paid-for breasts, testing the restraining seams of her gown. "We must always find the extra energy for our men, am I right? I imagine a man like Hayward has stamina, not to mention an insatiable appetite."

Belinda caught the not so subtle innuendo lacing her words. "Excuse me, I need to check on the auction."

"Oh yes, Michael and I noticed your little bowl when we came in." Angelique blotted her lipstick. "Petite and muted for my taste but pretty enough to raise some money." She snapped her purse closed. "What organization are we supporting tonight?"

"The Inner City Arts Club." Belinda shook her head. The people attending didn't even realize why they were there.

She scanned the room in search of Celeste and spotted her standing much like a sculpture herself beside the art display.

"Belinda, you're so pale," Celeste lifted a glass of ice water from a passing tray and offered it to her. "Do you need to step out for a bit of air?"

"Hayward needs me… needs my face anyway, for a few more hours."

"Forget that." Celeste led her to the elevator. "Go to the roof and steal fifteen minutes. I'll run any interference."

"I shouldn't."

"Don't argue." Celeste nudged Belinda inside. "There's more than enough time before the bidder dance. Stretch it to thirty—I got you covered."

Couples milled about the heated, glass enclosed, rooftop terrace. Lush potted greens and elaborate beds of flowers married with an audio track of birds and created a near perfect replica of nature, stories above the earth.

Belinda drank in the illusion and worked to shake off her conversation with Angelique. She followed the path and discovered a fountain created with loose river rock. Spotlights highlighted the clever assembly of stone and bathed the cascade as it traveled and dropped into a pool of floating candles.

On a whim she slipped off her heels, hiked her dress above her knees, and stepped in. She closed her eyes to fully absorb the sensation of the cool water and soothing sounds.

Belinda sat on the edge and allowed her feet to dangle. Memories of simpler times, bonfires, splintering wood, and pounding surf washed over her. She tipped her head and absorbed the constellation-rich heavens. Ripe for wishing.

Once-upon-a-long-time ago she'd dreamed of little except leaving the island. She'd been determined to follow the bright lights to the city and live grand. The alliance with the Livingston Foundation and the relationship with Hayward happened so effortlessly, she never thought to question.

It was becoming increasingly clear how deliberate and calculated their courtship had been. Each extravagant trip, public event or personal introduction had been orchestrated to fortify Hayward's personal agenda. The recent triumphs and recognition of Belinda Cole were beginning to overshadow his vision of her role as his partner in life, whatever that meant.

The terrace emptied around her. Belinda studied the endless ceiling of paneled glass and found she longed for an unhindered view. A giggle floated over the serene rooftop and invaded her thoughts.

"No one will miss us, sweetheart," Angelique's Texas twang and signature snap of gum amplified her sultry tease. "I promise to make it worth your while."

The last thing Belinda wanted was a front row seat to Angelique's sordid tryst with her ancient husband. She lifted her toes from the water, hooked the strap of her shoes, and prepared to dash to the elevator on the opposite side of the room.

"I'll give you five minutes to impress me, and twenty if I feel it's worth my while."

Hayward's distinctive voice stopped her. Belinda froze and watched in stunned silence as Angelique brazenly unzipped her dress and let it fall beyond her waist.

"I won't need five and you'll have wished for an hour." She rubbed seductively against him. "In my opinion you've been settling for a little less than you deserve."

Belinda cleared her throat. The sound cut through the silence of the rooftop.

"Hello, darling."

Angelique looked over her shoulder with a pout of disappointment. She adjusted her gown and turned for Hayward to assist with the closure.

Hayward held Belinda's gaze as he squeezed Angelique's ample bottom then lowered his lips to her ear and murmured, "I'm certain we can find an hour before you head back to Texas."

She ran her hand along Hayward's lapel. "Make it two." Angelique sauntered past Belinda and stepped into the elevator. "I'll tell Michael to get his checkbook out." She smiled as the doors began to slide closed. "A little clay pot would be a nice memento to mark the night."

Hayward adjusted his tie and flattened the front of his pants. "Put your shoes on, darling. We're needed downstairs."

Belinda crossed her arms over her chest.

Hayward snared her wrist and pulled her roughly against his chest. "Influential men enjoy an array of perks while holding powerful positions." Icy indifference coated his words. "And their women learn to look the other way."

Chapter 33

Hayward beamed with self-importance as Belinda gave her spiel to encourage donations. He added a wink for the crowd and offered his arm in a gesture of chivalry.

She brushed past him and descended the platform.

"Mind yourself." He caught her hand and tightened his grip when she attempted to draw away. "Many children are counting on the success of your little auction."

Belinda relaxed her posture as his threat radiated over her.

Hayward remained glued to her side as the bidder dance began. The latest concept to liven the fundraising process, donations were made anonymously and the five highest patrons received a one-minute dance with the featured artist.

She fought the headache blooming at her temple and made cordial chitchat with her cycling dance partners. Hayward was always the highest donor supporting Belinda's cause. The audience booed effectively when Hayward was announced as the second highest bidder of the evening.

Belinda held herself rigid as he drew her close.

"Smile, darling." Hayward squeezed her hand forcefully. "You have raised quite a sum for the Inner City Arts Club." For the crowd's delight he spun Belinda in a practiced flourish. "Don't be a child," he cautioned through his veneers, "or I'll happily scold you in front of everyone."

Belinda narrowed her eyes coolly. Applause erupted as the highest donation was announced and Michael Russo, Mr. Texas Oil, moved toward her.

"Well, aren't I the luckiest man in the room?" He settled his hand well below the base of her spine.

"Placing a lofty donation is hardly luck, Mr. Russo."

"Perhaps." He intensified the contact between their bodies. "But look at my prize."

Belinda lifted her lips to his ears and whispered, "Unlike your wife, I'm not for sale."

"On the contrary, my dear. I do believe Hayward understands tit for tat, although you'll need to visit my Angelique's plastic surgeon to be on equal footing there." He ground his pelvis against her hip. "I'll have you any way I choose, and Hayward will happily cash my check."

Bile flooded her mouth. Belinda executed a quick flourish to camouflage her abrupt exit and motioned for Celeste to join her at the private elevator. "Refuse his check. I don't want one cent of that bastard's money contaminating the children's program. I'll cover the donation myself."

"Done," Celeste nodded without question.

Belinda pressed the button to the penthouse and willed the doors to open and separate her from any additional humiliation.

"The event is not over, Belinda." Hayward clenched her arm.

She jerked away, drawing attention from the crowd. "It is for me."

"I'm sorry you're not feeling well, darling." Hayward's words dripped with concern. "I'll escort you to our suite." He placed his arm around her waist as the doors opened.

Celeste followed closely behind.

"You'll leave us." Hayward's words crackled with controlled ferocity.

"I don't work for you, Hayward." Celeste straightened her spine and looked toward Belinda.

"It's alright, Celeste," Belinda nodded. "I'll meet you tomorrow for brunch as planned." The steel box sealed and Hayward's displeasure turned lethal.

"What could possibly be strutting around in that space assigned for your brain?"

The doors opened to the lavish sitting room. Hayward strode to the bar and poured two fingers of whiskey.

"Your little display may have threatened the flow of information from a lucrative financial insider."

"Mr. Russo implied I was to sleep with him in exchange for your ongoing association."

"Did he?" Hayward chuckled. "The old devil."

"He also suggested I visit Angelique's surgeon, but let's not get off point. Just how many adulterous indiscretions am I expected to excuse?"

Hayward's brow lifted. "We are not married."

"And this ring was a promise of what?"

"The life every woman desires." Hayward waved a dismissing hand. "Michael was joking." He poured another drink. "You'll need to improve your sense of humor. I'll not be embarrassed in public by your reckless behavior."

"My behavior? A rooftop lay is acceptable?"

His hand connected. The force propelled Belinda into the corner of the table and onto the floor. Her fingers twisted in the plush white carpet as the metal tang of blood bathed her tongue.

A weft of hair, jarred loose from pins, shielded her vision. Belinda sensed Hayward's presence. She braced as his shadow loomed like an ominous cloud over her. A memory from her childhood filled her mind... her mother bruised and bleeding huddled by the stove while her father hovered above her.

"Why do you push me to behave this way?" Hayward's cool and polished tone arched like a rainbow after the passing storm. "Up you go, let's have a look." He gripped her arm and hoisted her from the floor, ignoring the wince of pain as she straightened her leg.

"You must have bumped your hip on the way down. So clumsy." Hayward assessed her torn gown. "Difficult to explain a second outfit at this point in the evening."

He pursed his lips considering a resolution.

"It offends me, the way you treat your things." Hayward reached behind her, drawing the zipper down. The gown rippled to the floor leaving Belinda clad in nothing but the silk of men's fantasies. "Better," he hummed and traced the edge of the delicate material. "Get rid of the dress and ready for bed." He placed a kiss between her brows as if to erase the burst of brutality. "I'll return to the party and make your apologies. Just another hour, maybe two, then we'll make this all better."

She trembled. Cruelty had become Hayward's preferred aphrodisiac. When he returned he would expect to find her naked within the satin sheets and grateful for his attention.

The door to the suite closed. Minutes passed with only the sound of her heart drumming in her ears.

Belinda stepped from the pool of ruined fabric, limped to the bathroom and turned on the shower. Steam swirled, filling the room in a mystic haze. She balanced on the rim of the vanity and stared into the vacant eyes of a woman who'd lost herself.

She lifted a hand to her battered face. An impressive welt had already gathered in the tender flesh beneath her eye. Her mouth was distended and her lips were lined with drying blood.

Was this how it had been for her mother?

The child she'd been judged without experience. Shame surged from a forgotten depth, a glacial tide that snapped her back to the present moment.

Belinda swiped her hand through the gathered steam and asked her reflection, "Who are you?" She leaned her forehead against the mirror. "I have no idea."

But you do, her mother's voice echoed in her heart. *You're stronger than you know, stronger than I ever hoped to be. Look again.*

She took a steadying breath, eased back and faced herself. "Who are you?"

The image of Belinda Cole wavered in unshed tears while somewhere deep inside someone was fighting to have a say. "Who am I?" she asked again, and this time the answer arrived in a confident burst.

"I am Lindy Colton."

Lindy's pulse hammered in her throat. She shut off the water and rushed to the bedroom closet. In record time she dressed and collected her things. She hitched her overnight bag high on her shoulder and reached for the door.

A brisk knock nearly stopped her heart.

"Housekeeping," a woman announced as the lock disengaged. "Pardon me, madame." She averted her eyes but not before the shock of the obvious injury registered. "I'm here to turn down the bed and prepare Mr. Livingston's nightcap."

Lindy stepped into the hall. "You may want to make it a double."

Chapter 34

Lindy hailed a taxi and relayed the address to the loft. Her adrenaline spiked as she nodded to the doorman and moved quickly down the corridor, stepped inside her apartment, and bolted the door.

She opened her lingerie chest and dumped bras, underwear and socks into the canvas duffle. Lindy stood in the center of the walk-in closet and stared at acres of gowns and expensive suits, cubbies of neatly stacked cashmere, a myriad of coordinating accessories, and enough shoes to outfit a third-world country.

The wardrobe belonged to Belinda Cole. A woman she'd never pretend to be again.

Lindy raced upstairs to her studio and knelt in front of the scarred mirrored dresser. Inside were the rags Hayward pretended she didn't own. Well-worn jeans, tattered sweatshirts, and hand-knit sweaters. She scooped out the entire drawer and deposited the items into her bag. Next she added her classic rock t-shirts. The threadbare and stained cotton was more priceless to Lindy than the jewels Hayward had chained around her throat.

In the bottom drawer, tucked in the back, Lindy grasped the shoebox she'd hidden several months before. The tape securing the lid released with a snap and she ran her fingers through the contents—$2,000 in cash, a folder of personal banking documents, a booklet with passwords, an old iPad, a manila envelope of mementos and keepsakes, and the contract for her storage unit.

She removed every snapshot from the mirror, placed them in the center of her holiday wreath and added them carefully to the bag. She scooped her pillow and blanket from the twin bed and hugged the cloth to her chest. Fear fluttered in her stomach.

You're stronger than you know. Her mother's voice overwhelmed her once again.

Lindy slashed the moment of panic with a heavy sword and nipped the spare key to Celeste's car from the peg. She engaged the studio security and hurried down the steps.

No longer concerned about Hayward's standard of ruthless organization she strode to the master bath, flung open the medicine chest, and scattered the meticulously arranged bottles of skincare and perfumes across the counter.

Giddy now, Lindy closed the door. The likeness reflecting in the mirror startled her. The vacant expression had been replaced with fire. The intensity rivaled the riotous blaze of gems circling her neck and dangling from her ears.

Lindy stripped every adornment and piled the jewels beside the sink. She topped the heap with the multi-carat skating rink that had shrouded more than her finger for the past two years.

The quiver in her stomach bloomed into a mass of strength. She pulled on sunglasses, zipped her bag, and left the loft.

The cab ride to the parking garage took less than fifteen minutes. Lindy entered the security code then joined a group of guys waiting by the elevator.

"Told ya to write it down."

"Who writes anything down?"

"I think it's on five cause there are five of us."

"Four, five, just flip a coin."

"I'm not sure we're even in the right garage."

Lindy chuckled as the door slid open. "Four, please."

"She knows where she's going," the men laughed.

Lindy lowered her gaze as the men continued to debate the location of their vehicle. She wished them luck as the doors slid open on the fourth level and began to rummage in her tote. Her fingers grasped everything but the single key she needed to start the car. "Serves you right for picking a no-pocket, cavernous…"

A hand clamped roughly around her arm. "Going somewhere?"

"Hayward."

"Yes, darling," he said coolly.

"How did you know where…?"

Hayward spun her toward him. "You thought you could storm out of a significant function while reporters were milling about and move freely in this city?" He laughed. "You really thought I wouldn't be notified? That I wouldn't put a stop to your little adventure?"

Her eyes scanned the lot for anyone who could help her. "You shouldn't have bothered, Hayward." She hated the tremor that laced her words. "I'm not going with you." Lindy glanced over her shoulder as the chime announced the arrival of the elevator.

"Told you it was on four."

"Seriously dude, you don't know anything."

Hayward's clasp weakened her knees. "Don't get brave, little mouse." He shoved her toward his car. "I think we'll finish our discussion in private."

Caught in the jaws of a deadly beast, Lindy mustered her courage, twisting away from him.

Hayward's hand connected with her cheek in an explosion of pressure which sent her sunglasses flying.

The men moved as a unit and closed the distance. "Everything okay here?"

Hayward cleared his throat. "This is a private matter."

"That smack made it public, dude."

"How 'bout you let her go?" Their combined attitude and potency had Hayward releasing her.

"I have a car." Lindy scooped up her glasses and staggered toward her champions. "If you could keep him busy for twenty minutes I would greatly appreciate it."

The men tightened their circle. "Busy or bloody?"

Lindy unlocked Celeste's car and tossed her bag on the back seat. She opened the driver's-side door and cast one last look over her shoulder. "Your choice."

Chapter 35

The drive to Newark Airport took less than thirty minutes. On the way Lindy realized Hayward had most likely intercepted her by tracking her phone. She decided to use his arrogance to her advantage.

She drove into the long-term parking lot, pulled out the credit card he provided and booked a first-class ticket on the redeye to Phoenix. Next she secured a rental car and stretched the fantasy a little further with a hotel reservation in Flagstaff.

Lindy boarded the shuttle and rode the loop to the terminal. On a bench beneath the sign for departures she sent a brief text to Celeste canceling brunch and apologizing for her impromptu trip to Arizona. She asked forgiveness for stealing her car, relayed the recovery location, then powered off the device before Celeste would have an opportunity to reply.

Feeling steadier, Lindy dropped the phone in the trash, walked to the curb, and hailed a cab.

In East Brunswick, New Jersey, Lindy had the driver stop at an all-night drug store. She grabbed a small first-aid kit, protein bars, bottled water, and a prepaid phone. A few miles farther she paid cash for two nights in a hotel where she was guaranteed to remain anonymous.

The breath she'd been holding for the past three hours released as the deadbolt clicked. She dug out the ancient iPad, plugged it in, and prayed it would charge. The shower was big and the water was hot. Lindy lathered her hair with the hotel shampoo and willed the night's dread to join the suds on the journey down the drain.

She pulled a Pink Floyd t-shirt over her head and wrapped her hair in a turban so she could treat the cut on her face. Lindy snapped the ice pack to activate the cold and pressed it against her injured lip.

"Now what?" Lindy had expected to be drained but instead was re-energized. She snagged the complimentary notepad and listed everything she needed to do to break ties with Hayward Livingston, including forfeiting her loft and pottery studio.

The punch of regret was swift and painful. She'd left so fast. Even with the security engaged, Hayward would certainly gain access. What would he do after he got inside? "Better not think about it," she sighed. "Can't do anything about it anyway."

Lindy grabbed her shoebox and spread the contents across the bed. She spied a small, satin pouch among her keepsakes. Holding the fabric tenderly, she opened the snap and poured the tiny star necklace into her palm.

Her thumbs fumbled with the clasp, but as Lindy fastened the delicate chain and pressed the pendant to her chest, the world... for just a moment... slowed down.

Lindy opened her investment portfolio. Thank goodness she'd stuck to her original plan of maintaining independent accounts in her birth name. "I may be homeless but I'm certainly not penniless." The ridiculous sum of money she'd earned had been invested and grown substantially.

She closed her eyes and tried to visualize where she'd like to live. "Where do you want to go?" West—Sedona or Arizona? South—Florida or Georgia? "Who do you want to be near?"

Lindy kissed her iPad for luck as she pressed the power button. The device churned to life and the screen-saving picture was from the last summer she'd spent on Chincoteague. The image captured Nina, Mike, Tucker and Lindy full of youthful joy where it all began, her garage studio.

"My where and who." Lindy ran a finger over each of their faces, then hunkered down to establish her new life.

Real-estate was the first item on her list. She perused the listings for townhouses and condos, then decided leasing felt temporary, like indecision. "This is not a whim," she mumbled and refined the search. A moment later the screen populated with available homes.

The simple saltbox house hooked her immediately. Nestled in a cubby of tall trees on the north end of the island, the home was secluded and had an amazing view of the water.

Perched on a stone foundation the first floor was higher than many on the island, providing additional protection from rising water during coastal storms. The wraparound porch extended and joined a planked walkway which led to an oversized garage that would work perfectly for her studio.

She clicked through the additional pictures and something stirred in the back of her mind. "The McCoy house," she whispered. "Is that possible?" As a child she'd ridden her bike past the property nearly every day in the summer. A sand and gravel lane that ended with a circle of crushed shells just wide enough to turn around before you'd fall into the bay.

Lindy had spent many lazy afternoons in the cove beyond the shore floating away the heat of the day. She'd used the view to dream of her future, whispering her wishes to the setting sun. The orb of fire was an amazing listener not to mention a loyal keeper of sacred secrets. Her mind drifted to the night she'd spent with Tucker following the loss of her mom.

"Memory Lane indeed."

The property had been upgraded over the years. There were raised beds in the side yard for gardening and a large children's swing set. The virtual walkthrough showed the home was outfitted with basic bedroom and living room furniture that suited Lindy's taste. With a few clicks she wired the money for a deposit from her private account to the realtor. She made an additional offer to have the furnishings included.

Lindy sent an email to her broker requesting a phone consultation at her earliest convenience. "House… check." She smiled and drew a line through item number one.

Hayward's connections would make securing transportation a bit trickier. Lindy wanted to take extra precautions to be certain not to toss up any red flags. She knew she could trust Celeste but it was likely Hayward would assign one of his henchmen to monitor her movements.

Her eyes fell on the picture from her sixteenth birthday—she and Nina eating ice cream sundaes on the porch of the B&B. If she was going to toss her life into anyone's hands Nina would be top of the list. As children they'd vowed to stand together in any circumstance. Lindy could only hope the systematic separation over the last few years hadn't fractured Nina's trust.

Lindy hesitated then powered up her prepaid phone and placed the call.

Hayward was not accustomed to answering questions about his personal affairs. After his failed attempt to intercept Belinda at the garage he'd returned to the penthouse and learned the maid had reported to her supervisor that Belinda had been injured. In the end, management decided the relationship with the Livingston Foundation outweighed the opinion of one member of their service staff.

He'd tracked her phone to the airport and according to her credit card she would be landing in Arizona within the hour. Running off to that ridiculous schoolmate's home, no doubt. He made a few calls and sent the private jet to have her collected at baggage claim.

Chapter 36

Lindy timed her arrival on Chincoteague for the wee hours and crossed the causeway just after two in the morning. Elevated billboards stood just off the shoulder in the marsh. They advertised seafood restaurants, mini golf, and luxury vacation properties. The thoroughfare offered a view across the water to where the island slept. A stark contrast to the bustle of the city whose sky never dimmed and streets never stilled.

She turned on Memory Lane, pulled into the crushed shell driveway, and turned off the engine. Lindy unfolded from the car and stretched. Silence lay over the night like a quilt sewn with love. She looked at her new home silhouetted in the moonlight, and smiled.

Lindy gathered a grocery bag from behind the seat then loaded her arms with her blanket, pillow and bathroom tote. The porch light was on and the door was unlocked as promised.

Fatigue greeted and welcomed her inside. Lindy dropped her bedding in the foyer and walked to the kitchen. On the counter she found the keys along with the final settlement paperwork.

Too tired to unpack she placed the bag of food in the refrigerator and wandered into the living room, collapsed on the sofa, and slept.

On the other side of the island… damp flesh and pounding hearts tumbled across the narrow bed. The moon shone through the window and provided just enough light to accent the line of her cheek, the shape of her mouth, and her eyes lost in his. Home was all he could think as his mouth captured hers once more.

Tucker came awake as if a gun fired. As the intensity of the dream began to fade, he unwound the tangled sheet and tossed his leg over the side of the bed.

Boop, his Chesapeake Bay Retriever, stretched until her cool nose bumped Tucker's side. "Sorry to wake you, girl." He stroked her head then pushed up from the mattress. Chilled tile met bare feet. He walked to the kitchen, jerked open the refrigerator, and grabbed the gallon of orange juice.

Tucker filled his favorite chunky mug and carried it to the breakfast nook. From the window he had a clear view across the channel to the Assateague Lighthouse. He was surprised to discover the water calm, the sky clear.

"Would have sworn a storm was brewing," he said as Boop joined him. "Well, we're up." Tucker opened the container of kibble and filled her dish. "Might as well get to the day."

"Anyone alive in here?"

Lindy stirred. Was someone knocking?

"Hellooo," the word dribbled like syrup. "It's just Lois from Island Properties. I've got muffins."

The realtor? Lindy refrained from screaming.

"Oh, there you are." Lois closed the door and bustled to the kitchen. "Just checking to be sure you got in alright."

Lindy's fatigue-laden brain cleared. She pushed upright and threaded her arms into her denim shirt.

"Gracious, did I wake you? It's nearly nine."

"I got in late," Lindy yawned.

"I'm not a fan of traveling at night. How was your drive? You had so far to come… New-York-City." Lois savored each word as if confectioner's sugar were dusting the syllables. "Coffee? I have hazelnut, vanilla cream, Caribbean kick? Or tea if you prefer—black raspberry or chamomile?"

Lindy stared vacantly as Lois waved tea bags and Keurig cups in the air. "Did I forget to sign something?"

"Sign?" Lois's brow creased. "No, dear." Her laughter echoed through the house. "Heavens no, just welcoming you to your new home. Thought you'd appreciate an in-person tour."

Lindy raked her finger through her mussed hair as she made her way to the kitchen. "Can we do this another time? I'm not feeling well, migraine," she lied and twisted her hair into a loose knot.

Lois's eyes widened. She averted her gaze but not before she got a good look at the blooming color beneath Lindy's eye and the five-finger handprint marking her forearm. "Sure dear, you take your time." Welcome shifted to sympathy. "Just give a call if I can be of any assistance." She placed her card on the counter and backed toward the door. "The muffins are all-natural, by the way. I read that article about you taking care of your health and all."

Lindy winced as the door closed. News of her arrival on the island wouldn't be Lois's biggest tidbit of gossip. It would be that she'd arrived battered and bruised. "Not the hometown impression I was going for."

Lindy fixed a cup of tea and opened the door to the back deck. Newly updated, the walkway followed the edge of the garage and continued to the dock. The wooden structure spanned the marsh, extending into the bay, and ended where the depth would support a small boat.

She cradled her mug and settled on the planks by the water's edge. She greeted the day the way her mother had nearly all her life. The morning ritual had given her mom perspective in a season of change.

Lindy breathed the fragrance of earth and sea as the tide shifted in a natural dance to baptize the newly exposed mud. "Not a bad spot to begin again, if I do say so myself."

The breeze swirled in a sweet caress that lifted her hair, tickled the length of her arms, and teased her fingertips.

Lindy smiled. "Hi, Mom."

Tucker's feet slapped the street in a steady rhythm. With Boop at his side, he allowed his mind to turn off as he ran to the southern end of the island. The sun was peeking through the tall pines as he passed the park. He followed the bay along Main Street where the marina was stirring with daybreak fishermen.

160

His course led past the house he'd helped renovate. There were two cars in the drive. One belonged to the listing agent, the other was a rental car with Jersey plates.

"We're not the only ones getting a jump on the day," Tucker said to Boop then continued along the narrow road. The unique property had been on the market less than a week. A quick sale wouldn't surprise him. Island living held an alluring appeal.

He wondered who the new residents would be. Summer vacationers or weekend warriors? Maybe retirees looking for an island community or new adventure. Anything was possible. He passed the private drive where a big city developer had built an extravagant residence. The house had been vacant since completion and was seeking a buyer with very specific taste.

Tucker reached the turnaround circle and looked over the bay. He had a ton of memories on this stretch of road and a few more in the cove beyond the shore.

Fragments of his dream stirred on the edges of his mind.

Boop whimpered and tugged against the lead.

"Gonna be pretty chilly." Tucker indulged and unhooked her. She bounded in with a splash and swam in delighted circles.

Tucker laughed as she barked at him from the water. "Although a cold shower might help clear my head, I'm not up for a swim today." A stiff spring breeze rushed across the cove and pushed against his sweatshirt. "Sending me luck?" Tucker thought of his grandfather. "I could use a little today."

He'd recently closed escrow on a building in Ocean City, Maryland. The old structure needed a major overhaul before he could consider expanding his business. Today Tucker would meet with another contractor to see if what he visualized was a possibility.

Boop climbed from the bay and shook the sea from her coat.

"We have a big day, pretty lady. Are you ready for a road trip?" Tucker reached down, attached the leash, then together they turned for home.

Through the trees Tucker glimpsed a woman sitting on the dock behind the McCoy house. Steam lifted from the mug in her hand as she surveyed the water. If she turned he'd wave, but she didn't so he continued on.

———⁓⁓⁓———

Hayward poured a generous portion of Scotch and savored the burn as the liquor raced to his stomach.

She'd parked the car, purchased the ticket, but never boarded the plane. It didn't matter. What was she without him?

Nothing.

Everything Belinda was, he had provided. She'd miss the exposure his name and the Livingston Foundation had brought to her little pots and vases. When sales dried up and no one so much as glanced in her direction, she'd come crawling back.

Chapter 37

Nina couldn't contain her happiness.

She'd resisted the urge to camp out on Lindy's front porch the previous night. She continued her display of extreme restraint by waiting until noon before loading an insulated bag with food and treats and climbing on her bike.

"But time's up," Nina grinned as she pedaled through the alley and onto the main road. "My best friend is home and I'm going to see her."

Nina grabbed the soft cooler and tote from her bike basket and headed to the door.

She whacked the screen. "Ready, wanted or not, I'm coming in."

She turned the knob and wandered through the foyer, spotting Lindy on her yoga mat in the center of the large glass-enclosed back porch. She had earbuds in to block the outside noise and was positioned to look over the water.

Nina watched with wonder as Lindy balanced steadily on one foot while she reached back to capture the other, then tipped effortlessly forward.

"Amazing," Nina whispered then stifled a yip of distress as she noticed a speckling of fingertip-sized bruises on Lindy's bicep. She pressed her hand to the ache in her chest and backed from the room.

Nina placed the baked treats and snacks in a basket beside the sink then unloaded the single-serving portions of soup, casserole, and quiche into the freezer. She grabbed a notepad from her purse and made a list of essential pots, pans, dishes, and utensils Lindy would need.

The pen rolled off the counter and bounced across the tile. Nina turned to retrieve it and found Lindy standing in the archway behind her.

Nina worked hard to mask the shock as she took in the injuries to Lindy's face.

A butterfly bandage secured broken skin dangerously close to her eye. The damage to her cheek had begun the shift from plum to dark purple.

Lindy waited for the inquiry, but Nina just opened her arms. Whatever concerns she had about Nina being angry dissolved as she moved into the circle.

"I really love the house." Nina sipped hot tea with honey. "Mike did the HVAC upgrade and Zak and Tucker helped with the new construction on the garage. They're going to be so thrilled when they find out you bought it."

Lindy paled. "Not ready for any reunions just yet."

"I'm not pushing, just saying, and I completely understand." Nina wedged a pillow under her elbow. "Tucker is off-island for a few days, not that you asked, but I wanted you to be aware. I spoke to Kate this morning... she and Rudy will be back from their cruise Friday afternoon. She threatened to call the National Guard and be airlifted home immediately, but I talked her out of that idea."

"Good, gives me time to figure a couple things out."

"Seems to me you've figured a lot out already."

"Well, it's amazing what you can accomplish with the proper motivation and a sturdy investment portfolio." Lindy's fingers feathered over her bandage. "I'm sorry I called in the middle of the night and dragged you into my drama."

"I'm not." Nina laid her hand open between them and smiled as Lindy's fingers linked with hers. "So, what's the plan?"

Lindy allowed the connection to roll through and ground her. "I'd like to take a few days and," she gestured to her face, "heal. Then I could use your help returning the rental car."

"Of course."

"My storage pod should be dropped off by the end of the week. I've been filling it with random items and have no idea what I'm going to find inside. It's going to feel like Christmas."

"That will be fun." Nina sat quietly allowing Lindy to lead the conversation.

"I need to work. It's like breathing and therapy all rolled together."

"What do you need to get started?"

"I secured my studio before I left but I have no idea what I'll find when I go back." Lindy absorbed Nina's flinch. "Not in that way. I'm never going back to him."

"Okay," she breathed a sigh of relief. "Studio supplies, continue."

"I started an order for the basic tools and equipment but need to sit in the garage and get a feel for the space before I click *buy*." *That's the easy part*, Lindy thought. "Before I can actually do any serious work I'll need a contractor to renovate the garage into a workspace, an electrician for the kiln and ventilation, and a plumber to modify the outdoor shower to include a utility sink. I'll also need somebody to install a really good security system."

Nina swiped open her phone and tapped contacts. Seconds later from the kitchen Lindy's phone chimed. "Done."

"You're amazing." Lindy set her cup aside and faced Nina. "My last request is… well… what I really need is a…" Her face flushed. "I'm embarrassed to ask."

"Come on, it's me," Nina giggled at her friend. "You know you can ask me for anything."

"A makeover, or more accurately a make-under. Would you call whoever you see and ask if she can work me in next week? If I'm going to be myself, I need to look like myself, and that means this facade has to go."

"No problem. Anything else?"

"Do you have an extra bike I could borrow?"

"You'll keep mine for as long as you want." Nina popped open her cell phone and tapped the screen. "Hey honey, I'm at Lindy's and I need a ride." She listened a moment. "Yes, feeling much better, thanks." Nina winked at Lindy. "No problem, she's great. I will. Perfect, see your sexy buns shortly." She ended the call. "Mike says welcome home."

"Still got the hots after all these years?"

"You better believe it."

"Were you sick earlier?"

"Uh-huh." Nina rested her hand over her stomach.

"Really?" Lindy felt the surprising punch of envy.

"Fourteen weeks and almost over the morning sickness."

"Wow, Eric's going to be a big brother." Lindy felt the tears rising. She hadn't met her honorary nephew yet. "I'm really looking forward to meeting Eric."

"Remember that when you're covered in unidentifiable goop." Nina laughed as dread washed over Lindy's features. "Boys come with goop." She lifted her palms and let them fall. "I don't know what to tell you, it's a modern mystery."

"I've missed so much of your life." Lindy's eyes filled and spilled.

"Hey now, shh…" Nina gathered her close. "None of that."

"I… I've made su-ch a mess of ev-erything."

"You're just tired. Rest for a minute." Nina guided Lindy until her head lay on her lap. She rubbed a hand over her friend's back and sent Mike a quick text to tell him to take his time.

Chapter 38

Lindy carried her dinner to the garage for the third consecutive night to visualize her studio one final time. She double-checked the list for the hardware store and added additional sheets of plywood, a few yards of heavy canvas and basic tools, a staple gun and hammer as well as a broom and dustpan.

Her wish list for functional furniture would be ongoing. Lindy preferred to up-cycle whenever possible. She would be on the lookout for tables and shelving that suited her taste and made her smile.

"Need to stumble on a flea market or repurpose warehouse," she muttered to herself but knew the right pieces would fall into place a moment at a time.

Lindy adjusted the items in her online shopping cart and completed the transaction. Feeling confident, she left voice messages for the contractors Nina recommended.

Thankfully three days had done wonders to restore her energy, not to mention improve her appearance. Lindy looked at the sun's position in the sky and decided she had just enough time for a quick bike ride.

When was the last time she'd done something as basic as riding a bicycle? As a child her bike was her freedom. She'd ridden everywhere, often with Nina by her side, but as she straddled the metal frame she had a moment of healthy adult panic.

"Here goes nothing." Lindy pressed the pedal, wobbled, but found her balance as the tires moved from shell to macadam.

She passed a couple walking hand in hand enjoying the spring sunshine. Settling into an easy rhythm she made her way to the school, rode along the football field, then turned south following the road to town.

The silhouette of the B&B came into view. Nina had added a stained glass window to the second-floor balcony. Suspended above the railing the panel burst to life in the afternoon sun.

Little had changed, she thought, as she navigated the shops on Main. The signs were faded and weather-worn but unlike the ever evolving canvas of New York, the town held many of the same small businesses.

Lindy followed the familiar narrow streets toward the heart of the island and found herself in front of her first childhood home. A tattered for rent sign lay flat on the neglected lawn.

The state of disrepair was shocking. The siding was discolored and the roof was partially draped with a tarp. The front porch planks were buckled, trapping the screen door between open and closed.

Unsure why she felt compelled to look closer, Lindy hopped off the bike and crossed the lawn of the vacant property. She carefully climbed the damaged steps and used the sleeve of her jacket to wipe the grime off the window.

The kitchen was deserted except for a small enamel table. The countertop was cut where appliances had been and in the corner a chair lay in pieces. The dirty glass muddled the sight and a memory filled in the scene.

Lindy trembled in the closet while the storm raged. Something shattered and splintered. Fragments of glass tinkled over the linoleum floor. She remembered leaving her hiding place and discovering her mom lying in a heap beside the stove.

The haze from Frank's unfiltered cigarette polluted her mind. "Look who thinks she's something special." His words dripped like venom. "Feeling brave? You're not. You're nothing."

The warped planks groaned as Lindy stumbled away from the filthy pane. She turned her back and walked away.

Lindy rode home, lost in thought for the girl she had been. It was interesting how, despite every intention to pursue a life without the ugliness and control, she'd partnered with a man like Hayward. A polished version of the cruelty she'd been so determined to avoid.

Tucker placed the day's receipts in the bank bag and zipped it tight. He did a final walk through the store, adjusting merchandise and straightening displays. If the recent spike in online traffic was any indication, he'd be right where he needed to be for his planned expansion.

He was humbled by the support and success Sea Surge was experiencing. Tucker's small dream was growing up. Now that he'd landed a contractor who understood his vision, Tucker was hopeful everything would fall into place.

He flipped the open sign to closed, turned off the lights and locked the door. "Time to go home, Boop." His faithful three-year-old Chessie scurried from her bed behind the register and joined him by the door.

Boop wagged and wiggled then offered a small bark of greeting. "No, we're not chasing..." Tucker's sentence died on his tongue as he caught a glimpse of the bicycle crossing the intersection.

"Lindy Colton." *No*, he corrected. Belinda Cole was what she called herself now. "For once, the buzz around town is true." Lindy was on the island. She had done quite well for herself through the years and had landed right where she had always aimed.

Tucker led Boop away from the window. "Come on, girl." He opened the doorway to his private residence on the second level. He'd only seen Lindy twice since she set out to pursue her dreams. Both times he'd gotten his hands on her... and both times she'd slipped through his fingers.

Chapter 39

"You were exactly right." Nina's face filled the laptop screen. "Christmas on steroids."

"Once upon a time I attempted to keep inventory." Lindy gestured to the half dozen totes she'd carried in from the storage pod. "But somewhere along the way my need for organization was swallowed by enthusiasm. Where do you want me to start?"

"Just pick one and dive in."

"Brutus," Lindy hooted as she unwrapped a chalkware pug piggy bank. "Hello, big boy. I've missed you."

"Where did you find him?" Nina laughed.

"Roadside market, upstate New York." Lindy grinned. "He has a twin sister in here somewhere." She discovered a plastic measuring spoon for instant coffee, an oversized clock made from license plates, and a set of Looney Tunes character glasses.

There were at least three dozen old books, an understandable weakness. Lindy opened the cover of *The Cat and the Fiddle.* The 1802 first edition had an inscription which read, *"To Harriet at Christmas."* Lindy's vision swam as she unearthed the pink hardcover copy of *Misty of Chincoteague* her mom had given her on her seventh birthday.

"You're going to need a bookshelf," Nina said. "Turn the screen so I can have a better view."

Lindy re-positioned the laptop. "Better?"

"Much. What's next?"

"This is the last one for tonight." Lindy dragged another tote into view. "I'm overwhelmed. Besides I'd rather you were here in the flesh to help me get organized."

"You don't have to ask me twice," Nina laughed. "How about I come over Saturday after your salon appointment?"

"Perfect." Lindy popped the next bin open and knew instantly it held items she'd packed after the funeral. "Too many emotions in this box, Nina." She lifted the bowl and note her mother had written, and held them to her chest.

"Then quit until Saturday. I need to get Eric in the tub."

"Sounds good. Night." Lindy disconnected the call and looked over the eclectic mix of treasure from thrift stores and flea markets filling her living room. Hayward had called her assortment "secondhand trash" and said none of it would ever have a place in his home. *Exactly*, she thought now. Not in *his* home.

Lindy carefully returned the bowl to the tub and spotted a length of silver chain. The links unfurled as she lifted it. Two tiny keys dangled from the end. They fit the lock on the box Tucker made to guard her wishes.

Chasing stars. Lindy rubbed her hand over the sudden ache in her chest. After the transfer of the B&B, the little box had mistakenly been sent to auction and was long gone.

Tucker exited the Sea Surge lot and jerked the wheel to the right. Up to this point he had resisted the urge to drive by the old McCoy house, but the village was small and he wouldn't need to circle too far out of his way.

He drove past the school and eased onto Memory Lane. The McCoy house came into view. The sign in the yard now boasted SOLD. The idea of Lindy and the polished peacock she was hooked up with rambling around town, or worse, raising refined society brats on the island, blew through Tucker like a bad day at sea.

Beyond the tall trees he could see a light bouncing around inside a storage pod. Lindy emerged, backlit by the moon. She appeared etched in silver light. Tucker's heart looped in his chest.

She spared a glance toward his vehicle, then hefted an oversized tote higher on her hip.

He watched her carry the container inside and close the door behind her. "Spying on her." Tucker shook his head. "I'm no better than the busybodies at the pub."

He continued to the end of the road, put the Jeep in park, and looked across the water. It was the place he and Lindy had come countless times in their teens to extend an evening or toil away an afternoon.

The last time Tucker and Lindy had anchored in the cove, a gale of heat and history fueled the night. Grief paved the way and their definition of casual friendship had been shattered.

The image of Lindy highlighted by moonbeams filled his mind. Maybe he'd been dreaming then, maybe he was dreaming now. Either way, he'd been right. A storm had come to the island and it was raging inside him.

His pencil rampantly rebounded off the glossy desk. The robo voice came on the line, *"The mailbox you are trying to reach is full."* Hayward's knuckles whitened and the pencil snapped in two.

Belinda was behaving like an ill-mannered child. There were many things requiring her attention, not to mention her physical presence. He would not allow her impulsive actions to tarnish opinions surrounding him.

No doubt she'd run straight back to her hometown to cower in the rent-by-the-night shack facing the bay. He had no desire to make room in his itinerary to travel to that rinky-dink island and fetch her.

He scooped up his phone and dialed Baxter.

"Sir," Baxter answered.

"Belinda's having a moment. I need you to take a trip." Hayward relayed the details. "Be discreet and follow up with me directly."

"Yes, sir."

Chapter 40

Traffic on the dead end road had picked up. Lindy doubted it was prospective buyers for the overpriced mansion at the end of the lane. Regardless, she wanted to check out the hardware store for the remaining studio supplies, but even more, she needed food.

Grateful for Nina's bike, Lindy pedaled along Church Street to Chapel's Produce.

"As I live and breathe, it's Lindy Colton," squawked the woman behind the register. "Back from the big city. You probably don't remember me, being famous and all."

"Sure I do, Mrs. Chapel. I've missed your produce and your tomato pie."

"Come July, I'll hook you up," she grinned in delight. "What can I get you today?"

"I would love some veggies."

"From Georgia and Florida, but anything beats hothouse, am I right?"

"You are." Lindy added a jar of honey to her basket then turned her attention to the selection of jams and preserves.

"All local berries in the jelly," Mrs. Chapel commented. "Last year's harvest was the best we've had in several years." She angled her head and studied Lindy. "Never thought you looked much like your mom, but now that you've grown into those legs, you resemble her."

"Thank you."

"She's missed, your mom, as were you." Mrs. Chapel smiled. "So, now tell me..."

"How's your family?" Lindy neatly interrupted. She knew the best way to avoid the interrogation was to be the one asking the questions.

Mrs. Chapel swallowed the bait with gusto and regaled Lindy with stories of her adult children and their kids. "Too bad you didn't get back sooner. You could have married my boy. Now his eyes are all over Heather, your friend from high school. She's a nice girl." Mrs. Chapel bagged Lindy's items. "But she's not a famous big city artist."

Lindy paid for her produce and hoped she would be several blocks away before Mrs. Chapel realized she'd blundered her chance to nab the latest gossip.

Mrs. Quinn, the local bakery owner, wasn't as easily distracted. She spotted Lindy's bare ring finger and pounced. "Having your ring sized? I hear it's a beauty. Your fancy man did his shopping at Tiffany's. I guess he'll be coming to the island more often with you buying the McCoy house."

Lindy paled. Was it too much to hope for a bit of personal space? She selected a fresh baguette from the bin beside the counter as Mrs. Quinn rolled on.

"His handsome face will certainly be a welcome addition to our community. Those loaves came out of the oven less than an hour ago. Best in three counties. There's fresh pesto in the cooler if you're after a tasty treat."

"That would be lovely and I'll take a petite lemon pound cake too, please." Lindy hooked her tote on the handlebars and pedaled toward home. The breeze was cooler than she'd anticipated and her fingers were freezing. Hoping for a shortcut she turned at the alley behind the fire station and stumbled on a bustling flea market.

"Ooh, jackpot." Lindy hopped off the bike and for the next hour she strolled through the tables. She bought a pair of hand-knit gloves, found five-gallon buckets for glazing, and a canvas boat cover.

She was just figuring out how to carry everything on her bike when she spotted Zak standing on a trailer, wrestling with a vintage enamel-topped table. Lindy engaged the kickstand and chuckled at Zak's creative string of profanity. His long beard and sunglasses masked his face, but his t-shirt made her smile—*Trash or Treasure, you decide.*

"That table is treasure for sure."

174

"She could be yours," he said without looking. "If I can convince her to release her stubborn legs." The table popped loose. Zak cursed again as he was thrown off balance.

He vaulted to the ground and slid his glasses to the top of his head. The grin that split his face was pure pleasure. "My truest of true loves." Zak crossed to Lindy in stalking strides and scooped her clean off her feet. "You ready to marry me yet?"

She laughed as he set her down. "I'm out of your league, remember?"

"Damn truth, even more now than when I last held you in my arms." Zak retrieved the table. "She's sturdy, but a bit of rust on the corner."

"Rust is such a dirty word." Lindy frowned playfully and stroked the shiny metal surface. "Character and life experience is what I call it. How much are you asking?"

"Before we get to the dollar discussion, let me show you one other piece I pulled from the same house."

Lindy followed Zak to the opposite side of the trailer. "Mike told me you mentioned a sink install for your garage studio. Now that I see you have an impeccable eye, you may be interested in this."

"Oh well," Lindy sighed, clearly smitten. "Hello, beloved."

Her reaction made Zak's morning. "If your crush blooms and you fall all the way in love, I'm happy to deliver, no extra charge. I could walk through the security system I have in mind while we're at it."

"Done and done."

Chapter 41

"You can't hide out forever." Nina crossed her arms.

"I'm not hiding." Lindy hugged the throw pillow tight to her chest. "I'm just not going out of my way to be visible."

"Do you really think Hayward will be stalking the Bayside Inn on the off-chance you might drop in for a bite to eat?"

Lindy shrugged even as her internal voice cautioned that anything was possible.

"We're going."

"I'm dirty."

"No one cares." Nina tapped her foot. "Put your shoes on and grab a sweater. The breeze off the water will be chilly."

"You've gotten bossy." Lindy stepped into her soft leather ankle boots.

"Rearing a young boy does that to a person."

Lindy scooped up her sweater and tugged it over her head. "You're very good at it."

Tucker felt the air shift. A moment later Lindy strolled across the deck. He leaned against the pillar and allowed his eyes to take a parched man's gulp. He knew seeing her unobscured was going to kick him square and he was right. Lindy was beyond beautiful. Her hair was darker but still long. He wished she'd tied it from her face. It was a spectacular face.

Nina gripped Lindy's hand firmly in hers and weaved through the bodies to a round table in the back of the dining area. Lindy snuggled her chair tight against Nina's. Their lips moved in a constant stream as if they plotted and planned world domination. Just like old times, his heart warmed for their friendship.

Tucker swallowed the last bite of his burger as Trish, the town easy, entered the bar. She signaled the bartender, "Screaming Orgasm please," then fluttered her lashes and wiggled onto the stool beside Tucker. "Should I make it a double?"

Tucker sputtered as he finished his ginger ale.

"How's my favorite guy doing?"

"I'm doing alright." Tucker wiped his mouth and pushed the glass across the bar.

"You're not leaving me here all by my lonely self, are you?" Trish pouted.

"We both know you won't stay that way for long."

Trish's deep and throaty laugh jiggled her abundant cleavage. "I could come back to the apartment for an hour." The bartender set the shot in front of her. "Or maybe you'd prefer a quick ride around the harbor."

"I wouldn't be good company tonight, Trish."

She lifted the glass and sipped the coffee flavored concoction. "I could be entertaining enough for both of us."

Tucker knew the girl wasn't without skills, but he hadn't given in to her charms for quite some time. His eyes tracked toward Lindy. Even with her back to him she pulled.

"I see how it is." Trish tossed the remaining liquor back then placed her hand on Tucker's shoulder. "Your forever crush has returned." She eased off the stool and pressed her curves against him. "I'll be around if you change your mind."

Kate, the owner, bumped Tucker's hip with hers. "Can I get you anything else, handsome?"

"No thanks, I'm heading home." Tucker tossed a few bills on the counter and ducked out the side door toward the dock.

"Coward," Kate frowned in the wake of his rapid exit.

Kate scooped up two menus and moved toward the ladies. "My dearest girl," Kate's eyes were brimming with affection. "It cost me, not coming to you the minute Rudy and I got home. Stand up and hug me like you mean it."

Lindy hugged Kate firmly.

"Excellent, now step back and let me get a good look at you." Kate gripped Lindy's hands in hers and took in every detail. Her skin was pale and her eyes were shadowed with weariness. Kate leaned close and brushed a kiss over the fading bruise on Lindy's temple. "Nothing love and rest won't mend, sweetie."

Lindy sank into another embrace. "I'm sorry… an all-encompassing sorry."

Kate held Lindy a bit tighter. "Everything will be fine now. You're home." She inched back. "You are home, right?"

Lindy lifted her shoulders and let them fall. "Looks that way."

"Good, I have one invasive question. No, I have two." Kate grinned as Nina scowled. "Back down, girl. It's my nature to know what's what and meddle when I see fit." Kate focused on Lindy. "First, is that excuse of a man who put a ring on your finger and marks on your skin setting foot on this island?"

"Not by my invitation."

"Good. Second…" Kate continued. "Are you happy?"

"I will be," Lindy answered softly.

"That's my girl." Kate enveloped Lindy again. "The remainder of the inquisition will be held tomorrow morning over fresh-baked pie and coffee. Does nine work for you?"

"Eight would be better. I have a big day planned."

"There you are." Kate squeezed Lindy's hand. "Now let's tend to the business at hand. Food and drinks? What can I get for you?"

From the shadows Tucker watched.

Kate's comment chewed at him as he walked along the planks of the deck toward his boat. So what if he decided not to approach Lindy right at this moment? It didn't make him a chicken.

It had been a long time since they'd seen one another and they were vastly different people. Lindy was practically a stranger.

Tucker scrubbed his hand across his face. His argument sounded lame even to him. Years may have passed but emotionally he was right where he always was where Lindy Colton was concerned, neck deep in complicated feelings.

Their ancient history was his problem. She bought a house and was staying. He'd have to get a grip on himself before he attempted to talk with her.

"Hey, boy-o." Retired Fire Chief Rudy hustled up the planks. "They run out of food and beverage in this joint or are you cutting out for a hot date?"

"Neither," Tucker chuckled.

"Well, then why are you running off?"

"Just been a long day." Tucker studied Rudy's guilty face. "Kate called you, didn't she?"

"Woman's always calling me about some damn thing." Rudy's sheepish smile wavered beneath Tucker's steely stare. "Alright, alright. Kate thought you might be needin' a man to talk with since the girl who swallowed your heart like a goliath grouper drove over the bridge."

Tucker blew out a short breath. "She didn't swallow my heart."

"No shame in it, boy. Sometimes it's damn delightful to let a good woman gobble you up." Rudy had carried a torch his entire life for Kate. Somehow they finally found one another and by some miracle Kate's endearing sass was the perfect ingredient to balance Rudy's gruff demeanor.

"Kate has made you weak in the knees." Tucker untied the bowline and tossed it into the boat.

"I thank the Lord every day for it."

"Blink those stars from your eyes, Rudy. Life isn't a Nicholas Sparks novel. Not everyone gets the girl."

"You're right. More times than not, Stephen King picks up the pen and everyone dies dreadfully." Rudy opened his tobacco pouch and shrugged. "Kate's got me reading."

"What's next?" Tucker snorted. "Crocheting doilies?"

"Mind your tongue, son." Rudy looked over his shoulder. "My woman's got superhuman hearing. You want a brew buddy or not?"

"I'll take a rain check." Tucker released the stern line and hopped aboard. The engine rumbled and the boat eased away from the dock.

"Anytime." Rudy raised his hand in salute.

The lights were dim around the stage and the music kicked up. Local talent took turns at the microphone.

Kate walked slowly toward Rudy and slipped her hands in his. "Is he going to be okay?"

"Of course. Tucker's tough." Rudy hugged Kate. "But it's hard when the one you want is right in front of you and still out of reach."

"And sometimes one step closes the distance." Kate leaned her head on Rudy's sturdy shoulder.

"You planning on meddling in Tucker's business?"

"Me?" Kate's eyelids fluttered. "I'm just a sucker for love. Tucker's been lonely long enough, don't you think?"

Rudy's brow lifted. "What do you know?"

"No engagement ring, no wedding, no Hayward."

"Makes my little tidbit icing to your éclair." Rudy leaned close and lowered his voice. "The house is in her name only."

"Going to be a lovely thing to watch, don't you think?" Kate placed her hand on her husband's chest and brushed her lips over his. "I think we'll nudge, not push, just nudge them in the right direction."

"Can we let her finish unpacking first?"

Chapter 42

Lindy filled the bike basket with her woven blanket and blocks then threaded her arm through the strap and wiggled until her yoga mat settled between her shoulder blades. The crisp air cleared her mind as the pedals circled. The morning sun was climbing, painting her shadow on the road beside her for company.

Familiar sights greeted her as she rode downtown—Don's Seafood, the T-shirt Emporium, and Main Street Coffee House. Green Goodness caught her eye. Lindy slowed and propped her foot on the curb to study the innovative storefront.

A stained glass panel was hanging over an antique washstand. The wide wooden frame was filled with united circles in a wide range of shape and color. Beside it a bucket bench displayed a grouping of unique crocks. The porch was jam-packed but tastefully arranged with architectural and industrial metal works.

"My kind of trouble," Lindy happily added Green Goodness to her must-visit list.

She continued past Island Theater and the library until she reached the old square and the cheerful yellow icon holding the corner, Sundial Books and Music. Lindy secured her bike in the rack then grabbed her water bottle, blanket, and block from the wire basket.

Overhead, birds babbled as the glug of want and wane lifted and lowered boats tethered to the pier. The sigh of stretching rope blended with the prattle aloft and the simplicity soothed her. Ease fueled her steps as she followed the wide brick walkway into Robert Reed Park.

The community courtyard offered a view of the vast channel separating the island from the mainland. In the distance, cars raced across the bridge and causeway like ants at work.

Lindy moved to the center of the open lawn and for the next several minutes simply breathed in time with the environment around her.

Stillness arrived.

Lindy unrolled her yoga mat and sat. She draped the blanket over her lap and invited her body to discover tranquility as well.

Her surroundings softened and became vague impressions. Lindy moved through a basic seated sequence and warmth spread to her limbs. She shifted, found her feet and pressed firmly into the mat. Vertebrae unfurled one after the other until she was fully upright in mountain pose.

Grounding, her teacher had always said. *Pay attention to the soles of your feet.* Profound awareness filled Lindy as she welcomed the gift of true wakefulness. Even with many aspects of her life upside down, she felt more anchored in this moment. She shifted her weight and placed her foot against her upper thigh in tree pose. As her arms circled and fingertips reached to tickle the rising sun, a smile bloomed across her face.

When Lindy completed her practice, she noticed a woman in a bright maxi-dress watering flowers on the back porch of Green Goodness, the shop she'd admired.

"Good morning." Lindy walked closer. "Is this your shop?"

"It is." Her joy radiated. "My second year."

"Your porch is amazing and I love the window display. I look forward to coming back when you're open to see what else I love."

"You want to look now?"

"Really?"

"Why not? You're here, I'm here." She set her broom aside. "I'm Candi, by the way."

"Nice to meet you, I'm Lindy."

Lindy walked up the wooden steps and through the double front door. Inside was an eclectic world of primitive and fine art, including hand-lettered signs and scenes painted on a variety of architectural salvaged pieces, barn doors, piano tops, and shutters.

She was greeted by a wool hooked rug of a whimsical octopus. Periwinkle and teal, the cartoon-style character sported a bow on her bulbous head.

Lindy grinned. "This is so fun. The design feels Seuss-inspired."

"The crafter is a young mother. Her children draw critters for fun then she transfers them to wall hangings."

"Clever." Lindy wandered deeper into the remodeled fisherman's cottage. The floors tilted with age and the exposed hatchet-scarred beams itched to share the secrets of time.

Beneath the narrow staircase Lindy found a ten-gallon Ohio Stoneware pickling crock she had to have. "Ooh, I may have a spot for you too." She ran her hands over a petite pine church pew. "Would you mind measuring this for me?"

Candi took a business card from her rack and jotted the dimensions.

A gallery of framed and stretched canvas photography overflowed into the enclosed back porch. Lindy smiled as she noticed the scrolling "Z" in the corner of many. Clearly Zak hadn't lost his touch behind the camera.

Lindy rounded the corner. An array of stained glass punctuated the natural light. Drawn to the panel of spheres she'd seen from the street, Lindy turned the tag. The piece was titled *Full Circle* and was marked with Candi's name. "This is your work?"

"It is."

"I imagine you face a lot of hazards working with cut glass."

Candi held up two bandaged fingers. "Preventative," she laughed. "I'm grinding a sixty-piece custom order today."

"Wow." Lindy walked to the counter. "I really love your eclectic inventory, and appreciate you letting me look. I definitely want the large crock and octopus wall hanging, but I'll need to come back with my wallet. Do you mind holding them?"

"Not at all." Candi unfastened the quirky rug. "Let me know if you decide you want the church pew, and we can connect to settle up whenever it suits you."

Lindy studied the large panel again. *Full Circle. Not yet*, she thought, but she was on her way.

Chapter 43

Lindy pedaled into Kate's promptly at eight.

"You've had a busy morning," Kate said. "My man saw you doing your fancy exercising in the courtyard, then at Green Goodness. You start the day with a bit of bartering?"

"Small towns." Lindy shook her head. "I'd forgotten."

"Had you?" Kate asked quietly. "Forgotten?"

"I tried to," Lindy shrugged.

"Was it so awful living here?" The sadness in Kate's tone tugged Lindy's heart.

"No, but even at sixteen everything felt so small. I knew there had to be more," Lindy sighed. "When you all came together and gifted me with the tools and space to create, you unlocked something inside of me. The academy scholarship was my ticket to see a bigger world."

"It certainly was."

"You can't be angry about me taking the chance and making the most of it."

"Not angry, sweet girl, not in the least. I just didn't expect you'd turn your back on all who loved you."

"I didn't mean for it to be that way." Lindy's throat was suddenly dry. There was no point trying to explain that pursuing art had never been an option. She would have followed her passion anywhere at practically any cost.

They sat in silence enjoying the movement of the swing.

"I needed to succeed. And after Mom…" Lindy rested her head against Kate's shoulder. "Creating was an escape and New York was simply where I landed. Before I knew it, weeks became months, and months rolled into years."

"I'll always be proud you began in my garage," Kate smiled. "Everything's still in there, you know. Just as you left it."

"What?" Lindy raced to the small detached garage. Her tools, her wheel, even notes for projects she'd envisioned before she had the knowledge to bring them to fruition.

"I'm sure the clay is dryer than dust. The wheel will likely need serviced and oiled, or something." Kate leaned against the doorway. "Rudy will load everything, whenever you give the word, and deliver it to your house."

"I can't believe it's all still here." Lindy lifted the sheet covering the piano stool, lowered to the wooden surface and buried her face in her hands.

Devastating sobs echoed in the small room. "You were only supposed to be gone a few months." Kate moved to her and stroked her back. "Tell me something. Does that twisty bending burn fat?"

Lindy sniffed and nodded her head yes.

"Good, 'cause we need pie."

Lindy's laugh was more of a gurgle.

Kate shot her a playful wink. "What would you think about an old gal like me giving it a whirl?"

"You'd never be the same." Lindy threaded her arm through Kate's and returned to the deck.

Kate laughed richly and disappeared into the house.

Rudy returned from his morning walk. "There's the famous artist I've been reading about." He held out the daily paper. "Right here on the front page—*Belinda Cole returns home*. Of course I don't know who that is because Lindy Colton is the girl I remember."

Lindy glanced at the article. "Is there nothing else to report?"

"Rudy, leave her be," Kate chastised as she balanced two slices of pie.

"I see I'm right on time."

"You go in and fix your own," Kate clucked her tongue. "Troublesome man."

"Speaking of men," Rudy said, "I'd consider it a huge favor if you could take it easy with my friend Tucker."

"I haven't seen Tucker yet." Lindy looked puzzled.

"Precisely my point, Lindy girl." Rudy placed the tip of his finger under her chin and lifted until her eyes met his. "You hurt him by pretending he's not important. Go see him and make nice." He kissed Lindy square on the forehead and then looked at his wife. "I'm going inside to check on my NHL scores."

"Rudy looks out for those he cares about and Tucker would be high on his list." Kate patted the seat beside her. "Sit a bit and eat your pie."

"I'm not hungry, Kate."

"Don't get prickly. Your mama was my dearest friend and you were my sweetheart. I paddled your tush when you needed correction and sang your praises when you weren't close enough to hear."

Lindy scooped up a bite of pie. The simple sway of the swing made the pastry taste sweeter.

"Do you consider Tucker your friend?"

"Yes," Lindy answered instantly.

"How many other true friends do you count on this island?"

"Nina and Mike of course, and Zak."

"And in the past week have you seen Nina, Mike and Zak?"

"I hear you." Lindy's head dangled like a scolded two-year-old. "But with Tucker it's complicated."

"Wouldn't mean much if it weren't."

It had taken Lindy years to master the untamed tight-rope tethering her to Tucker Brandt. In truth, distance was what made balancing her feelings for him possible. "I'll go see him today."

"That's my girl." Kate gave a brisk nod. "He'll be on the water 'til dusk, not at the store." She chuckled as Lindy raised a single brow. "Just minimizing your run around, sweetie. Now, finish your pie."

Chapter 44

Lindy rode to the marina and leaned her bike against the pylon. Anytime between now and sunset Tucker would end his day and return to the dock. She placed a towel on the bench, opened her book and settled in to wait.

A boat raced through the mouth of the bay. The operator cut the speed. The wake softened, the vessel leveled in the water and angled toward the marina. Lindy's heart took a slow, lazy turn in her chest and she knew without a doubt it was Tucker.

Lindy watched as he expertly eased the boat into the slip, reversed the engine and aligned the stern. He made quick work of securing the lines then turned his attention to her.

"You'll want to grab hold of something." Tucker's mouth tipped upward in a crooked smile. "Land," he said, and the massive dog at his side propelled overboard with an impressive splash. "Boop tends to say hello with her whole body."

"Oh!" Lindy gripped the scarred wooden pylon as the sopping dog shook furiously then plopped down on top of her feet. "Well, haven't you grown to be a gorgeous girl?" She released one hand to stroke Boop's head.

"We're still working on manners." Tucker hopped nimbly to the deck. Boop quivered in delight, and in an effort to get even closer, pressed firmly against Lindy's legs.

"You're a very good girl." Lindy continued to pet Boop while she postponed facing her master.

Tucker pulled a tennis ball from his pocket and gave it a hearty toss. Boop chased after the toy.

With the barrier between them vanished, Lindy straightened. "Hi."

"Hi back." Tucker offered a towel.

"Thanks, I'm sorry I didn't come by earlier. I was just taking my time trying to get more settled."

"And are you?" Tucker studied her. "More settled?"

"I am, sort of, well not quite, but more than I was a few days ago."

"Relax, Lindy," he said gently.

He would make it easier, she realized. Lindy looked at Tucker and swallowed her nerves. "I wanted to stop at the store but…"

"Yeah, I was going to drop by your place too," Tucker said. "Well, actually I have, I just hadn't worked up the nerve to let you know I was there."

Lindy smiled. "Stalking me?"

Tucker shrugged. "I didn't want to cause any trouble with your fiancé."

"That would be difficult since I no longer have one."

Genuine shock washed over Tucker's face making Lindy laugh.

"For once the island news circuit missed the scoop." She shifted her weight anxiously. "It's no big deal, really. People break engagements all the time. We just…" Her voice died out as Tucker's eyes locked on hers and he moved closer.

The planks beneath her tipped. She leaned or he leaned… his lips were a fraction from brushing hers. Tucker placed a stray tendril behind her ear and in a voice ripe with emotion whispered, "Welcome home."

Boop chose that exact moment to thrust between them and return the tennis ball.

"I told you we were working on manners." He pitched the ball away. "Wanna go grab some dinner? A buddy of mine makes a mean shaved brisket. Stacked high on fancy rolls, then tops them with fresh cut slaw and fries."

"Can't."

"Breakfast tomorrow?"

"No, I have a salon appointment, then Nina's coming over to help me set up the house." Lindy fought the unreasonable urge to escape. "Bought a house. But you knew that. I'm not sure… I mean, I don't know if or when…" She fumbled to turn the bike around.

"It's just food, Lindy."

"Of course it's just food." She climbed on the bike. "But I think I better..." Her brain and her tongue had parted company. "Another time, okay?"

Tucker hooked his thumb in his front pocket and watched her hasty retreat. Lindy had always been a master at dodging his invitations.

He was glad she'd come to him and happier still to have gotten a glimpse of the old Lindy.

Boop leaned against his hip and whined.

"I know, girl. It hurts when she goes away." Tucker stroked the dog's head. "But this time she just might be planning to stay."

Baxter's report was thorough. Belinda was in Virginia just as Hayward had suspected. She'd purchased a home and acquired a new credit card. She had also placed an order for pottery supplies, hired a contractor, and met with a security specialist.

Hayward fanned out the images across his desk. Belinda at a restaurant and riding a bicycle to buy groceries. His hand crinkled the print of her flirting with some unshaven vagrant and buying secondhand garbage. There were more photographs of her on a yoga mat in public and eating pie with some old woman.

Mindlessness, Hayward sniffed. Her pout would be over soon enough and she'd be back in the city, on his arm, and more importantly in his bed.

Chapter 45

The heat from the screaming blow-dryer worked to chase the moisture from Lindy's hair. She'd been in the hydraulic chair for three and a half hours, and every strand had been stripped, cut, toned, and sealed.

"So gorgeous," Crystal said. "Go on and toss it back."

Lindy flipped the mass and for the first time in years recognized the reflection in the mirror. Her shoulders relaxed.

"Whew, that's a relief." Crystal wielded the round brush proficiently. "I've never seen anyone so tense in the styling chair." She smoothed small sections around the frame of Lindy's face. "I was about to have the receptionist fetch some whiskey and place an emergency call to your bestie for emotional reinforcement."

Crystal rattled off a list of products she recommended to maintain, condition, and manage the natural waves. Lindy bought everything, tipped outrageously, and scheduled a repeat performance in eight weeks.

Lindy texted Nina to let her know she was alive and on her way home. She opened the front door and found Eric stretched out on the floor playing quietly with matchbox cars. His killer dimples engaged.

"Hi, Aunt Lindy. Wanna play?"

"You bet I do." She kneeled and gathered him into her arms. "You're so big."

"I eat good-for-me food."

"I bet you do." Lindy snuggled him close and breathed him in. "Where's your mommy?"

"Right behind you," Nina sniffed. "Hormones." She snagged a tissue. "Who's holding you, Eric?"

"My Aunt Lindy." His little hands cradled her cheeks. "She's pretty."

"I agree. I mean, wowza." Nina fluffed Lindy's freshly styled hair. "You look like a supermodel."

"Better than that." Lindy settled Eric on her hip. "I look like me."

"Your collection is so you too." Nina lifted the snow globe she'd given Lindy years before. "I grouped things that may suit different areas of the house, but I didn't place anything yet."

Lindy glanced into the living room and the disarray she'd created unpacking the pod was now separated into neat piles. "You've been busy. Thanks in advance for helping." She walked toward the kitchen. "What do I smell?"

"I'm heating some soup for whenever we take a break."

Lindy lifted the lid, and the aroma was even more enticing. "Your mommy is the best."

Eric laid his head on her shoulder. "I know."

Nina built Eric a fort using pillows and blankets, then she and Lindy got to work. In virtually no time, the living room emptied and her house became a home.

Lindy poured a glass of iced tea and joined Eric on the back porch.

"Aunt Lindy, you have a real fort in your yard."

"I do."

"Can I play on it sometime?"

"You sure can. Whenever you want."

"Whew." Nina flopped on the chair and propped her feet on the ottoman. "I forgot how tired pregnancy makes me."

Eric led Lindy to the sofa, waited for her to sit, then climbed on the cushion beside her.

Lindy stroked his hair. "Kate made me go see Tucker yesterday."

"Tucker…" Eric said through a yawn.

"Yes, Tucker's your best guy," Nina smiled. "So how'd your reconnection go?"

"It was fine. A little intense, but that's our recipe."

"When are you seeing him again? Maybe we could all go out for pizza like we used to."

"No set plans, but it's a small island." Lindy stalled. "I'm not interested in going backward, and in the spirit of moving forward, I need to get in touch with someone in New York. I'm sure my abrupt absence has caused some problems."

"Someone? Haven't you checked in with any of your friends? What about your agent?"

"I don't have a professional representative anymore." Lindy shrugged. "A story for another day. I don't really have any friends and my business contact list went into the trash with my phone."

"It's only been a week." Nina pushed the sadness aside. "I think even folks in your fancy world won't question a spontaneous vacation." Nina glanced at the clock. "Lord have mercy, where has the day gone? I'm running out of minutes." She pushed up from the seat. "Mike still has a few hours of work and I have to get to the store and get a quiche made. I have guests arriving tomorrow morning, a family of four."

"You can leave Eric with me if you want."

"Really?" Nina froze mid-movement. "You'd watch him for me?"

"I think I can keep him alive for a few hours."

"He can be a H-A-N-D-F-U-L."

"That means handful." Eric nestled into the crook of Lindy's arm. "I'm a busy boy."

Lindy chuckled and ruffled his hair. "Seriously Nina, I have peanut butter and jelly, and popsicles. We can play with these." She held up an action figure of some kind. "Or make something."

"Eric," Nina narrowed her eyes, "you must nap." She turned to Lindy. "If he doesn't, he will become a M-O-N-S..."

"Monster," Eric nodded. "That's the truth."

"I have a bed. A few beds, actually," Lindy smiled. "And a swing set."

"A fort," Eric corrected.

Nina studied her friend. "You sure? It's not as easy as you may think."

"We'll be fine. Go do your stuff."

"You're a lifesaver. I promise I'll be quick." Nina dashed to the front door. "Let me grab the emergency bag from the car."

"Eric?" Lindy lowered her voice. "What's in the emergency bag?"

"Cool stuff like snacks and movies and a soft blankie Daddy says is magic and makes me sleep through anything."

"Well then, I definitely want the emergency bag."

Nina tried to haul the box she'd found on the front mat inside but the delivery weighed a ton. She abandoned her effort and followed sounds of laughter to the kitchen.

Eric was sitting on the counter beside the sink eating an icy treat. His pants were rolled above the knee and his feet were bare.

"Hi, Mommy."

Lindy jolted then winced. "Eric buddy, you were supposed to be my lookout." She shrugged in apology. "You get everything finished?"

"I did." Nina rounded the corner suspiciously. "What have you two gotten into?"

"We played on the swings and walked to the secret cove." Eric grinned. "Then Aunt Lindy let me help with a project and I'm gonna have paint between my toes 'til I'm twenty."

"Between your toes?"

"Wanna see it?" Eric asked.

"I do." Nina lifted Eric to the floor. "By the way, there's a package by the door that weighs a million pounds." She followed her little boy to the studio to see their collaboration.

Lindy had cut a canvas boat cover into a rectangle then used the bottom of the five-gallon bucket to trace rows of circles to make a twister mat.

"Pretty great, right?" Lindy considered the design with satisfaction. "Somewhere along the way a little man knocked over a cup of paint and thought he'd splash like Daddy lets him do with mud puddles."

"Oh, Lindy." Nina's shoulders began to shake with restrained laughter. "I'm sorry. Your vision has become…"

"A magnificent, messy masterpiece." Lindy buzzed a kiss over Eric's cheek.

"One of a kind," Eric said proudly. "Best day in my whole life."

Chapter 46

Lindy began her day at Kate and Rudy's packing the garage.

"Things are starting to come together for you, Lindy girl." Kate passed another set of bubble-wrapped tools. "Rudy will deliver everything after lunch."

"I'm grateful." Lindy snapped the lid on the tote. "As soon as I get my hands on a solid secondhand pickup truck, I'll stop pestering you."

"Nonsense, we old folks need to be useful." Kate scooted another empty container forward. "I'm guessing you and Nina made good progress unloading the pod."

"We did. The container is empty. The unit will be removed tomorrow which is great because FedEx uploaded the tracking information for my new wheel and kiln. Which reminds me," Lindy straightened and stretched her back. "I need to buy or borrow a hand-truck so I can get them situated in the studio."

"Rudy will bring one with him today, but you're not tackling that project by yourself." Kate frowned. "I still remember how we struggled as a group to set the one in here."

"It's no trouble. I'm sure I can handle it."

"What you're capable of is a different conversation." Kate waited until Lindy looked at her. "I'm sure you're excited to have everything situated, but your friends want to help. The empire will not crumble if you drop a layer of your fierce independence and allow the ones who love you to lend a hand."

"Promise?" Lindy wrapped her arms around Kate. "What would I do without you?"

"Not a worry for today, sweet girl."

Bursting with contentment Lindy cruised toward home. She rounded the corner and drifted down Memory Lane. Mike's truck was in the drive. Fingers crossed, the sink installation would be finished today. She could hardly wait to get her hands into clay.

Lindy decided to let Mike work without interruption. She fixed herself a cup of tea and settled into an Adirondack chair at the end of the dock. A heron was fishing along the edge of the marsh. Its likeness reflected perfectly on the water's glassy surface.

The peace and warmth of the morning were waging a battle and Lindy allowed herself to drift into a soft and soothing daydream. Her mom was sitting beside her smiling, healthy, and whole. In the haze of half sleep her presence felt like unfiltered rays of sunshine.

Lindy reached toward the mind mirage hoping to grasp a fragment of something tangible. The illusion swirled and passed through her fingers. Goosebumps rose on her forearm as she wakened fully and trailed her hand over the vacant chair at her side.

Mike finished the sink just as Rudy arrived with the totes from the garage. It took effort but Lindy stood aside and watched the men unload her boxes and carry her things into the studio.

She waved goodbye as they backed out of the driveway then welcomed the guys from the pod retrieval company. The storage pod was loaded with efficiency and removed in minutes.

Sometimes things do just fall into place, Lindy thought, including the phone number nestled in her pocket for a truck Rudy had located through his mechanic.

Lindy worked for an hour to organize her supplies. She squatted and zipped a razor through the tape sealing the million-pound box that had arrived the day before. The top popped open and revealed her first order of unblemished clay.

"Time to get my hands dirty."

Lindy turned on classic rock, adjusted the piano stool, and positioned her body behind the wheel. The motor hummed and the figure at her fingertips developed contour and character.

It had been a long time since she felt connected to the movement and even longer since she'd created simply for the love of it. She rediscovered beauty in the tangible process, embracing the imperfections and unpredictable outcomes.

The phoenix quality of clay stimulated Lindy's thoughts. Was she willing to shape her own renewal? She wasn't resistant to all facets, she conceded. She was living in a new house and establishing a customized studio as part of a lovely island community.

"And there's the rub." Lindy released a weary breath as she guided her sponge.

All her life she'd preferred solitude but had never felt lonely. In recent years privacy had become a masquerade of spiteful separation. The masterful execution by Hayward, and the company he kept, had taught Lindy it was possible to feel lost in a room of hundreds.

Complex associations were not something she planned to prioritize ever again. Lindy turned off her wheel and studied her first official thrown piece. Clay, water, pressure and motion… it was basic, simple, and that, she understood.

"Nothing wrong with my personal rekindling having boundaries," Lindy spoke to the empty room. "Only simple friendships," she said as she lifted the wooden bat off her wheel and carried it to the rack to dry.

Her mind drifted to Tucker and the disk bobbled. There was nothing simple about her feelings for Tucker Brandt.

Lindy scrubbed the clay from her hands and forearms. She'd have to face him again sooner or later. She hung her apron on the hook then blew a kiss toward her firstborn work. "But I vote for later. Much, much later."

Chapter 47

Progress is like dancing the cha-cha, Lindy thought as she drove her newly acquired Toyota Tacoma home from Green Goodness. Forward and back, forward and back, but at least she was learning to dance.

Her new routine included peaceful early mornings on the dock followed by a walk or bike ride through the nature loop. Each day, Lindy entered her studio by ten o'clock and remained a happy captive of creativity, often working through lunch and dinner. The crowded shelves of the antique baker's rack showed the result of her dedication and a body in desperate need of a massage.

Lindy backed the truck into the driveway. She hopped from the cab and released the ratchet strap securing the cargo in the narrow bed.

The church pew unloaded easily and fit, as she'd hoped, on the short wall in the foyer. Lindy returned to the truck and muscled the thirty-eight-pound stoneware crock from the lip of the gate to the porch.

"Oh," she groaned and pressed her fists into her aching back.

Kate's lecture on fierce independence resonated loudly. "Alright, Kate, you win." Lindy retrieved the hand-truck and wheeled the breakable beast to the mudroom.

Light danced through the back door, marking the spot she'd reserved for the whimsical octopus wall hanging. She grabbed a hammer and fastened the tack-strip to the wall. Lindy adjusted the edge then pressed the canvas firmly into the spiked board. "Welcome home," she tickled the cheerful critter's chin. "I hope you'll be happy here."

Lindy carried a giant glass of ice water to the studio. She cranked the music, grabbed the broom, and swept the concrete floor for the hundredth time. Sand, a delightful curse of coastal living, was impossible to keep outside.

Tucker assumed the truck he didn't recognize belonged to a subcontractor helping with Lindy's studio upgrade. He picked up the carton lying beside the front door and followed the strains of classic rock to the detached garage.

For a moment Tucker thought he had the wrong house, but then he remembered the salon appointment Lindy mentioned. He grinned as she thrashed a mass of blonde hair and waited for her air guitar solo to end.

A figure moved at the corner of her vision. Color leached from her cheeks as panic squeezed her throat. The broom escaped limp fingers and slapped the cement. In one motion, Lindy sank to the floor and scurried backward like a crab seeking safety. Her arms banded tightly around her legs as she fought to steady her breathing.

Tucker took a single step toward her.

"Wait." Lindy issued the sharp command then lowered her head to bent knees and trembled.

The flashback clouded Tucker's mind... he had driven Lindy home and discovered her mother bruised and bleeding in the midst of shattered dishes. His stomach sank like a doomed ship as he realized someone had hurt Lindy like her father had hurt her mother.

Seconds ticked until a full minute had passed. Tucker moved with extreme care and kneeled beside her quaking body.

Lindy turned her head and rested her cheek on her knee. "Scared me."

He eased a hip onto the floor and pulled his long legs beneath him. "May I touch you?"

Instead of answering, Lindy crawled into his lap and curled tight into his body. Tucker wrapped his arms around her as Freddie Mercury crooned a ballad.

When the chorus ended Tucker released the circle of his arms and Lindy climbed from his lap.

"Sorry about that." She offered a trouble-free smile. "New place, new shadows. I've always startled easily."

"Stop." With cool control Tucker got to his feet. "Please... just don't." Lindy's floundering and excuses would cut him as deeply as her fear. "I'm slow, but I'm putting it all together now." He paced to the window. "You're here alone, no Hayward. Arrived in the middle of the night and bolted yourself into this house for nearly a week." Waiting for bruises to heal, he realized now. "Does he know where you are? Of course he does. Are you going to take him back? Of course you're not."

"Do I need to be here for this conversation?" Lindy laughed weakly. "Or have you become a mind reader since I left the island?"

Tucker's expression swam with the unanswerable questions, *How* and *Why*, but his focus remained serious. "Will he come for you?"

"Doesn't matter if he comes, I'm not go-i—" Lindy cleared her throat when her voice wavered. "I'm not going back." She picked up the broom and leaned it against the wall. "Maybe it's true we are what we are born into. I have some of my mom in me after all." She shrugged. "It wasn't always bad between me and Hayward but in the end..." She trailed off as Tucker tensed. "I stayed because I was weak."

"No."

"Yes, Tucker." Lindy walked to the back door and stared toward the water. "I was alone, so I excused and accepted."

Tucker stuck his hands in his pockets. "Are you safe? I mean do you feel safe here in your new home? Zak is in security... we can get you an alarm or whatever you need."

"I met with Zak and discussed everything a few days ago. The studio renovation is my first priority. He'll get to the security in a week or two."

He nodded but silently amended, *Zak will be here today after I give him a call.* "So," Tucker deliberately relaxed, "you had enough of this discussion?"

"I have." Lindy blew out a weary sigh. "I'm a mess, Tucker."

"Who isn't?" he shrugged. "Let's go get some pizza."

"You shift gears fast."

"Actually, when it comes to you, I've always been steady and straight. You still go for meat lovers?"

"Uh-huh."

"You might be a mess, Lindy Colton, but at least you're not a vegetarian. I'm looking forward to taking you for ice cream because you have to admit, ice cream is perfect anytime. Our second date you ordered a mint chocolate chip shake and when I took you home I got my first rock-me-back-on-my-heels kiss."

Lindy smiled and this time it brightened her amber eyes. "You hoping ice cream does the trick again?" Her laughter bubbled over as Tucker wiggled his brows.

"What do you say, Lindy?" He held out his hand toward her.

"To what? The pizza, the shake or the kiss?"

"Start with pizza?"

"Why not?" She stepped forward and linked her fingers with his.

He'd take it and hope for the rest.

Chapter 48

They got their order to-go, drove to the beach, and claimed a table overlooking the ocean.

It wasn't easy but it wasn't awkward either. Tucker talked about his mom and dad, his sister and new niece. Lindy wondered if he realized how his blathering calmed her. Of course he did. Tucker could always read her. He was filling in every blank so she didn't have to think.

Despite their uncomplicated conversation, Lindy sensed his detachment. She figured it would happen and wasn't surprised. In her experience sooner or later everyone saw her for what she was, damaged.

"Where did you go?" Tucker said gently.

"I'm here." Annoyance laced each word.

"Your head isn't."

No use trying to keep anything from the man. Lindy set her drink aside and faced him. "I'm not sure what you expect or what I'm willing to give, but I do know I'm not interested in your concern or pity."

"Okay."

"I'm not trying to be mean, I'm grateful for your friendship. I'll always be appreciative for your kindness… but, Tucker, if you pretend for another minute you're not angry with me, I'll lose my mind."

"Angry?" He pushed off the picnic table and took a deep breath. When he stalked back to her his eyes were filled with fire. "You want to do this now? Here in front of small town eyes and ears?"

"Why not?" Lindy's temper flashed. She jammed her trash in the bag. "Go on, tell me what you think of me. I can take it."

"Don't push me, Lindy." He reached for her elbow. "I'm taking you home."

She jerked her arm away and straightened her spine. "I'm done being ordered."

"Glad to hear it." Tucker absorbed her fierce fury as they stood toe to toe. The image of Lindy facing her father at sixteen rippled through him. The girl he'd tripped and fallen for, only grown and more potent. The punch of awareness snapped his brewing tension and frustration vanished. His posture softened and his smile was full of understanding as he stepped toward her and cradled her face in his hands.

Lindy leaned into him. "I'm sorry, Tucker."

"Never apologize for your strength." His voice surrounded her in a bubble of sanctuary. "It steals my breath." Tucker looked into Lindy's eyes. "What do I expect? I haven't decided. What are you willing to give? Hundred percent up to you. Damaged? Wounded maybe. Pity? Never. My concern? Deal with it, and what was next? Oh yeah, angry? At you? Don't be foolish."

Lindy's mouth dropped open.

"I can't say I'm happy I missed watching you succeed. What you do fascinates me. I also won't say I'm happy I'm not the only man you gave your heart to, but I was the first. I have every intention of being patient and giving you time to work through whatever this thing is with Hayward. But make no mistake, my anger is warranted. When and if Hayward is fool enough to cross the causeway and set foot on this island, I'll know exactly where to place my anger."

His voice was soft and devastating.

"Oh Tucker, he's not…"

"…A concern of yours any longer." He pressed a tender kiss to her temple. "You thought because you moved away that you were alone? Because you couldn't reach out that you were weak? You're wrong on both counts." His thumbs trailed along the sides of her neck up to the line of her jaw. "Regardless of the miles, Lindy, I was here for you. I'm here for you now, if you'll let me."

The man had always been a master of cutting to the core. Lindy closed her eyes and held the treasure offered in his words.

"Feel like taking Boop for a walk? Or do you…" Tucker's phone rang. "It's the store. Hey Natalie, what's up?"

Lindy stepped away and looked across the ocean. In the distance a tanker cruised along the fabled edge of the world. The vessel moved without concern or anxiety over the peril lurking beyond sight.

Experience had given Lindy a greater perspective of here and there. The horizon's alluring appeal was nothing compared to the sphere of Tucker Brandt's undivided attention. She may have lost pieces of herself during her years with Hayward, but Tucker was mistaken, her heart had never been one of them.

"Sorry about that," Tucker said as he joined her. "The second shift cashier didn't show. I need to get to the store and relieve Natalie. If you don't mind dropping me, you can take the Jeep and go home."

"Or I can stay and help." Lindy smiled. "I haven't run a register for a few years but I can fold clothes and straighten the racks."

"Really?" Tucker grinned. "You're hired."

Tucker gave Lindy a Sea Surge sweatshirt and put her to work. She examined the apparel as she tidied the racks and was impressed by the quality and brands represented.

Sea Surge was more complex than she'd expected. The store had several social media pages and a highly interactive Instagram account featuring Boop's weekly special. Software managed online shopping and bookings for recreational experiences including surf, skim and paddle boarding.

A promo loop was running on a screen above the dressing rooms. Zak's photography and video footage, overlayed with text, outlined different packages. She had to admit she was intrigued by the paddle boarding.

From the register Tucker watched Lindy help a woman from Canada select a pair of board shorts for her husband. Boop bumped his leg then ran to the front door and rang the string of sleigh bells. "That's her signal for a bathroom break," Tucker explained as he rang up the swim trunks.

"I'll take her." Lindy snagged the leash from under the counter and led Boop to the grassy section behind the store. She hugged the soft sweatshirt and realized she'd found a new favorite. Boop's tail engaged and she let out a happy *woof-woof* as Zak pulled into the residential parking area.

"Hey there, my first love." He slammed the car door and scooped Lindy off her feet. "Ready to marry me yet?"

Lindy laughed. "I'm not marriage material, Zak."

"Hogwash." He set her down and pinched the fabric on her shoulder. "The old man hire you to cover the evening shift?"

"Just filling in."

"Shame. Your smile alone raises the stock, and I'm invested."

"Now who's full of hooey?"

"No joke, you should buy in, sugar. Your man's goin' places." Zak ruffled Boop's ears and unhooked her lead. "I'll take the four-legger upstairs. Tell Tucker I'll get her fed. Come on, Boop, wanna eat? Will you be around tomorrow morning? I'd like to do a little work in the main house, if it's okay with you."

"More than okay." Lindy smiled. "I have another project to discuss with you."

"Cool." Zak dashed up the steps to the apartment.

Lindy carried Zak's easy going nature with her as she followed the walk to the front entrance. Her good humor faded as she spotted a car parked at the end of the lot. The driver, obscured by ballcap and dark sunglasses, had a camera aimed in her direction.

Her hand trembled as she reached for the door, then she squealed as the glass opened and Tucker's customer exited.

"Oh no, you lost the dog."

Fighting the urge to hurry inside, Lindy gripped the door and smiled politely. "I handed her off to a friend."

"What a relief. Thank you again for your help."

"Anytime." Lindy scanned the parking area as she closed the door. The car was gone.

"You can lock the door."

Lindy jolted.

"Everything alright?"

"Of course." Lindy flipped the sign to closed then turned the bolt. "Zak took Boop to the apartment to feed her."

"She's sweet on him."

"Don't know a female who isn't."

"True enough." Tucker transferred the day's sales to the bank bag. "Thanks for staying."

"I had fun." Lindy ran her hand over his shoulder as she passed behind the counter and returned Boop's leash to the hook.

"I'll run you home then come back and finish the paperwork," Tucker grumbled. "It's the worst and best part of the day."

"I can wait, if you don't mind. I'd like to finish."

Tucker watched Lindy dive back into the display of t-shirts, picking up where she'd left off. He turned off the promotional video and changed the music to Big Hair ballads.

Lindy hummed along with Jon Bon Jovi as she sorted and stacked the screen-printed hoodies. "Your store is amazing, Tucker. I'm so proud of you."

"Thanks, more than I expected when I drew up the business plan." Tucker shook his head. "Starting to think I'm crazy to expand, especially when the second location is an hour away."

"I imagine there will be challenges. How is that coming?"

"My contractor is a genius. I have to run up early tomorrow morning for another inspection. Maybe one day you'd like to come along. I'd really like to show you the building."

"I'd like that. What do you do with Boop when you go?"

"I take her with me when I stay a few days. My parents still have the rental cottages, which makes traveling back and forth easier. Tomorrow should be quick so I've asked Zak to be in charge of her."

"Why don't you leave her with me? I'll be in the studio most of the day and she'd be good company."

"You sure?"

Lindy nodded. "She can come home with me tonight, if you can sleep without her. You'll be able to get an early start and take your time with the inspection. Besides, Zak is planning to spend time at my house tomorrow, so it may help him out too."

"Sounds great."

205

Boop stretched across the back seat. Her head rested on the fleece-lined dog bed Tucker had packed for her sleepover. Pink ribbons streaked the sky over Wallops Island and reflected in a stunning spectacle across the water.

Tucker dodged evening shoppers and early diners strolling Main Street and turned onto Memory Lane.

Lindy stifled a yawn, then sat up straight. A line of solar lights edged her property. "Zak didn't mention this when I saw him earlier. Wow." A motion sensor activated and a bright beam streamed across the narrow walkway leading to the front porch. "He must have found room in his schedule."

"Something like that." Tucker hopped out and grabbed the dog's gear. "Thanks again for watching Boop."

"No problem, she's my very first overnight guest." Lindy juggled the lead and unlocked the door then smiled as Boop set out to investigate her new surroundings. "Put her bed wherever you think is best. I'll take her dishes and food to the kitchen."

"You do understand the dog bed is a hopeful suggestion. Boop will probably crawl under your covers at some point during the night."

"I'm looking forward to it." Lindy filled the water dish and placed it on the floor beside the island. "I never had a dog growing up."

"Remember that when you're hanging off the edge of the mattress." Tucker smiled. "You may want to keep her on the leash when you take her outside. Your dock and the water beyond will be a temptation she'll find impossible to resist. I packed extra bath towels in her overnight bag."

"You're giving me more instructions than Nina did when I watched Eric," Lindy laughed. "We'll be fine."

"Okay, but if you're not, pass her to Zak." Tucker studied the assorted furnishings spread through the room. "You're settling in, Lindy Colton. I like it." He tugged the hem of her sweatshirt. "And I like how this looks on you too."

She flushed. "I know the owner. He gave it to me in exchange for a few hours of my time."

"Quite a bargain." Tucker rubbed Boop's head as she angled her body between them. "She's not used to sharing me." He snatched Lindy's hand and walked to the foyer. "But she'll adjust." Tucker gave Boop a signal. She sat and wagged her tail. He held up his palm and she lowered to the floor.

"Impressive."

"That's all we've got." He winked and opened the door. "I had a nice time tonight. I look forward to taking you for ice cream one day real soon."

As the door closed between them, Lindy whispered, "Me too."

Chapter 49

The mattress had proven big enough. Lindy decided sharing her bed with a beast was everything she'd hoped for and more. Boop was an early riser. The Chessie happily walked through town and joined Lindy's yoga practice in the park, demonstrating a perfect down-dog posture.

To Lindy's surprise, Candi, the owner of Green Goodness, carried her yoga mat to the lawn and moved through her own practice a few feet away. Afterwards they visited on the porch over a cup of tea.

Boop picked up the pace on the way home and ended her walk with a sprinting dive from the end of the dock. Lindy snapped a picture of the morning swim and sent it to Tucker along with a message of encouragement for his inspection.

Lindy heard Zak pull into the drive. Boop heard too and raced to say hello.

"Hey canine, been skinny dipping already this morning?" Zak rubbed her bay-soaked coat. "Where's my first love? Ah, there she is. How's your day going, sugar?"

"Very nicely, how about you?"

"I haven't had a swim or participated in a public yoga session. Saw you in the park," he explained. "I did, however, enjoy a bit of vigorous cardio before I left the house."

Lindy swatted him with the towel.

"Get your brain out of the gutter," Zak chuckled. "Resistance training. You and Candi meet often?"

"First time, but we've decided to connect a few days a week."

"Cool. I have a soft spot for women who begin their day getting limber."

"I'm not surprised," Lindy grinned. "You want me to start coffee and fix you some breakfast?"

"You mean it?"

"I do. Figure I better get on your good side before I tell you my idea for shelving in the living room."

"Gorgeous, you're all over my good side. It's my bad side I'd like to sway you toward." Zak held the door and followed her to the kitchen.

Lindy prepared a full skillet of eggs and bacon while Zak leafed through pictures she'd collected of floating shelving constructed from pipe.

He chewed while he jotted notes and offered suggestions. The exchange reminded Lindy of when they worked on her portfolio together. His intensity and attention to detail was extraordinary.

"Doable," he mumbled.

"Which part?"

"All of it." He wiped his mouth and noticed she was nibbling her lip. "What are you holding back?"

"A few other ideas for the studio, one rational, one ridiculous."

"Give it to me," he gestured with his fingers. "Start with the ridiculous, it's more fun."

Lindy told Zak of her concept of a convertible workspace. "It's something I dream about which is why I know it's extreme. I imagine working outdoors occasionally, but hauling the wheel outside by myself is difficult. Plus I want to be able to put it away easily too so I don't expose the equipment to the elements overnight. Just say it's unfeasible and I'll let it go."

"Alfresco artistry," he hummed. "I like it. Tell me the vision in as much detail as you can."

Lindy pursed her lips.

"Not making fun, sweetheart. I want to see what you see. The picture your imagination painted when your mind was free."

His hand scribbled and sketched as she spoke.

"I get where you're going." Zak tossed back the rest of his coffee. "Now give me the rational."

"Those massive oak horse stall doors I saw on your trailer at the flea market," Lindy paused. "I'd like something similar installed like a French door, which opens to the water."

"Security?"

"Yeah," she sighed. "Maybe not sensible after all." She watched again as Zak turned his notepad to the side and drafted a quick layout of her workspace, the back deck and dock. He nodded, made little pondering noises, then asked her a few questions about her kiln placement and natural light.

"Lots of good stuff rolling around in your beautiful skull." He popped off the stool and rinsed his dishes and loaded the dishwasher. "You done?"

Lindy smiled as Zak tidied the kitchen like a pro. "You're quite a catch, you know that?"

"Should I call the clergy?"

Lindy rounded the island and wrapped her arms around him. "If only I was the kind of girl who believed an 'I do' would do it."

"Someday, you're gonna explain to me why you don't." Zak lifted her off her feet, pivoted, and set her down again. "I'll work up a few sketches and see what we can come up with."

"Appreciate it."

"I'll be here an hour, give or take. Just prep work and measurements today. You want me to take Boop with me when I'm finished?"

"I'm good, but tomorrow I could use some muscle. My kiln is arriving in the afternoon." She wrung her hands. "I'm paying in steak and beer."

"Baby, I'm yours. Text me a definite time, and thanks for breakfast."

Chapter 50

Tucker grunted as he, Mike, and Zak hefted the kiln into place.

"Holy cannoli, Batman, that sucker was heavy." Zak groaned. "You are feeding us, right, sugar?"

"I am, after you guys assemble the grill." Lindy lifted her palms.

"If we were married," Zak spun Lindy in an impromptu dance, "I'd do anything you asked without complaint."

"But you'd require deviant sexual favors, am I right?"

"Without question," his grin flashed.

"Zak," Tucker snapped. "Go get your tools."

"Now who's talking dirty?" Zak's rich laughter filled the room and echoed even after he'd gone.

"The man's relentless," Mike chuckled.

"He's a child." Tucker tried to shake his annoyance before he focused on Lindy. "Anything else in here?"

"Just my hammock." Lindy lifted the compressed silk from the packaging and hugged it to her chest. "Thanks for helping today." She passed the bag of hardware to Tucker. "I'm sure there are many places you'd rather be."

"I'm exactly where I want to be." He snagged her wrist and tugged her closer. "Well, maybe not exactly. I'd rather we were alo—"

"Seal the deal or pass the prize." Zak's tool bucket hit the floor. "Awesome, I was hoping you'd hang another nap nest. Where do you want it?"

"In the far corner." Lindy moved around Tucker and explained her vision for her sitting area then ducked inside to prepare the steak and salad before Nina and Eric arrived.

The guys' banter floated through the open windows as they tackled the grill. Swearing one second, laughing the next, their bond exceeded casual friendship.

Lindy had always been cautious of relationships. She didn't take time to form many close attachments. If she was being honest, she didn't see the point. Eventually all relationships changed, and generally not for the better.

She rinsed the lettuce and spinach. It was one of the reasons she'd been determined to keep Tucker at a distance all their lives. There had never been anything tranquil or composed when it came to her feelings for him. From childhood he'd sparked something inside her that was wild with promise and hope—two sensations in Lindy's experience that ultimately led to pain and disappointment.

She began to peel the carrots with a bit more force than required.

"You mad at root vegetables in general or that carrot in particular?" Nina stood beside her with a covered casserole in her hands.

"Hi, sorry, didn't hear you come in."

"The guys ran for propane, so we have about fifteen minutes. Want to tell me what's going on?"

Lindy opened the low cabinet and dumped the shavings. "It's Tucker. Not really Tucker as much as what he represents. What he offers without asking for anything in return. There's always a price." Lindy paced to the sink and rinsed the minced carrot off her hands. "The sight of him in my studio and on my deck…" She lifted the cutting board to the counter and selected a chef's knife from the block. "Being here, looking at me…" The razor-sharp steel gleamed as she gestured to the room. "Saying heart melting things. It's requiring more adjustment than I can pretend to manage."

"So quit pretending and put the knife down. You're making me nervous."

Lindy surrendered the cutting edge.

"If you don't want to be friends with Tucker, then stop." Nina turned the dial to preheat the oven.

"Of course I want to be his friend, but you know he'll want more." Lindy sat with a dejected thud. "I don't do more." She pressed her cheek against the cool table. "Please talk me down, Nina. I can barely stand the sound of my own crazy."

"What I know is, when you were barely sixteen, you decided every relationship ends in hurt and abandonment."

"And?"

"And," Nina sat beside her, "you've grown up."

"If your goal is confusion, you're succeeding."

Nina snickered. "Does Tucker check your boxes?"

"My what?"

"Your after-ever boxes. You told me once you were looking for safety and security above everything. Do you feel safe with Tucker?"

Lindy stared blankly at Nina. "Of course I feel…" Boop barked and ran to look out the window. "What does that have to do with anything?"

"Perhaps nothing, but maybe," Nina scooped Eric into her lap, "just maybe, it's the door to everything. We'll talk more about this later. Go change your shirt."

"After-ever." Lindy dashed upstairs and pulled her soiled top over her head. "Such nonsense." Nina had never seen glimmering, hopeful affection torn and shredded to ribbons. She'd never heard harsh words replace endearments or witnessed cruel actions raining down until love spilled across the floor in jagged, bleeding pieces.

Lindy had.

She'd held ice packs to blooming bruises and watched flesh meld from purple, to green, then yellow, until flawless tissue erased the marred. She understood a heart thriving in the nurturing promise of love could suffer until it was withered and empty.

Checking boxes did nothing to prevent rejection or harm.

Lindy pushed the unsettling thoughts aside. Tonight was about friends and food, not swimming in the murky depths of complex entanglements.

Thanks to her experience navigating high society, Lindy knew how to stay afloat in uncomfortable pools. She pulled a Joan Jett hoodie over her head and faced the mirror. "You're an expert in small talk and pleasantries," she coached herself. "Just stay in the shallow end."

"I'm sorry to ditch but," Nina carried in an errant plate, "Eric needs to get to bed."

"Of course, thanks for all your help. It was nice to have a house full of friends. I can't tell you how nice."

"Get used to it." Nina wrapped Lindy in a tight hug. "You're stuck with us, and by us, I mean Zak."

Lindy chuckled. "I'm his truest love."

"You and every breathing female in the tri-state area," Nina laughed. "Speaking of Zak, he got a security call and had to rush out. I'm passing on his thanks for the perfect evening. Of course he phrased his gratitude more colorfully. I'll let you use your imagination."

Lindy finished straightening the house, then wandered to the studio to turn out the lights and lock the door. Tucker was stretched out in the hammock. His eyes were closed but his toes were tapping to the classic ballad, *Is This Love.*

"I can see why you love these things." He shifted. The ropes groaned as the fabric swayed. "Slide in with me."

"I shouldn't."

"Do it anyway," Tucker teased.

Lindy toed off her shoes and levered her body alongside his.

"I fear you may have to seek professional help for your '80s fixation. Brett Michaels and Annie Lennox just finished, and now Whitesnake."

"Journey is up next."

"Steve Perry, awesome." Tucker draped his arm over her shoulder. "Now how about you let the heavy stuff you're pretending not to carry slip away. For a little while, it's just you and me and this contraption hanging from the toggles Zak installed. I mean, come on. You've gotta agree, that's trust, am I right?"

The playlist cycled and Lindy was surprised to admit she felt no call to struggle or flee.

"Do you feel safe with Tucker?" Nina's question resurfaced and bobbed beside her. Lindy drifted into the deep end and pondered her best friend's words. *"Just maybe, it's the door to everything."*

"Can I walk you home?" Tucker's sleep heavy voice interrupted her thoughts.

"Seriously?" Lindy frowned but untangled herself, first from him then from the silk.

Tucker stifled his chuckle then followed her up and tucked her hair behind her ear. "You're not ready for me to stay, and I'd prefer to wait until you are."

He took her hand and whistled cheerfully as they crossed the forty feet separating the studio from the house. He kissed her cheek then closed the door between them and drove home dreaming of the next time.

Hayward cursed as he scrolled through the photos Baxter sent. Belinda in her baggy clothes and lightened, ratty hair. "She looks like a street urchin."

He'd been justifying her artistic liberty, telling everyone who asked she was off being inspired, or on holiday seeking her muse. Of course he always added the lie of how he had just returned from seeing her. How they'd stolen an evening in a secluded location.

Hayward slammed his fist on his desk. "Making a mockery of me."

Celeste wasn't making the situation any easier for him, claiming she hadn't spoken with Belinda for two entire weeks. What kind of manager handled a client so loosely? Any administrator with half a brain would insist Belinda return to where her business and future were golden. Not to mention, Hayward fingered the ring in his pocket, returning to her fiancé.

"Baxter, get me Belinda's phone number... no, I don't care how... You're clever, figure it out, damn it. We are dealing with a woman, for pity sake. How hard can it be?"

Chapter 51

Lindy held Boop's leash as she explored the building Tucker was converting in Ocean City, Maryland. A bait and tackle hub in its glory days, the structure had unique built-in features, high ceilings, and wide plank floors.

"You're just a shy gem," Lindy ran her hand over a knot in the raw cut pillar, "waiting patiently for someone to notice you."

"I see her." Tucker pointed toward the exposed rafters. "Guys worked like hounds to fortify and condition the parched wood."

"Worth it." Lindy strolled deeper into the room. Steel beams had been erected to support the second level. The renovation plan included two rental units and an efficiency apartment/office for the prospective manager of Sea Surge North.

"Excuse me a minute." Tucker stepped away and greeted a pair of sturdy gentlemen. The men moved to a table along the wall and bent over blueprints. They discussed modifications to the lower level bathroom and concerns about compliance standards.

Lindy eavesdropped long enough to be impressed by Tucker's knowledge and consideration to the smallest detail. At the rear of what would become the retail area, doors opened to the deck and pier. The pilings stretched to the bay, offering easy access for his water-sport boats.

"Impressive project, Mr. Brandt," Lindy commented as Tucker joined her.

"Insane is a better description." He took Boop's lead. "But worth it in the long run. I'm glad you were able to take a break and come with me today. Want to see the upstairs before we go?"

"Sure." Lindy scrutinized the extension ladder spanning the gap between levels.

"Where's your sense of adventure?" Tucker settled Boop in an area complete with a water dish and dog bed.

The aluminum creaked as she scaled the makeshift staircase. Tucker followed and was pleased to discover the promised progress. The crew had completed framing the units he envisioned and the rough-ins for the plumbing had begun.

"Not sure what I'm looking at, but the view from this window alone will be worth whatever price you decide to charge."

"That's the hope." Tucker led Lindy through the obstacle course and pointed out features and fixtures. "Zak's helping to locate architectural furnishings and will be doing the security install."

Lindy's mind was on overload. "You have incredible vision, Tucker."

"My dream also includes a fire pole from the office to the main floor," he laughed. "Actually to be fair, it's Zak's idea. He found a firemen's pole at an auction last month and has been trying to sell me on the idea."

"Sounds like Zak." Lindy's stomach flipped as she peered into the hole leading to the first floor. "But in this moment sliding down a pole would be more inviting than climbing back down that ladder."

Tucker and Lindy drove across the inlet and made a brief stop at the cottages owned by his family.

Lindy hadn't seen Tucker's parents in many years and was delighted to find them well and happy. Mrs. Brandt prepared a light lunch then scooted them along, promising to spoil Boop rotten while Tucker and Lindy enjoyed the afternoon on the north end of Assateague Island.

"I figure kayaks are our best bet today rather than the stand-up boards." Tucker chuckled when Lindy pouted. "Don't let the unseasonably warm day fool you. The water temperature is only fifty degrees. If you fall in, the shock may give you a heart attack."

"While that certainly doesn't sound like fun, I'm anxious to try the paddleboards, but you're the professional."

The tone of sadness hit its mark. "In the spirit of adventure, I do have wet and dry suits here. Give me a minute."

The barrier island's pocketed coves and narrow peninsulas offered shelter from the coastal wind. Lindy pulled on the hooded second skin. Tucker attached the board leash to her ankle and they stepped into the shallow water.

He held the board still as she climbed on. He guided her through the balancing process modeling knee placement on either side of the carry handle. "Kneeling is a great place to start. When you paddle, make sure to fully submerge the blade."

Lindy mimicked his action and followed him in a small loop.

"Ready to stand up?" Tucker offered his instructions in a straight-forward manner as he moved into position. "Look at the horizon and put your feet where your knees are."

Lindy concentrated on duplicating his example. The wide buoyant plank wobbled as she shifted and found her feet.

"Good," Tucker said. "Now push down firmly and evenly."

Lindy compensated for the ever moving surface, made adjustments, and pressed to her feet.

"Excellent, now trim out to find your ideal sweet spot." He watched and encouraged. "You're a natural."

"I'm sure you say that to all your participants."

"No, I'm usually fishing them out of the water for the first ten minutes."

Lindy took to the board without difficulty. She mirrored Tucker's actions and cruised the shoreline. The sun was warm and the scenery peaceful. "What do you do when people don't acclimate?"

"They stay on their knees, or I can attach a cloth seat. Either way they slow down, trepidation slips away, and they have a quality experience." Tucker paddled into a deeper channel. "Your turn. Relax, let everything go and just be."

The water was clear below her paddle. Lindy could see blue crabs and skates scurrying over the soft sandy bottom. She was amazed at the bustling life below the surface.

"In the summer even the larger fish wander in from the sea to explore the warm shallows."

Lindy narrowed her eyes. "How large?"

Tucker laughed. "Striped bass and drum fish can be three feet, but thanks to satellite tagging, we know Mary Lee enjoyed a morning tour of the bay a few years back."

"And Mary Lee is?"

"A big fish with bigger teeth."

Lindy bobbled at the thought of sharing the water with a toothy giant.

Tucker navigated toward the beach and modeled a successful dismount.

Lindy couldn't wait to shop for her own board. "Launching off my dock wouldn't be a problem, right?"

"Different since the water is deeper but not a problem." He tipped the board toward him and grabbed the handle. "The back bay wouldn't be heavily traveled by boats either. You ever want a part-time gig taking folks out, let me know. I've been getting calls about board yoga. You're certified, right?"

"On dry land."

"You'd be great."

Lindy wriggled out of the wet suit, then pulled her t-shirt over her sports tank and tugged her sweats over her compression shorts. "Something to consider," she said.

Tucker pumped his fist.

She shook her head. "I'll need some help ordering a board and wet suit. I'm not going to wait for warm water, I know that much."

Chapter 52

Lindy worked through the day mixing glaze while her first full load processed in the kiln. Her pottery had taken on an earthy quality, heavy forms and natural color. It was functional not fussy, Lindy not Belinda.

Her paddleboard arrived. She'd purchased the grapnel anchor device and began experimenting with a floating yoga practice. Despite the occasional polar plunge, Lindy loved the challenge.

Her phone rang for the seventh time in an hour. She pinched it between her ear and shoulder as she finished washing her hands. "Hello?" There was no one on the line. "Why call if you've got nothing to say?" She tossed the device on the chair and it rang again. Lindy huffed and answered, "Talk or stop calling, I'm a busy lady."

"Too busy for ice cream?" Tucker chuckled.

"Sorry," she laughed. "The phone's been going crazy, tons of hang-ups today. It took three weeks but I think telemarketers have finally gotten my number."

"Boop wants to bring you a shake. She's been in the store all day. I promised her a boat ride, a tennis ball, and a swim. Okay if we swing by for a visit?"

"A mint chip shake from the Creamery will grant you access anytime." She checked the kiln. "The kiln still needs a half hour, so come over whenever you're ready."

Tucker and Boop arrived by boat and tied up to Lindy's dock. "My first water guests," she laughed as Boop leapt overboard and swam to shore.

"Making good on your promises, I see." Lindy turned away as Boop shook the water from her coat.

"Sorry," Tucker hopped from the boat and offered Lindy her milkshake.

"Forgiven." She sank the straw into the cup. "Still the best anywhere."

"No doubt." He passed her a spoon. "Triple thick."

"Just the way I like it," she smiled. "Want to walk to the cove and give it a chance to melt?"

Tucker fastened Boop's leash and they carried their treats to the cove. "Is this your first full load in the new kiln?"

"Yes." Lindy kicked a shell as she walked. "I'm always a little nervous but this batch feels more significant." She leaned against the pylon and stared thoughtfully across the bay.

Boop whimpered and Tucker turned her loose for another swim. Her delightful barks carried across the water as she splashed and paddled in big circles.

"Want to tell me what else you're worrying over?" When she stayed quiet he lowered to the grass beside the dock and waited.

"The way I left the city, walking out without explanation, it's been bothering me." Lindy lifted the lid from her cup and scooped up a taste of cool flavored cream. "I have one final contractual obligation in association with the Livingston Foundation to fulfill. I could care less about any breach of contract repercussions, but the organizations I've partnered with are important to me. I don't want my impulsive behavior to affect them negatively."

Tucker pulled a tennis ball from his pocket and tossed it for Boop. "What about the programs you started out west, with the veterans and the kids?"

"My workshops are separate." Lindy was pleased he knew of them. "They belong to me exclusively. The sessions break for six weeks so as much as I've enjoyed my time off the grid, sooner than I'd like, I'll have to face the symphony. My friend Cal, you met him in Baltimore, is running the Phoenix and Flagstaff sessions. I'll need to see if he wants to handle more or…"

"Take one step at a time."

"Funny, Cal always reminds me of that." Lindy stirred her shake and sat beside him. "I recently plugged into a group in New York. Many of the kids are dealing with so much, like I was after Frank. I know somewhere in the sea of faces is a boy or girl on the verge of figuring out the greatest secret ever."

"What's that?"

"That they are enough." Lindy drew her knees toward her chest. "Not the crap of the world, or the hurt they've handled. That discovery will make the rest fall away. It's the golden ticket."

"Wonka," Tucker smiled.

"Exactly, minus the chocolate bar," she sighed. "I love seeing it happen and now I'm here, so I won't be there." Lindy waved her hand. "It's not important."

"Don't dismiss it."

Lindy soaked in his sincerity. "The Livingston Foundation funded my first workshops because of my relationship with Hayward. We're tangled and not in a good way."

"Contact your manager and have them unravel it."

"I no longer have representation." Lindy shrugged. "And even though I know business isn't personal, things could become difficult if I remain on her client roster. That's the last thing I'd ever want. It's complicated." Lindy picked up the soggy ball and threw it. "I'm an expert in complicated alliances."

Boop leaped from the dock and landed with an impressive splash.

Lindy rested her head on Tucker's shoulder. "I don't want to let the kids down. When I was in their position, one more disappointment could be the straw that shatters it all."

Streaks of color celebrated the sun's dive toward the horizon. Lindy laced her fingers through Tucker's. "Is there anything better?"

"No," he said quietly. "Absolutely nothing."

Tucker attached Boop's leash and they started the walk home. "Are you going to unload the kiln tonight? I'm happy to hang around and help."

"No, I'm going to let it sit till morning. It's a very precise process of heat and degrees. The temperature can't just be switched on and off like…" she snapped her fingers. "I believe in deliberate degrees and managed steps. I believe in intention and patience."

"I think I share some of those traits." Tucker flashed a crooked smile. "Maybe I was a kiln in a former life."

"Go ahead and poke fun." Lindy's sneakered steps echoed in the night. "My kiln and I trust and understand one another."

"Uh-huh." Merriment danced in his eyes.

Lindy thrust her chin high. "It's a very special relationship."

"I'm sure it is. You need a porch swing."

"I'm on the lookout for two actually. I don't want the back porch to feel left out. I asked Zak to keep me in mind if he finds any sturdy ones."

"He'll certainly deliver. The guy's a magnet for good loot." Tucker continued to hold her hand as they followed the solar lights to the dock. Boop jumped into the boat and immediately lay down.

"She's played out."

"She sure is." Tucker waited for her to face him. "May I kiss you, Lindy Colton?"

Lindy put the straw in her mouth and nibbled on the end then took a drawn out sip as if considering his question.

"Taunting me," he whispered and stepped even closer. "Just like the old days."

She set the cup aside and looked into the familiar ocean of Tucker's blue eyes. "You may kiss me, Tucker Brandt."

The potent mix of then and now did indeed rock Tucker back on his heels.

Lindy gripped the fabric covering his shoulders, holding him in place when he would have broken their connection. The ice cream and the kiss, neither were their first, but she couldn't quite dismiss the longing simmering below the surface.

Tucker slid his fingertips along her arms, circled her wrists and tugged gently. "I better get home." He pressed her hands to his lips. "Don't want to miss curfew."

From the shadows, Baxter grinned. "There's the money shot." He snapped a dozen frames of the surf/paddleboard teacher locking lips with the boss's woman. "Add these to the others and I'll be getting a fat bonus." He hopped in his car and headed for the drawbridge.

Chapter 53

Kate studied the woman crossing the parking lot. She was city slick and teetering on pencil thin heels. "Bad choice of footwear, honey."

"I know, but they are so cute and make my legs look like magic."

Kate laughed. "How can I help you?"

"I'm Celeste Wilde." She extended her hand. "My friend Belinda Cole has spoken so highly of this establishment and I can smell why." She inhaled deeply. "I mean seriously, yum. Perhaps you know her?"

Kate continued to wipe the bar top.

"Belinda Cole, the elite pottery artist who lived here on the island as a child?"

Kate glanced around the patrons in the restaurant. "Nobody here by that name. I can help you with a cold drink and hearty meal if you'd like to have a seat."

"Unfortunately I have a conference call in fifteen." Celeste's brow puckered. "But I'd love a bowl of whatever sinful soup that gentleman is enjoying, to-go."

"Coming right up."

Celeste's phone chirped. "Excuse me." She walked to the window and deleted another blistering text from Hayward. "Belinda, my sweet friend, you're making it difficult for me to help you."

"Here you are, Ms. Wilde." Kate offered the brown bag. "Fresh chowder and a corn muffin to-go."

"My mouth is watering already."

"Join me at the register and we'll square your bill."

"I can see you don't want to help me, Mrs. Cocheran." Celeste paused as Kate's head tipped. "Belinda is my friend, and I'm only here to help. May I leave my card?"

"Suit yourself." Kate strolled to the end of the bar.

The phone alert announced the meeting was about to begin. Celeste dug out her money clip. "No change, thanks." She scooted outside and noticed a hunk tying up his boat. She tipped her sunglasses down. "Tucker?"

Tucker scrutinized the ice-blonde Amazon with a screaming streak of red hair shadowing her eyes.

"Tucker?" she repeated. "It is you. I'm a friend of Belinda's. I recognized you from the photo she had hanging in her studio." When Tucker said nothing Celeste huffed in frustration. "I get the small town protect-your-own routine, but heaven's glory, you're all making this so difficult." She brushed her bangs to the side. "I'm Belinda's agent, Celeste Wilde. I need to reach her. Be a dear, will you?" She thrust a takeout bag at him and dug a card and pen from her tote.

Tucker watched as she jotted a quick note then pinched a card between perfectly manicured fingers and waved it at him.

"Please pass my card as soon as you see her. I'm staying at the Rochelle on Madden until Sunday." Celeste fluttered her lash extensions. "Pretty, pretty please."

Tucker traded the card for her lunch.

"You're the best." She pivoted on sky-high heels. "Gotta run, conference call."

Tucker watched Celeste glide up the planks. He scanned the card: Celeste Wilde, Personal Representation for Extraordinary Artists. On the back she'd drawn a heart and written *Call Me*.

Lindy had been on the island for nearly a month and no one had come looking for her. Until today, the agent with the bleeding bangs.

"Who's the chick?" Zak sauntered toward the boat. "That's what I call an appetizer. Superb stems, the hair, the clothes… I wish I'd gotten a look at her face. Hot?"

"When are you getting out to Lindy's to finish the security install?"

"Later today. I should wrap up by dusk." Zak strained to catch a final glimpse of the exiting goddess. "Come on, man. Feed me some details. Sipping coffee hot or seek medical attention hot?"

"Call 911."

"Blistering. Damn, I knew it." Zak blew out a breath. "Where do you think she's headed?"

"The Rochelle."

"My lucky day. I have an install scheduled there. I think I'll navigate in her direction after lunch."

Tucker laughed at his buddy. "And do what with her?"

"*What* would be a fine place to start, then I'll work my way through *this*, *that*, and *anything else* she says yes to."

Chapter 54

The Rochelle was low on luxury but Celeste wouldn't be staying long. A power drill screamed. "Not long at all if this keeps up," she muttered.

The manager told her when she'd checked in that the two-story motel was sprucing for the upcoming season. Fresh paint and new carpeting were being added to wash away the staleness of winter. He also promised any intrusive noise would end before six.

Celeste pushed the commotion aside and imagined she had a window with a broad view of the water. She delighted in the idea of inviting the island's energy into the room. She longed to hear the waves and feel the salty breeze against her skin.

Kate's seafood chowder was a scrumptious compromise.

She finished her lunch then powered up the laptop and spent an hour tidying email and updating marketing files. Belinda's next contracted commitment was the May Day Majestic. Even though Celeste no longer officially represented Belinda Cole, she was determined to remain devoted to the vision she'd begun.

"If only I could find her." Celeste pushed from the bed. She should have acted the first time she'd suspected Hayward's influence was hurting Belinda. "But you didn't." She carried her heavy heart across the room and opened the door.

The racket from the construction rolled inside. Celeste drank in the sight of the hunk wielding the noisy tool. Snug Levi's, muscled forearms, and a bearded jawline that appeared sculpted from iron. "Yes, please." She snagged the ice bucket off the dresser and stepped onto the open walkway.

Zak kept one eye on the job and the other on her legs as the container filled.

Aware of his gaze, Celeste angled toward him, braced the bucket against her hip, and smiled. She fed a few bills into the vending machine then bent slowly to retrieve her bottle of Coke.

Zak absorbed every stride of her return.

"Hello, Island Boy."

"Hello, City Girl."

"Is it that obvious?" Celeste leaned against the open railing. "Tell a gal where she can pick up a bit of rum to go with her Coke?"

"If I said my place, you'd run scared." Zak grinned. "Ruppert's Liquor is one block north on Second Street."

"And if I'm standing in front of the office, facing Madden?" Celeste dipped her chin sending a chunk of cherry bangs over her eyes. "North would be which direction?"

"North would be to your right," he chuckled.

"I'm Celeste." She tucked the soda under her arm and offered her hand.

"Nice to meet you, I'm Zak."

Celeste braced for the sizzle and when their palms linked she wasn't disappointed.

Zak released a low whistle as Celeste clipped down the hall and disappeared into her room.

Zak was loading his tools when Celeste walked back from Ruppert's. She noticed the logo on the truck's front door, *Safe and Sound Island Security*. If Belinda was concerned about Hayward coming to Chincoteague, appropriate safety measures would be high on her to-do list. "You install all kinds of security systems, even residential?"

"Sure," Zak said. "I'm finishing a full install today. Doors, windows, motion detectors, the place will be a fortress when I'm done."

Jackpot, Celeste thought. "Odd this time of year?"

"New purchase," Zak said. "People always want to feel protected, so my work is steady. How long are you in town?"

"The weekend, just passing through on my way to surprise my friend in North Carolina." Celeste instantly regretted the lie. She lifted the little brown bag. "I'm not driving anywhere tonight."

"Do yourself one better and go down to the Bayside Inn for some live music, good food, and plenty of locals for company."

Celeste leaned against his tailgate. "Will you be there?"

Zak did nothing to mask his appreciation of Celeste's figure. "I'd make a point, if you'd like to find me." His phone rang. "Excuse me a minute. Hey, Tucker... I'm headed there now... As a matter of fact I did." Zak grinned at Celeste. "What's that?" He angled his body away. "Sure, right... got it. See ya."

The island was closing ranks. "So," Celeste straightened, "should I expect to see you at the Inn?"

"No, sorry. Something's come up." Zak opened the driver's side and hopped behind the wheel.

"That's a shame, it was nice to meet you."

"You too. Have a safe trip to North Carolina."

Celeste watched Zak's truck leave the lot. "Very interesting," she said to herself as she strolled to her room. Even after her prolonged absence, Belinda still had a tight, not to mention handsome, circle of loyalty.

Celeste mixed her first cocktail and replayed the sparring banter with Zak. When was the last time she had so much fun flirting with a stranger? Not a complete stranger, she qualified. Zak knew Belinda and was protective of her. "We have that in common." Celeste jiggled the ice in her short glass and decided her time would be better spent digging into the background of the local security expert.

A solid knock at the door made Celeste jump. Maybe Zak was feeling the same way. After a quick glance in the mirror she tousled her hair, boosted her cleavage, then pulled the door wide.

Lindy laughed at Celeste's shocked expression. "I hear you're looking for me." She stepped into the room. "Kinda difficult to remain inconspicuous with legs like a Bond girl."

"If you'd told me you were skipping town and tossing your cell into the nearest body of water, I wouldn't have had to snoop around," Celeste replied.

"Wasn't planned." Lindy flopped across the bed. "I stayed here once."

"Wild night?" Celeste asked.

"Depends on your definition, I guess. When I was a teenager, *wild* meant breaking curfew. My evening at the Rochelle definitely makes my top five of all-time memories."

"Well, if the hot first love was involved, I can see why." Celeste wiggled her brows. "Met him by the way, your Tucker."

"He's not *my* Tucker."

"So he's available?"

"No."

Celeste chuckled. "You're a smart girl."

"So what gives? Why are you crashing my vacation?"

"Is that what you're doing, taking a holiday? People don't usually purchase a home and install total security, unless they're planning to spend a fair amount of time living somewhere."

"Okay, it's more and it's complicated. I have a lot of balls in the air. It's an intricate juggle of old and new, of vague and defined. I'm just trying my best to keep them from dropping around me."

"Pass me a few." Celeste sat beside her. "Hayward wanted you to feel alone, but you're not. I've only been on this island for a few hours. You have an entire squadron of loyal friends eager to stand shoulder to shoulder with you."

"Yeah, I'm lucky in many ways. Celeste, you have to know that phasing you out," Lindy waved her hand, "was all Hayward. You're my representative for eternity, if you still want the gig."

"I do, for all eternity." Celeste patted Lindy's thigh. "And just so we're clear, I wasn't going anywhere. So when you're ready, pass me a ball or two."

"The fundraising event in May…" Lindy felt anxiety beginning to build.

"Majestic," Celeste nodded, "yes."

"I haven't decided if I'm attending, although I'm not sure I have a choice. So many people are counting on me. The organization needs the exposure and the monies generated." Lindy pressed the heel of her hand into the center of her chest.

"My ball, let me do what I do. But while we're on the subject of balls, make no mistake, I'll lead the charge to kick Hayward into permanent falsetto whenever you give me the green light."

Lindy laughed. "After Majestic, I no longer want to be linked, or funded, by the Livingston Foundation."

"I'll call legal and have the proper paperwork drawn up, then modify the press kits to feature your artwork and strip any Foundation branding."

"You're amazing."

"That's the truth." Celeste grabbed her laptop and began to type at a feverish pace. "Belinda Cole is the draw, honey. The remaining details will fall into place."

"Lindy Colton."

Celeste's fingers paused. "What's that?"

"Your first adjustment." Lindy got to her feet. "My name is Lindy Colton."

"I knew her once upon a time." Celeste's eyes filled. "It's really nice to see you again, Lindy."

Chapter 55

Zak heard Lindy pull in. He descended the ladder, then turned and saw Celeste. He crossed his arms over his chest, and braced his legs. "Everything all right, Lindy?"

Celeste dipped her chin and studied Zak over the frame of her sunglasses. "Is he always so protective? It's hot."

"Down, girl," Lindy snickered. "Zak's not used to city women."

"Maybe I should educate him." Celeste wiggled her brows.

"Lindy?"

Celeste patted his muscled chest. "Easy, Island Boy."

"I'm fine, Zak," Lindy chuckled. "Celeste's my friend and she's spending the weekend, so please try and play nice."

Zak watched until they vanished into the home. "Oh, I'll play."

"Welcome." Lindy opened the door and kicked her sneakers into a wire basket. "What's mine is yours."

Celeste stepped into the cozy dwelling and followed Lindy into the kitchen.

Lindy tossed her sweatshirt over the chair. "You want a drink?" She opened the cupboard and placed two vintage character glasses on the counter.

"Ice water would be perfect." Celeste smiled at Bugs Bunny and Petunia Pig. "My afternoon cocktail would have been more fun in one of those."

Celeste followed the tile to the living room and stood in a channel of colored light cast by a spectacular panel of stained glass. "Wonderful," she whispered as her eyes roamed Lindy's stylish decorative mix. "Where did you get all these amazing works of art and antiques?" Celeste called to Lindy as she studied an intricate unit of suspended pipes. The gravity-defying form displayed vintage books, photographs, and more.

"Zak made the up-cycled shelving."

"Island Boy is good with his hands," Celeste hummed. "Lucky, lucky me." She turned into the room. "Is this the print you bought on our first trip to Arizona?"

"Good memory." Lindy handed Celeste her drink.

"Great trip." Celeste sipped her water. "You have an incredible eye… that window and this bench, and that chair."

"The chair I picked up along the road a few years ago."

"By the road?"

"Yep, I had it in my storage unit with much of what you're seeing. The church pew I found here on the island. Green Goodness, a store on Main Street, is a goldmine. The owner, Candi, is the stained glass artist." Lindy pointed to the Full Circle window. "That's her work. So is the dragonfly over the sink in the upstairs bathroom. I'll introduce you. You may even decide you want to manage her."

"Seriously?"

"Uh-huh, she's not open today but we can drop in tomorrow after I show you my favorite flea market."

"Sounds perfect." Celeste bounced on her toes. "Gimme the twenty-dollar tour. Leave nothing out, I want to see everything."

"You got it. Afterwards we'll head to the Bayside Inn and meet my friend Nina for dinner."

"Sounds wonderful."

Lindy led Celeste through the lower level, taking time to open every cupboard and closet door. They climbed the staircase to the second level and repeated the process.

"You're my first human sleepover." Lindy gestured to the guest bedroom. "I have no idea how comfortable the mattress is. Your bathroom's here and towels are under the vanity." She pushed open the curtain. "You have a lovely view of the water. Feel free to sit on the dock. It's magic, trust me."

Celeste moved to the window and felt the enchantment calling softly to her.

Lindy jogged down the steps and guided Celeste through the kitchen and out the back door. They crossed the planks to the studio. "Hard to believe I've only been here a month."

"And in that short period of time you've bought and furnished a house, have begun to work, hooked or re-hooked the Adonis, and revamped your entire personal image."

"My personal what?" Lindy looked herself over. "I got a haircut."

"Is that what it's called on Chincoteague?" Celeste laughed. "You're radiant and more relaxed than I've ever seen you. Maybe it's a twin thing. I knew one woman and now I'm meeting her identical twin. You resemble one another physically, enough to pass for each other, but are at the core very different people."

"I was in the womb alone, I assure you." Lindy punched in the code and the locks disengaged. "Belinda was Hayward's creation. The only thing I share with her is my talent."

"I'm not sure about that." Celeste crossed the threshold and entered an environment poised for positivity and production. Alive with character, the studio boasted comfortable furnishings, along with the tools and equipment of her trade.

In the far corner a hammock draped loosely from the rafters. The swath of silk partially masked a group of stunning photographs featuring a younger Lindy and her pottery on the beach. A leather recliner, steamer trunk, and a brass lamp with a marble base completed the cozy nook.

A painted canvas floor mat separated the sitting area from the workspace. The stenciled fabric, playfully marked with a combination of adult and child-sized footprints, resembled a game of Twister in progress. Celeste imagined the delighted laughter filling Lindy's creative space as the match unfolded.

A pair of pottery wheels were positioned near a large window. Beyond the glass, the verdant view of the yard begged to be captured on canvas. The studio's long wall represented the organized progression of raw clay to finished product.

Celeste stopped beside an old metal refrigerator. "May I?" On Lindy's nod, she pulled the handle and discovered wire shelves supporting works-in-progress. "Wet box?"

"Damp box, yes," Lindy smiled.

Celeste closed the door and moved toward a dowel-constructed baker's rack. The shelves were loaded with recently thrown green-ware in various stages of drying. More shelves held bisque-ware waiting to be doused with color and fired a second time.

Lindy's glazing buckets sat on a raised skid near an old farm sink. An array of sample tiles were positioned beside notebooks filled with formulas and recipes for colored finishes. A few feet beyond, neatly arranged fire brick surrounded a brand new kiln. Celeste peeked inside the open furnace and viewed layers of dipped pottery awaiting the soaring temperature of transformation. "You've been very busy."

Celeste completed her perusal in front of a large shelving unit. There was something very different in Lindy's current inventory. Her creations were tangible and enticing. They encapsulated a raw power that beckoned.

"I've always been a fan." Celeste was breathless. "But seriously, Lindy, I don't have the words."

Color rose in Lindy's cheeks. "I've just been fiddling around."

"Your recent work is fascinating." Celeste cradled a bowl and angled it toward the light. "The shapes are charismatic and captivating. The glazes feel alive... they ache." She carefully returned the piece to the shelf. "Trust me, Lindy, keep fiddling around."

Chapter 56

Lindy drove them to the B&B, picked up Nina, and headed to the Bayside Inn for dinner.

"Hello again, Kate," Celeste said through chattering teeth. "I'll have a cup of crab soup, a large black coffee, and a seat next to a hot man."

"How about I invite Jim Beam to swim in your coffee, and you…" Kate motioned to the far corner of the dining area, "take the table under the heater?"

"Fantastic idea." Celeste pulled the zipper on her borrowed fleece jacket higher.

"And let's make it a bowl of soup," Kate scribbled on her pad, "seeing as you'd benefit from a little insulation over your bones."

"What a nice thing to say," Celeste grinned.

"Same for you, Nina? Lindy?"

"Yes," they answered in unison, then Nina added, "Minus the liquored coffee, of course. Just water for me, please."

"Perfect, I'll bring warm dinner rolls to get you girls started. Would you like cinnamon butter?"

"Yummy," Celeste hummed in anticipation.

The music kicked up and the crowd thickened. Eager singles jostled along the bar surveying their prospects.

The unspoken language between men and women fascinated Celeste. "The show is about to begin," she winked at Lindy then tuned in, eager to watch.

"Celeste is an avid people watcher and a master at spinning a tale," Lindy explained to Nina. "She should really consider becoming a writer."

"Interesting hobby." Nina adjusted her chair and leaned closer. "Tell us, Celeste, what's the play?"

Celeste rubbed her hand gleefully. "Check out Blondie, by the door. She came in with the muscled stud, but he's quickly become inebriated so she's shifted to her backup man, Mr. Business Casual in the button-down collar, at the end of the bar." Celeste inclined her head. "Do you see him?"

"Mr. Self-important," Lindy remarked. "I'm familiar with the type."

"You certainly are," Celeste snickered. "Sadly, Blondie is unaware that Mr. B-Cas has a history of knocking boots with the waitress and they've got firm after-hours plans."

"Poor Blondie," Nina said, enjoying the unfolding live action. "She's going to have a disappointing night on all fronts."

"Hang in there, girlie." Celeste pointed to the side entrance. "Here comes a handsome fresh batch."

Nina looked toward the dock doors where Mike led the way, followed by Zak and Tucker.

The guys mingled on their way to the bar. Blondie perked up and trailed her hand over Tucker's arm. He smiled politely then lifted his hand to hail the bartender.

"Ouch, that hurt, but she's not going to give up that easily."

On cue, the woman shifted her posture. Her blouse slipped off her shoulder nearly spilling her ample bosom. Zak's head jerked toward the exposed line of flesh.

"Men will be men," Celeste chuckled goodheartedly. She smiled as Zak stepped neatly to the side, putting a barstool between them. Blondie's lips puffed in a practiced pout. "Two down, one to go. Come on. Re-bait your hook, honey."

Before the woman had a chance, the last man in the trio pinched the fallen fabric and slid it back in place with a brotherly pat.

"What a sweet refusal."

Nina scooted to make room around the table. "Mike is sweet, he's also my husband. Tucker is Lin…" she trailed off then lifted her hands.

"Sorry, Lindy. Tucker has always been yours. And Zak? Well, Zak's a pirate."

"A buccaneer, you say?" Celeste made a sound like she was savoring something delicious. "Pillage and plunder." She pushed her shoulders back and crossed her man-murdering legs. "Time for me to do a little fishing of my own."

"Ladies," Zak nodded to Nina and Lindy before he made a not-so-subtle study of Celeste. "City Girl."

"Island Boy." Celeste patted the open seat next to her.

Tucker slid into the chair beside Lindy. "Zak's always been such a cocky S.O.B. Gonna be fun to watch her take him on."

Zak moved closer to Celeste, staking his claim. "I was hoping you'd find your way to our little gathering."

Celeste crooked her finger, drawing him nearer. "Careful what you wish for, Island Boy," she whispered. "There's a good chance you'll get it."

Heat flashed in Zak's eyes.

Tucker let out a low whistle. "Really fun to watch."

Celeste's eyes twinkled. "And that concludes Act One."

Lindy filled the guys in on Celeste's gift for narrating the scene in front of her.

"More entertaining than reality TV," Nina said.

"I'd say it depends on the cast," Mike quipped, making the group laugh.

"Subtle, guys." Zak shifted uncomfortably. "I applied to be a contestant on *The Bachelor*. I'm still waiting to hear back."

"Really?" Celeste faced him. "I know the producer. Would you like me to pull a string?"

"Connections…" Zak's brows lifted. "Very sexy. I think before you offer me up to a swarm of marriage-minded hyenas, you and I should have a one-on-one and see if I deserve a rose."

Celeste snorted and was genuinely shocked at the sound. When was the last time a man coaxed genuine laughter from her? "I agree." She angled toward him. "I know you work in security and you're an artist. I saw the bookshelf at Lindy's," she explained. "It's remarkable."

"I dabble in what intrigues me." Zak leaned closer.

"He can't take a picture, that's for sure," Mike joked.

"True," Tucker said. "The man stinks with a camera."

Zak scowled at his friends.

"Boys," Lindy snickered. "Give him a break."

"Why?" Tucker scoffed. "He never gives us one."

"Even though that's true," Lindy smiled at Zak, "let's give Celeste a chance to discover a few things on her own."

"Thanks, sugar."

"Yes." Celeste placed her hand on Zak's arm. "No fun if someone opens your gift and tells you what's inside."

"I agree." Zak leaned close and lowered his voice. "I prefer to do the unwrapping for myself."

The music shifted. Nina and Mike excused themselves and joined other couples near the band.

"You order any food?" Tucker asked. "I'm starved."

On cue, Kate carried over three steaming bowls of crab soup and hot rolls. "Evening, Tucker." She served the table. "What are you after besides this pretty girl?"

"Steak, big and red, a loaded potato, and any vegetable that's hot and green."

"Broccoli," Kate made the note on her pad.

"If that's not enough, I'm sure I'll squeeze down some pie."

"Good man." Kate turned to Zak. "Same for you?" He nodded without shifting his full attention from Celeste. "Save your drooling for your steak. The soup's plenty hot, so take the girl for a twirl around the tiles."

"Yes, ma'am." The blush that had receded washed over his neck once again. Zak cleared his throat. "Want to?"

"Might as well see how we move together." Celeste unzipped her jacket and let it fall to the chair. "Vertically, that is." She stood, straightened the hem of her sweater, and cut a path to the dance floor.

"Mother of all things holy." Zak tipped his beer high and swallowed deep before he followed.

———

Masked by the shadows, Hayward sipped the shameful excuse for whiskey and observed the clusters of insignificant barroom inhabitants.

The public escapade disgusted him.

Belinda and her party were too busy stuffing their faces and flaunting themselves to notice anyone beyond their narrow scope.

Her arrogance would be her undoing.

Hayward zeroed in on the blatantly willing blonde jostling to the beat of the band. She would certainly be agreeable to an interlude with a handsome stranger. He deliberately softened his features and waited for her to look in his direction. When her prowling eyes locked on his, he winked and inclined his head toward the exit.

Painted red lips curved in a flash of triumph. She hooked her purse over her shoulder and walked with an extra swing in her hips toward the door.

Hayward cast one final look toward the corner table, then followed the town tart to the parking lot to test the limits of her tease.

———

After dinner Nina and Celeste stepped outside for a breath of fresh air.

"I'm looking forward to your anecdotal observation of tonight's second act," Nina said.

"Are you?" Celeste smiled.

Nina nodded. "Muddled brains and loosened inhibitions, it's gonna be epic."

Celeste laughed. "You decide to let me on the team yet?"

"I have."

"Perfect. Want to help me talk Lindy into doing a show or festival here on the island?"

"That sounds like a wonderful idea."

"What does the community need in terms of awareness and funds?"

241

"Hmm," Nina considered. "I think anything that highlights our people and the island would go over well."

"Okay," Celeste said.

"Just like that?"

"My business is to showcase our girl and her amazing talent. Lindy prefers to partner with organizations so the benefit spills over." Celeste rattled the ice in her empty glass. "She was born and raised here, left to expand her life experience, and now has returned to her roots. There's treasure on this seven miles of sand. Don't you think the world should know about it?"

"Maybe not the *entire* world," Nina said.

"Noted, but certainly the exposure could inspire a person to visit or plan a multi-day vacation. Publicity and feedback fuels tourism, which translates into revenue for the local retailers, restaurants, bookstores and…"

"Okay, okay, whew." Nina's head was spinning. "You're very good at what you do, aren't you?"

"I am." Celeste grinned. "Why don't we make time to brainstorm tomorrow before I head back to the city?"

Nina pulled up her calendar. "My guests check out at eleven and I'm pretty sure…" She tapped the screen. "Yes, no reservations. You'll come for lunch and then I'm yours until Eric goes to tumbling."

"Excellent." Celeste hooked her arm through Nina's and returned to the bar. "Now let's order another round of drinks, indulge in a couple more dances, and then, spoiler alert, you can watch me persuade Zak to tumble me back to the hotel."

"You checked out, remember?" Nina said.

"Well, shoot," Celeste laughed. "I guess I'll have to talk him into tumbling me back to his place."

Celeste handed Lindy the keys to her rental car and turned to Zak. "Ready to go, Island Boy?"

"You better believe it." Zak anchored his arm around Celeste's narrow waist and lifted her toes off the floor.

"Don't wait up," Celeste called over her shoulder as he carried her toward the exit.

"She's something else," Mike said dryly.

"You never have an opinion on such things." Nina wrapped her arm around him. "This was so much fun, a little like old times."

"Better," Mike's brows wiggled playfully. "My beverage was legal and my date is a sure thing."

Tucker took Lindy's hand as they walked to the parking lot. "Pretty night. You want to sit by the water?"

"No."

"Want to go back to my place?"

"Definitely no." She felt his fingers flinch in her grasp. "I didn't mean it that way."

"What did you mean, Lindy?" Tucker wedged his hands in his pockets. "What do you want?"

"I don't know."

"And we're here again," Tucker sighed. "Moving on... standing still... always circling back to the beginning."

"The beginning was easier, Tucker."

"Was it?"

"Friendship is always easier." Lindy's voice hitched with brewing emotion. "I never planned to pursue a romantic relationship."

"And yet you've had a ring on your finger and a man in your..." Tucker lifted his chin and studied the stars winking overhead. "You've always been crystal clear about what wishes you did, and didn't, want to catch, Lindy." His shoulders drooped. "This is one hundred percent my issue. It is past time I work on getting over it."

Lindy felt as if a massive sinkhole had opened beneath her feet.

Tucker crossed the lot and stood beside the rental car. "Hop in. I'll follow you home. Please," he added before she could reject him again. "I'll sleep better knowing you're home safely. Besides, it's what friends do."

While Lindy searched for the words to smooth the hurt she caused, Tucker closed the door between them.

The comfort from Tucker's headlights left her rear window as Lindy turned onto Memory Lane. She passed her house and drove to the dead end.

Tucker wasn't wrong, Lindy acknowledged. She had been crystal clear about the wishes she wanted to catch—independence, education, travel. What he didn't understand was how many stars she felt unworthy of holding. Love, *real* love, partnership, vow-bound forever love...

After-ever wishes weren't meant to be grabbed from the sky. They were too beautiful, too impractical. "You touch 'em, you mess 'em up," Lindy mumbled. After-ever love-laden stars were much safer left in infinite orbit.

Circling back, just like Tucker had said.

Lindy abandoned the warmth of the car, and strolled to the water's edge.

Long ago she concluded romance was an erratic and untrustworthy investment. This certainty became the mortar she'd used to fortify the walls around her heart, and was a boundary of protection she'd been determined to maintain.

Moonlight painted the salty bay's serene surface. Lindy tried to harness the peaceful sensation. Nina was right... Tucker had always calmed her. She wondered if she could lean into the discomfort and challenge her convictions.

She knew Tucker loved her, and deep inside, she knew she loved him too.

Lindy looked at the twinkling orbs partnering with the moon and felt a stirring inside her. Maybe it was time to reach for something new. Maybe it was time to be more clay-like, and if Tucker was in fact formerly a kiln, maybe they could find a path to firing.

What color would they become when they heated to max temp? "Woo doggie," Lindy fanned her face.

She decided to call Tucker and ignite the spark before she lost her nerve. Lindy dug in her pocket for her phone then jolted when it rang.

It would be Tucker, calling to smooth over the awkward end to their evening.

Lindy answered quickly. "I'm so glad you called."

"That's nice to hear, darling. Are you enjoying your creative holiday?"

"Hayward…" Lindy braced a trembling hand on the hood of the truck and worked to level her breathing. "I, ah, I…" Her words lodged in her throat.

"Many brides require a moment or two of frivolity, but you should know your tryst with your former special acquaintance is beginning to strain my tolerance. It is in the best interest of all parties that you return to the city promptly. We have many events to attend and you have several commitments to fulfill."

"I live here," her words quivered.

"Merely a vacation residence." Hayward's dismissal was swift. "A dwelling well beneath our position. If you insist on owning an island home, we'll move to the newly constructed property on the end of your little private lane. The builders are quite motivated. I'm confident they'll find my cash offer very appealing."

The phone slid from limp fingers and landed with a dull thud. Lindy braced her hands on her knees as her stomach twisted painfully. She raced to the tall grass and was violently ill.

Chapter 57

Tucker… Hayward… Hayward… Tucker… Was it any wonder she couldn't settle?

Lindy lay awake for hours picking through the complex tangle of unintended and calculated hurt. "Night and day… wicked and good." She rolled to her side and adjusted the pillow.

Why she'd held every childhood experience against Tucker, yet gone along so easily with Hayward, was baffling.

Not only were the contrasts confusing, they were intimidating. And for the first time in her life, Lindy felt something real was hanging in the balance.

In defiance of the turmoil lurking in her busy mind, Lindy abandoned her sleepless bed. She tiptoed to the kitchen and made a bold cup of coffee.

Lindy stepped into the darkness the world endured at four in the morning. Blackness prodded her to turn back rather than challenge the unseen. She forced her feet to connect with the damp planks, placed her thermal cup under the chair, and unrolled her yoga mat.

Partnering with the stillness of the marsh, Lindy moved through a deliberate sequence of strength and power. Her breath painted the air as her body warmed. Eventually, she kneeled, folded her torso over bent knees, and settled into child's pose.

Lindy shifted to the chair, hugged her sweater close, and sipped her cooling coffee.

The sun crept into the day. A beautiful reminder of how quickly the world around her was moving. "I'm just a thing within the things," Lindy whispered. "A small part of the whole." She reached for insight from the rising spectacle of light.

"Talk to me, Mom... tell me what to do." She waited for the environment to stir, but the air and water remained hushed and unmoving.

Behind her the porch door opened and closed. Moments later Celeste strolled to the end of the dock.

"Pretty spot to start the day." Celeste blew a steady stream of air across a steaming mug of coffee. "I'm still not sure what to do with all the silence." She dragged the other chair closer. "I mean it, how do you think?"

"Takes some getting used to." Lindy opened her blanket to share. "When I was a kid I craved the noise and energy of the city. I viewed every wide stretch of water like a barricade."

"And now that you're back?"

"I see it differently," Lindy said thoughtfully. "I guess a fresh lens has changed my perspective." She patted Celeste's knee. "Based on the cheerful whistling I heard when you came home, I'm assuming the rest of your evening went well."

"You would be correct." Celeste cradled her cup to her chest. "I'm having trouble getting a handle on Zak. He's so different from any man I've ever been attracted to. He's playful and unashamedly forward. He's extremely talented, but at the same time profound and enigmatic."

"Uh-huh," Lindy smiled. "Trust me, I know. You ready to search for flea market treasure?"

"Right now?"

"Best things sell first."

Celeste shot to her feet and raced toward the house.

Lindy laughed. "You can take a minute to finish your coffee."

"This is the best retail therapy I've ever experienced." Celeste cheerfully combed through another box lot. "Look at these little measuring cups. I have to have them."

Lindy shook her head. Celeste's enthusiasm brought smiles to everyone. She had no concept of bartering and was paying more than asking price.

Celeste plucked a few dollars from her money clip and passed the bills to the seller. "How is it possible I've never flea marketed?" She gushed and tucked her treasure inside her tote.

Zak came up behind her. "Generally it requires you leave the world of comfort and concrete." He leaned close and indulged in a lingering kiss. "Morning, City Girl."

Celeste's face flushed. "G'morning, what are you offering today?"

"This and that." Zak linked his fingers with Celeste's. He flashed Lindy a quick grin. "Follow me, my first love. I'm going to make your day."

Lindy stood beside the wooden porch swings. "They're very nice."

Her underwhelming reaction left Zak deflated. "No trouble if they aren't your style, I'll keep looking."

"Sorry Zak, I'm dealing with…" Lindy waved her hand. "I didn't sleep well. They're perfect."

Zak rubbed his palms together gearing up for the haggle.

"Whatever you're asking is fine. Make sure you add a little extra for delivery, fuel, and muscle."

"Man," he scuffed his boot heel in the dirt, "you're both off the game today. Bartering is half the fun."

"Again, sorry," Lindy smiled. "My mind's down the road. I'm going to grab a few things from the produce stand, Celeste. I'll meet you at the truck."

"Am I missing something?" Zak asked as Lindy moved off. He kneeled and fastened sold tags to the swings. "What went down after we left the bar?"

"Don't worry, I'll get to the bottom of it," Still woozy from his fly-by, Celeste ran her hand over Zak's arm. "We're headed to do a bit more shopping in town and then to Nina's for a power lunch. I can be available later, if you want."

"No question." Zak hauled her close and covered her surprised gasp with another sizzling kiss. "Better kick than coffee."

Celeste giggled.

Zak glanced over Celeste's shoulder and spotted a woman admiring a wicker rocking chair. "I have a customer. I'm going fishing with Tucker, but I'll be sure to track you down after."

Celeste watched Zak focus his charm on the unsuspecting shopper. She laughed quietly. "Might as well hand him your money now." An instant later the lady's cheeks pinked prettily, her wallet opened, and the dollars transferred.

Chapter 58

Lindy unleashed Celeste inside Green Goodness, then retreated to the porch to clear her head. She needed to shake her Hayward hangover before brunch or Nina would sniff out her mood and press for details.

Hayward's threat to purchase a property on the island was just an empty attempt to upset her. An effective shot, Lindy conceded. She'd be better prepared next time.

"Next time." Her heart sank. If there was one lesson she'd learned during her time with Hayward, it was that he would follow through on anything he considered significant. How important she was in his grand scheme remained to be seen.

Celeste's excited chatter flowed through the open windows. Lindy decided to escape further to the quiet of the courtyard.

The moment her soles impacted the soft grass, her senses engaged. The rally of untainted beauty waged a gentle assault on the funk camped in her heart. Lindy sat by the water and released the tension gripping her shoulders. With each breath the shackles of captive thought loosened.

Celeste bounded across the courtyard. Delighted laughter arrived before her body. "You're a terrible, beautiful influence, Lindy Colton."

Lindy soaked in Celeste's abundant joy.

"Green Goodness was everything you promised and more." Celeste plopped down on the bench, then rebounded as if she'd hit a trampoline. She twirled in a dizzying circle while waving a stack of business cards. "I could have a dozen new clients by the end of the week."

"You could also end up taking a swim." Lindy caught her hand. "Please come away from the water."

"The talent showcased under Candi's roof…" Celeste jogged to the safety of the grass. "I'm not kidding. I don't know where to begin."

"Any favorites?"

"Too many, their names are blurring." Celeste looked over the bay. "Candi's work of course, a watercolor artist, a jewelry designer, and reclusive photographer who goes by the letter *Z*."

Lindy covered her surprise with a cough.

"Gorgeous," Celeste gestured broadly to the vision before her. "Is it any wonder talent thrives here? Anyway, I think there are plenty who will play into what I have in mind for the event, but before I get sidetracked further," she sat beside Lindy, "I can tell something is weighing on you. Do you want to tell me what happened after Zak and I left last night?"

"Just history repeating," Lindy said quietly. "Nothing for you to be concerned over. I'll trudge through. I always do."

"Well, you don't need to slog along by yourself. Remember that." Celeste reached for her hand. "Think Nina's ready for us? I'm starved."

Nina set the small kitchen table in the family quarters. She served warm scones with fresh berries and what she called Trifecta Quiche— an egg soufflé, three inches high, boasting a trio of meats, topped with three kinds of cheese.

"You could retire on this recipe alone." Celeste's fork disappeared again. "I wasn't going to eat it all, and look."

"Eric would say you've made a happy plate." Nina smiled and began to clear the table.

Lindy took command of the sink. She enjoyed the view of the yard as she rinsed the plates. The fencing had been updated and a substantial patio added. The butterfly garden was thriving and now housed a small fish pond and fountain. *Past and present*, she thought with a contented sigh.

"I'm so excited." Nina placed a legal pad and pen at Lindy's seat. "Mike said he could hear the gears in my brain spinning all night." She positioned a pillow on the chair. "Celeste, before we start I just want to thank you for including me. I'm sure the last thing you need is input from a small event planner."

"Don't be silly, you're my ace. No one knows Lindy better than you." Celeste opened her laptop. "Disclosure, I didn't get as far in my prep work as I would have due to a delectable distraction last evening."

"The buccaneer?" Nina lifted her brow.

"Indeed." Celeste waited for Lindy to join them. "What I envision is a small show like your yearly Blueberry Festival." She beamed at their shocked expressions. "Everything's on the internet. Including a few hundred five-star reviews for the accommodations and award-winning breakfast served at your B&B, my dear."

Nina flushed. "Just building on Susie's legacy."

"I've perused the expanse of local talent featured at Green Goodness." Celeste placed a stack of business cards on the table. "This island is a gold mine."

"We'll want to add musicians and food to the tangible artistry." Nina's pen raced across her tablet.

"Our headliner will be Lindy Colton." Celeste tossed Lindy a sassy wink. "A teasing debut of your new work. I'd like input on any specific organization you'd prefer to highlight. After that, it's simply a matter of finessing the details." She rubbed her palms together with glee. "Let's choose a date."

"Should we wait until the end of summer?" Nina paged through her planner. "Definitely not in July, too much going on with the annual Pony Penning."

The keys of Celeste's laptop rattled. "The sooner the better."

"Can't be too soon," Lindy commented. "I don't have much inventory."

"You've got plenty." Celeste's dancing fingers froze. "Um, I might have forgotten to mention one small detail." A mix of worry and guilt painted her cheeks. "I packed the loft studio—your tools, completed work, and bisque-ware—before I left the city. Anything that wasn't dry enough to transport safely, I had transferred to the academy for safekeeping."

Lindy's mouth dropped open as Celeste's words swirled around her.

"The courier was waiting for a delivery address, which I sent yesterday. Everything you need will be here..." Celeste tapped a link on her phone. "...tomorrow by noon. So, in regard to ample inventory, you'll be good to go."

Lindy stood by the back door and looked at the flower bed she'd planted with her mom nearly ten years before. She smiled, remembering how they'd tended and watered the tiny sprouts through the blistering summer. In the fall they covered the plot with straw, and then worried the coastal winter would damage the resting roots.

The following spring they'd laid side by side on their bellies, scrutinizing the earth while urging the soil to reveal its secrets. The first fragile shoots were celebrated, like a child arriving from the womb, as were the blooms that erupted thereafter.

The echoes of her mom's happiness filled Lindy's heart. "Mother's Day," she murmured. "The focus will be domestic violence. An organization that specializes in art camps and programs designed to mend the trauma families face as they begin to rebuild." Lindy was amazed how clearly she could see it. "I want an area where kids can make things. Age-appropriate activities, coloring pages, sand art, sidewalk chalk, acrylic paints and canvases."

Nina and Celeste left their chairs and stood on either side of her.

"An Artist Expo, outside if the weather permits. Easels around the perimeter," Lindy continued. "Where the artists can be spoken to and interacted with. Artists are everyday people after all, and creative expression is for everyone."

The room fell silent.

Lindy snapped out of her trance. "What did I say?"

"Everything," Celeste said.

Nina wrapped her arms around Lindy. "You said everything."

Chapter 59

Celeste wanted to spend the last moments of her weekend watching the boats return from a day at sea. She was fascinated by the display of patience and care the captains showed as they lined up and waited for the drawbridge to open.

"The water wasn't kind to this guy today," Celeste's commentary began as an obviously impaired vessel lumbered toward the marina. "He's going to linger at the dock, bang some wrenches, then find a bar stool until his mood improves." A newer skiff buzzed happily across the water casting an obnoxious wake in the relative calm. "Here's a fella who wants to be seen. His belly isn't reliant on the day's work."

Lindy laughed. Celeste's play-by-play was as entertaining as ever. "I guess you'll be heading back tomorrow."

"This was a wonderful escape, but yes, I really should." She looked across the bay and sighed. "I'll continue to iron out the details for the Artist Expo and connect with you as usual on Thursday mornings. We can live chat, since a weekly in-person will prove difficult."

"I know a schedule is necessary for professional reasons, but friends call anytime for any reason, and they're welcome to visit without invitation."

"I like the sound of that." Celeste's attention shifted to the boat angling in their direction. "Now here comes my kind of trouble." Her cheeks warmed as Zak lightened the pressure on the throttle and aligned expertly with the dock. "I thought you were fishing."

"I am fishing," Zak grinned. "I'm hoping to hook a clever woman and take her to see the wild ponies on the north end of the island. Thought I'd fix her a nice dinner and catch a sunset view on the water. What do you say, City Girl? Have time for a ride around the island?"

"I may freeze."

"I'll be sure to keep you plenty warm."

Celeste clapped. "Wild ponies."

Lindy squashed the flicker of jealousy. Why were romantic relationships effortless for everyone but her?

There was no reason for Lindy to be annoyed. No one was stopping her. Nothing was holding her in place except old outgrown ideas.

"Everything moves," Tucker had told her years ago. *"You move forward or you stand still. No safe zones or guarantees… only balancing the parts that matter."* Tucker mattered. The only truth from the beginning was that Tucker loved her.

How Lindy felt for Tucker wasn't complicated, it was terrifying. Kate was right—it was terrifying because it mattered.

Tucker had begun the day hopeful that his full schedule would provide the mental unwind he desperately needed. Instead, his past had manifested at every turn.

His morning paddleboard tour, sorority sisters on spring break, chattered about their dreams and current relationships. The resounding theme was *you can't have everything*. They asked Tucker's opinion, as a man who appeared to be living the ideal life.

He indulged a million staged pictures for social media while skillfully dodging their relentless flirting and repeated invitations to Happy Hour. When the session ended Tucker was exhausted. He figured he'd more than earned each dollar of their outrageous tip.

After lunch, he had a couple booked for a ninety-minute boat ride to see the wildlife. The husband was superior and exacting, his wife enthusiastic and uncomplaining.

The woman spent forty minutes photographing a Great Blue Heron feeding in the shallow water, while her husband fussed about a bird being a bird.

On the return ride, Tucker anticipated the man's demand for his money back and wasn't disappointed. He avoided confrontation, issued a refund, and put the entire experience in his rearview.

Tucker liberated Boop from the apartment. He filled the cooler and met Zak to close out the day fishing. They cast line after line off the southern tip of the island only to come up empty. Zak abandoned the effort to sniff out Celeste and squeeze in a little more time before she returned to New York.

With Boop dozing at his feet, Tucker turned the boat for home. He drifted into the slip, secured the lines, and began to rinse the salt residue off the deck.

Bone weary, he considered bedding down on the boat, but as his mind drifted to Lindy, he realized memories were waiting below deck too.

Boop barked.

"Y'all done for the day?" Trish strutted along the planks with a bottle of wine in one hand and a bag of takeout in the other. "I brought you some dinner." She lifted the fragrant food away from Boop's seeking nose.

Tucker's cell phone rang. He held up a single finger to halt Trish's advance. "Hello." The telemarketer rambled information about current interest rates and debt consolidation. "I'm on my way, be there in ten minutes."

"I'm sure that could've waited." Trish cocked her hip and lifted her chest, reminding Tucker of her best attributes. "There was a time we would make good use of ten minutes."

"You should want more than a fast grope, Trish."

"You don't have to be mean." Her lips pushed into a full pout.

"You aren't taking subtle." Tucker scrubbed his hands over his face. "I tried to be nice the other night. I'm sorry, but I just need you to accept my no, and go."

"Can't blame a girl for giving it one last shot." Trish relaxed her posture and smiled with genuine understanding. "I know you love her, you always have." She closed the distance and offered her hand. "Friends?"

"Of course." Tucker hopped off the boat and gave her a hug then watched Trish's taillights disappear from the lot.

Lindy stepped from the shadows wrapped in a woven blanket from shoulders to shoes. Tucker drank in the sight of her strolling across the weathered wood. How often he dreamed of spending a day on the water and returning to find Lindy waiting for him.

"You going to send me away too?"

The wind lifted her hair and Tucker's heart began the inevitable tumble. "You shouldn't be here."

Lindy ignored his comment and stepped closer. "May I?"

Tucker's thoughts muddled as Lindy nimbly crossed from dock to deck. Despite his better judgment, he joined her. "I made a few upgrades since you were last on board."

Lindy poked her head inside the cozy cabin. "It's very nice."

Tucker moved behind the console, trying in vain to establish a thread of physical distance. "The bunks are small but…"

"I remember." Heat flooded her cheeks as desire swamped his eyes. Lindy lowered to the captain's chair. She took Tucker's hand and pressed it to her cheek. "Take me somewhere, Tucker."

He started the engine, tossed the lines, and left the channel.

They cruised along the shoreline to a stretch of beach where a band of ponies preferred to end their day. Foals frolicked in the tall grass and then disappeared into the thicket.

The motor silenced and the anchor entered the water with a splash.

In the stillness, the memory of the last time Lindy had been on Tucker's boat swam into focus. Tucker always believed they could have everything. She still wasn't sure.

Lindy kept her back to him. She gathered the blanket tightly around her shoulders and absorbed the fleeting display of loveliness painting the sky.

Tucker crossed the small deck.

The warmth from his body surrounded her. Lindy knew if he touched her right now, she'd take everything he was willing to give. "I've never meant to be careless with you, Tucker." Lindy faced him. "I owe you an apology. Several, in fact." The boat rocked with the shifting tide. "I always focused on what was coming next and worried over what may happen down the road."

"You dreamed big, Lindy." Tucker ran his hands over her arms.

"Yeah, well, my boldness often blinded me to influence and outcomes."

"It's the way we learn," he said softly.

"After Mom, after the funeral…" Lindy looked at her feet. "I knew what I was doing when I came to you. I knew it was unfair."

"Me too."

"You aren't going to let me apologize?"

"For that night?" Tucker framed her face with his hands. "Not ever." His lips cruised over hers.

Lindy allowed the tenderness to flood into her. She placed her hands on his chest and took a purposeful step back. "I can't think when you hold me."

The cool evening air swept in to fill the void. She snatched the blanket and wrapped her body in an attempt to replace the refuge of his presence.

Lindy stared over the water. "I don't understand how couples sustain a relationship. I watch Nina and Mike, Kate and Rudy, my friends Cal and Jane… I think it's a real possibility, I'm just not built for it." She stomped her foot when Tucker chuckled. "I'm being serious."

He held up his hands, clearing the way for her to continue.

"I'm not sure I'm capable. When I think of affection going south and bursting into a million pieces, I lose my nerve. I would never survive if you—"

"I've heard enough." Tucker scooped Lindy off her feet. "Stop squirming or we'll end up taking a midnight swim."

Lindy huffed as he carried her to the back of the boat and settled on the cushions.

"Your brain needs a break." Tucker kissed the top of her head. "What if you stopped trying to figure everything out? Look at the sky, nothing but stars to dream on."

Lindy adjusted the angle of her body and tipped her head back.

"Not so long ago I knew a girl who guarded her smile and protected herself fiercely. She reached for everything and dared anyone to slap her fingers. That girl became an amazing woman who discovered the strength to pursue what others would have believed impossible."

"I remember her." Lindy snuggled closer and rested her hand over his heart.

"What if, for just a moment, you take a spin among the stars?" Tucker covered her hand with his. "Catch one for us, Lindy. Any one you want."

The blanket fell from her shoulders as she sat up and surveyed the nuggets of promise winking against the night sky. She nibbled her bottom lip then reached high and captured the brightest speck between her fingertips.

Lindy lowered her arm and cradled the star against her chest. "Heavy little sucker," she said and settled across Tucker's lap.

He brushed the hair away from her face. "Then how 'bout we carry it together?"

Hayward scanned the email from Baxter.

Belinda was going to be displaying at some craft show the second weekend of May. Perhaps it was time he take a little vacation.

Chapter 60

Lindy clamped the lid of the pen between her teeth and pulled. The cap released with a pop. She drew another X on the calendar. "Eighteen days to go,"

The wave of interest and excitement for the Artist Expo had exceeded expectations. Nina and Celeste were handling the endless details. All Lindy had to do was show up. No fancy threads, no spiels or speeches required.

The kiln hummed as the temperature continued to climb. Inside were several new pieces sealed with a variety of original glazes. When added to her recovered inventory from the loft studio, Lindy would, as Celeste promised, be in good shape for her hometown debut.

Before starting the meticulous task of tidying her studio, Lindy surveyed the rack loaded with green-ware. In various stages of losing moisture, the pieces, once dry, would be enough for another full kiln load. There was no way around it, drying took time. She could try to cheat a few items in the kitchen oven, but rushing the process wasn't worth the gamble of having her work shatter during firing.

Lindy rinsed her glazing brushes and washed her hands. Her mind softened while she swept every inch of her workspace. Lulled by the bristle strokes across the concrete floor, she wasn't surprised to find herself thinking of Tucker.

Following their boat ride and in-the-moment dream session, Lindy and Tucker had continued to explore the weight of their star. They talked daily, met for walks and casual meals. She helped in the store and accompanied him to Ocean City to check on the progress of the renovation.

Each moment was a delicious, tension-riddled flirtation with the line in the sand.

Lindy checked the kiln's control panel. The firing cycle was nearly finished. Thoughts of maximum heat brought to mind her last friendly encounter with Tucker. She leaned against the counter, cued up the memory, and let it play.

They'd taken the paddleboards and spent an afternoon exploring the shallows between Assateague and Chincoteague. *Tucker pulled into Sea Surge to unload their gear. He set the brake then hunched over the steering wheel.*

Lindy unfastened her seatbelt and ran her hand over his back. "You okay?" Taut muscles rippled beneath her fingers. "If you want we can skip dinner and just go back to my place. I'm really not very hungry."

"I am." His eyes, hot and seeking, scorched hers. "You're safer in public."

Lindy squeaked in surprise as Tucker hauled her across the console, captured her mouth, and kissed her breathless.

"Whew." Lindy fanned herself. Her kiln's 1800 degrees was no match for Tucker Brandt.

The unit chirped, signaling the unhurried cool-down had begun. Lindy turned off the lights and engaged the studio's security system. She had just enough time for a hot bath before Nina arrived for Girl's Night.

It had been years since she and Nina spent an evening hanging and chatting until the wee hours. Although Nina informed Lindy the "wee hours" certainly weren't what they used to be.

Lindy dashed through the foyer and gripped the banister at the base of the stairs. The scent of lavender stopped her. Unease scaled her spine like an insect with multiple legs. Cautiously, she climbed to the second floor, scanning every shadow lurking in the narrow hall.

The door to the spare bedroom was ajar. Lindy's pulse raced as she approached and flipped on the light. Nothing was out of place, yet something was telling her to flee.

She rolled her shoulders and took a deep breath. "Get it togeth—"
A breeze lifted the curtain. Lindy stumbled and stubbed her toe on the

blanket chest at the foot of the bed. She cursed her over-active imagination and hobbled to her bedroom.

The cast iron doorstop, used to prop the closet door, was lying on its side. Lindy swallowed her anxiety and grasped the knob. In one motion, she dove into the small space, pulled the chain, and shattered the dark with light.

"I will not be afraid in my own house," Lindy declared to the hollows.

Silence pressed against her confident affirmation like an unwelcome embrace. Lindy huffed, then marched to the security panel and engaged the system. Part of her hated the comfort the flashing red light provided, but a larger portion was grateful.

Lindy spun the faucet and adjusted the temperature. While the water poured, she balanced on the porcelain edge and dug through a basket of bath-bombs.

Jasmine, peppermint, or lemon/basil. "Decisions, decisions…" Lindy unwrapped the pale yellow ball and tossed it into the belly of the tub. Humid, aromatic air punched through her worry. She stripped her clothing and sank into the deep warmth.

Thirty minutes later, pink and peaceful, Lindy rose from the cooling pool and rubbed her hair with a towel. She got dressed and went to the kitchen to finish making a pitcher of decaf iced tea. A knock on the back window startled her. Liquid sloshed over the counter and floor, splashing her sweatshirt and pants.

"Great." Lindy tossed tea towels atop the expanding pond and hurried to unlock the door for Nina. "Hi, come in. I just made a mess." She gathered the sopping towels and threw them into the sink.

"Is everything okay? You're shaking."

"When I came in from the studio, the house felt off." Lindy pulled her sweatshirt over her head. "I thought I smelled lavender upstairs. Hayward insisted we run a diffuser for twenty minutes before bed for quality rest," she explained. "I'll despise the scent for the rest of my life."

"Understandable."

"My imagination took over…" Lindy shrugged.

"Is your code a number he'd guess?"

"I don't think so."

"Is it 5309?" Nina recited the code Lindy had always used for everything.

"No, it's 9035. I reversed it, smarty."

Simple enough for anyone who knew Lindy well enough. "How about we change it anyway?"

"I can barely remember my own phone number."

"Who knows anyone's number these days? Electronic contact lists are dulling our wits." Nina walked to the security panel and started the reprogramming sequence.

"How do you know what you're doing?"

"Zak installed the same unit at the B&B." Nina faced Lindy. "Now let's create a new code, something fresh."

Lindy's brow furrowed. "I'm only going to forget it."

"How about something old then? What was my home telephone number when we were kids?" Nina grinned when Lindy rattled off the digits. "Impressive, your wits are clearly intact. Want me to change the studio code too?"

"I'd rather change my clothes and eat ice cream."

Nina balanced the bowl on her growing belly. "Built-in table," she laughed. "Jealous? I've popped so early this time, but the doctor assures me everything's right on schedule."

"More than halfway already." Lindy handed Nina a napkin. "Any inkling of gender?"

"I'm thinking pink, but another boy would be perfect too." Nina scanned the basket of movies Lindy had selected. "Interesting choices... action, horror, and documentaries. Where are the sappy romance and fun-loving chick flicks?"

"You have enough lovey-dovey in real life and I'm drowning in unending courtship. It's making me edgy."

"Do tell."

Lindy laughed and shook her head.

"Come on." Nina wedged a pillow under her hip. "Give a girl with swollen ankles some juicy tidbits."

Nina listened intently as Lindy filled her in on the past two weeks. "So other than his brief loss of control after paddleboarding, Tucker's been determined to take things slow?"

"Understatement of the century," Lindy muttered. "His pace is dawdling, his patience excruciating. The man makes my head spin, reeling me in and winding me up. He drives me home, kisses me on the porch, then walks away whistling."

"Aww, he respects you."

"Well, I wish he'd knock it off."

"No, you don't," Nina laughed. "You can't be surprised that Tucker would move cautiously. He knows what being without you feels like."

"I'm not going anywhere."

Nina placed her bowl on the end table then laid her hand open on the cushion between them. "You may not have plans to leave, but do you have plans to stay?"

Lindy gripped Nina's hand and squeezed. "I'm not going anywhere."

"You do understand even Tucker is looking for after-ever."

Lindy wiggled uncomfortably. "At this rate we'll never get close to after anything."

"Then do something about it."

"Like what?"

"When does he get back from Ocean City?"

"Friday."

"Pizza night at Famous," Nina hummed wistfully. "Squeezed into the corner booth, vintage jukebox, loaded deep dish, good memories."

"Tucker and I spend too much time navigating the old days."

"So get your order to-go and make everything new. I'll give you the spare key to his place and you can ambush him."

"Bold," Lindy considered. "Unexpected." She grinned. "I like it."

Chapter 61

Fragrant hot bread and Italian spices greeted Lindy as she walked into Famous Pizza. The owner, Marco, winked then tossed a disc of dough into the air. The rapid spinning circle skipped across his knuckles and took flight a second time. His mustache tipped up at the corners. "I haven'ta loss my tooch, ah Lindee?"

"You certainly haven't."

Lindy placed her order, then wandered to the jukebox. The quarter disappeared through the slot and clinked as it dropped into the channel below. She selected the music of her mood and pushed the numbered buttons. Moments later, Pat Benatar's "We Belong" swelled into the dining room.

Fuzzy images accompanied the melody, guiding Lindy to the vacant corner booth. She slid across the re-upholstered bench and for once didn't shove the memories aside.

Nina squeezed close, giggling in girlish delight as Mike and Tucker refilled their fountain sodas. She whispered into Lindy's ear, projecting her future with Mike in elaborate detail then switched her focus to Lindy.

"You and Tucker will be the golden couple." Nina smiled, dreamily tracing a heart around the initials Tucker had carved into the wooden top. "He'll go to the Rose Bowl and the cameras will pan to you in the stadium cheering him on."

"Be serious," Lindy scoffed. "When I break free of this floating pile of sand the last thing I'll do is wave pom-poms."

"Not smart to run away from your after-ever."

When the song ended Lindy placed her hand on the shiny laminate tabletop. "Everything changes," she murmured. "That's how you arrive at whatever comes next."

What would be next for her? One way or another she'd find out tonight when she forged ahead and attempted to drag Tucker with her.

Marco carried her to-go order to the table. "We make-a update a few years ago. New seat, replacea de old scarred tops."

She flushed, knowing she'd been part of the damage. "Looks beautiful."

He tapped the bag. "Direction ina here to finish de pasta cook. I adda two salads an a sweet treat."

"Thank you, Marco." Lindy stood and opened her wallet.

"Keepa your doollars." He customarily kissed each of her cheeks. "Your beauty in-a my resturante' affa all deez years, is payment enough."

Lindy texted Zak to let him know she was on her way after a brief stop at the liquor store. She selected a simple wine and then snagged a bottle of Hornitos.

Nerves simmered as she crossed the island. She parked in the lot behind Sea Surge and looked at her loaded front seat. Cooler, overnight bag, and a basket Nina had packed with linens, fancy dishes, and candles. Lindy sighed, "So much for keeping things simple."

"Hey, sugar." Zak jogged down the stairs. "It's not too late to abandon your plan and profess your surreptitious love for me."

Lindy lifted the basket and cooler from the truck and handed them to Zak. "Never been a secret how I feel about you."

Zak scanned the contents of the basket. "Nice," he said recognizing the props of seduction. "This everything?"

"Yes," she blushed then raised the bottle of tequila. "For you, just a little thanks for letting me kick you out of your home for the night."

"Happy to help, plus you inspired me."

Lindy hooked her tote over her arm and followed him up the steps. "Inspired you how?"

"Called my City Girl." Zak's brows wiggled. "Sweet talked her into meeting me in Odessa." He opened the door. "I'm hitting the road in fifteen so if you want to stay, you can set things up the way you'd prefer."

"I have a few more things to do. If you wouldn't mind, just put the bag in the kitchen and the wine in the fridge." Lindy turned her back and looked toward the lighthouse. "What if dinner wasn't delicious or the wine wasn't... her mind swirled with worry and she started to doubt her bold move.

Zak deposited the bags inside then joined Lindy along the rail. "No time for second guessing, sweetheart." He draped his arm companionably around her shoulder. "Your plan is a good one."

"Still wouldn't hurt for you to wish me luck."

"You don't need any." Zak dropped a kiss on the crown of her head. "Tucker's due and so, my truest of true loves, are you."

Lindy delivered Boop to Kate and Rudy's then hurried home to drown any trace of apprehension in the shower. She wound the towel around her body and faced the steam-fogged mirror. There in the haze she confronted her truest concern.

What if Tucker was content with their friendship as it was? What if he didn't want to step into what came next?

Lindy dressed with more care than usual. She added simple jewelry before going downstairs to grab her sweater. "No turning back," she said and drove across town.

The key clicked and the lock gave way. Lindy walked into the living room of Tucker's home. Simple furnishings and a big screen television occupied the space. The art on the walls was diverse and the framed photos were Zak's.

Lindy recognized the low table in front of the leather couch. Cleverly shortened and modified it was the surfboard she'd ridden when she was sixteen. The fins pointed toward the floor and the polished top held an assortment of magazines and books. She ran her hand across the smooth epoxy and remembered the dolphins dancing beneath her.

The warm summer day had been important in many ways. It had marked the beginning of her friendship with Tucker and the ending of her relationship with her father.

Lindy walked to the surprisingly spacious kitchen and unpacked the cooler. She put the pasta in the oven to warm, plated the salads, and set them in the fridge beside the wine.

Beneath the table linens, Lindy discovered a package tied with a satin ribbon. She pulled the end of the bow and lifted the lid. Under a nest of teal tissue Lindy discovered a soft tank top and matching boy shorts.

She shook her head then sat the transparent ensemble aside and returned to the work at hand.

The tablecloth billowed then fell across the round oak table. Lindy centered the candles and laid the matchbook where she'd be certain to find it. The last item in the basket was a pastry box. Nina had drawn a heart on the corner and a note that said, *"Pastries are perfect for breakfast."*

"Subtle, Nina." Lindy smiled. "Very subtle."

She carried the treats to the breakfast nook and admired the view of the lighthouse. The box bobbled then skidded across the narrow table. Lindy blinked in an effort to clear her vision. Her fingertips fanned across the familiar wooden surface, tracing letters etched years before— *TB & LC.*

Chapter 62

Tucker sent Lindy a brief text before leaving Ocean City. He hoped the hour drive would shake loose the dregs of his rotten day.

The permit for the parking lot had been filed incorrectly. The warehouse delivered the wrong flooring and the new kid on the crew had broken a window on the second floor. Just as Tucker was going to string him from the rafters, Joel, his design contractor, arrived from Pennsylvania.

Joel immediately took charge and pledged to stay in town until the project's loose ends were tied up tight. A task, he assured Tucker, would take less than three weeks.

"I can survive three weeks." Tucker crossed the inlet and headed south. He longed for a cold beer and a hot shower and planned to indulge in both before he picked Lindy up for dinner.

Tucker pulled into the lot behind Sea Surge and was surprised to find Lindy's Toyota truck occupying Zak's space. He climbed from the cab and caught sight of her smiling from the top of the stairs.

Light danced over the delicate chain around her neck. Tucker's eyes followed the dangling links to where they vanished beneath the scooped neckline of her shirt.

Lindy descended the stairs and stopped one step from the bottom. "You've had a difficult day."

"It's improving," Tucker sighed as she ran her fingers through his shaggy hair. "I expected you to be busy in the studio."

Lindy rested her hand on his shoulders and tugged him close. "I'm not working tonight." She feathered the words over his lips, stirring layers of sweetness, then took his mouth and sank in.

The intensity washed through him, fueling the craze he worked constantly to restrain. Tucker gripped her hips and, with great effort, eased back. "You look beautiful. Did we have plans I forgot about?"

"We're having an urban picnic."

"A what?"

"A hearty meal, a movie." Lindy kissed him again to keep from adding *and hopefully more.* "Boop is having an overnight with Kate and Rudy, and Zak is on his way to Odessa to meet Celeste."

The information bumped around in Tucker's brain. "I really need a shower."

"And you'll have one." Lindy led him up the steps and gestured to his apartment. "We're staying here."

"We are?" Tucker walked inside and looked at the table set with flickering candles. It seemed the challenges of his day weren't over.

Lindy scrutinized his somber expression. "You want a beer for your shower?" She opened the refrigerator, popped the top, and offered it.

He tipped the chilled bottle and swallowed a hearty gulp. "Something smells really good."

"Food assist goes to Marco, and Nina helped with the pretty stuff. I just…" Lindy smoothed the linen tablecloth. "I invaded your house without invitation."

"Let's be clear about one thing." Tucker sat the bottle on the counter and crossed to her. "I welcome any raid that results with you in my home."

Lindy relaxed and turned toward him. "So you're okay?"

"Very."

She lifted on her toes and pressed an easy kiss to his lips. "Go get cleaned up." She patted his chest. "Dinner will be ready in twenty minutes."

Tucker escaped to the bathroom and braced his hands on the vanity. Having Lindy under his roof was a slippery slope.

He stripped his shirt over his head and tossed it in the hamper. *You can handle a romantic dinner. Candlelight isn't kryptonite after all.*

Tucker scowled. "And you're not Superman." He adjusted the water temperature to ice, gritted his teeth, and ducked beneath the spray.

Fifteen minutes later, Tucker stepped into the bedroom and discovered Lindy sitting in the center of his bed, scarcely covered in flimsy fabric. "I...ah..." He attempted to retain his failing equilibrium. "I thought we were..."

Lindy shifted to her knees. Her hair fell over one shoulder revealing the necklace which had teased him earlier. Again, he followed the length of chain until his eyes settled on the star pendant he'd given her years ago. "Dinner?"

"Pasta..." Lindy reached toward the towel fastened low on his hips, "...is easily reheated."

"I apologize in advance for my lack of finesse." The towel slid to the floor as Tucker stepped into her embrace. "I promise I'll make it up to you."

Chapter 63

Day was breaking over the lighthouse. Lindy skipped down the steps and climbed into her truck. She turned the ignition and replayed the events of her successful siege.

It was after midnight when she and Tucker stumbled from bed and reheated dinner. They'd eaten straight from the containers at the surf table in the living room. A matter of practicality, Tucker assured her as he tossed a blanket across the floor and served Lindy his luscious version of dessert.

"Clearly, it's my turn to drive home whistling."

Lindy pulled into the driveway. She couldn't wait to get into the studio and channel energy into the clay. The kiln was ready to empty. Celeste was arriving for the Artist Expo midweek, and Lindy wanted to have everything ready for her.

She lifted the date night basket from the front seat. She needed to call Nina. Although they hadn't used the dishes, the candles and lingerie had certainly come in handy.

Lindy jogged up the front steps and discovered a bouquet, tied simply with a piece of twine, leaning against the door. She buried her nose in the colorful faces and didn't even attempt to figure out how Tucker pulled off such a sweet surprise.

The card slipped from the petals and fluttered to the kitchen tile. Anxious to read the sentiment, Lindy bent and pinched the paper between her fingers. A shiver climbed her arm like a scaled boa and draped across her shoulders.

Anticipating your return. ~Hayward

Lindy gripped the counter. How dare he contaminate her home with his veiled offering?

She pivoted to the stove and turned the knob. A series of rapid clicks sparked the flame and the tip of the card caught fire. Lindy raised the paper and watched Hayward's name be overtaken by ash.

Lindy dropped the charred remains into the sink, turned the faucet on, and systematically fed stem after stem into the garbage disposal.

While her temper revved, Lindy unlocked her phone, swiped the screen, and engaged the call.

"Belinda darling, did you enjoy your flowers? Not what you deserve, but I imagine you're growing accustomed to settling for less in all manner of things."

"You've never had any idea what I value."

"I received your proposal to dissolve our alliance," Hayward rolled on. "Ill-advised to think so little of the terms of the contract you signed, not to mention the organizations you pretend to adore. The Foundation will take no pleasure stripping your credibility."

"I think…"

"Darling," Hayward interrupted, "thinking has never been your forte. Enjoy your flowers and what remains of your little trip."

The phone went silent.

Chapter 64

Celeste arrived at Lindy's early Wednesday morning. She'd brought chocolate croissants from Lindy's favorite New York bakery along with the final pieces of green-ware the academy had safeguarded.

They sat side by side on the dock nibbling and sipping as the sun climbed into the day.

"I could hardly wait to return to your little slice of heaven." Celeste smiled over her mug.

"I'm sure the fact that my paradise comes with a side of Zak doesn't hurt," Lindy laughed.

"The man is certainly a quality draw. Did your evening with Tucker go as well as I hope?"

Lindy blushed. "It did."

"Superb news. Speaking of splendid news, the tickets for Majestic are selling fast."

Lindy placed her mug on the planks and turned up the hem on her pants until the fabric reached her knees. She reclined into the Adirondack chair and closed her eyes, absorbing the warmth.

Celeste followed suit, gathering the bottom of her skirt and wrapping it around her thighs. "Also the buzz surrounding your hometown launch has reached the city."

"Is that news complicating matters?"

"Not as far as I'm aware." Celeste tipped her head to the sky and embraced the flood of vitamin C. She filled Lindy in on their plight to separate Belinda Cole from the Livingston Foundation and assured her a resolution would be reached soon. "Honestly Lindy, I feel you have many allies within the Foundation that surpass the Livingston bloodline."

Lindy kept the flower delivery and her conversation with Hayward to herself. There was no reason to upset Celeste. "Even if that's true, it doesn't change my mind."

"Didn't expect it to, but I thought you should know."

"I owe you an apology." Lindy tipped her head to the side. "When we selected the date for the Mother's Day event I hadn't thought about Majestic being the following week."

"No worries, I'm always up for a challenge." Celeste smiled. "Especially one that makes you shine like the star you are."

"Regardless, I promised myself I would stop burdening you." Lindy rested her hand on Celeste's arm and squeezed. "I'll do better moving forward."

Lindy drew the razor blade through the seal and pushed the paper and bubble wrap aside. She lifted a large platter accented with scrollwork from the box. "Hello, dear one." Her finger traced the etched pattern she'd doodled on the flight home, after her first trip to Sedona.

The systematic unpack of her New York inventory took three days. Lindy's shelves were now loaded with dozens of forgotten children. She busied herself preparing the kiln, while Celeste worked to catalog her finished work.

"*LindyColton dot-com* is a masterpiece, if I do say so myself." Celeste closed her laptop. "The moment we 'go live,' all things Belinda Cole will seamlessly transfer to Lindy Colton."

"Excellent."

"I'd like to add a blog thread for your workshops. Give you an avenue to share success stories, and encouragement." Celeste pushed up from her chair and strolled toward the kiln. "Wow, that's a full load."

"Thanks to you," Lindy smiled.

"You should poke around and make sure you're comfortable navigating the site and the online store." Celeste pulled two pieces of fruit and a container of granola from a basket of snacks.

"You don't want me touching the website." Lindy bit a chunk from the Gala apple. "I'll mess things up for sure."

Celeste wandered among the framed photographs in Lindy's studio. "Why didn't I notice this before?" She pointed to the bold *Z* in the corner. "I've been trying to identify this artist for weeks."

Lindy lowered her gaze and filled her mouth again.

"You know who it is," Celeste said, her eyes narrowing. She tapped a finger to her lips considering. "You told me a friend had taken the shots for your portfolio."

Lindy saw the moment the clues dropped into place.

Celeste crossed her arms over her chest. "That clever, talented, gorgeous pirate." She snatched her purse from the stool and stalked toward the door.

Lindy winced. "Go easy on him."

"Not my nature."

Chapter 65

Robert Reed Park was bustling with activity. People had gathered well before the official opening to watch the craftsmen set up their displays. Overflow parking was arranged at the high school and shuttles were helping to manage the crowd.

Lindy wrapped a mug in tissue and placed it inside a brown paper bag. She handed the purchase to a woman from New Jersey.

"Another happy customer," Celeste clapped her hands.

"I wish there had been enough time to finish another kiln load."

"Leave people wanting," Celeste grinned. "The silent auction bids are climbing. We should easily meet Nina's goal for the women's program."

"That's wonderful," Lindy said. "Are the other vendors doing well?"

"They are. Have you seen the display at Hippie Chic?"

"I love her bracelets. Did you stop by the essential oil stand?"

"I did. They really offer a unique line of diffusers and blended scents."

"There truly is something for..." Lindy gathered her sweater closer and glanced toward the funnel cake cart. A man with dark glasses stood off to the side and appeared intently focused in her direction.

"What is it?" Celeste noticed Lindy's unease. "Is everything okay?"

"I'm fine." Lindy rearranged her display. "I just got a chill." The band struck up, and she jumped then laughed. "Good heavens, I startle so easily."

"How about I run things here and you take a stroll in the sunshine? Enjoy the Expo firsthand and see for yourself what's going on."

Local artists were positioned throughout the park and worked to capture the view. Lindy sipped fresh squeezed lemonade while she observed a man in a wide brimmed hat manipulating a pallet of watercolors. He toiled with incredible patience to duplicate a ship anchored in the distance. The picture, barely begun, was already stunning.

The breeze off the water teased the nape of Lindy's neck. A clutch of panic squeezed her belly. She scanned the crowd and jolted a second time when a child's scream pierced the day.

Tracking the sound, Lindy saw the inconsolable toddler in the arms of her mother, reaching in vain to catch the string of a red balloon. Her wails continued as the wind captured the colorful orb and carried it across the bay.

Lindy was halfway around the courtyard before the child's cries and the tension in her stomach faded. She spotted the display for Hippie Chic jewelry and decided to do a little shopping.

She stepped beneath the canopy and spied Tucker holding a group of silver bracelets in one hand and a heavy hammered bangle in the other. Lindy winked at the artist then stepped to his side. "Hey there." She kissed his cheek.

"Hi." He flushed and returned the items to the table. "Great day. Glad you're taking a break."

Lindy picked up the trio of narrow bracelets and put them on. She lowered her arm and shook her wrist, making the metal sing. "Just for a few more minutes. Celeste is covering for me." She slipped off the set and tried on a leather cuff.

Tucker watched as she repeated the sequence. "How do you choose one?"

"Well, we rarely pick just one." Lindy winked at the artist. "I'd be happy to explain in abbreviated, man-friendly terms, the process of selecting the perfect bangle."

Tucker rolled his eyes. "I know it's more than them being pretty, because they're all awesome."

The designer smiled.

"I think the piece has to suit the woman and what she wants to do while she's wearing it." Tucker lifted one bracelet and then another comparing and examining, then paused on a petite band with a flattened oval accent boasting a dragonfly with etched wings. "There was a time when the dragonfly would have been your pick, but now," he selected a wide hand-hammered band, "I think this one."

Lindy tried not to be charmed as Tucker took her wrist and slid the bracelet into place.

"Do the twisting thing and see where it falls." He waited a moment. "Pass your test?"

Lindy nodded and ran her fingers over the textured metal. "It's perfect."

Tucker paid then took her hand. "Ready to rejoin the festivities?"

"Aunt Lindy, Aunt Lindy." Eric raced across the lawn and launched his body into her open arms.

"Are you having fun?"

"The best fun. Hi Tucker, wanna see something cool?" Eric's legs collapsed into an awkward *W* as he sat on the grass. He rummaged in his bag and held up his sand art creation. "I shook it by accident, but it's still cool."

Tucker studied the swirling color. "Very cool."

"I think mistakes make the art more interesting." Lindy ruffled Eric's hair.

"That's what Mr. Cal said."

"Mr. Cal?"

"Yeah." Eric pointed over his shoulder. "He said he's a friend of yours from school. Is that true?"

Lindy's mouth dropped open as she spotted Cal and Jane strolling toward her wearing Chincoteague sweatshirts and broad smiles. "It is absolutely true." She pushed to her feet.

Cal grinned and gathered her close. "Couldn't let you keep this island all to yourself." He eased back and extended his hand. "Tucker, good to see you again."

"This is a surprise." Tucker clasped his hand.

"Where are you staying? How long are you here?" Lindy fumbled to make sense of her friend's presence. "I would have made arrangements or reservations, or done something. How did I not know you were coming?"

"Simple," Cal's laughter rolled, "we didn't tell you."

"We're on vacation." Jane buzzed a kiss over Lindy's cheek. "We booked for the week with Nina, of course. She called us the minute the date was confirmed."

Lindy was having trouble keeping up.

Jane lifted the bags at her fingertips. "Your event is outstanding. So many talents. How on earth did you pull this together in such a short time?"

"My three secret weapons, Celeste and Nina and Kate," Lindy smiled.

Cal boosted Eric to his hip. "Your mother would be bursting with pride today. She was so pleased with everything you did, but this event would have sent her over the moon."

"We need to keep moving, still have a few vendors to see." Jane admired the bracelet circling Lindy's wrist. "Beautiful."

"Hippie Chic, right here," Lindy inclined her head.

"I'll be there in a minute, my love." Cal jiggled Eric and made him giggle. "Jane and I are meeting Rudy and Kate for a late dinner at the Bayside Inn."

Lindy was still in shock. "Can I meet you later?"

"We'll see you tomorrow afternoon. Nina's organizing a family picnic."

"Oh… okay." Lindy gaped as her own personal rogue wave of happiness dissipated as quickly as they'd appeared.

In the shadow of the crab shack, Hayward clenched his fingers into a tight fist. *Jumpy little mouse, you probably think you look eccentric in your tattered jeans and ratty sweatshirt.*

After all he had done to provide for her. *Where's the gratitude? The respect?*

He'd show her, but not today, too many people underfoot.

Chapter 66

Lindy convinced Nina to shift the location of the backyard barbeque from the B&B to her house. While she gave Cal and Jane the grand tour, Kate decided to formally christen the kitchen by baking apple pie.

Celeste balanced on the stool at the end of the counter. She sipped a chilled glass of wine while scrawling dubious notes with the hope of duplicating Kate's technique. "Do you think I'll be able to do it?"

"Of course," Kate said as she added cinnamon and sugar to the cut apples.

"But you don't measure anything." Celeste frowned.

"Really?" Kate's brows lifted. "I guess you're right." Her laughter rippled through the room. "I assure you pie is the most forgiving baked dessert."

Nina and Mike turned up after Eric's nap. The youngster commandeered the swing set, officially dubbed Fort Lindy, and was actively defending the territory from all invaders, namely Zak.

Within the hour, Lindy's home smelled of comfort and love. Conversation floated on the breeze, and the afternoon passed in a blur of calories and conversation.

"Regretting inviting us all here?" Nina stacked the plates on the counter.

"The opposite actually." Lindy smiled as she rinsed and loaded the dishwasher. "I was wondering how I've gone so long without all of you."

Rudy and Kate ducked in, said their good nights, then retuned Cal and Jane to the bed and breakfast.

"You mind if I settle Eric into the spare room?"

"Not at all."

Nina carried the child down the hall. Boop followed to oversee the tuck-in ritual, then she jumped onto the bed and curled up tight beside him.

"You throw a pretty good party, Miss Colton." Tucker joined Lindy in the kitchen and wrapped his arms around her. "You seen Boop?"

"She's nestled herself in with Eric."

"The kid wore her out," he chuckled, then pressed a hand to his stomach. "Oh, I ate too much."

"Hard not to do when Kate's slicing pie," Lindy laughed.

They stood at the window and looked over the backyard. Celeste and Zak were on the dock, making the most of the sunset.

"I think she really may be falling for him," Lindy said quietly.

"That's good to hear 'cause Zak's jumped without a chute."

"You think?"

"No doubt."

"I wonder how they'll manage the distance and their differences. Relationships are so complicated."

Tucker turned and pulled her close. "They don't have to be."

Lindy met him halfway, then moaned as Tucker lifted her off her feet and pressed her against the cabinet.

"Fire in the kitchen," Mike whistled and opened the fridge. "We were going to have one more round, but say the word and we'll clear out."

"Word." Tucker hooked Lindy under the knees and began to stride from the room.

"Tucker," she laughed and swatted his shoulder.

"We'll be out in a minute," Tucker grumbled and returned her feet to the floor. He leaned his forehead against hers. "What you do to me."

Lindy placed her hand on the side of his face. "We have all night."

Tucker nipped her bottom lip then satisfied himself with one more ravaging tangle of tongues. "If our friends know what's best for them, they'll drink fast." He grabbed her hand and dragged her to the deck.

Solar lights flickered to life, casting a soft glow over the yard. Wood popped as smoke swirled from the chiminea's narrow stack and lifted toward the heavens.

"Hey, Tucker." Mike adjusted the pillows on the chaise to make Nina more comfortable. "How are the renovations of Sea Surge North coming along?"

"Joel has exceeded my expectations."

"The man's a wizard," Zak remarked. "I consulted him regarding your ridiculous project, Lindy. Should have some drawings to show you in a week or so."

"What ridiculous project?" Tucker asked.

"Just a little fantasy concept I have for the studio." She patted his leg. "I'll tell you about it later. Tell us more about the expansion."

"The end is finally in sight. I'm headed north first thing tomorrow. It's time to shake hands, sign papers, and begin hiring staff. We're shooting to have the soft opening by Memorial Day."

"Aggressive," Zak nodded. "Like it." He smiled sweetly as Celeste refilled her wine. "Hey there, gorgeous. Primo sky tonight." He tapped his thighs. "Reserved the best seat in the house for you."

Celeste settled across Zak's lap and rested her head against his shoulder. On cue, the clouds broke and framed the climbing super moon. "Looks like an enormous flashlight. I completely understand why people are drawn to celebrate her energy."

"Stick around, City Girl. Two more days and she'll be full. I'll take you on the boat and we can have our own energetic celebration." Zak hugged her close and whispered, "Clothing optional."

"As lovely as that sounds I have a previous engagement."

"Lucky for me, the cycle repeats." Zak nuzzled her neck. "What do you say to penciling me in for June?"

"It's a date."

"I like this settee," Nina said. "I've been looking for something similar for the B&B."

"I stumbled on it at the Kiwanis Club barn sale." Lindy draped a throw across her and Tucker's legs. "Zak hooked me up with the porch swings. Now all I'm missing is a mint-green metal glider with vinyl cushions."

"What a happy coincidence." Zak lifted his phone and cued up some pictures. "Whatcha think of this?" He passed Lindy the device.

"Looks just about right." Lindy tipped the screen so Tucker could see the images.

"Shameless opportunist," Tucker muttered.

"Figure after the success yesterday, your girl's got some fresh dough in her pocket." Zak set his phone aside.

"I still wish the other load had been ready for firing," Lindy said.

"Keep 'em wanting." Zak shot Lindy a wink.

"That's my line." Celeste bumped him with her elbow. "You'll have an eager crowd next year," she smiled at Lindy. "But I'm thinking, why wait? An indoor festival in October or November would be very well received."

"Oh yes." Nina sat up straight. "Kick off the holiday season. Let's meet tomorrow and brainstorm."

"Sorry, I'll be racing to deliver Lindy's featured piece to the city. Curtain rises on the media junket for Majestic in four days." Celeste's hand quickly covered her mouth.

"What's Majestic?" "Sounds fancy." "When's this?" everyone seemed to ask at once.

Lindy pushed up from the swing and added a small log to the fire. "It's just a fundraiser."

"Oooo," Nina clapped her hands. "Is it a formal party with tiny food and endless champagne? If yes, can I please, please, please, come with you?"

Lindy straightened and brushed the dirt off her hands. "I'm not attending in person, just sending a donation."

"Bummer," Nina whimpered. "I would have enjoyed an adventure before I'm bigger than a house."

Mike kissed her cheek. "Your idea of adventure is putting on fancy clothes and snagging dinner off moving silver trays?"

"Yeesssss."

Nina's wistful sigh made everyone laugh.

Long shadows from the swollen moon streaked the deck and ended beneath the glowing coals in the base of the bulbous chiminea.

Tucker's thumb traced lazy circles over Lindy's thigh. "If you want to go into the studio and work for a while, I'm happy to stretch out in the hammock and watch."

"Actually I had other plans for tonight's Flower Moon." Lindy left the swing, picked up her phone and adjusted the playlist.

The first notes of Richard Marx's "Right Here Waiting for You" joined the night. Tucker followed each movement as Lindy's hips began to sway back and forth like reeds in the wind. He cleared his throat as she returned to him. "I think the fire's gone out."

Mischief danced in Lindy's eyes. "Has it?" Her hair fell like a curtain as she bent and propped her hands on his knees. She savored the feathered touch of her lips against his, then took his hands and pulled.

Tucker claimed her mouth on the way to his feet then aligned his body with hers.

Lindy rested her cheek over Tucker's heart. The steady rhythm synced with hers and they moved together, as they always had, easily, effortlessly.

Clouds drifted and dimmed the lunar light. The song ended and sounds from the island filled the space. Lindy caressed Tucker's shoulders then allowed her fingers to travel over his arms.

She turned inside the circle of his embrace and pressed against him. Tucker's hands drifted from her waist to halt her teasing hips. He gathered her hair and feasted on the line of flesh at the base of her neck.

The tone of their dance shifted. Bodies entwined and mouths fused, they staggered toward the house.

Lindy's sweatshirt whooshed up and over her head. They stumbled inside. Shoes rebounded off furnishings and scattered across the kitchen tile.

Tucker strained for control as Lindy's fingers worked the line of buttons securing his shirt.

"Too... many... clothes." Urgent kisses punctuated each word. She cried out in victory as the fabric splayed wide and she found flesh.

Tucker gripped the back of her thighs, boosted her body and pinned her against the front door.

Lindy locked her legs around his waist and sighed as his weight held her firmly in place. Triumph gleamed in her eyes. She lifted her arms over her head and her camisole took flight. "Upstairs," she panted.

Tucker nearly missed the bottom step when her hands skimmed low over his belly. "I may kill us first."

Amusement bubbled. "At least we'll die happy."

Tucker smothered her laughter with a smoldering kiss then carried her safely to the second floor. He released her legs and gripped the railing as Lindy's busy fingers fumbled the button at his waist.

His jeans were the next casualty of their unyielding impatience. Tucker stepped free of the denim and watched Lindy strip away the last remaining barriers between them.

She stood radiantly in front of him.

Tucker trembled. He thought he'd fallen before. He'd been wrong.

Words formed in his heart and traveled to his tongue. To thwart any threat of spoiling the moment, Tucker pulled her into his arms and covered her mouth with his.

He strode through the hall and turned into her room.

Eagerness and surrender merged as they toppled across the bed.

Chapter 67

Beyond the pane, morning prepared to counter the night. Boop whimpered softly.

Trapped beneath the delicious weight of Tucker's body, Lindy attempted to wiggle free and roll to her side. His voice, layered with sleep and satisfaction, tickled her ear.

"Where do you think you're going?"

"Boop needs to go outside."

"I'll take her." Tucker snagged her hip and drew her beneath him. "In a few minutes."

Lindy left Tucker in the shower humming under the hot spray. She pulled on a pair of yoga pants and a Fleetwood Mac tank top and stepped into the hallway.

A trail of discarded clothing littered the corridor. She lifted Tucker's shirt from the floor and hugged the soft fabric to her chest. Images of their passion dance washed over her. She threaded her arms into the sleeves then draped his jeans over the handrail where he'd be certain to find them.

Boop raced to the first floor and into the kitchen. Lindy followed close behind giggling as she unhooked her cami from the deadbolt. She collected errant shoes on the way, tossed them into the catch-all basket in the mudroom, and opened the back door.

Boop leapt onto the dew-soaked grass, paused briefly for relief then lifted her nose, examining the breeze. In a flash the pup raced toward the dock. The splash of her body shattering the bay's glossy surface echoed over the marsh.

Goosebumps shivered to life. Lindy hugged the oversized shirt close and stepped into the soft light of morning. Tucker's voice, rich and strong, carried from the upstairs window and married with the rising mist.

Lindy's heart was full. She knew it was greedy to want anything more, but she was hungry. She remembered the quiche Nina had given her in the freezer.

While the oven heated, Lindy measured coffee into the French press. The kettle screamed. Water infused the dark grounds and the fragrant, caffeinated, siren's call filled the kitchen.

Boop's sharp bark cut the peaceful air. Her tone was one of warning not welcome. Lindy fumbled to close a few buttons of Tucker's shirt and slid on her sneakers and rushed outside.

Lindy's wail of distress pierced the breaking day.

Tucker dragged his jeans over his hips, bounded downstairs, and sprinted to her studio.

Her beautiful workspace had been ransacked. Puddles of glaze streamed from toppled buckets. Broken tools and shards of pottery littered the floor.

Tucker cradled two jagged halves of what he supposed was once a vase. "Someone did this on purpose."

Not someone, Lindy thought. *Hayward*. She took the sharp fragments from Tucker's hands and laid them aside.

"How'd they bypass the security?"

"I probably forgot to set it." Lindy rested her cheek against Tucker's bare chest and allowed her eyes to fully survey the damage. She had swept up brokenness all her life and knew wreckage could be cleared.

His arms banded around her. "I'll go call the police."

"No, it's done." Lindy stepped away. "I need a minute, if you don't mind."

"I'm going to help."

"You need shoes," she said quickly. "I don't want Boop to get hurt. Would you take her in the house and check her paws for cuts?" Lindy knelt and sifted a handful of dust through trembling fingers. "The first-aid kit is under the kitchen sink with the towels I use to dry her."

Heartache threatened to strangle him. "Lindy, I—"

"Please, Tucker." Her breath hitched. "Just a minute."

"Of course." Tucker hooked Boop by the collar. "Whatever you need."

Tucker backed out of the studio. He checked Boop's paws thoroughly before entering the house and was relieved to discover her unharmed.

In addition to the towels, he found a heavy wire basket filled with treats and plush squeaky toys, designed to make Boop feel at home. He swaddled her and vigorously buffed the bay from her coat then tossed her a treat.

Tucker returned the bin to the cupboard and stared across the backyard. As he washed and dried his hands, the current of sorrow coursing through him changed to anger.

Hayward had made a grave miscalculation. It was time he understood Lindy wasn't standing alone.

Lindy wandered through the debris and allowed her feelings to swell. Hot tears spilled over her cheeks and fell in fat droplets to her shirt.

The door to the damp box was open. Reduced to rubble, the green-ware would have offered little resistance to pressure and crushed with barely a pop.

Misery expanded as she discovered her own baseball bat, silenced with an apron, resting atop the gravel remains of her bisque-ware. The antique rack bore splintered scars from repeated impact.

Lindy tiptoed through the spoils to retrieve cleanup cloths and a plastic tarp from the storage closet. She laid the stack on her painted dresser and kneeled to roll up the twister canvas. Gratefully intact and unharmed, she dragged both away from the sea of swirling color.

All in all, it could have been much worse.

She exchanged Tucker's tear-dampened shirt for canvas coveralls, crossed to the doorway, and unfolded the tarp.

"One step at a time." Lindy took a deep breath, blew her nose, and turned on her music.

The acoustic guitar carried her through the first chore—stacking the glazing buckets inside one another. Next, she layered a dozen rags over the muck then stepped away to give them time to absorb.

Lindy carried a clean bin to the damp box, cupped her hands, and scooped the pebbled, unfired clay from the wire racks. She shifted the salvage tub to her hip and moved to the fractured baker's rack.

Stones gathered in her stomach. Even though Lindy knew it was impossible to reclaim what was destroyed, she lowered to the floor and began to sort her broken work into piles.

The sound of a car interrupted her task. Doors slammed and feet pounded. Lindy surged to her feet and grabbed the baseball bat.

Tucker caught Lindy as she bounded through the studio door. He released quickly and held up his palms. "I called Zak."

Lindy blew out a weary breath and turned her back. "That wasn't necessary." She preferred to keep the embarrassment to herself. "I'm capable of cleaning up the aftermath by my…"

Celeste crashed into Tucker then stumbled into the room. "Oh, Lindy," her voice quivered with distress.

Zak crossed beyond the threshold. A vicious string of inventive profanity rebounded from the walls.

Lindy found Zak's outburst refreshing and surprisingly comforting.

"You call the police yet, sugar?"

"No." Lindy propped the bat in the corner. "We're not involving the police. There won't be any proof it was Hayward. Besides, he wouldn't dirty his hands."

"He's certainly behind it," Tucker said.

"Probably, but I don't have the energy to counter Hayward's version of the truth, which would certainly be that I did it myself."

Celeste stepped to Zak's side, gripped his hand, and squeezed.

"How can we help?" they said at the same time.

Lindy opened her mouth to run them off, then faced her trio of champions and really looked. She wasn't alone, just like Tucker had always claimed. Tears began to rise for completely different reasons.

Lindy took the coffee she hadn't realized Tucker was holding and set the mug aside. "Thank you," she said and kissed him fully, then turned to Celeste and Zak. "Thank you for being here."

"Where else would we be?"

———∞———

Belinda's cries and blubbering had been music to Hayward's ears. Thanks to the backyard barbeque, he'd been in and out without anyone noticing.

If only he had more time. It would have felt good to shatter the entire lot. He would settle for damaging the soft sculptures and making a mess, for now.

He'd barely made a dent in what she owed him, and he planned to collect.

Chapter 68

They worked together half the day to put things right. Even with the damage cleared, the impact remained. Lindy understood the wounds of such nastiness accrued like loose coins in a handbag—out of sight and seemingly trivial, but accumulating with burdensome weight.

Celeste insisted Lindy take a break and a long hot bath. Lindy set her coffee within reach then sank to her chin. She willed the steam to eliminate the lingering violation to her home and spirit.

Her thoughts drifted to her mother.

Throughout childhood Lindy had seen the injuries of mistreatment erased like chalk on a slate slab. She'd observed the effort required to shed the powdery residue in order to rebuild strength and confidence.

"You're stronger than you know," her mother's voice whispered. *"Face it, finish it."*

Lindy pulled on fresh clothing and stretched across the bed. The dream arrived like a powerful storm.

Shards of pottery propelled into flight and sliced her flesh. The next crushing blow cast her to her knees. The heels of posh polished shoes clicked against the studio floor. Through tear-laden lashes she pleaded, but his expression remained aloof and superior.

The scene twisted and Lindy was seated at her wheel.

A gruesome mix of blood and clay dripped over her wrists. Darkness stalked the hollows of the room like a ravenous predator. The steady thump of a baseball bat kept pace as it prowled. Teasing and taunting, her father stepped from the shadows. The form at her fingertips collapsed. "Think you're something special?" Frank's howling laughter flooded the room. "You're not, you're nothing."

The strength Lindy had forgotten lived inside her flickered to life. The spark penetrated her horror and shoved back the murk.

Lindy's hands were suddenly clean, her skin unblemished. She stood toe to toe with Frank and saw him for what he was—a tired, bitter man. The bat slipped from his grip and clamored to the floor. The features of Frank's face distorted, reshaped, and became Hayward's. His practiced smirk and arrogant posture dominated the center of her studio but failed to incite a scrap of worry.

She saw Hayward clearly. A bully underneath layers of shine.

"Face it, finish it." Her mother's voice ignited and caught fire. "You are stronger than you know."

Delicious scents entwined with light-hearted chatter and chased away her dream. Lindy wakened slowly. She followed her nose, and noise, to the kitchen and found Kate, Jane and Nina preparing a feast.

"What are you three doing?" Lindy circled the island and placed her mug in the sink.

"I should think it's obvious." Jane dumped chunks of pineapple into a large glass bowl.

"We're having an old-fashioned brunch." Nina gestured broadly. "I heated the quiche you set out to defrost, added some broasted chicken, cut fruit, and a selection of pastries."

"Good grief, that's enough food for an army."

"No fussin'." Kate tapped the spoon on the stainless vat. "Come here, sweet girl." She turned from the stove and opened her arms. "Nasty business you faced this morning."

Lindy walked into her embrace. "I didn't face it alone."

"And isn't that a lovely thing?"

Lindy felt her sorrow begin to fade as the group gathered around the table. While she'd rested, her band of able-bodied allies had grown. Mike, Cal and Rudy had mopped the remaining spilled glaze and rolled the first coat of slate-colored paint over the stained concrete.

The leisurely meal and casual conversation filled Lindy as much as the scrumptious food.

Jane and Kate shooed everyone outside. The warm spring day seduced them to the water's edge. Tucker convinced Lindy to show off her floating yoga skills. It didn't take much coaxing for Zak to hop on the paddleboard and give it a try.

They laughed as he struggled to balance on liquid glass. They rooted for him as he persisted, then cheered as he successfully moved through a progression of warrior postures.

The comrades celebrated with high-fives and fist bumps. Additional attempts led to further baptisms. Ultimately, stamina and sunlight waned and the bulk of the forces headed home.

Lindy stood by the open studio door.

Celeste joined her and offered a glass of wine. "Aside from the empty shelves and lingering paint fumes, it's almost like it never happened."

Lindy lifted a shoulder and let it fall. "I'm sorry this morning's commotion delayed your return to New York. I know you have many things to finalize for Majestic. I've cost you valuable time."

"Rest easy. Forty-eight hours is all I need. Besides," Celeste grinned, "if I had gone back I would have missed seeing Zak wave his arms in vain before dumping into the cold bay."

"True."

Celeste leaned against the door frame. "I heard rumors that Hayward's pristine image was cracking. His endorsements are falling through and the Livingston Foundation has put him on probation."

"None of my concern what people whisper about."

"No, but I should have warned you he was becoming more unstable." Celeste's eyes filled. "I've known for years what he was capable of... known and done nothing."

Lindy turned off the lights and secured the door. "You are not responsible."

"Maybe not for today." Celeste rested her hand on Lindy's arm. "I've done something, and hope with all my heart it won't damage our friendship."

"You have my attention."

"The night you borrowed my car and left the city," Celeste swallowed. "I called in a favor and secured copies of the surveillance video from the parking garage."

"Leverage is power," Lindy mumbled. "Go on."

"I also tracked down the fraternity brothers who came to your aid and procured official statements, discreetly," Celeste added quickly to soften the blow.

"I'm sure that made for interesting reading," Lindy scoffed and walked to the end of the dock.

Celeste hurried after her. "I violated your privacy, and I'm sorry."

"You didn't." Lindy sat with a thud then motioned to the other chair. "You were smart, Celeste, very smart. I wish I had thought of it."

Relief coursed through Celeste. "If the time comes when you need to add weight to your word, or push back against Hayward..."

"I'll have the means to shove hard." Lindy rested her hand on Celeste's arm. "I hope it doesn't come to that."

"Me too."

"Thanks Celeste, for always doing what's in my best interest."

"Easiest part of my job," she smiled. "I love you."

Lindy frowned. "I have trouble with love."

Celeste's laughter erupted and echoed into the night. "Nothing could be further from the truth. You may have a problem with the undersized syllable, but you, my dear friend, know love." Lindy's baffled expression amused Celeste further. "This entire weekend has been a celebration of rallying love. If the word trips you, then come up with another way of saying it."

"Nina calls legendary love *after-ever*."

"After-ever? Like happily-ever-after but backwards?"

Lindy lifted her hands. "I guess."

Celeste smiled. "Has a nice ring to it."

Chapter 69

One movement... Lindy pressed her hands into the mat, inhaled, and arched her back to the soft blue sky. *One breath...* Air expelled slowly and her belly dipped toward the dock. *One movement...* She anchored her toes, tucked her hips, and lifted to down-dog. *One breath...* She flowed forward to plank, completing her exhale, and held.

Tucker savored the last of his coffee as he watched Lindy move through her morning yoga practice. The intricate display of power and flexibility ended when she wrapped a woven blanket around her shoulders and settled on the end of the dock.

He washed his mug, set his overnight bag by the door, and joined Lindy on the dew-soaked planks. "Your mom had a fondness for staring over the water."

"I've been thinking about her a lot lately." The wind chased ripples across the surface. "I can feel her with me when I sit here. I know that sounds crazy."

"Not really."

"What kind of woman do think she would have become, if she'd been given a chance to grow old?"

"I don't know." Tucker jammed his hands in his pockets.

Lindy mustered a cheerful tone and got to her feet. "You all set to make friends and hand out marketing information?"

Tucker hated the idea of leaving her alone in exchange for overpriced salads and weak iced tea. "I can reschedule."

"Don't be silly. Networking and community alliance are vital for small businesses." Lindy folded the blanket and placed it on the chair. "You've already missed a full day by holding my hand."

"I like holding your hand." Tucker snagged Lindy's wrist and pulled her against him. "Come with me." He kissed her tenderly.

"Tempting." She kissed him back. "And mildly unfair." Lindy rolled up her mat and placed it under her arm. "I'll have no trouble filling my minutes. Boop will be an ideal distraction and studio companion."

"You sure?"

"More than sure. I have a ton of inventory to replace. Working will keep my mind off New York."

Tucker knew she was feeling bad about missing Majestic. He cradled her cheek. "We can still go, if you want to."

"No." Lindy smiled. "We're moving forward."

Boop barked and ran toward the driveway.

"That'll be Kate," Tucker said. "She texted to say she was bringing breakfast."

Lindy tried not to fuss. She didn't need company, she needed to work.

"Morning, sweet girl." Kate lifted the kettle from the stove. "Want honey and milk for your tea?"

"Sure." Lindy scanned the counter for the calories she knew accompanied a visit from Kate.

"Only cookies," Kate chuckled, "and they're already on the table." The spoon rattled in the cup. "Come sit with me and give me all the burdens you're pretending not to carry."

Lindy frowned but followed Kate to the windowed back porch.

"This is a lovely space. First time I'm seeing it in the morning." Kate sipped her tea. "Was this the first time Tucker was seeing it in the morning?"

Lindy blushed.

"Lovely and long overdue." Kate pulled an afghan over her legs. "Now tell me what's going on."

Lindy shook her head. Kate knew her too well. "A few weeks ago Hayward contacted me. He caught me completely off guard. I wasn't prepared to handle the conversation." She swirled her cooling tea. "Several days later, I found flowers on the porch. Arrogant bastard even signed the card. I was furious, reacted, and contacted him."

"I'm sure he appreciated getting a response," Kate commented and passed Lindy a peanut butter cookie.

"He most certainly did." She took a bite. "And then the studio." Lindy sighed. "I was uneasy a few times during the Artist Expo. Felt like someone was watching me but dismissed it. When Cal and Jane showed up, I fell into the joy of it all." She shrugged. "I'm sure my triumph was a jab to Hayward's fragile ego."

"You'll never apologize for embracing happiness, or celebrating your accomplishments again," Kate said sternly.

"Yes, ma'am."

"Hayward is a sad, small man." Kate sat her empty cup on the side table. "What's your plan?"

"I hoped to avoid making one." Lindy gave a half-hearted shrug. "I wanted to believe Hayward would get the hint and just go on with his life."

"Your mother wished Frank would stay away too," Kate said quietly. "I watched Susie heal and regain her strength. When the time came for her to face him, she was ready. What was it she used to say?"

"Face it, finish it," Lindy whispered.

"Yes…" Wistful and watery, Kate patted a trailing tear. "Face it, finish it… that's precisely it. Oh Susie, how I miss you."

"I dreamed about her after the mess in the studio." Lindy passed Kate a tissue. "She said those exact words to me."

"How lovely and encouraging." Kate gathered the dishes. "You are stronger than you know, Lindy girl. When the time comes, you'll be ready too."

Kate discussed her plans to revive Lindy's landscaping, then spent the day puttering in the yard. She tugged weeds around the house and turned dirt in the raised garden beds. Her husband, Rudy, arrived an hour later with mushroom soil and vegetable plants.

Through the studio window Lindy watched the pair. Elbow deep in earth, they worked to nestle young tomato plants and place wire cages to support future growth.

Kate and Rudy sweet-talked Lindy to the deck for a late lunch. Afterward, they gave her a tour of her updated garden. The fresh produce would be a welcome gift to her table come July, provided she kept the plants alive and thriving 'til then.

Lindy enjoyed a peaceful evening working in the studio. Boop snored beneath the hammock, occasionally twitching in response to a dreamland adventure.

Tuesday and Wednesday passed much in the same manner. Visitors showed up often and unannounced.

Zak had persuaded Lindy to take a break to paddleboard on the bay, and then he commandeered the hammock for an indulgent nap.

Nina popped in as Lindy was cutting and weighing six hunks of clay. She was delighted to learn the mounds were to become signature mugs for the B&B. She sat on the chair and leafed through a magazine while Lindy worked.

Later that evening, Mike brought pizza and played with Eric in the yard. Lindy knew she was being tended, but she didn't care.

Even with the interruptions, Lindy had two very productive days. Her shelves were filled with simple and complex shapes. In the damp box several pieces awaited further attention. In the days ahead, she would add cambered handles and whittled texture, infusing her imagination to make each distinctive, and implicitly Lindy Colton.

"Hey, doggie." Lindy stretched to loosen her back. "You want to go outside for a few minutes? Wanna play fetch?"

Boop galloped across the yard, snatched the tennis ball from the grass, and returned to drop it at Lindy's feet.

"You speak English?" Lindy laughed as Boop reared up and bathed her face. She tossed the ball until Boop's legs grew weary, then she took her inside for a cool drink and a bowl of kibble.

While her own dinner heated, Lindy called Nina. Her friend had been to see the obstetrician, and was excited to report all sorts of detailed information, most of which made no sense.

"So, in summary, you're cooking on schedule, the tech could see what brand of human you're housing, but you asked them not to say."

"That's right," Nina laughed. "Gender is one of the only true surprises left in the world."

"I guess you're right." Lindy tidied the kitchen, made a cup of tea, then returned to the studio.

Lindy worked long after the moon claimed the sky. Mud streaked her forearms and splattered the apron covering her thighs. Tired in the most delicious way, she flipped the switch cutting the power to the wheel.

She hung up her protective clothing and washed her skin clean. The next gaping yawn drained the final energy from her body. Lindy staggered across the room, grabbed a cotton throw, and stretched across the canvas mat.

Boop shifted, aligned with Lindy, and then they both fell soundly to sleep.

Chapter 70

A low rumbling sounded beneath Lindy's ear. "Shh," she rubbed Boop's side and squinted at the security panel. The red light shone brightly. "It's just a boat. We're okay." She reached for her phone.

Boop surged to her feet. Her muzzle quivered then drew back exposing white teeth. She lowered her head and released a long, steady growl.

Lindy squealed when her phone vibrated against her palm. "Hello," she said sharply.

"You okay?" Tucker's warm laughter filled her ear. "Sorry to call so early. I hope Boop isn't giving you trouble."

Sensing her master, Boop's demeanor instantly softened.

"She's fine," Lindy yawned. "I'm fine too." She rolled her head from side to side, releasing the stiffness from her neck. "We slept on the concrete floor."

"The hammock would have been a better choice."

"No question." Lindy looked out the window and spotted a Great Blue Heron proudly perched on the end of her dock. She disengaged the alarm and opened the door.

Boop barreled full speed toward the stately creature. Six feet of feathered muscle unfurled, propelled into flight, and cruised above the water in search of a roost with a less bothersome neighbor.

A tremendous splash shattered the peaceful morning, as Boop's pursuit went airborne with much less success.

"Did you hear that?" Lindy laughed.

"Hard to keep a Chessie out of the water. You may want to confine her to the porch until she dries fully."

"Nonsense. After her swim I'm going to give her a spa treatment instead."

"She'll never want to come home if you spoil her like that."

"All girls love to be pampered now and again. How's the networking coming along?"

Tucker grumbled. "The interviews for Sea Surge are more fun. I have the final one this morning, a candidate for manager. If she's half as good as her resume claims, I'll hire her on the spot."

"That sounds promising."

"Fingers crossed. I need to drop by my parents' before I head out of town. I'll be back by lunch or slightly after."

"How do you feel about takeout from Woody's?"

"Pulled smoked pork, corn fritters… music to my ears. I'll shoot you a text when I'm on my way."

"Perfect."

Lindy snapped a few pictures then ran inside to grab towels while Boop finished her swim.

Her phone rang again. She scanned the caller ID. "Hi Celeste, everything going alright with the setup?"

"Better than alright." Celeste must have stepped away from the commotion as the background noise dwindled. "I wanted to share the good news… Majestic has sold out. Every ticket! Three hundred for dinner, plus fifty standing passes for cocktail hour only."

"That's wonderful." Lindy pulled a large bath sheet from under the sink. "Almost erases my guilt for not being there in person. Tell me quickly. What's the fallout over my nonappearance?"

"Zilch." Celeste paused. "Sadness of course, because the board members adore you."

"That's nice to hear but…"

"You aren't interested in anything beyond tonight," Celeste completed her sentence. "Understood. I bumped into Hayward yesterday. The spin he's putting on your absence is well…"

"I don't want to hear Hayward's concocted story," Lindy said. "You are my representative, Celeste. I trust you to speak and act as you always have, in my best interest."

"You should know, I wasn't as eloquent as I'd hoped to be."

"Passionate truth is still the truth." Lindy could feel Celeste's worry vibrating in the silence.

"I do, and okay." Celeste covered the phone and called out instructions to someone onsite. "I'm needed. Time to go and make everything fabulous. Bye."

Lindy gathered the doggie towels from under the sink. Her phone rang again. "Hello."

"Belinda Colton? This is Raquel Martinez, *New York Post*. Any response to the comments made earlier today by Hayward Livingston regarding your breakdown?"

"My wha...? No comment." Within minutes Lindy had fourteen missed calls and a dozen emails. Even though she knew better, she opened her browser and scanned the statement Hayward had given.

We at the Livingston Foundation are saddened by the news that Belinda Cole will not attend the event she inspired. Talented individuals are often susceptible to debilitating self-criticism.

I am brokenhearted over the insecurity this may cause the children she's attempting to motivate. The Foundation will continue to do whatever we can to encourage their young hearts. I will immerse personally with the most gifted artists, to make certain they have the support needed to navigate the creative community successfully.

Lindy closed the screen and slid the device across the island. Hayward had certainly established the first word. Turmoil churned in the pit of her stomach. Could she rally and claim the last?

Lindy walked to the living room. Morning light was streaming through the panel of suspended glass. The hopeful channels of beaming color cheered her. She remembered how the Full Circle window inspired her when she'd returned to Chincoteague.

Face it, finish it. The words swirled in Lindy's heart. It was time to stand and face her bully. She hustled to the kitchen and dialed Celeste.

"Hi, sorry to interrupt. I need a favor and it's, as Kate would say, a doozy."

Celeste remained quiet while Lindy outlined her plan.

"So, what do you say, Celeste? Feel like finding the energy to pull a string or two?"

"I'm all over it. I'll let my doorman know to expect you. Text me when you arrive in the city."

"Okay, I'm not..." Lindy's mind went blank. "I don't know what to do next."

"Call Tucker, make arrangements for Boop, and get yourself to New York. I'll handle the rest. Safe trip. See you soon."

Rather than interrupt Tucker's interview, Lindy decided to collect Boop from the bay. The backyard was empty and the water was calm. She whistled, as she'd seen Tucker do when he called for her. "Boop. Come here, girl."

Muffled barking drew Lindy to the studio. "Boop?" She opened the door slowly and stepped inside. "Are you in here?"

A strong hand closed over her upper arm. "Hello, darling."

Chapter 71

Any natural response to fight or flee was extinguished in a wave of fear. Lindy stood paralyzed as Hayward moved beyond the shadow of the door.

"I've been waiting patiently for you to return to the city." He brushed the hair away from her face then leaned close and kissed her cheek.

She began to tremble.

"I've missed you too, darling." Hayward glanced toward the supply closet where Boop was barking frantically. His grip tightened. "Come along now." He forced Lindy out of the studio and towed her to the house. "Your holiday adventure has concluded."

Lindy's refusal took shape in the recesses of her mind but failed to float past her lips. She willed her wits to engage as Hayward's reasonable tone slithered along her spine.

"As much as I'd love to take the time to celebrate our reunion properly, people are expecting us." Hayward stepped inside her home and wrinkled his nose. "Much to my surprise, your little Majestic party has become the event of the season."

"I'm not going with you," Lindy whispered in a rush.

"Of course you are. We're needed for publicity photos." Hayward stroked her shoulder. "Leather, tsk-tsk, you've been neglecting your moisturizer." His fingers wrapped around her ponytail and tugged hard. The mass fell in a cascade around her shoulders. He wound a section of blonde around his index finger and frowned. "Good thing Madame T is expecting you."

Lindy's vision drifted to the security panel. If she could get to the alarm box, she could hit the panic button.

The tint of anger began to inch along the sides of Hayward's neck. "Belinda darling," his teasing tone dripped with warning. "Don't do anything foolish or I'll be forced to discipline you."

"This is my home." Lindy forced her chin high and braced for Hayward's wrath. "You're not welcome here."

He gripped her shoulder possessively and painfully. "This house will be sold, and these furnishings disposed of."

Lindy's knees buckled and she sank to the floor.

"I have photos of you and the island bum licking ice cream cones and licking each other." Hayward placed his foot on Lindy's inner thigh and pressed. "What sort of businessman plays in the water and operates a store from an old fisherman's shack? Ancient timbers, old wiring." He shook his head. "Misfortune is bound to occur. Accidents happen all the time, especially to careful types."

Lindy's dread doubled. She folded over her legs and stripped the bracelet Tucker bought her from her wrist. "I came here on a whim." She deposited the bangle under the end table and shifted to her knees. "It was foolish. Tucker means nothing."

"Of course, he's nothing." Hayward jerked her to her feet, then kissed the mark he had made on her skin.

"I'll go with you." Lindy bowed her head in compliance. "May I get my personal things from the bedroom?"

"You left everything of value at home."

Chapter 72

Tucker was riding high as he crossed the inlet and pulled into his parents' rental cottages.

He'd landed his manager. She was twenty-eight years old with a marketing and design degree. If her references checked out, she wanted the apartment and was eager to start immediately.

"Hey, Mom." Tucker hurried to meet her.

"I visited your building last week. Joel has certainly worked a small miracle in a short time."

"He has." Tucker hugged her. "I'm going to owe him a fat bonus."

"I think this is the tote you wanted. Not sure what you're looking for… it's mostly childhood things, yearbooks and photos."

Tucker snapped the lid open and spotted the beach towel parcel he hoped would be inside. Digging deeper, his hands skimmed a creased envelope. "It is. Thanks, I'm sorry to grab and go, but I'm meeting Lindy for lunch." He buzzed a kiss over her cheek and lifted the keepsakes to his hip.

"Mind your speed on the trip back." She patted his shoulder. "Your father and I were sorry to miss the Artist Expo last weekend. I'd like to plan a long visit soon, over the holiday weekend perhaps? Maybe you could speak to Lindy and we could have an unhurried dinner."

"That sounds great."

Tucker loaded the tote into the front seat and texted Lindy he was on his way. Halfway to Chincoteague he called and got her voicemail. She was probably in the studio. He could picture her leaning over the whirling wheel, clay at her fingertips, with the music turned up loud and Boop at her feet.

The image carried him through the next thirty minutes. He hopped from the Jeep and stretched to loosen the kinks from his spine. Tucker whistled for Boop and was slightly insulted when she didn't bolt around the corner to greet him. He tossed his bag on the porch and followed the walkway to the deck. Lindy's studio was dark and locked tight.

The door to the back porch was slightly ajar. Not wanting to startle her, Tucker announced himself as he entered and whistled again for Boop.

The house remained quiet.

Tucker dialed Lindy's number and waited. Seconds later he heard the phone ringing in the kitchen. He couldn't shake the feeling something was off. He dashed upstairs and systematically combed every room, but found nothing out of place. He pulled his phone from his pocket and called Zak. "Are Lindy and Boop with you?"

"No, what's up?"

"We were supposed to meet for lunch." Tucker hurried down the steps. "Her truck's in the driveway and the studio is locked. What's really weird, when I got here, the back door was standing open."

"Do you think she took Boop for a walk?"

"Maybe." Tucker ran a hand through his hair. "But her phone and backpack are too. Text me Celeste's number."

"On it." Zak hung up.

While Tucker stood in the kitchen waiting for Celeste's contact information, he noticed the sweatshirt Lindy habitually tossed over the chair hanging on the rack in the mudroom. Her shoe basket was empty and each pair was lined up in a tidy row beside the back door.

The hair on his neck stood tall. Tucker entered Celeste's number and waited for the call to connect. "Celeste, it's Tucker. Do you know where Lindy is?"

"On her way to me, of course. I expect she'll be in the city any minute now. Didn't she get in touch with you before she left?"

"No."

"That's odd."

A spectrum of light reflected across the wall. Tucker rushed into the living room and swept his hand beneath the table. His stomach plummeted as he gripped the bangle he'd given Lindy at the Expo. "He came for her, Celeste."

"Hang on, let's not get ahead of ourselves. I'm calling her now."

"Don't bother, her phone is here." Tucker strode from the house, crossed the deck and disengaged the studio security. The moment he entered Lindy's workspace Boop began to whimper. Tucker cursed and rushed to open the storage closet. Boop leapt into his arms. "I've got you." He rubbed his hands over her body. Then to Celeste he said, "He shut Boop in the closet, Celeste. That's not an accident."

"I agree." Celeste took a deep breath and tried to process the information.

"I'm calling the police."

"The police won't help us, Tucker, not yet."

"The hell they won't." Tucker pushed fear aside and followed Boop to the deck.

"Tucker, listen to me. I spoke with Lindy this morning. She decided to come to Majestic. She was going to call you and get on her way. I was to meet her at my apartment, I'm on my way there now. Give me fifteen minutes."

"Fifteen, not a second more."

Celeste parked the car and raced into her building. No Lindy. She tossed her purse and keys on the counter. "Come on, Celeste, think." She paced and worked it through. Majestic was set to start in seven hours. If Hayward did in fact have Lindy, it would be for appearances. She stopped abruptly. "Appearances."

As much as Celeste appreciated Lindy's new look, Belinda she was not. If Hayward was anything, it was habitual.

Celeste's fingers raced over the keys on her laptop. She opened the online booking link for the Madame T Salon, entered Lindy's password, and nearly cheered when the account unlocked. Following a brief series of clicks, Celeste had all the information she needed. She picked up her phone.

"Lindy is here, Tucker. In the city, that is. She's scheduled at the salon, a private suite for full treatment."

"I have no idea what any of that means. I'm calling the police."

"We won't need to involve them. This is my territory, and I have connections of my own."

Tucker sighed. "She could be in danger."

"Not while she's at the salon. You need to trust me, Tucker."

"I'm coming to New York."

"Good, come." Celeste knew she wouldn't be able to keep Tucker away. She opened a second tab and emailed her inside connection with the Livingston Foundation. "Bring Nina and Mike, Kate and Rudy, bring whomever... Lindy will need the support. Rally the troops and be at the airport in one hour."

"Airport?"

"Yes, Ocean City Municipal, on Route 611, in Berlin. I'll make all the arrangements and call you with the itinerary and final details."

"It's not a damn vacation, Celeste."

"You're absolutely right, Tucker. It's not a vacation, it's a liberation."

Chapter 73

"All ready for you, Ms. Cole," Gayle, the salon practitioner, led Lindy down the hall to the private styling suite. "We've got you scheduled for the works today. Massage, facial, full color and style. Mr. Livingston reserved four staff members and spared no expense."

"Sounds great." Lindy followed while she formulated a plan for escape. "Gayle, if I could use your..."

Hayward's security goon stepped into the hall.

"What's that?" Gayle asked.

"Nothing." Lindy dipped her head. "I'm just anxious to get started. I'm carrying a lot of stress these days."

"Don't you worry. I'll work out those knots." Gayle smiled. "Although I can't imagine why you're so tense. Surely you know by now, the event will be wonderful. Everything you've put your name behind has been a tremendous success."

Not my name. Lindy stepped into the room and acknowledged the additional staff. So many people... too many. She released her robe and stretched out on the heated table.

"What does your new artwork look like?" Gayle draped the sheet over Lindy's back. "I read how you were traveling to seek a new muse and expand your vision."

"My new pieces are..."

"Stunning to be sure, but one must've been very heavy. Your arm is marked from handling it."

Lindy had never been sure if Gayle was either incredibly dim or incredibly kind. After working on her body for years, she'd seen bruises in all matter of places, and never let on if she suspected anything other than Lindy's clumsiness.

Gayle brushed a mint-infused body mask over Lindy's entire body then covered her with hot towels. "Time for you to drift and snooze. I'll return in twenty minutes to finish with your body polish and cucumber aeration." The door clicked behind her.

Lindy knew this was her opportunity. She opened her eyes and nearly screamed in frustration. She was swaddled like a mummy and covered in goo. The current situation was not going to make for an easy escape. She rolled to her side and attempted to bend in half to get to a seated position.

"What type of overpriced body cast is this?"

It took a moment for Lindy to recognize the voice behind her. She burst into tears. "Help me, Celeste. We only have seventeen minutes."

"We have more than that. Gayle's playing for our team. Right now she's telling the receptionist you're going directly into the steam sauna for cellular detox." Celeste unwound the cloth binding her legs. She handed Lindy a hot towel. "Scrub your face and arms."

Lindy followed directions like a pleasing child. "How are we going to get out without Hayward's guard dog noticing?"

"A disguise, of course." Celeste pulled a maxi dress and long brunette wig from her tote. "Put these on."

Lindy trembled but obeyed.

"I'm going to go to the front desk and demand to see you." Celeste handed Lindy a tube of lipstick. "Madame T has strict rules assuring the privacy of the clientele so of course I will gain nothing except the attention of Hayward's man." Celeste laid an envelope in Lindy's hand. "Put this in your pocket. It's money and a key card."

"You're going to take the elevator to the lobby, walk straight out of this building, and hail a cab and go to the Archibolt Hotel." Celeste slid dark sunglasses over Lindy's nose. "Everything is written on the envelope. Are you hearing me?" Celeste asked gently. "I need you to answer."

"An envelope, the key, a cab to the Archibolt Hotel."

"Good." Celeste hugged her fiercely. "I'm right behind you, I promise."

"Celeste, I don't know if I can—"

"You can. Now, count to twenty, then go. Elevator, lobby, cab…" Celeste left the room.

Lindy's heart was pounding so loudly she could barely think. She took a deep breath and began counting.

…*sixteen…seventeen… You can do this.* Lindy pushed the tinted lenses tight against her eyes, forced her painted lips forward in a faux collagen-induced plump and opened the door.

"I'm her agent, that's why," Celeste barked at the receptionist. "I need to speak with Belinda regarding the event tonight. It's urgent."

Lindy watched as Hayward's henchman took a step toward the counter.

"I assure you once Ms. Cole's session is complete I will make her aware of your need to converse with her. If you are capable of remaining quiet, you are welcome to wait."

"Unacceptable," Celeste said. "I would like to speak to Madame T."

"I assure you the result will be no different. In fact, she may have you escorted from the building."

That was the last thing Lindy heard as the elevator door closed. She forced herself to remain calm as the chamber descended, then moved through the lobby to the open street.

Lindy hailed a cab and conveyed the hotel information to the driver. Fifteen minutes later the key card slipped into the lock and the light turned green.

Before she could reach for the handle the door flew open. Lindy was pulled into the room and thrust firmly against Tucker's chest.

"Thank goodness," he pulled the wig off her head and rained kisses over her face. "Are you okay? Did he hurt you?"

"Tucker?" The stress of the last several hours crashed over her. "Tucker," Lindy whispered again as her vision swam. She heard him curse a moment before the world went dark.

——————

"Explain yourselves," Hayward's wrath peppered the security team.

"She just vanished, sir." His harsh grunt echoed the firm strike from Hayward's hand.

The towering, muscled giant wobbled. "Don't speak unless you have something worthy of my ears."

"Ms. Cole's agent was demanding entry. The staff told Ms. Wilde she'd have to wait until after the appointment. They gave her a cappuccino, and an hour later Ms. Cole was gone."

"Find Belinda." Hayward crowded close. "Or I'll make sure you never work in this city again."

The men scurried from the room.

Hayward poured a generous portion of small-batch whiskey into a Harmonie Crystal tumbler. The caustic liquor warmed his tongue and heated his belly.

He should have anticipated Celeste's interference.

He gripped the decanter and refilled the heavy-bottomed glass. The exclusive liquor swirled rapidly, riding the walls of the tumbler, then trailed the glass in wide legs, and rejoined the pool.

Hayward refused to be outmaneuvered, and he'd be damned if he'd stand in the room alone. He picked up his phone.

"Sir," Baxter answered.

"Change of plan."

Chapter 74

"She's stirring," Celeste motioned to Tucker. "I'll start the bath, you get her some juice."

Muffled voices swirled around her. Lindy rolled to her side and encouraged her eyes to open. "Celeste?"

"Well, hello there." Celeste walked to the bedside. "Stay still a moment. Tucker is getting you some juice."

"Thanks for the rescue." Lindy propped on her elbow. "You're a miracle worker."

Celeste nipped a tear before it fell, then rested her hand against Lindy's cheek. "Your bath is nearly ready." She glanced over her shoulder as Tucker returned to the room. "I'll give you some privacy."

"Before you go, Celeste, would you contact someone who's not on Hayward's payroll? I want to file an official report."

"Already done. I've also arranged a private pre-press junket one hour before the doors open for Majestic. I figured you may want to refine your scripted statements in person."

"Good idea."

"There's one more thing." Celeste nibbled her lip. "I want you to be completely relaxed tonight, so I contracted private security to escort you to the hotel, and shadow you all evening. They're reputed to be as discreet as they are proficient. I know your impulse will be to reject immediately, but I'm going to beg you to let the idea marinade."

"Yes," Tucker spoke for the first time.

Lindy looked at Tucker's face, pale and lined with worry. "No marinade needed, Celeste. Thank you."

"Don't let the water get cold." Celeste quietly disappeared into the next suite.

"Adjoining rooms," Tucker said as the locks snapped in place. He passed Lindy the cup and tried his best to keep his hand steady. "Celeste is a clever girl. Even if Hayward finds her, he doesn't find you."

"Come here." Lindy patted the comforter. "Hey." She caught his wrist when he started to move away.

Tucker settled beside her. "Are you hungry?"

"Actually, I am." She sipped her juice. "But I need to get this stuff off my skin first."

Tucker lifted her and carried her to the bathroom. He was twice as strong as Hayward and infinitely more gentle.

Contrasts, Lindy thought as the tips of her toes touched the tile.

Tucker's arms banded around her. "I was so frightened."

Lindy rested her cheek against his chest. "Me too." She raised the hem of his Henley, found flesh, and held tight.

"That bathtub looks more like a swimming pool to me."

"Maybe you should stay and lifeguard?" Her fingers drifted to tease the waistline of his jeans.

"You're probably in shock," he said hoarsely. "Celeste is ordering some food. It'll be here any moment."

"Food isn't what I'm hungry for." Lindy pressed against him and sought his lips.

Tucker drank her in like a parched man, then regrettably stilled her busy fingers. "But food is what you need." He kissed her knuckles and stepped into the safety of the other room.

Lindy met the attorney and police representative in Celeste's suite. They recorded her statement and photographed the fresh bruising on her thigh and arm.

Celeste also gave a sworn declaration, and with Lindy's approval, furnished the footage from the parking garage.

After the officials left, Lindy stayed in Celeste's suite and tried to eat. She made it through half a sandwich before losing her appetite altogether.

Lindy walked to the window and tried to still her mind. She replayed the accounting of truth she'd shared, her truth. Hayward, if given the opportunity, would definitely paint the picture with different strokes.

"Want a bite of fruit?" Celeste asked.

Lindy tossed a chunk of pineapple into her mouth. "Mmm, maybe two bites."

"How about we put the first part of this day far behind us," Celeste glanced at the clock, "and get to work dolling you up?"

Lindy groaned. "I hate the fussy dress-up part."

"That's because you've never done it my way." Celeste rubbed her hands together. "I promise it'll be more fun than ever before."

"Don't make promises you can't keep."

"Oh, dear friend." Celeste strolled to the adjacent suite and placed her hand on the knob. "You must know by now, I always deliver."

Confusion and curiosity stirred. "How many rooms did you book?"

"Enough," Celeste winked.

The door opened and revealed Nina, Kate and Jane, wrapped neck to knees in hotel robes. They were sipping mimosas and being tended by a professional stylist.

Celeste guided a dumbstruck Lindy into the room.

"There she is," Jane said. "Lindy, look at my nails." She waved polished, hot-pink tips.

"Having the time of my life over here." Nina's hair had been teased and twirled into a complex wrap at the base of her neck. "Don't worry." She lifted her glass. "100% orange juice."

Kate turned slowly from the lighted mirror. Her lips quivered as she scanned Lindy from head to toe.

"No tears." Lindy crossed the room in two strides. "You'll spoil your makeup."

"Lashes can be fixed." She held and sniffed. "False lashes on these old eyes, can you believe it? Rudy will probably walk right by me."

Lindy allowed them to swarm. She answered each question and reassured every concern. Their overflowing love and support gave her the strength she needed to effectively turn the page.

"So…" Lindy balanced her hip on the arm of the chair. "It appears I'm not the only one who's had an interesting day. Fill me in."

"Celeste is our Fairy G-Queen," Nina gushed. "She arranged everything. We flew here on a private jet, ate lunch overlooking the city, and now we're getting primped and pampered. The guys are downtown getting hot shaves and meeting with a tailor."

Lindy glanced over her shoulder. "Fairy G-Queen?"

"If the stiletto fits." Celeste strolled to the closet. "Ladies, I know you've all brought dresses for this evening, however, I have one final Fairy G-Queen gift." With a grand flourish, the double doors swung wide and revealed a selection of gowns for them to consider.

Nina squealed in delight and dove toward the taffeta, silk and satin.

Chapter 75

Lindy stood before Tucker dressed in endless inches of shimmering midnight blue. He ached at the sight of her. "You are the most beautiful woman I have ever known."

"Celeste picked it out."

"And don't I have an eye for it?" Celeste held up two sets of jewelry for Lindy's inspection.

Lindy fastened the earrings while Celeste hooked the necklace.

Tucker caught her wrist. "I don't like the idea of you going alone, Lindy."

"Schmoozing the press is necessary." She brushed a soft kiss to his worried lips. "And remember, I won't be alone." She gestured to the sturdy gentlemen by the door. "Everything will be fine. I'll see you both in the lobby in an hour."

Tucker stepped into the hall and watched Lindy disappear into the elevator. "Tell me again why we aren't going with her?"

"Because I have one more piece to add to the game." Celeste opened her clutch and dropped her hotel key inside. "I hope you aren't one of those men who need hours to pull himself together."

"I'm not."

"Good," she patted Tucker's arm. "Get showered and put on your party pants. I'll be back in a jiffy."

Forty minutes later Celeste tapped on the door and entered the room wearing a column of fire red that would've stopped any man's heart.

Tucker let out a low whistle. "Zak's going to swallow his tongue."

"You think?" Celeste's laughter twinkled. "Maybe I'll send him a picture and see if I can entice him to join me for a pre-party cocktail." She stepped close and adjusted Tucker's tie. "Don't you make the mouth water. If Lindy didn't already love you…"

"I sure hope she does."

"She may struggle to wrap her tongue around the word, but don't you doubt it for a minute."

―――※※―――

Hayward looked down from the mezzanine and devoured the growing crowd. Angelique sipped champagne and babbled at his side. He indulged the view of her ample bosom while muttering an occasional response to maintain the illusion of conversation.

Baxter had yet to locate Belinda. She'd been absent for the media assembly and ignored her contractual obligation to present her donations for board approval. She wouldn't dare embarrass him further by showing up late for the Foundation's opening remarks.

Hayward's jaw clenched as he spotted Belinda moving to the center of the lobby. "They're about to open the doors, cupcake." He patted Angelique's bottom. "Why don't you run along and powder your nose? I want you to be perfect when we enter the ballroom together."

"Anything you want, lover," Angelique purred and hurried away.

Like an arrow seeking a target, Hayward moved swiftly to the elevator.

―――※※―――

The Majestic was ripe with activity. The media circus was unlike anything Tucker had ever witnessed. He climbed from the car and offered his hand to Celeste.

"Everyone's buzzing now, wondering who we are." Celeste flashed a killer smile and maneuvered through the throng. "Typically I keep a low profile but I figured our grand entrance would ruffle Hayward's feathers."

"Do we need to add fuel to this particular fire?" Tucker blinked as another round of flashes erupted.

"If Hayward's focus is on you and me, it's not on Lindy."

"I don't like it," Tucker said.

"I know," Celeste patted his arm. "We'll go inside, connect with our crew, and find our seats for dinner. Easy breezy."

"Nothing is ever as simple as it sounds," Tucker muttered.

"There," Celeste slanted her head to where Lindy was standing, then squeaked and held on as Tucker cut a path through the mass of people. "Slow down." She scurried to stay balanced. "In case you hadn't realized, I'm not wearing track shoes."

Lindy saw them coming. "Wow. You look like movie stars, all legs and glamour, all brooding and serious."

"Everything going okay?" Celeste asked.

"Better than." Lindy's phone vibrated. She glanced at the screen. "The gang has arrived. They're grabbing cocktails and heading to the table. Celeste, if you want to join Zak," she squeezed Tucker's arm, "we're good here."

"Just a quick hello. I'll be back in a flash. You want me to bring you a drink, Tucker?"

"No."

"Try to relax." Lindy pressed a kiss to Tucker's cheek. Shutters snapped capturing the intimate exchange.

"Belinda, darling." Hayward snared her elbow. "You look beautiful."

"She does, doesn't she?" Tucker drew Lindy even closer to his side.

Hayward had been so focused on the artist he'd failed to see her escort. A well-bred smile veiled his annoyance. "Mr. Brandt, nice of you to attend this evening."

"Stuff it, Hayward." Tucker angled his body and crowded close.

"No apologies for my interruption." Celeste joined the tense trio. "Lindy, I'm certain you remember Mrs. Kimberly Keyport."

"I do," Lindy beamed. "How lovely to see you again."

Kimberly enveloped her in a warm hug. "Jon and I were so honored by the invitation to join you for dinner."

"My pleasure." Lindy masked her surprise, and introduced Tucker.

"Celeste told me about your successful Artist's Expo last weekend. I wish I would have known. I've been dying to visit Chincoteague and also the vanishing island of Tangier."

"When you make your travel plans," Tucker said, "add Smith Isle to your list."

"Tucker," Celeste continued to transition the situation seamlessly. "Why don't you and Kimberly continue your conversation on the way to the table? I have this covered," she whispered sensing his refusal. "Lindy, the photographer is ready for you."

"Thank you, Celeste." Lindy squeezed Tucker's arm and nodded toward the personal security. "I'll join you in just a moment."

Hayward waited until the senator's wife was ushered away. "I believe what you meant to say, Celeste, is the photographer is ready for us. This is a Hayward Livingston Foundation event."

Celeste ignored Hayward's tantrum. "Will five minutes be enough time to conclude your business, Lindy?"

"Plenty." Lindy kept her protective detail in her peripheral as she walked to a small alcove along the wall.

Hayward snarled as he followed her. "*Conclude* our business?"

"Since I've returned your engagement ring, my obligation to spend any additional time maintaining this charade has ended. In the event you doubt my sincerity to sever all ties with you, and the Livingston Foundation, the documents your attorney received this afternoon will make everything quite clear."

Hayward crowded close. "How dare you address me with such disregard?"

"You should also be aware," Lindy didn't falter, "included with my statement regarding today's abduction—"

"Abduction," Hayward chuckled, "that's quite an embellishment of the facts. You seem to have developed a flair for the dramatic, Belinda. I merely arranged transportation to an event—your event, to be specific—and delivered you to the salon for a luxurious afternoon of pampering. A tradition clearly documented for several years, and a fact to which any member of the Madame T staff could attest."

"Versions of the truth," Lindy shrugged. "I expected as much, which is why a copy of the surveillance footage from the parking garage, taken the night I left you, was also furnished to the authorities."

Hayward's smug expression twisted.

Lindy continued to look directly into Hayward's eyes. "In cooperation with members of the Livingston Foundation's current board of directors, papers have been drafted to ban you from the premises this evening. I thought given the opportunity, you'd choose to see the big picture. The need to enforce the restraining order remains up to you. Stay and behave or…" she nodded to the security duo, "…be removed."

"You self-righteous bi—"

"Pardon me," a deep voice interrupted.

"Senator Keyport." Hayward morphed into a genteel politician. "I hear we have the great honor of dining with you and your lovely wife tonight."

The Senator ignored Hayward. "It's wonderful to see you again, Belin… pardon me, Lindy. Kimberly is looking forward to discussing the event Celeste mentioned. We can't thank you enough for lending your face to the domestic violence platform. Your support will triple awareness and change many lives."

"I'm delighted to help. Kimberly is already seated." Lindy motioned to Celeste. "Would you please accompany the Senator to our table? I'll be just another moment."

"Do-me-stic," Hayward stammered as the Senator moved off.

"Try not to make a scene, *darling*," Lindy cut off Hayward's sputtering.

"Who do you think you are, dictating to me?" Hayward's face reddened. "I'm a powerful man with influential connections and limitless resources. I will have the final word."

Lindy lifted her chin and waited. "I'm sorry, was that it?"

Hayward snared her elbow. "I will not come to a heel like a trained canine. Especially when told to by a woman so beneath me."

Lindy jerked her arm free. *Face it, Finish it.* "Take a moment, Hayward." The men stepped forward to bookend her. "Consider the big picture." She turned her back, dismissing him.

"Belinda."

Lindy continued walking. "There's no one here by that name."

Chapter 76

Lindy ducked into the bathroom, braced her hands on the counter, and started to laugh. The acoustic amplification tickled her even more. She'd faced him. Regardless of her churning belly and weak knees, she'd faced him.

"Belinda?" Angelique stepped toward the sink. "You're blonde."

Lindy's fit of giggles renewed. "Yes Angelique, I am, in fact, blonde."

"I hardly recognized you. Hayward told me you weren't attending tonight."

"Hayward has trouble discerning the truth." Lindy grabbed a tissue and tried to save her makeup.

"He also said you and he were no longer together."

"Now that is absolutely true." Lindy freshened her lip-gloss.

"You're being awfully insensitive." Angelique frowned. "Are you trying to hurt his feelings? You embarrassed him and had him fired from his very own board."

Lindy sighed. "And we're back to fiction." She picked up her clutch, and left the room.

Tucker was waiting in the hall. Lindy crossed to him in confident strides and gripped his lapel. "You should know, this intense, protective thing is working for me."

The potent punch of her kiss surged through him. Tucker reached for reason and regrettably broke the connection.

"I wish we could skip out right now." Lindy rubbed her thumb over his bottom lip, removing the transferred sheen. "I'd like to speak with the leaders of each of the art programs."

"Certainly."

"It's important they see me, the real me," she laughed as they wandered into the deserted atrium. "Hardly anyone has recognized me tonight. It's been refreshing to reclaim a small degree of privacy. Anyway, I'm not in the presentation lineup, so we don't have to linger after dinner."

Tucker stopped and wrapped his arms around her. "We'll stay as long as you want, and leave whenever you're ready." He lowered his mouth to hers and savored one final private moment before entering the ensuing hustle. "Ready?"

She lifted her shoulder. "Or not."

Lindy entered the ballroom and her jaw dropped. Her face, her real face, was everywhere, along with candid shots of her most recent pottery in a variety of settings.

She recognized the talent responsible for capturing her work immediately. "Zak." Lindy looked at Tucker. "Did you know?"

"That he was taking pictures? Yeah, but this?" Tucker was nearly as shocked as Lindy. "I had no idea."

"You have to admit, the scoundrel did a remarkable job." Celeste handed them each a glass of champagne.

"He sure did. How did you get the Livingston Board to go for this?" Lindy asked.

"I wasn't kidding when I told you many people are dedicated to your vision. But no business tonight." Celeste lowered her voice. "I'll tell you more next week. Tucker knows where we're sitting. I'll join you in a minute."

Zak tracked Celeste to the lobby. His artist's eye captured her figure in still frames as she navigated the posh furnishings in fitted silk and spike heels. He stayed out of sight until her conversation with the banquet coordinator ended, then made his move to intercept.

Celeste's smile bloomed. "There's my sharp dressed man." She ran her hands over his broad shoulders.

Zak gripped her hips. "I need to photograph you."

"You *need* to?" Celeste tossed her head back and laughed with delight.

"Yes, need." He crushed his mouth to hers.

Celeste was off balance and breathless. "I'm not sure you can afford me."

"I'll pay anything," Zak said, and meant it. "I swear to handle you gently, and show you off beautifully. Name your price."

"Really." Celeste eased back. "Name my price?" She raised her brows. "Let me represent you professionally."

Zak paled. "I don't like attention."

"Don't be shy, Island Boy." Celeste aligned her lean body with his. "I promise to handle you gently, and show you off beautifully."

Zak blushed. "Not concerned about conflict of interest?" He pinned her tight against him. "Mixing mediums, business and bliss?"

"I think we can handle it," Celeste giggled.

Hayward stalked into the atrium with Angelique trailing close behind.

"Can we hit pause for a second, Zak?"

Celeste didn't wait for his answer. Focused on her target, she was across the room in a flash.

"Leaving early, Hayward? Not very mannerly." She shook her head in disapproval. "The event has barely begun."

Hayward detached from Angelique and aimed an accusing finger at Celeste. "You think you're slick, stealing Belinda away while lining your pockets and getting rich off my name?" He crowded close and bumped her with his chest. "Overconfident twit. Kiss your career goodbye."

Celeste dipped her head, looked Zak dead in the eye, and winked.

Everything happened so fast Zak nearly missed it.

He watched as Celeste gripped Hayward's jacket and tugged hard. Her skirt fell open to mid-thigh, her knee emerged, and rammed Hayward soundly.

Zak winced, then enjoyed every slow motion second as Hayward buckled and sank to the polished floor. Man, how he wished he had a camera in his hands.

Celeste motioned to a muscular man a few feet away. "Can you finish this for me?"

"Yes, ma'am."

Zak vaulted the lobby furniture and stepped to Celeste's side. He teased his finger along the silk slit framing her thigh. "I thought this design was meant to entice, not cripple."

"Multi-functional," she laughed.

Zak kissed her. Tenderness weaved a thread of connection he thought was out of his reach. "I would have loved to capture that exchange frame by frame."

"And I, as your representative, would've enjoyed marketing every image."

"I haven't signed yet."

"But you will." Celeste took Zak's hand and led him to the ballroom.

Flickering lights danced off crystal champagne flutes and silver serving trays. The decadence was all Nina had hoped for and more.

Lindy beamed as Zak and Celeste joined the table. "Everything okay?"

"Yup." Zak pulled out Celeste's chair. "Just watched my girl take out the trash."

"Thank you," Celeste said over her shoulder, then smiled at Nina. "How's your adventure so far?"

"Perfect." Nina nibbled on a succulent crab stack. "Everything is so beautiful."

Celeste raised her champagne flute. "To friendship, joint ventures, fine art, and fancy food. May each grow and spill over to generations beyond our own."

Nina rested her hand on her belly and lifted her water glass. "Cheers."

The plates were cleared. The lights in the ballroom dimmed. A member of the Livingston Foundation took the stage and offered opening remarks.

Lindy gripped Tucker's hand. The support was humbling and exceeded any wish Lindy could have ever imagined.

Sentiment welled in her chest as Cal stepped to the podium and read the accomplishments of the veterans workshops and outreach in Arizona. He shared the history of their friendship, smiled at her and said, "Please join me in recognizing a remarkable visionary for expanding art. My dear friend, Lindy Colton."

The ovation swelled and expanded like a tsunamic wave. Cal gestured for Lindy to join him on the podium.

Tucker squeezed her hand. "So much for no speeches."

"I have nothing prepared."

Nina wiped her tears. "Just give them your heart."

"Thank you." Lindy took a deep breath and allowed her eyes to travel over the faces in the room. "Thank you all so much. Seasons of life. What we experience, retell, and remember. Bits we leave out or embellish. Situations we add splashes of color to or diminish. What we show the world, what we camouflage, or bury well out of sight. All the pieces and parts come together. The flaws and imperfections somehow fit. Whether they align perfectly or not, are palatable or not, are pleasing to ourselves or others or not, matters very little.

"When I was a child I looked to the sky. The vastness and speckled light made me feel little, which really meant I was part of something bigger.

"I wished, like many do, for things I never thought would come true. I wished to get beyond my circumstance and find purpose. When the stars began to answer me, the dream gifts were packaged differently than I expected. I looked to the sky again and was reminded that my part was small but the splendor was vast.

"Tonight, as I look around this room, I can't begin to…" she cleared her throat. "I was lucky to have support." Lindy gestured to her table. "Support beyond actual bloodlines. The people in my corner showed me resilient love.

"I learned stars also live on the inside. We forget to look for those," she laughed quietly. "For me, through art, I learned my stars could be as radiant as the ones shimmering in the sky.

"I've been fortunate to have a community who encouraged me. They still encourage me…" Lindy glanced at Cal, "…to take one step at a time.

"We have one life… beginning, middle, forever… after-ever." Lindy winked at Nina. "I hope I'm in the middle. I hope I have an opportunity to make more wishes, have more experiences, and share more time. To be part of something bigger… I want to catch more stars." Lindy's eyes landed on Tucker. "I hope you do too."

Chapter 77

"Back where we started." Lindy climbed onto the hood of Tucker's Jeep and looked across the water. The night sky was dotted with orbs of promise and possibility.

"Wanna catch another one?" Tucker unhooked Boop's leash and smiled as the dog followed her nose into the reeds.

"It's not polite to be greedy." She began to unpack the moonlight picnic Nina had prepared. Her hands bumped a box at the bottom of the basket. She lifted the bundle, swaddled in a beach towel. "I hope Nina doesn't expect us to go swimming."

"I'm game."

Lindy chuckled. "Wait a minute." She recognized the Van Halen towel. "This is mine."

Tucker stood beside her. "Unwrap it."

Tears fell as the cloth dropped away, revealing the wooden box Tucker had made for her. "I don't understand… how… where…" Lindy traced the stars on the lid. "I thought it was gone forever."

"I helped Zak transport the remaining items from the attic of the B&B to auction. I stumbled on it when we were loading… hoped you'd left it behind by mistake."

"I kept the key," Lindy laughed softly. "Probably the only thing I've never lost. It's at the house."

"I told you I made spares." Tucker offered a chunky sealed envelope.

Lindy looked at him skeptically. "You want me to believe you never peeked inside?"

"Won't say I wasn't tempted," Tucker chuckled, "but they weren't my dreams." He cradled her cheek. "They were yours."

She leaned into his caress. "Some we shared."

Lindy tore a corner from the envelope and pulled out a small key. "It'll be fun to read through them." The lock clicked, the top opened. "But I'll save that for another day." She sifted through the cut paper stars, looking for one in particular. "Found it," she said, passing one to Tucker.

A heart revealed itself as the seams unfolded. He held the paper toward the headlight and read the faded ink.

After-ever = Tucker Brandt

In a flash, Tucker scooped Lindy into his arms and spun in dizzying circles across the packed sand. Boop joined the joyful dance, yipping and leaping at Tucker's hip.

Lindy snuggled tightly against Tucker's chest as her feet found the ground. "Well, Tucker Brandt? What do you think?"

His rumbling laughter vibrated against her cheek.

"What do I think? I think I should've opened the damn box years ago."

Other Titles by the Author

Available at Amazon

 Devoted sister to Murphy, Tory Kean encourages him to take a vacation and champions his heart when he finds more than relaxation on the sandy shores of Chincoteague, Virginia.

Flourishing with beauty and life, Chincoteague is the perfect place to lose time in person or within the pages. Don't miss Book One, Murphy and Jess's story ~ *Saltwater Cowboy,* a sweet romance featuring Chincoteague's annual roundup and Pony Penning.

 *Late to Breakfast* ~ Ranch owner and animal advocate Tory Keen's repeated encounters with veterinary intern, Avery Rush, entice her to make time in her hectic work schedule for a little play-time.

 *Invisible Woman* ~ inspirational fiction ~ a thought provoking celebration of friendship awaits when Jillian, Arie, and Sarah attend the Awakening Goddess Retreat and uncover pure joy and embrace their inner radiance.

 *"Here's the Thing..."* ~ humorous fiction ~ a thrill ride of delightfully destructive mishaps overtakes a family wedding weekend where the only life preserver 'for better or for worse' is bloodline.

Connect with Laura

Digital reviews go a long way in helping me reach new readers!
I invite you to join me online and spread the love through any
and every social media shouting box you have.

Facebook.com/LauraRudacille

Blog - http://laurarudacille.com/

Made in the USA
Middletown, DE
01 July 2021